PRAISE FOR THE NEW IRIS THORNE MYSTERY FROM DIANNE G. PUGH

SLOW SQUEEZE

"Iris Thorne is back again in SLOW SQUEEZE, confronting a hyper-zaftig and florid Southern lady with oodles of money to invest. Pugh has a raucous sense of humor, a satiric eye and an assured way with construction."

—Charles Champlin, *Los Angeles Times Book Review*

"Pugh serves up an exhilarating cocktail of high finance and mayhem and in Iris Thorne has produced a character who can hold her own with Gekko and yet still retain her femininity."

—Sue Fox, *Northern Echo* (Darlington)

". . . fascinating. Iris Thorne is here to stay."

—*The Observer* (London)

"Gritty.... Those who come to SLOW SQUEEZE ... are in for a surprise.... Pugh has captured the essence of modern-day business, and . . . the Los Angeles ambience as well."

—*Deadly Pleasures*

D1487923

Books by Dianne G. Pugh

Cold Call
Slow Squeeze

Published by POCKET BOOKS

SLOW SQUEEZE

AN IRIS THORNE MYSTERY

DIANNE G. PUGH

POCKET BOOKS

New York   London   Toronto   Sydney   Tokyo   Singapore

This book is a work of fiction. Names, characters, places and incidents are products of the author's imagination or are used fictitiously. Any resemblance to actual events or locales or persons, living or dead, is entirely coincidental.

POCKET BOOKS, a division of Simon & Schuster Inc.
1230 Avenue of the Americas, New York, NY 10020

ISBN: 0-671-77844-7

First Pocket Books paperback printing October 1995

10 9 8 7 6 5 4 3 2 1

POCKET and colophon are registered trademarks of Simon & Schuster Inc.

Cover design and illustration by Michael Schwab

Printed in the U.S.A.

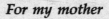

For my mother

ACKNOWLEDGMENTS

Special thanks to my intrepid and astute editor, Dana Isaacson.

To Rowland Barber, for listening, advising, and letting me tap into his muse when mine had gone home for the day.

To my diligent agent, David Chalfant, for keeping the faith.

To friends who had the courage to give me their thoughts on the manuscript and the grace to speak diplomatically: Ann Escue, Mary and Don Goss, Jeff McLellan, Jennifer Urick, and Linda Webster. A special thanks to Mardi Bettes who read two drafts—a gesture that was truly "above and beyond . . ."

To my mother, Theda, and my sister, Sheila, for attending signings and readings as if they were at the hottest venue in town. Thanks to other family members: Jeanine, Mark, Carl, Craig, Dad, Marie, Bill, June, David, Eric, and many others whose delight over having a published author in the clan delights me.

To Charlie, who stood by through riots, fires, earthquakes, and step aerobics, and through the good times, too.

PROLOGUE

It was Easter Sunday. Barbie Stringfellow was lying on her back in bed, propped up against fluffy goose down pillows, wearing a negligee of many yards of fabric, some sheer and some slippery satin, all purple. Barbie was not a slender woman. Her breasts and thighs tested the sheer fabric. Her pose seemed casual and relaxed in spite of her dishabille. She had a pleasantly surprised look on her face, the look of someone who had won five dollars in the lottery or who had been tapped on the shoulder by a friend at the supermarket.

The morning light filtered between the wood shutters. A moment before there had been silence, but all at once the birds came alive and started chirping merrily. Outside the bungalow, the air was fresh. A rainstorm had moved down the coast during the night, raising the scents of the pine, eucalyptus, and cypress trees and of the musty soft soil underneath the fallen pine cones, seed pods, leaves, and needles.

Barbie's red Mercedes convertible was parked next to the cabin. The rag top had been left down during the night. The white leather interior of the car was now wet and covered with leaves and needles. Curious squirrels had gathered their courage and were exploring the car's interior, periodically lifting their heads and sniffing the air.

The ocean had been stirred up by the storm, and it pounded the cliffs bordering the central California coast town of Las Pumas. Barbie was in the central coast's best

1

hotel, the Mariah Lodge, and in the lodge's best bungalow, the one called the Cabin in the Woods, nestled in the forest with a garden fronting the cliff.

At the base of the cliff in a sandy alcove out of reach of the waves, a flock of sea gulls had lighted. Several gulls were fighting over something that lay in the sand. Something fleshy. Another gull flew up to the group, landed, then circled around the others, intimidating them until they scattered. This gull grabbed the prize in its talons and ascended the cliff. One of the gulls that had been chased away rallied. The two gulls struggled in midair. The object was dropped in the fracas and fell against the side of the cliff. They tried to retrieve it, skimming close to the cliff, but it was lost. They flew away, side by side across the ocean, and were soon joined by the others.

Inside the cabin, Barbie's expensive clothes had been carelessly tossed around the room as if there were plenty more where they had come from. A purple silk blouse lay across the back of a rough-hewn wooden chair, which had snagged it. Designer jeans were in a twisted heap on the floor. Leather cowboy boots sat close to the fireplace, where the fire was now dead. A full-length red fox coat was spread across the bed, near Barbie's feet, like a faithful dog.

A platter of untouched fruit and cheese withered on a wheeled table near the door. The table also held a bottle of bourbon and another of soda water. An almost empty bottle of flat champagne rested in a silver bucket full of melted ice next to two cut crystal champagne flutes. The rim of each flute had a lipstick imprint, one hot pink, the other red.

Barbie still lay in her negligee on top of the patchwork quilt that covered the bed. The quilt was handmade, sewn in the broken star pattern with scraps of red, blue, and green fabric. The Mariah Lodge spared no expense in decorating its cabins in rustic Americana.

Dark purple and red bruises circled Barbie's neck. Her hand was lying palm up next to her on the comforter, the fingers curled inward in repose. Blood had pooled underneath her hand in an irregular circle. There was a stump of red flesh and white bone where the little finger of her left hand had been.

SLOW SQUEEZE

A key jiggled in the lock and the bungalow door was pushed open. Police Chief Charles Greenwood stepped inside, his cowboy boots on the hardwood floor conspicuously announcing his arrival. He rolled a milk chocolate Easter egg around his mouth, lodging it against his cheek, where it made a small protuberance. The rich color of the chocolate that he enjoyed regularly matched the color of his skin. He walked heavily to the bed. A maid peeked behind him through the doorway.

Barbie didn't stir. A dead woman wouldn't.

1

IT WAS TWO WEEKS BEFORE CHRISTMAS, AND IT HAD JUST stopped snowing in Salt Lake City. The sun sparkled on the fresh cover and reflected off the flakes, creating a trompe l'oeil that made the fluffy white layer seem dense and solid.

Lorraine and Charlotte were snug inside their apartment, sharing a crocheted comforter and watching daytime television. Lorraine had called in sick to work that morning even though it was Monday, the allure of playing hooky stronger than the threat of her boss's giving her a hard time come Tuesday morning. Charlotte had talked her into it. Charlotte wasn't employed. There was a recession, after all, and jobs were scarce. Lorraine understood.

She sat on one end of the couch with her feet in Charlotte's lap. Charlotte massaged them through Lorraine's thick socks. Spooky, a gray tabby cat, lay curled in Lorraine's lap. A small Christmas tree stood on a table in a corner of the small apartment, its multicolored lights twinkling. There were a few wrapped gifts underneath. Just a few, but they'd been selected with particular care.

Cheerful, energetic music filled the room as the Susie Santé talk show began. Applause, applause, applause. Susie Santé was middle-aged with sensibly cut, short, blond hair, an open face, and an energetic demeanor. She stood in the audience holding a microphone.

"Today we're going to meet four women who work in an industry that's still a bastion of the old-boy's club—the high-

5

flying world of stocks, bonds, and financial instruments. They've made it in a man's world and haven't let that world make them over. And, boy, the stories they have to tell you, right after this."

The show broke for a string of commercials advertising laundry detergent, a personal injury attorney with testimonials from clients for whom he had won big money, a dental assistants' school, and a weight-loss center where people danced behind the huge garments they used to wear.

Susie Santé brought out her first guest, who talked about how she got started in the industry and the dues she paid before attaining her current position. She was now—finally—handsomely compensated for her talent, perseverance, and savvy. In response to leading questions by Susie Santé, she titillated the predominately female audience with stories about Neanderthal male bosses, cretinous male coworkers, and oversexed male clients. The next two guests shared even worse horror stories.

A man in the audience dared to venture a comment. "It seems to me the guys you work with prefer women coworkers who aren't trying to be men." He was resoundingly booed and hissed by the audience's distaff members.

"They plant those bozos in the audience, don't you think?" Charlotte asked.

Lorraine shrugged.

Charlotte reached for a round tin, lined with crumpled wax paper, sitting on the coffee table. "Course, takes all kinds. Your mother makes the best fudge."

"She makes good fudge," Lorraine agreed.

After another string of commercials advertising sink and tile cleaner, a computer school, and a firm that assists in filing workmen's compensation claims, the show resumed. Susie Santé stood in the audience, her face somber.

"Now I'm going to introduce a woman who is only too familiar with the price paid for making money a god and greed a catechism." She strolled toward the stage. "This woman uncovered a money-laundering scheme in her office. A scheme with tragic consequences that cost the life of several of her coworkers and nearly cost her own." The audience was hushed. "Ladies and gentlemen, meet Iris Thorne."

Iris Thorne walked across the stage, wearing an elegantly tailored suit, looking poised and chic. She smiled and waved at the audience before taking her chair next to the other three women. The audience warmed to her and heartily applauded her fortitude.

"She's cute!" Charlotte exclaimed.

"She's all right," Lorraine sniffed. The dozing cat purred on her lap.

Charlotte turned and looked at Lorraine, then at the television, then back at Lorraine. "Rainey, she looks like you. She sure does. There's definitely a resemblance."

"Think so?"

"Sure do."

Lorraine watched the polished and composed figure on television with more interest.

Susie Santé led Iris through a litany of the atrocities that had occurred the previous year at McKinney Alitzer, the investment management firm where Iris was still employed. The camera panned the audience, whose members listened with horror. There was a lighter note when Iris revealed that one of the detectives on the case, John Somers, was an old college boyfriend and that they had resumed their relationship after the case was solved. The conversation grew somber again when Susie Santé asked Iris about the murders. Iris stepped lightly around the grisly details.

Since delicacy doesn't earn ratings, Susie Santé pressed her. "It must have been horrible when . . ." "Tell us how you felt when . . ." "Is there anything worse than . . . ?"

"She's losing it," Charlotte said. "All that poise don't go too deep, does it, Iris?"

Iris's voice broke, and a tear painted a line down her cheek. She removed it with the back of her finger. The sister securities trader sitting on Iris's right put a reassuring hand on her arm. The camera panned the audience again. The women wiped their eyes and noses with paper tissues. The men looked aghast. Everyone felt lucky that these things hadn't happened to them.

"And quite a bit of the embezzled money is still missing, isn't it, Iris? How much?"

"About a million dollars."

The audience gasped.

"Rumor has it that since you were good friends with the murdered mailroom boy who stole the money, you know where it is," Susie said forebodingly.

Iris's momentary loss of control passed. She touched the last tear on her cheek. "People keep looking for more scandal, but there isn't any."

The show broke for commercials.

"A million bucks," Lorraine said. "Wouldn't that be nice?"

"I'm gonna call," Charlotte said. She pushed Lorraine's feet off her lap and leaned across the couch to grab the telephone sitting on a small end table. She dialed a few times before she was finally put through. The program staff queried her about where she was calling from and her purpose.

"We have a caller from Salt Lake City, Utah," Susie Santé said. "Are you there, caller?"

"Hi, this is Charlotte. I just wanted to tell Iris that you're a hell of a woman to have gone through what you did and to just keep on rollin'. My hat's off to you, sugar."

The audience applauded enthusiastically.

"Thank you." Iris smiled.

Charlotte hung up.

"Happy now?" Lorraine asked.

"Rainey! You're not jealous, are you?" She put her arms around Lorraine. "You got no reason to be."

There was a knock at the front door.

"Who in Hades . . . ?" Charlotte said. "I'll get it."

She walked across the living room and looked through the peephole in the front door.

"Who is it?" Lorraine asked.

"Some guy. Looks like he's selling something."

"Don't open it."

"Let me just see what he's got. It's Christmas, after all."

Charlotte pulled open the door, stepped outside, and quickly pulled the door closed behind her. She patted her arms against the cold. "Well, Jack Goins. To what do I owe the pleasure?"

"I was in the neighborhood and thought I'd stop by and wish you a Merry Christmas."

"This is nowhere near your neighborhood."

"The world's my neighborhood."

"Hmmm. How did you know I was here?"

"I always know where you are. You keep making that mistake, don't you? Thinking people are stupid."

"I paid you this month. Didn't you get it?"

"I got it. But I'm a little short."

"That's your problem."

"No, my dear. It's yours."

"I'm not giving you any more."

"I think you are."

Charlotte ran her hands up and down her arms. She was wearing only a thin sweater.

The man ran the back of his fingers against Charlotte's cheek. "Your face is cold." He looked at her chest. "And your nipples are perked. Maybe we ought to go inside and get warm." He moved his fingers down her neck and across her chest. "Like we used to, remember?"

"I'm not alone. How much do you want?"

"A thousand would do it."

"A thousand?"

He shook his head sadly. "Prices are going up all over. Terrible, isn't it?"

"Come back tomorrow at two o'clock." She rubbed her hand against his face, drew her thumb across his lips, and stuck it in his mouth. He sucked on it. "I'll be alone then."

Charlotte went back inside the apartment.

"Who was it?" Lorraine asked.

"Someone selling ... encyclopedias."

"Today?"

"Well, I guess everyone's gotta make a living. Oh, shoot. I missed the end of the show." Charlotte covered herself with the comforter, picked up Lorraine's feet, and placed them on her lap. She retrieved the tin of fudge and put another piece into her mouth. "So, what's on next?"

2

THE TRIUMPH'S THROW-OUT BEARING FINALLY BLEW ON THE Ten just east of Crenshaw Boulevard. It had been whizzing loudly whenever the gears were engaged for the past several months. Now it had blown within tantalizing, just-out-of-reach miles of Eric's British Car Shop. No other mechanic would do. A long history had been built. Eric understood the Triumph, which demanded a great deal of understanding along with everything else that was precious: time, money, patience, fealty. Iris Thorne persisted, refusing to give up this close to Eric's. She drove the remaining miles stuck in third gear, gunning the engine like crazy when lights turned from red to green. She and the give-me-a-ticket red 1972 Triumph TR6 finally reached the mechanic. Several hundred dollars later, the Triumph had a new clutch.

It was January 3 and the first Monday of the new year. The sky was clear and blue and the sun shone hard. As in any desert, the temperature of the warm day dropped with the setting sun. There was little humidity to hold the heat. It had been a sunny and warm Christmas, with the kind of weather that made transplants to Los Angeles moan that it wasn't "Christmasy" enough. The natives didn't know any differently and would be as unprepared for real weather as they were for any crisis.

Iris was following up on a lead, a potential new client who might turn money over to her on the promise that she would return even more money. More, anyway, than would be received by stashing it in a safe but boring passbook savings account or CD. Mrs. Stringfellow, who requested in a slow Southern drawl that Iris please call her Barbie, had suggested they meet at a restaurant called Wave.

10

Iris took down the Triumph's rag top. She left Eric's and continued west on the Ten, riding it until it dumped out onto Pacific Coast Highway and ran shoulder to shoulder with the ocean. She turned on the radio, driving north.

The Pacific was an energetic green. Emerald waves splashed against tan, sandy beaches. There were few people. Iris spotted a jogger, a dog owner, and a person strolling with hands behind his back, eyes seaward, footsteps deep in the surf-smoothed sand.

The beach was bordered with tall houses built on precious, tiny oceanfront lots, exclusive members-only beach clubs, skate and bicycle rental shops, parking lots, and snack shacks closed for the season. Farther north, the topography grew more dramatic, more expansive, and more expensive.

In Malibu, the water was crowded with surfers, locals only, young men wearing knee-length sleeveless wet suits shot with bright colors against black. Their long, wet hair lay in strings against the thick neoprene. A few girls huddled together on the beach watching them, wearing bright bathing suit tops and shorts in spite of the chilly air. Even though the sun's rays were the gentle rays of winter, they were rays all the same. Scouts from modeling agencies cruised these beaches hoping to spot young blood with that Californian *je ne sais quoi* rising from the sea foam.

The radio station broke for news. "Jury selection began today in the trial of the four white Los Angeles Police Department officers accused of using excessive force in the arrest of black motorist Rodney King. The incident was videotaped by an eyewitness. Today's weather . . ."

Iris turned off Pacific Coast Highway and drove down the steep driveway by the restaurant, past the outer river rock wall covered with fuchsia and salmon-blooming bougainvillea vines, now mere twigs as they slept during the California winter. The entrance to Wave's driveway was marked with just a tiny sign, the smallness of the type implying that if you don't already know the restaurant's here, you need not stop by.

Wave was a Malibu cliff-hanging confection financed by a group of L.A. investors—a movie star, two television stars, a movie producer, an entertainment attorney, and a hairdresser—all exploring their creative and business potentials. There were designer linens on the tables and original art on the walls, some of it the creations of the investor group's famous friends. The chef of the moment was busy in the glass-walled kitchen.

Iris reluctantly turned the Triumph over to the valet, grimacing but not looking back when he ground the gears. She walked across a bottle green, fired Mexican tile patio, her pump heels shallowly resounding against the brittle clay. She was wearing her Chanel knockoff, a pink mohair suit with a jewel collar and big gold buttons connected by chains. She had splurged on the real thing for her handbag.

She flipped one side of her chin-length, blunt-cut blond hair behind an ear. People watched her as she walked through the restaurant. Not because she cut a striking figure—she was tall and slender and attractive in a WASPy, white-bread way—but because people were fascinated by women in suits, especially the way Iris wore a suit. Like a man wore a suit, as if she'd been born with it on, which was how she felt on her worst days.

The restaurant grounds were landscaped in politically correct, drought-resistant, indigenous plants. Busy waiters traveled to and fro, men and women dressed in white tops and black bottoms, a straightforward enough dress code perverted here by an L.A. interpretation—too tight, too baggy, or too short.

Stout beams suspended the patio a hundred feet above surf-smoothed boulders and crashing waves. It was a demonstration of the power of architectural design over earth in constant motion from earthquakes and erosion. This unstable land influenced the attitudes of the denizens who lived upon it; they were never at rest and never left well enough alone.

Iris sat at the bar. Barbie Stringfellow was even later than Iris was. The bar was off the patio, surrounded by sliding glass doors now pulled open to let in the ocean breeze. The bar top was a large half circle of lacquered blond wood. Matching blond stools stood underneath. Silver "mind-bender" puzzles were placed along the bar top, games where one attempted to form odd-shaped pieces into a T or remove a ring that was wrapped inside a silver pretzel or some other task. Iris ignored them.

She ordered a glass of chardonnay from the bartender, who was of a square-jawed, blond and buffed California design. His name tag identified him as William. He'd probably been just plain Bill once upon a time in Michigan or Nebraska or Kansas before he started California dreamin'.

Barbie had said she'd be wearing purple. Iris imagined a proper Southern lady in a tailored suit with outdated hair, big diamonds, and careful makeup. She nursed her wine and observed the women entering the restaurant alone. There was a blond with 8 percent body fat wearing a white cat suit, white cowboy boots, and wild string-permed hair. She pranced around, vogueing while looking for her party.

Okay, everyone's seen you, Miss Melrose, Iris said to herself. *You'll grow old too—if you're lucky.*

"Is she acting like a cat because she's wearing a cat suit or is she wearing a cat suit because she acts like a cat?" William, the bartender, mused. He busied himself refreshing plastic jugs with fresh juices brought from the kitchen.

Iris laughed. "The former, I think."

William gave Iris a searching look.

Iris knew what was coming.

"Don't I know you from somewhere?"

She looked at William coyly. "I bet you say that to all the girls."

"No, really. You look familiar. You an actor?"

"Not officially."

He looked puzzled.

"I'm an investment counselor. Got any money stashed in a mattress you'd like me to put to work for you?" Iris batted her eyes.

William set a plate of toast circles, radish flowers, and herbed olive oil in front of her. "I'm not coming on to you or anything. It's just that I never forget a face."

Iris turned the wineglass by its stem against the cocktail napkin. "Too bad. I could use a good come-on."

He smiled at her, a guy who knows he's attractive.

"You an actor?" she asked.

William leaned against the bar with his arms crossed,

which pushed his biceps out. "Yep." He rubbed his square jaw with his hand. "Actually, I'm a bartender. I'm trying to break into acting."

Iris raised her wineglass toward him. "Good luck."

A beefy, dark-haired, middle-aged woman with collagen-smooth skin and mannequin-perfect makeup entered the restaurant, trailing fragrance and carrying a big designer handbag over her shoulder, the same designer's date book in one hand and the matching briefcase in her other hand.

"Beverly Hills? Encino?" Iris said.

William nodded. "Definitely."

Then Iris saw a bird not native to these parts.

She was pretty, with a diamond-shaped face, wide-set brown eyes, full cheeks, and a puckish mouth, all of it just past ripeness. She was short and a bit round and walked with quick, mincing steps on purple Frederick's of Hollywood shoes with ankle straps and three-inch heels. Her white suit had a bolero jacket with bright faux jewels scattered across the lapels. Her skirt was short and tight with a high back slit. Her blouse was purple silk with a low V neck revealing serious cleavage. She wore big gold jewelry, a large, white, hobo-style purse, false eyelashes, many shades of eye shadow, and hot pink lipstick. She had very big, very black hair teased into a style suggesting a bird's nest.

"Now there's someone who marches to her own drummer," William said.

"I have a sinking feeling she's my client."

The host had wandered away from the podium, and the woman pranced around on those heels looking for him, twisting the oversized watch on her wrist with long, hot pink porcelain nails. She skipped to the front of the podium, picked up the reservation list, held it to her forehead to shade her eyes, and peered into the bar. Iris tentatively raised three fingers in greeting. The woman fluttered the reservation list at her and started walking quickly, her pace constrained by her tight skirt, waving the reservation list in time with her hips, holding her other arm out to the side as if to balance her top-heavy proportions. Iris slid from the bar stool and started her own noisy walk across the tiles.

"Ma'am?" the host said, hopping behind the woman. "Excuse me, ma'am?"

She stopped, turned around, grabbed his arm with one hand, and waved the list with the other. "Oh my goodness! Barbeh girl, you're losin' your marbles. Here ya go, buddy." She gave the host his list and continued walking toward Iris, her now free right hand extended in front of her, a smile stretched from ear to ear.

"I-ris! I-ris Thorne! I'm so sorry I'm late." She shook Iris's hand firmly. "I just can't get used to these Los Anglelees freeways, Lord Almighty!" She continued to hold Iris's hand. It wasn't Iris's style to release first, so they stood there, hand in hand, as diners nearby casually watched. "It is you! My gosh. You're much prettier in person than you were on TV. Not that you didn't look pretty on TV, of course! What am I sayin'! Where's the bar? This town's gonna drive me to drink and I've been here but a week."

"Nice to meet you, too," said Iris.

Barbie climbed onto the bar stool with difficulty, the short skirt now hiked well up on her fleshy thighs, restraining her. She grabbed Iris's wrist. "Iris is such a lovely name. You don't hear it no more. I bet you were named after your grandmother or somethin'. You know you're even thinner in person than you were on TV? I'd just die to be tall and thin like you. I'd just die."

William placed a cocktail napkin in front of her.

"Whatchy'all drinkin'?" Barbie finally let go of Iris's wrist. She sat with her back straight, folded her hands in her lap, and exuded anticipation.

"Chardonnay."

"You Californians and your wine." She stretched the *i* in wine. "I'm a bourbon drinker myself." Barbie leaned slightly forward toward William and pressed her hand on his. He glanced down her blouse. Anyone would have, just from curiosity. "Hey, bud. I'll have a bourbon and ginger ale in a tall glass. Thank you. So, was it your grandmother, Iris?"

"Grand . . . ? No, my great aunt is named Iris."

"I bet she's a kick in the pants."

"She's eighty-nine and buys a new Cadillac every year."

Up close, Iris could see that although Barbie's jewelry was big and garish, it looked like the real thing.

"Well, bless her heart. Let's toast to dear Aunt Iris."

They clinked glasses.

The bartender set a glass filled with slender breadsticks next to his previous hors d'oeuvre offering.

"Well, aren't you just the attentive one, Billy." Barbie placed manicured, jeweled fingers on top of William's hand. She made eye contact that surpassed friendly. "I just *love* California men. Ain't nothin' like 'em where I come from."

William freed his hand from underneath Barbie's. He blushed and started washing glasses. "Thanks."

"I'll bet William's not from California," Iris said.

Barbie opened her eyes wide. "Really? That true, buddy?"

"I'm from Wisconsin."

Iris raised her eyebrows a little and smiled, being careful not to be indelicate in her victory.

Barbie put her hand on Iris's knee and leaned close to her ear. Her lips brushed Iris's hair. "Lady, you're a good judge of character."

"Thanks, but that was easy. I think the more typically Californian someone looks, the less likely they're from here."

"I'm going to have to think about that one," William said.

Barbie's expression was suddenly serious. She grabbed Iris's hand. "Honey, don't sell yourself short like that. You *are* a good judge of character." She maintained eye contact with Iris and squeezed her hand while she nodded, expecting assent.

Iris just smiled.

William continued washing glasses. "If I can interrupt, you said you saw Iris on TV?"

"Of *course* you can interrupt, Billy." Barbie dunked a toast circle in olive oil and crunched it noisily. "Mmmm, that's different. Iris was on the Susie Santé show."

"That's right." William brightened, having solved his puzzle. "Before Christmas. 'Women in Finance.' And you were in the paper, too. That money-laundering thing at . . . what's the company?" He snapped his fingers. "Kinney . . ."

"McKinney Alitzer," Iris answered. "So. I've been unmasked." She sipped her wine.

"Someone at your office was murdered, right?" William continued enthusiastically. "And they never accounted for all that money."

Iris tossed back the last of her wine.

"Let's stop talking about this," Barbie said. "Lord knows this poor woman's been through enough."

William left to wait on a man and a woman at the other end of the bar.

"So, you got a boyfriend, Iris? You're not married, are you?"

"I've got a boyfriend."

"He in business?"

"No, he's a cop."

"That's right! I remember that from the show. Well, that's a job if there ever was one. Betcha he's a big, strong kinda man."

Iris nodded and smiled, her eyelids dropping a little with the thought of John Somers.

"Well, of course he is. What else could he be?"

William returned, wiping his hands on a towel. "So you went on the show to talk about the murders?"

"Billy!" Barbie exclaimed, hopping up a little on the bar stool. "We're droppin' the subject!"

"It's all right," Iris said. "I'm used to it. A friend from my MBA program is the producer. She told me it'd be fun and I might get some new business."

Barbie gestured toward herself with both hands. "And here I am. When I moved out to California, I said to myself, 'Barbeh, you gotta get that Iris Thorne to manage your affairs.' See, honey, it wasn't a total loss." Barbie patted Iris's thigh.

"My friend promised we'd just talk about the old-boys' network, the famous clients I've had and stuff like that. But Susie Santé brought up the scandal in my first five minutes on camera."

"Oh, it was awful," Barbie said. "I felt so sorry for you. Even Susie Santé with her heart of stone shed a tear."

"It was good television." Iris shrugged.

William ran glasses through a hot bath, then a cold one. "It's an amazing story."

"I just want to put it behind me."

"How did the people at your office react to you being on TV?" William asked.

"They weren't thrilled. The firm's trying to put the scandal behind them, too. But I'm still their top salesperson in L.A., so . . ."

"So fuck 'em," William said.

Barbie blinked her eyes as if someone had hit her in the face.

"Sorry. I get too familiar with the patrons."

"That's okay, Billy. It's just that I could never get used to vulgarity." Barbie tugged at her tight skirt, which had inched even farther up her hips. "Enough of this sad talk." She waggled an accusing finger playfully at the bartender. "It's all your fault. Treat Iris to some more wine."

"Oh, no, thank you. I'd prefer some mineral water."

Barbie widened her eyes. "She's always on top of her game, isn't she? Well, I guess that's how you gotta be in this world. You either hunt with the foxes or run with the rabbits, isn't that right?"

"True words," Iris agreed.

William filled a glass with mineral water from a green bottle.

"But I like your style. Bein' timid never got a woman nowhere except to the kitchen sink."

"The female please disease." Iris squeezed lime into her glass.

"That's it! That's it." Barbie shook her finger. "Tryin' to keep everyone happy. But you and I, we're independent. But the world takes its price for that, don't you know?"

"Yep," Iris said emphatically.

"Are you two going to break out in a chorus of 'I Am Woman'?" William asked.

"No, a chorus of 'I Sacrificed Marriage and Family for a Career,' " Iris said.

"Really?"

"Sure. Just ask my mother." She winked at him.

"I admire ya, Iris, for being out and amongst them. You're

making it easier for all the girls who come after. A toast to you, darlin'."

Iris touched her glass against Barbie's. The full glasses clinked dully.

"Gee, I thought I was just paying the mortgage."

Barbie rubbed her ample belly. "I'm starved. I started a diet today but guess I'll get back on it tomorrow. Should we get a table? Can you eat something, Iris?"

"I can always eat."

"A woman after my own heart."

William picked up the check that was sitting on the bar in front of them. "Drinks are on the house. I really got a kick out of you two ladies, and I'm sorry for bringing up bad memories."

"You don't have to do that," Iris said. "Thanks."

"Well, that's real nice, Billy. Thank you."

Barbie stretched one leg down until her spiked heel touched the floor, then heavily slid her hip off the bar stool. She hoisted her large hobo bag onto the counter, dug her hand around inside, and pulled out a twenty-dollar bill. She extended her hand with the twenty and crooked her fingers at William. He stepped up to his side of the bar. Barbie shoved the twenty inside his shirt pocket, then patted his pocket with her hand, caressing his pectoral, her long fingernails against his shirt.

"Just a little something to show my personal appreciation for the good service. Maybe we'll see you later, huh?" Barbie turned and started walking toward the restaurant, swinging her hips.

Both Iris and William watched her.

Barbie turned back. "Iris, y'all comin'?"

Iris looked at William and raised her eyebrows. He shook his fingers as if they were hot.

3

THE GAS FLAME CANDLE IN THE MIDDLE OF THE TABLE FLICK-
ered in the wind. Floodlights underneath the patio illuminated the rocks, the narrow beach below, and the phospho-
rescent white sea foam. The setting sun painted the ocean
and sky in Jell-O shades of red and orange. Sea gulls were
starting to disappear as the sun went down. Tall heat lamps
on poles kept the restaurant's diners warm.

Barbie lifted her bourbon and ginger ale to her lips. "I
love this, the ocean rollin' and crashin' underneath our feet.
I just took a li'l place down at the marina. Do I love it! I've
always wanted to live by the water."

"You've just arrived in L.A.?"

"Just a week ago. Fresh from Atlanta."

"Making a fresh start after your husband's death?"

Barbie exhaled slowly and looked across the ocean. She
sipped her drink.

Iris stumbled. "I'm sorry. I didn't realize your husband's
death was recent."

Barbie looked at her, her eyes tinged with red. "That's
okay, honey. It wasn't that recent. Just takes me by surprise
sometimes. It's a funny thing. One day a person's there, and
the next they're gone for good. It takes a long time. I go
along and I'm fine, then all of a sudden I think about him
and I . . ." She dabbed at her eye with the linen napkin. Iris
dabbed at her own eye.

"Don't you cry, sugar. It'll just make me cry more."

"I always cry if someone else is crying."

"Boy! You and I sure know how to cut straight to the
quick, don't we?" Barbie sniffed and dabbed at a tear and

laughed. "Sitting here cryin' and carryin' on and we only just met."

Iris laughed too.

"Iris, you and I have more in common than you think. Bet ya saw me and thought, 'What in the world have I gotten myself into?' Didn't ya, huh?"

"You do cut a . . . unique figure."

"Darlin', you reach a point where you learn you just gotta please yourself. People are gonna nip at your heels no matter what."

"Isn't it the truth?"

Barbie sighed heavily, her chest rising up and down. She draped the napkin across her lap and smoothed it. "Mr. Stringfellow passed on a year ago."

"Barbie, I'm sorry I brought it up."

"But I want to talk about it. I've been kind of lonely since I've come west. Got no friends here, no one to talk to. I'm enjoying the company."

The waiter brought a basket of hot rolls. Barbie slathered one with butter, took a big bite, and dabbed her hot pink lips with a napkin, leaving lipstick on the linen.

"I was thirty years old when I met Hal. He was sixty."

Iris raised her eyebrows in polite surprise.

"I know. But I'd rather be an old man's lover than a young man's slave, know what I mean? I was a waitress in his restaurant. Hal's. Real high-class Atlanta place in this big old plantation house. That was my first legitimate job. I was a stripper before that." Barbie paused.

"Supposed to pay well."

"It does, darlin', it does. But you don't meet the class of people you'd like to hook up with. And if someone nice does wander in, who wants to bring a stripper home to Momma? Know what I mean? Hal was divorced. We got married after a coupla years and I helped him run the business. When he started havin' heart problems, I took over runnin' the place. Did that for five years. When Hal died, I lost the taste for the whole thing. I sold everything, packed up, and moved out."

"Do you have any children?"

"Nope. You?"

"No."

"Hal had a coubla grown kids. Hated me. So did his ex-wife. Real society type. Tennis lunches and bridge brunches and charity balls and debutante balls and balls balls. She got remarried to some big executive at the soft drink company. Had everything she wanted and still hated me." Barbie shrugged. "Just no tellin' about some people."

The waiter brought their food. Barbie's seared New York strip steak was surrounded by baby summer squash and edible flowers. Iris's swordfish steak was grilled without butter or oil and circled with flowers and a halo of raspberry sauce.

Barbie picked up one of the yellow flowers. "What's this flower doin' here?"

"Try it. It tastes spicy." Iris popped a flower into her mouth.

Barbie tentatively nibbled on the petals. "Well, I'll be damned! They wouldn't have gone for flowers on the food at Hal's, let me tell you!" She picked up her knife and fork, eyed the steak lasciviously, then dug in. She closed her eyes. "Mmmmm ... delicious. How's your food?"

"Wonderful," Iris answered.

"So, Iris. Say I have a million dollars to invest. What could you do for me?"

"Do you have a million dollars to invest?"

"Say I do. What could you do for me?"

Iris sipped her mineral water. "I don't know you well enough to say. I need to know your financial goals, your risk aversion. I need to get a feel for who you are."

"C'mon, Iris. You have a feel for who I am."

"We only just met."

"You're hedgin'. You've at least got a first impression."

"Well, sure."

"Let's have it."

"First impressions aren't always accurate."

"But they're usually dead straight, aren't they? C'mon. Let's see how much guts you got."

"Okay. I think you're very warm and personable. You have a great sense of humor. And I appreciate what you've accomplished in getting from where you were to where you are now."

Barbie watched Iris with heavily made-up brown eyes creased with crow's-feet. She chewed another hunk of steak. "That's very sweet. Thank you. But you're holdin' back the good stuff."

"Why do you care what I think of you? You told me earlier you've learned to just please yourself."

"And I do. But if I'm gonna give you my money, I got a right to see what you're made of, don't ya think? Believe me, you're not gonna tell me anything I don't already know."

"All right. You like showing you have money, but that's not unusual for someone who's not used to having it and something that I completely understand. You lack a certain . . . polish, but it's part of your charm. Since schooling tends to round off rough edges, I'll guess you haven't had much beyond high school, which only shows how far you've pulled yourself up. You're certainly memorable. The flirting and flamboyant clothes contribute to that. People enjoy being with you."

"Flirting? Flirting how?"

Iris paused, struggling for a diplomatic response. "Well, like being touchy-feely. Maybe I misinterpreted your inter-action with the bartender. If I did, I apologize." Iris took another bite of her cooling food.

"Being touchy-feely bothers you?"

Iris shrugged. "Whatever works for you."

Barbie reached across the table and put her hand on Iris's hand. "So if I touch you, you think I'm flirting with you?" She looked into Iris's eyes.

Iris returned Barbie's gaze and didn't move. "Of course not."

"Does it bother you?"

Iris pulled her hand from underneath Barbie's and reached for her glass of mineral water. "No. It doesn't bother me," she said confidently. "All this provides some interesting possibilities in terms of an investment strategy. My feel is, since you got your money quickly you think it'll keep coming the same way. I'd like to balance something high-risk, high-return with a few more conservative choices. But I hope I haven't offended you by some of the things I've said. You may want to shop elsewhere, but you won't find anyone in this town who will do a better job for Barbie Stringfellow."

"Waiter? Honey, could I have a cup of coffee, please? Iris?"

"Yes, thank you."

"Don't worry, Iris. You'd have to go a long, long way before you offend me. You're nice to say I'm not polished. What I am is poor white trash. I came from dirt. A little place in Mississippi that you could hardly call a town. Wore clothes the town folks gave me. I'd remake them to fit. High school education? Good Lord, you flatter me. Daddy worked for the railroad. Momma took off when I was twelve, leavin' me to take care of my three snot-nosed brothers and my father and that shack we called a house. I left home at fifteen. Got a guy I knew to drive me to Atlanta. Ain't never been back. Got my first job as a stripper, even though I was underage."

The busboy brought the coffee.

Barbie poured in artificial sweetener. Iris drank hers black.

"Iris, you're wrong about one thing. My money did not come easy. It may have come all at once when I married Hal, but it did not come easy. I used whatever god-given talents I had to get ahead, to make somethin' of myself. Just like you. See, you and I aren't all that different. You just went about it different."

Barbie pulled her large handbag onto the table top, plunged her hand inside, and dug around. "Hal left me well set. I didn't even have a bank account before I met him. He taught me to manage money. He taught me that you need to put your money to work for you."

She took out a purple wallet, flipped it open, and began writing a check.

Iris watched her silently, remembering that a good salesperson knows when to talk and when to shut up.

Barbie held the checkbook down with the flat of her left hand and tore the check out with her other hand. She held it between two long nails toward Iris.

Iris took it. It was made out for fifty thousand dollars.

"This good enough to get us started, darlin'?"

4

IRIS SAID GOOD-BYE TO BARBIE IN THE PARKING LOT OF WAVE and took Pacific Coast Highway south to Topanga Canyon Boulevard. She left the top down on the TR. The night air helped sober her up from the buzz of closing the sale. Her purse sat unzipped on the passenger seat and she caught a glimpse of Barbie's check. She fingered the paper.

"Damn, I'm good!" One of the Triumph's spark plugs misfired as an exclamation point.

At Topanga Canyon Boulevard, she turned east and headed into the canyon. It was about nine o'clock and there wasn't much traffic. The air temperature rose as she drove higher and deeper into the hills and farther away from the ocean. Her tires clattered over a wooden bridge that crossed a normally dry, small stream that now ran high due to the recent spate of winter storms. The canyon's pine trees scented the air. The Pacific faded to the east; the asphalt sprawl of the San Fernando Valley was a threat to the west. The center of the canyon was a world apart.

She drove past a ramshackle fish restaurant where the shifting earth had tilted the building, slanting the wooden walls like a fun house. Patrons stepped over a large hound that slept across the doorway and were served fresh fish dinners on paper plates. Down the road, in front of a rock and roll emporium, chromed and polished motorcycles stood like dominoes. The bass downbeat of the house band rumbled through the Triumph's chassis. Bikers were sprawled across redwood picnic tables scattered in front of the place, drinking beer, holding the bottlenecks between their crooked fingers, and carving yet more marks on the table tops with vicious knives. Some looked for real and some

25

looked like white-shirted bean counters by day trying to be born losers by night.

Iris turned onto Withered Canyon Road, John Somers's street. There were no streetlights, and she navigated the narrow, winding road by memory, by the TR's bright beams and by the light of the crescent moon shining blue-white in the smogless January sky. She passed rustic houses nestled into the hillside or clinging to cliffs on the canyon side. The beat-up broken asphalt gave way to gravel that crunched under the TR's tires until the gravel gave way to dirt and pine needles marked with tire tracks.

She parked in the residents' visitor parking lot overlooking the Santa Monica Mountains, rolling hills black against the night sky. Beyond the mountains was a patch of twinkling lights that marked the Pacific Coast Highway. Beyond that was the dense, damp blackness of the Pacific. At night, there was more to feel and hear than there was to see.

Iris put the top up on the TR, took out a duffel bag, and locked her briefcase in the trunk. Two brown squirrels ran a few feet away from the car, then turned to watch her, their cheeks unevenly packed full of squirrely treasures.

She climbed the gravel road that led to John Somers's driveway. The gravel was damp, its normally dry, crackling retort muted by recent rains. The house was built in several levels against the side of the hill and could be seen from the top of his steep driveway but not from the road. It was a redwood-paneled rustic affair. John had replaced the shake roof with fire-resistant tile and each summer dutifully cleared the brush from a thirty-foot semicircle around the perimeter of the house to provide some protection against the canyon dwellers' perennial fear: brush fires.

Iris walked around to the side of the house and used her key to enter the side door that led to the kitchen. The kitchen was brightly lit but empty. When the bull terrier, Buster, didn't rush in to bark and growl at her, never having warmed to her even after a year, Iris thought that maybe John had gone out and taken the dog with him. There was a pot on the stove and a ladle encrusted with red sauce lying in a spoon rest on the yellow and magenta tiled counter. There were more spoons and dirty white porcelain bowls in the sink. Iris lifted the pot lid and an aroma of cayenne pepper and onions arose. John had made chili. Iris was still hungry. She'd talked so much during dinner, she'd left most of her meal untouched.

She sat her bag down on the kitchen's wood and brick floor and was ladling chili into a bowl when she heard laughter from the living room. She paused, holding the ladle in midair. She separated John's voice from a second, female voice. It was Penny, John's ex-wife.

"Oh, joy," Iris muttered. She sat the bowl on a matching white porcelain plate. Simple and utilitarian. Clean and practical. Like John.

She walked down the polished hardwood hallway, stepping more firmly than usual so that her footsteps announced her in advance. While she was walking past John's scrubbed pine table in the dining room, Buster met her, barking all the more ferociously at the indignity of having been caught off guard. The dog's short white hair stood up on the back of his thick neck. He sniffed her feet and ankles, looked at her challengingly with one blue and one brown eye, then turned his head to give her the blue-eyed stare. His throat rumbled.

Iris smiled through clenched teeth. "Good dog."

He attempted to sniff her crotch. She pushed his big head away and walked into the knotty pine–paneled living room, the dog close on her heels.

John was already on his feet, walking toward her. His wiry red hair had been carrot-colored in his youth but had mellowed to auburn and was now gray at the temples. His complexion was red-tinged and freckled. He had a long face with a square jaw, narrow green eyes, and a Cupid's bow mouth. He stood just over six feet tall and was broad-shouldered and long-legged. Physically, he was a mixture of childlike imp and imposing male. Mentally, the same was true. When they dated in college, it had been a combination that Iris found both attractive and exasperating. When circumstances brought them together again fifteen years later, she was chagrined to discover she felt the same way.

"You found the chili. Good."

Iris puckered her lips. John avoided them and kissed her chastely on the cheek.

"Hi, Iris," Penny said cheerfully. She sat on one of the two couches that stood perpendicular to one another. Her shoes were off and her feet tucked underneath her, sitting familiarly on furniture that had once been hers. When she and John split up eight years ago, John had kept the house and the furnishings. At that time, Penny hadn't wanted him, his lifestyle, or anything that went with it.

Penny resettled herself on the couch. She held a white cup and saucer in her hands and was smiling contentedly. Her cheeks were rosy. She had retained a fresh-scrubbed, flower-child, chamomile-tea-and-patchouli wholesomeness into her forties. She'd filled out a bit but was still in good shape. She wore well-worn denims and a navy blue turtle-neck sweater. Her face was lined beyond her years due to many sunny seasons of outdoor activities. Her thick, dark hair, cut sensibly short, was beginning to show some gray and, of course, Penny was leaving it alone. She wore no makeup.

Iris greeted her and then said hello to their daughter, Chloe, who was sitting in an oversized pine rocking chair with one denim-clad leg tossed over the chair arm, the other leg stretched forward on the floor. She pressed the floor with her bare heel to rock the chair. Chloe had inherited John's height and red hair and coloring but had her mother's facial features. The years were beginning to smooth Chloe's gangliness and she was a pretty girl if one looked beyond her adolescent angst. It hurt to greet Iris. It hurt to be nice. Life hurt. She mumbled "Hi" and didn't look up.

Iris sat on the couch across from Penny and next to John. Buster continued to sniff her ankles. Iris resisted the urge to jam her pump toe into the soft flesh underneath his neck. She just smiled and tried to push his big head away with her hand.

"Buster!" John said. "Leave Iris alone."

The dog dutifully retreated and sat next to Chloe's rocking chair. Chloe put her dangling foot on his back and scratched it with her bare toes as she rocked back and forth.

"Penny," Iris said. "Long time no see. What have you

been up to?" She ate a spoonful of the chili, frowning as she chewed.

"Busy with my classes. Christmas break is over next week. The kids'll be coming back hyper from all the sugar and excitement." She grimaced in mock dismay.

Iris grimaced to commiserate. "You have fifth graders this year?"

"Sixth. It's different. They're almost in junior high, so it's fun for them." She opened her eyes wide and nodded enthusiastically.

"I miss teaching sometimes," Iris said. "The business world has its own challenges and rewards but they're different. I guess whenever you choose a road in life, you get something but you leave something behind, too."

Penny sat the cup and saucer on the coffee table. "Personally, I've never wanted to do anything other than teach. To me, molding young minds is the best job a person can have. It's not only personally rewarding, it's so socially relevant, especially these days. Iris, didn't you teach hearing-impaired children?"

"For eight years, until I decided to get my MBA."

"What made you want to give up teaching to do what you're doing with"—Penny molded something in the air with her hands, grappling for the right word—"money?"

Iris gave Penny a cool look. "I was ready for a new challenge."

"Speaking of that," John interjected, "how did you do on your sales call tonight?"

"Closed it." Iris opened her purse, took out Barbie's check, and tossed it face up on the coffee table. "Nice way to start the week off."

Penny glanced at the check from where she was sitting, then leaned closer, the better to count the zeros. "Fifty thousand dollars?"

"Fifty K," Iris confirmed.

"It's amazing that some people have that kind of money," Penny said.

"Some people do."

"How's the chili?" John asked.

"Good," Iris said, "but it needs salt."

"Penny helped me in the kitchen." John said. "She stopped me when I went for the salt."

Penny sat straighter, assuming a more forceful posture, as if she were about to express an opinion that no one else in the room held but she felt compelled to voice anyway. "Without all the salt, Iris, you'll find the food's natural flavors come through. I haven't used salt for years. No caffeine or booze, either. I've felt so much better, like I'm clean inside." She smiled in a way that alluded to her inner glow.

Iris took another small spoonful of the chili, chewed it a little, and swallowed it quickly.

John said, "I've decided it wouldn't hurt me to clean up my act, too. New year and all."

"So you helped John cook, Penny?"

"I came over earlier this afternoon to pick up Chloe to go camping. John and I got to talking . . ." Penny smiled robustly at John. "You know. Old times. The new year, it makes you reflect."

"Seems like the new year has a lot of ramifications in this house," Iris said. "So, where are you going camping?"

"The Grand Canyon, with my brother and his family. Ever been there, Iris?"

"Never made it there."

"Iris in the Grand Canyon?" John said with amusement. "Paris is too rustic for Iris."

Everyone laughed good-naturedly. Iris too. "Oh, that's not completely true, John. Paris is tolerable when I stay at the Ritz."

Chloe rolled her eyes theatrically.

"Chloe's looking forward to camping out under the stars." Penny reached to pat Chloe's leg. "Aren't you, sweetheart?"

"If you say so," Chloe said.

"Well," Iris said. "I'm sure you'll have a good time. How long did you say you were going to be gone?"

"I didn't say, but we'll be gone a week. Until next Sunday. I'm trying to talk John into coming with us. I think I've just about got him convinced."

"Really?" Iris said flatly. She stood up, holding her bowl. "Excuse me." She walked down the hallway toward the kitchen.

She was digging through the spice cupboard when John came in.

"Iris . . ."

Iris turned away from the cupboard and looked at him. She waited for him to speak.

He took a step toward her. "I haven't decided to go. I wanted to talk it over with you first."

"That's considerate."

"It was Penny's idea."

"Of course."

"So, I started thinking, with Chloe and her . . . problems lately, she needs both her mother and father."

"And Penny needs a man."

"It's not that."

"Oh, isn't it? Penny sure as hell knows how to punch your buttons. Some coincidence that she suddenly wants all this family closeness right after she got dumped by Phil. Oh, sorry, *Philip.* Chloe was screwing up months before that happened."

"You'll be mad if I go?"

"*Yes.* Wouldn't you be mad if I went camping with another man?"

"Penny's not exactly another woman."

"Puh-leese. She's the ultimate other woman."

"It's not like we'd be sleeping together."

"I trust you. It's just that it would hurt my feelings if you went."

"Okay." John put his arms around her shoulders and kissed her. "I won't go."

"Really?"

"Really."

She kissed him, long and hard. When they broke, his eyes were half-mast.

"Wow," he said. "That's right. You just closed a deal. It always makes you frisky."

"Too bad we're not alone."

"They're going soon." John found the salt shaker that Iris had been searching for and handed it to her. He held her around the waist as she salted her chili.

"Did you ask Chloe about my bracelet?"

John's grip loosened slightly.

She turned to look at him. "What? You're mad now?"

He let go of her completely. "My daughter did not steal your bracelet."

"Did you ask your daughter about it?"

"She said you were out to get her."

"That's pretty much the response I expected."

"I don't want to talk about this."

"That's part of the problem, John."

He turned and left the kitchen.

Iris let him leave with her lipstick still on the corner of his mouth. She picked up the bowl of chili and the salt shaker and rejoined the party.

5

LATER THAT EVENING, JOHN WAS IN THE BATHROOM MAKING familiar water sounds. Iris looked through the dresser drawer where she kept a few clothes. She picked up a slinky, short turquoise gown. John liked her in that number. He liked to wrap his arms around her and rub the slick fabric against her bare skin.

Not tonight.

She opened one of John's drawers and found plaid flannel pajamas that were threadbare in the seat. She put them on and rolled up the waist to take in the length. They felt worn and cozy.

The dog sniffed Iris's crotch through the pajamas. Iris shoved him away. "Damn dog."

"Buster, go to bed!" John shouted from the bathroom. The dog dutifully walked to the other side of the room and lay down with a groan in a basket lined with a cedar-chip mattress.

Iris climbed onto John's water bed, propped a pillow against the headboard, and leaned against it. Small waves undulated beneath her.

John came out of the bathroom wearing boxer shorts and an old sweatshirt. He climbed into the water bed. "You cold or what?"

"Both."

He propped a pillow against the headboard and leaned against it. "You're not still thinking about this Penny thing, are you?"

"Yes. Why did you make fun of me in front of her?"

"Iris. I was just teasing." He slid his arms around her and pulled her closer to him. "I love you."

"I know. But Penny hanging around so much lately rattles me."

"Why? There's no romance there."

"That's not what rattles me. It's you feeling like a failure as a family man. If you hooked up with Penny again, you could put your family back together."

"Iris, c'mon." He shook her. "Don't worry. Everything's fine."

She gazed into his eyes for a long time.

He playfully shook her again. "Tell me about Ms. Fifty Thousand."

"Barbeh Stringfellah," Iris imitated Barbie's accent. "A blowsy Southern belle. Dragged herself up from the dirt. Widow. Married well. Ran this high-class restaurant in Atlanta with her husband. Lots of dough, no class, but she has this old-world propriety like being embarrassed by profanity."

"She'll enjoy herself with you."

"She's actually kind of fun." Iris chuckled, remembering the evening. "She's a character. She's got street smarts. She's fragile but she's tough, too."

"You have something in common."

"She played that up. This is no dummy. But a couple of things bug me."

"What?"

"For one thing, she wanted to know what I thought of her. I mean, *really* thought of her."

"Did you tell her?"

"Sort of. I tried to be diplomatic."

"That's an odd thing to ask someone you just met."

"She said she wanted to see what I was made of, but it was more like she wanted to see how *she* was doing. Like she was selling herself to me. Hell, I would have taken her dough anyway. I need the business. The fact that my sales have been off hasn't gone unnoticed at the office."

"Think her money's good?"

"I'll soon know. I won't act on it until it clears the bank. Money talks and bullshit walks. But why go through dinner and everything just to give me a bad check?"

"Well, you're sort of a minor celebrity. Maybe she's a stalker."

"Thanks, Mr. Policeman. I feel so at ease now. You know what else? I think she made a pass at me."

"You *think* she did? What did she say?"

"She asked if it bothered me when she touched me. Then she touched my hand."

"That's a pass?"

"There was definitely something sexual there, between the lines."

"You're always finding something between the lines."

"That's where all the action is."

"Want me to check her out?"

"Yeah. Thanks."

"Maybe you should invite her over."

"Why?"

"A little two-on-one."

"You're disgusting. Fucking men."

John pulled Iris on top of him. "Fucking men. Can't live with us and can't live with us."

"Screw you." Iris slid the loose pajama bottoms down her hips and kicked them off. She straddled him.

"That's what I'm trying to do." He put his hands underneath the flannel pajama top. "I thought you were too mad for nookie."

She grabbed the hem of the pajama top, pulled it over her head, and threw it off. She held his face between her hands, looked at her hands against his cheeks, and realized again how different he was from her. She touched his wiry red hair, touched the few strands of gray at his temples, and looked into his eyes. "I *am* mad."

They kissed. She traveled to that place where warm water and warm sand rushed over her body and settled into every crevice.

"I'm giving you an opportunity to make it up to me," she said.

"Oh, are you?"

"So, are you gonna?"

"Gonna what?"

"Make it up to me."

"Man's gotta do what a man's gotta do."

"Good boy." Iris suddenly sat up on her elbows and looked over her shoulder. "Jo-ohn."

The dog was lying with his head on his crossed paws, staring at them.

"But he likes to watch."

She looked at him incredulously.

He laughed. "Buster, let's go."

The dog slowly rose and left the room, giving John a baleful look over his shoulder as he crossed the threshold.

John aimed a pillow at the door and knocked it closed. "Now, where were we?"

John was snoring, but it wasn't his snoring that woke her; it was the dog's, whom John had let return to his cedar bed. Normally, Iris slept through the cacophony, but her meeting with Barbie Stringfellow and the evening with Penny kept replaying in her mind.

She quietly slid out of bed and tiptoed out the door and down the hall. She opened the door to Chloe's room, went inside, and closed the door behind her before turning on the light. She surveyed the room.

It was an updated version of what Iris's own room had looked like when she was a young teenager. There were posters and pictures of singers and actors cut from magazines, there were tapes and CDs, books and magazines, school paraphernalia—play programs, pennants, booster buttons from athletic events, ticket stubs—and stuffed toys cluttered on the bed.

Clothes, shoes, jewelry, and hair ornaments seemed to be everywhere except in their proper places.

Iris surveyed the mess with her hands on her hips. She walked to the dresser and lifted the lid of a pink jewelry box. A tiny plastic ballerina sprang up. A preteen relic. Fortunately, Chloe hadn't wound the music box, so the ballerina just wobbled silently on its spring. Iris dug through the box, then closed it.

Too obvious.

She casually looked through some of the dresser drawers. Nothing. She looked at the stuffed toys on the bed. One of them, an alligator, was fatter and broader than the rest. She picked it up. There was a zippered opening on the bottom. It was a pajama bag. She unzipped it, put her hand inside, and retrieved her bracelet.

She found a spiral notepad of colored paper and a pen. She wrote: "I won't tell your father about this, but don't steal from me again. Let me know when you want to talk. Iris."

She tiptoed back to John's room, slipped the bracelet into her purse, and climbed back into bed. After she was snuggled in, Buster woke, dreamily raised his head, and halfheartedly growled at her before dropping his head heavily back onto his bed. Finally, Iris fell asleep.

6

ON FRIDAY MORNING, AT 4:25 A.M., THE NEW AGE MUSIC selected to gently nudge Iris awake clicked on. But she was already awake, having long grown used to her early hours that matched the East Coast stock market schedule. She climbed out of bed, pulled on the robe hanging from a hook in the attached bathroom, walked down the corridor past the condominium's second, smaller bedroom that she'd set up as an office, and then past the guest bathroom, walking by the light of the small lamps she left on each night. In the living room, the floor felt prickly, then cool under her bare feet as she walked over the oriental rug, then the hardwood floor. In the long, galley-style kitchen, the coffee maker had already brewed her coffee, its red light shining energetically. Iris poured a cup into a squat-bottomed commuter mug and took a few sips.

"Friday," she said to no one. "Whoop-de-doo."

She pulled open the drapes covering the French doors that led to her terrace, rattling the string of brass bells that she'd hung from all her doorknobs to warn of intruders. She'd installed the bells and extra locks after the McKinney Alitzer murders the previous year. She looked through the glass windowpanes at the Santa Monica beach. It was an hour before sunrise, and the waning moon hung pale and low in the sky, right above the inky black ocean. Iris sipped her coffee. Thinking about the day that lay ahead made her tired. She chose not to think about it. She'd just do it. She clicked into high gear.

"Meet with Dexter at ten."

She walked back through the condo, turning off lights and opening drapes and blinds.

"See the Khalsa family. Turban fiesta."

She picked out a woolly suit and examined a blouse that she'd worn once since stripping it from the dry cleaner's plastic. She smelled the armpits.

"It'll do."

She showered, moisturized, combed and curled her hair, put on her makeup, and dressed in half an hour.

"Finish Barbie's proposal. Dinner with her. Early night, I hope. Then home. Home, Toto! Home!"

In the garage, she set the commuter mug on the ground, unshrouded the Triumph, and stashed the cover in the trunk. She got inside the car, pulled out the choke, stepped on the accelerator twice, and turned the key in the ignition. The engine fired and the Triumph's loud baritone roared in the empty garage. The owner of the Porsche parked alongside had finally adjusted his car alarm so that the Triumph's rumbling didn't set it off. The neighbors had complained.

Iris put the car into reverse, creating enough clearance to slide the pull-out stereo into its chassis. She backed the car out and looked disinterestedly at the Triumph's nightly excretions that had oozed onto the two drip pans positioned underneath its length, her grip on life's details having relaxed by the end of the week. She'd check its bodily fluids on Monday. She clicked the garage gate, which slowly rolled open.

She paused at the end of the driveway before pulling out onto the street. A movement in the shrubbery to her left caught her attention. She glanced in that direction and was startled to see a homeless man rising from the camp that he'd made underneath her terrace. He ignored her.

She gunned the Triumph's engine, feeling both angry and afraid, and quickly pulled into the street.

She entered the Ten at its mouth, near the sign that said CHRISTOPHER COLUMBUS TRANSCONTINENTAL HIGHWAY, at the edge of the new world, and headed east. At 5:15 in the morning, traffic was sparse.

Forty-five minutes later, the elevator opened on the twelfth floor of the office tower. Iris pulled open the large glass doors affixed with brass letters that said MCKINNEY ALITZER FINANCIAL SERVICES and walked through the mauve-hued lobby. Once inside the suite, she picked up her pace and moved with precision and purpose. The heels of her pumps left small, round indentations on the plush carpet.

"Fake it till you make it," she muttered.

"Morning!" she sang at the receptionist, snagging her mail from the slot labeled with her name as she sped by. She turned left into the sales department and walked briskly past the investment counselors' cubicles. They were wearing telephone headsets. Everyone was on a line.

"I got sixteen bid, what can you do for me?"

"Let it go to fifteen and three quarters, then we'll move."

"I told you I wasn't paying cost of carry, asshole!"

"Look, braindead, don't give me nine when I need twenty!"

"Morning, hi, how are ya, happy Friday, ça va?" Iris snip-snapped along, waving, winking, nodding, and making eye contact with everyone who looked her way.

Sean Bliss watched her legs. Dark and slender and fresh out of college, Sean had been with the firm just a few months. He had a good background, came from a good family, wore expensive, discreet clothing, and was appropriate in every way except one. He couldn't look Iris in the eyes but felt no compunction about staring at every other part of her anatomy.

Amber Ambrose waved a perfect French manicure in greeting. Her cute name belied her businesslike persona. She was the only other professional woman in the office, having joined McKinney Alitzer from a competing firm. She was in her late twenties, with a square face, small nose, hazel eyes, and short, stylish, auburn hair. She wore a forest green coat-style dress that had a conservative round neckline and was belted around her slender waist.

Sam Gold was the office's oldest sales rep. He'd worked in the industry his entire adult life and was retiring soon. He was wearing his favorite tie, a broad, shiny model with big diagonal stripes, with a twenty-year-old brown plaid suit. He smiled at Iris with tobacco-stained teeth.

Art Silva was leaning back in his chair, forcing the spring mechanism so far backward that he was almost horizontal. His hands were clasped behind his head, his elbows akimbo and biceps stretching the sleeves of his crisp white button-down Oxford cloth shirt. His thick, wavy black hair was brushed back from his forehead. His even teeth shone white as he smiled into his telephone headset. "It's shirts and skins at fourth down and goal. It's a gut check." He gave Iris a thumbs-up as she walked by. She returned it.

She reached the part of the corridor where the trajectory with Herb Dexter's office gave her a view of him sitting at his desk. She looked up at him at that precise intersection, and he looked up at the same moment. She waved energetically and gave a cheery smile. He waved and smiled back.

Dexter was tall and narrow with a cheerful, honest face and an accessible, folksy look enhanced by his round, tortoiseshell glasses and trademark bow tie. He had an Ivy League background and had served in the Nixon administration as assistant to the assistant to the secretary of something or other. He'd sold a large farmhouse in Westchester County in New York to come west and put the L.A. office back on track. He was reading one of the myriad new reports that he now required from his staff in an effort to keep all his ducks in line and make sure the firm was scandal free, or at least to find out about any scandal before the rest of the world did.

"Read those reports," Iris said to herself.

"Sign of senility, Iris. Talking to yourself." Billy Drye walked up behind her, his briefcase in his hand. Drye had been with the firm as long as Iris. He had thinning blond hair and was of medium height and medium build. He had an impish smile, pointed eyebrows, and pointed ears and was pointedly misogynistic.

"At least it's intelligent conversation," Iris responded.

"Pardon me." Drye put his hand on Iris's waist as he walked by, even though there was plenty of clearance for both of them.

"Maybe in the next administration, Drye."

She reached the corner of the suite, fished her keys from her purse, and unlocked her office door. The cursor on her computer terminal pulsed mindlessly at her in the semilight. She felt for the light switch.

"Top of the dung heap."

She put her purse inside a drawer in the tall filing cabinet that stood in the corner, hung up her jacket behind the door, hoisted her briefcase onto her desk, clicked open the brass clasps, took out her thick, leather-bound date book, several yellow pads with rolled-back, scribbled-on pages, and a few manila files and threw everything on her desk and on the credenza behind it next to the window. When she turned to the credenza, she roused herself from autopilot and looked out the window. She'd earned this view. She might as well enjoy it.

The floor-to-ceiling windows in her corner office faced west and south. From the west she had a view of the shiny, spanking-new buildings of downtown and Wilshire Boulevard. On the rare clear day, she could glimpse a sliver of the ocean glittering in the sun and the silhouette of Santa Catalina Island thirty miles offshore. Today was a clear day.

From the southern window, tall office buildings blocked

her view. She could see into the cells of the other worker bees in the neighboring buildings. Most of the windows were dark, as it was still early. Books and papers were stacked on some of the window ledges. Commerce waiting to begin.

If she pressed her cheek against the southern window, she could see the rolling hills of the lower-middle-class neighborhoods of East L.A.: El Sereno, Lincoln Heights, City Terrace, Eagle Rock, Highland Park. She grew up there. Home wasn't far, but she was a long way from it.

Another set of windows overlooked the suite and gave a view of the investment counselors' cubicles and Herbert Dexter's larger office directly across from Iris's in the opposite corner.

Back on autopilot, she grabbed her BUDGETS ARE FOR WIMPS mug from her desk drawer and walked down the corridor and into the lunchroom, where she peeked in the refrigerator just to see if it held anything interesting. She lifted the lid of a pink cake box. The frosting on the remaining hunk said:

PPY FIFTIETH BIRTHD
GEO

She ran her finger over the slick paper liner where the cake had been cut away, gathering the gooey remnants. She put her finger into her mouth, then ran it against the box lining again. The lunchroom door opened and she quickly closed the refrigerator door.

"I saw you." Art Silva smiled his winning quarterback's smile and winked at her.

"Who's Geo?"

"George, over in Accounting." Art picked up the coffeepot and held it out in an offer to pour for Iris.

"Thank you. A well-trained man."

"I aim to please." He grinned ingratiatingly.

Something on Art's shirt sleeve caught Iris's attention.

Art followed her glance. "Shoot! It's the one I burned."

"You iron your own shirts?"

"Like you said, I'm well trained."

"Take a tip, Art. Send them out."

"Too expensive."

"Not as expensive as letting your clients know you don't have the dough." Iris took a sip of her coffee.

"You're right. In the six months since I was promoted to Sales, I've bought more clothes than in the whole two years I was over in Accounting."

"I didn't know you were there for two years."

"Worked there while I finished my degree and studied for my license at night." Art flicked his sleeve. "Great. The day I'm having a big meeting with Oz."

"Oz?"

"Dexter. You know. Smoke and mirrors."

Iris nodded impassively.

"I'm gonna make a play for Sam Gold's accounts when he retires."

Iris topped off her coffee mug. "Good luck. Just be aware that a couple of those accounts already have my name on them."

Art smiled broadly. His white teeth contrasted with his olive skin. "Hey! Sometimes even the guys on the bench get a chance at bat."

Iris smiled limply. "Right. See ya."

She walked out of the lunchroom and back down the corridor to her office. *Try to move in on me. Chew him up and spit him out.* "Does his own shirts!" she said out loud.

Sean Bliss looked at her legs as she passed his cubicle.

At the next cubicle, Billy Drye stood and pasted a concerned look on his face. "Just awful what happens to you when you get older." He tsk-tsked. "Talk to yourself, get flabby, lose your touch. I guess even an Ice Princess grows past her prime."

"Shaddup, Drye."

Iris got to her office in time to answer the ringing phone. The phone's LED display indicated it was an outside call.

"Iris Thorne."

"Good morning."

"Good morning yourself," Iris said to John Somers.

"I finally heard back from the Atlanta Police Department. They didn't come up with anything on Hal or Barbie Stringfellow. No priors. The guy I spoke with had eaten at Hal's restaurant. Said it was a nice place but he thought it had been sold. You want me to call the new owner, see if they knew Barbie?"

"If the cops don't have anything on her, that's good enough for me."

"Nothing under the name of Barbie Stringfellow. She might have used aliases."

"The Accounting Department deposited her check on Tuesday. Thursday afternoon they told me it cleared. Her money's good. If she coughs up the million bucks she was talking about, she could be an ax murderer for all I care. Bringing in some big money would stop the noise around here that I've lost my touch."

"You've never lost your touch with me."

"That's true. You've never had any complaints."

"Let's go away for your birthday. Let's take a long weekend."

"My birthday? That's a couple of months from now. You're planning ahead? What's gotten into you?"

"Just wanted to do something nice for the Ice Princess."

"I thought you wanted to go with me, not Penny."

"Ha, ha."

"You have any place in mind?" Iris opened her date book and began flipping through the pages.

"A guy at work was telling me about the Mariah Lodge up the coast in Las Pumas, about a four-hour drive from here. Heard of it?"

"Sure. It's a yuppie hideaway. A lot of the glitterati go there. It's *very* expensive."

"You're worth it."

"Worth it? You mean you hope I'll make it worth it for you." Iris studied her date book. "We've got time but we should still make a reservation."

"I've already called."

"Already called? My, my."

"Booked their best room, called the Cabin in the Woods. It's all by itself on this point overlooking the ocean."

"So we can be loud?"

"If you feel the urge."

Iris wrote in her date book. "It's in ink."

"Great. You still coming over to barbecue on Saturday?"

"Unless I get a better offer."

" 'Bye."

Iris hung up the phone, smiling. As soon as she did, it rang again. The LED display said H. DEXTER CALLING. She glanced out the window that overlooked the suite and saw him on the phone in his office.

"Morning, Herb," she answered cheerily.

"Iris! I just saw the paperwork on this new sale. Congratulations! Snagged a live one, huh?"

"She looks real good."

"Cold call?"

"Actually, she saw me on that TV show."

"Is that right?"

Iris saw him leaning back in his chair. It was swiveled to face the northern window, his back to the suite, the ankle of one leg on the knee of the other, one arm crooked behind his head. The posture was carefree and the conversation light. Iris chuckled with him, but she knew that he hadn't made it to that office by simply being pleasant.

Dexter reversed the position of his legs. "I'm glad to see you're bouncing back. You were in a bit of a slump after"— he lowered his voice reverentially—"the scandal. Frankly, I was a bit concerned about giving you those accounts of Sam Gold's we talked about. Some of them need to be handled with kid gloves and I wasn't sure whether you . . . still needed more time to regroup. But this is wonderful news. No one's happier to see it than I am, Iris. Keep up the good work."

7

IT WAS EARLY AFTERNOON, AND IRIS WAS WORKING HARD.

"Hi. This is Iris Thorne with McKinney Alitzer. I wanted to get some information on your limited partnership in the recycling plant. How many have you sold? My client is prepared to spend twenty-five, thirty grand, with more later if things work out."

Iris took notes on a clean page of a yellow pad. Used pages that she'd scribbled on sat in a pile on the corner of her desk.

"Thank you very much. I'm just evaluating different options at this point." Iris smiled into the telephone receiver as if it were an animate object. "I'll let you know. Good-bye."

She made a few closing notes, tore the sheet from the pad, grabbed the pile of pages she'd already worked, added the new sheet, and tapped the pages' edges even against her desk top.

"Okaay . . . for Barbeh," she said to herself, mocking Barbie's accent. "Three risk levels: high, I mean hiii, mod'rate, and low." She looked at the sheets and chewed her lower lip as she thought. "No . . . for Barbeh, gotta be very hiii, then mod'rately hiii, and mod'rate with different turnarounds." She started dividing up the pile. "Recycling plant. Very high and long-term. Medical stocks mutual fund. Moderate risk, short-term. Precious metals commodities . . ."

Amber Ambrose rapped quietly on Iris's door frame. Iris didn't hear her and continued muttering to herself, "Li'l ol' virtual reality company, new issue . . ." Amber rapped more insistently, and Iris jumped.

"Amber! Hi. Come in."

Amber took a long look over her shoulder before she

walked in. Iris glanced out her inside window and saw Billy Drye peeking around the side of his cubicle. He puckered his lips at Amber. Amber pulled Iris's door closed hard. Iris saw Drye laugh, his face crinkling into his Beaver Cleaver grin. Then he righted himself in his chair and disappeared inside his cubicle.

"Can I sit down?" Amber said distractedly, after she'd already seated herself in one of the two chairs facing Iris's desk.

Iris gestured affirmatively. Her phone rang. The LED display read B. DRYE CALLING. Iris let it ring. After five rings, the phone mail picked up.

Amber crossed her legs, looked at Iris, and delivered her message with dispatch. "Has Billy Drye ever . . . touched you?"

Iris knew immediately what Amber meant. "Yes. He's touched me."

Amber sighed and her shoulders dropped. "I'm so glad to hear you say that. At least I'm not alone." Her story, now exposed to the open air, spilled out. "Right after I came to McKinney Alitzer, a few months ago, Drye started making these little comments . . . you know. I didn't like it, but the guys over at Pierce Fenner used to give me a hard time too. I know they're testing you and you don't want to look like a bad sport or a baby. It comes with the territory. But then Drye starts getting very . . . explicit? I think, 'Okay, now what?' So I asked him to stop, told him I found his comments offensive. He just laughed. Then in the lunchroom, right before I came in here, he kind of jostled into me and sort of accidentally on purpose put his hand on my breast."

"What did you do?"

"I backed away and said, 'Don't *ever* do that again.' He just laughed, you know, that creepy giggle. I should have smacked him. Hell of a thing. He goes over the line, but I can't bring myself to respond in kind."

Iris's phone rang again. The LED display said, B. DRYE CALLING. She picked up. "Yes, dear. Don't flatter yourself. We're not talking about you." She hung up, then got up and turned the rod to close the miniblinds over the window that overlooked the suite.

"What is wrong with him? Is he nuts?" Amber's voice was shrill.

Iris nodded. "Yeah. I've known him for four years and he hasn't changed one iota."

"You never complained about him?"

"I used to complain to the guy before Dexter. He never took it seriously. Told me it was part of the environment here. Drye did things like leaving dildos in my briefcase and dropping pornographic snapshots of himself with women on my desk, all in front of his buddies. They'd laugh, but I think they just didn't want to stand apart from the herd. The touching, of course, Drye always did in private.

"I documented everything and avoided being alone with him. And I tried to give as good as I got. He finally stopped doing the more outrageous stuff, but he still taunts me all the time. I've gotten so used to him, I don't even hear it anymore. I'm really sorry he's after you. I know how upsetting it is."

"Iris, forgive me, but you seem untypically passive about the whole thing."

"I know it looks passive but at the time it was a hassle to do anything official, and risky, too. I was the first female investment counselor in this office. All eyes were on me. People loved telling me, 'If it's too hot, get out of the kitchen.' "

"I think we should go to Dexter."

"Right. All he's interested in is squashing controversy."

"We shouldn't have to take this."

Iris paused. "Let me think on it. Evaluate the trade-offs."

"Trade-offs? What Drye's doing is against the law!"

"I know. But outing him's not going to come without a price. He's not just going to roll over. Plus, I don't need the negative attention at this point in my career. You can always go to Dexter on your own."

"But we're stronger together, Iris. You've been here a long time. Everyone respects you."

"I promise I'll think on it, okay?" She stood up and grabbed her coffee mug. Amber took the cue and also stood. She opened the door, and Iris walked with her down the corridor. Drye poked his head out of his cubicle to watch them.

Amber went back to her desk, and Iris continued to the

lunchroom. She filled her mug with the last of the coffee and took a sip. It was very hot from having sat on the warmer for a long time and tasted burnt. She took another distracted sip and puckered her lips, looked at the coffee, and dumped it into the sink. She began to make a fresh pot. It was something to do as she gathered her thoughts. As she ran water into the pot and grabbed one of the premeasured packages of coffee, the lunchroom door opened behind her. The cologne and the arrogant footsteps placed the person before he even spoke. An office is so like a household, Iris thought, steeped in familiarity and routine.

"Hello, Drye," she said with her back still to the door.

The footsteps approached. He was standing very close behind her. She was used to this. Drye's life was a power play. He stood in your space so that you'd step back. She wondered whether he did it consciously. Maybe it was the only way he could get close to another person. She took her time finishing her job, pouring the water from the pot into the brewer before turning to face him. "What's going on?" She still held the package of coffee in her hand.

He was still standing very close to her. At any time of day, Drye's breath had a unique and distasteful sour smell. His dental hygiene had been a subject of morbid speculation among Iris and her office cronies. She wanted to gag, but refused to step back.

"What were you and Amber Ambrose"—he said her name derisively—"up to in your office?"

"That's none of your business, Drye."

"You guys aren't buddies. You don't have closed-door chats."

"Very observant. Too bad you can't channel that into something positive."

"You weren't talking about me, were you?"

"Now why would we talk about you?"

"Because Amber's out to get me."

"Why would she waste her time?"

"Because she has an attitude about men."

Iris shook her head bitterly and turned back to the coffee-maker. She pulled the plastic and foil coffee package between her hands, feeling Drye close behind her. The package wouldn't give. She slammed the package on the sink, turned her head to the side, and said, "Drye, for Chrissakes, why are you standing so fucking close to me?"

She didn't expect him to move, but yelling at him felt good. She was surprised when he took a step back.

She put the package between her teeth and managed to tear a gash in it. At the same moment, Drye threw himself against her and pressed his pelvis against her buttocks. Iris could feel he was aroused. The coffee grounds showered over her face, down the front of her blouse, and onto the floor, scattering everywhere.

She kicked Drye's shin with the heel of her pump. He released his grip and grabbed his ankle.

"Bitch!"

Iris stared at him open-mouthed.

Drye laughed.

Iris spoke evenly. "I thought you and I had come to an understanding, Drye, but that tore it."

He laughed even harder. He grabbed his ribs and bent over in mock hysteria, backing up until he ran into the aluminum and plastic lunchroom chairs. They skidded against the linoleum.

Some of the bitter grounds had fallen into Iris's mouth. She tried to pull them off her tongue, then brushed at the coffee that clung to the front of her blouse and skirt.

Drye watched her. She stopped brushing and looked at him. "What?" she said accusingly.

He straightened the knot in his tie. "You can't prove anything."

"You're wrong."

"Just be careful, Iris. You don't know who you're dealing with."

"Oh, I'll be careful, all right, because I know exactly who I'm dealing with."

They stared at each other for several long seconds until Drye turned on his heel and walked out of the room. Iris wet a paper towel under the tap and mopped up the errant coffee grounds from the floor, cursing under her breath. "Two-bit bastard. Bully."

She walked back into her office, locking the door behind

her. The miniblinds were still closed. *Lousy son of a bitch. Try to intimidate me.* She stood over the trash can and brushed the grounds from her blouse, finally unbuttoning it. Coffee grounds had fallen inside and were stuck to her skin, which was moist with nervous perspiration. *Wants to play hardball . . .* She used a tissue to brush the grounds off, reaching underneath her brassiere. The coffee left brown smudges against her skin. *We'll play hardball.*

After she'd cleaned up as best she could and put herself back together, she pulled open one of the drawers in her filing cabinet and ran her fingers across the tops of the manila folders. She'd filed the documentation under a phony client name to disguise it from prying eyes. The file for C. GUMBAS had worked its way to the back. It was an anagram of SCUMBAG. Iris pulled out the file, then reopened her door and miniblinds, not wanting to arouse suspicion.

Inside the file were several pages of lined yellow paper. A list of times and events was written in blue ink, pencil, black rollerball, whatever was at hand.

8/23   Drye suggests I sleep w/ him. We're alone in elevator.

9/15   Drye puts hand on my ass in lunchroom. Alone again.

Iris had kept track of the incidents for a year before she stopped. She brought up the word processing program on her computer, typed in everything on the list, then added the events of today. She saved the file to the hard disk, then made a copy on diskette, which she put in her briefcase. She put the C. GUMBAS file back into the filing cabinet.

She looked at her watch. It was time to leave for her appointment. She turned off the computer, gathered her things, and started to walk out of her office. She paused with her hand on the light switch, changed her mind, went back inside, and turned on the computer again. She deleted the file from her hard disk, then opened the filing cabinet, pulled out C. GUMBAS, and put the file in her briefcase. She left the office, turned off the light, and closed the door.

8

IT WAS 3:30, AND ALMOST EVERYONE HAD LEFT THE OFFICE for the weekend. Art Silva was typing client follow-up data into his computer. He kept meticulous records on all his clients and frequently stayed late to update his files. His computer keyboard answered with a shallow plastic retort as he touch-typed, the long fingers of his quarterback's hands making small space of the keyboard. He sat tall in his desk chair, the woven leather braces that crossed his back making his shoulders look even broader in his white Oxford cloth shirt, which had lost its morning crispness. It was a discordant image, Art's primeval physique working the dainty plastic of the computer.

He ran his hand through his black, wavy hair, which he kept a bit long at the back and high on the top. He looked at his watch, a gold concoction with a bright band that was not cheap but was far from a status piece. Art wore a class ring from his alma mater, a local state university, on his right hand. It was set with a red stone simulating his birthstone, and his initials were inset on either side of it.

Art tilted his head up and looked over the top of his cubicle across the empty desks toward the corner office. The door was open and the light was still on. He checked the time once more, then stood up. He picked at the burn mark on his shirt, then took his suit jacket from the hook on the cubicle wall and put it on. His suit was gray with a chalk stripe that was neither too broad nor too thin, neither too far apart nor too close together, a fabric that was not designed to make a fashion statement. Like his watch, the suit was not budget and not the best, but it was the best that Art could afford at this point, and he bought the best that he could afford, knowing that appearances count, confident that eventually he'd be able to buy whatever he wanted. He had, however, spent a lot of money on his tie. It was silk and printed with a fashionably splashy pattern of Las Vegas icons: dice, card fans, roulette wheels, numbered keno balls, and slot machines. It was his favorite tie because it reflected his philosophy of life—roll the dice, spin the wheel.

He grabbed a yellow pad and started walking down the corridor toward Herbert Dexter's office, rolling his shoulders as he walked, marking the beat of his progression, a gait left over from the high school football field and the barrio, a motion that suggested bravado, that the best defense is a good offense.

At Dexter's doorway, Art rapped on the door and waited to be invited in.

Dexter was reading *The Wall Street Journal,* holding his head in his hands with his fingertips spread against his temples, the plain gold wedding band on his left hand resting loosely between the knuckles of his bony ring finger. There was a pile of several back issues of the *Journal* from the previous week squared against a corner of his desk.

He looked up when Art knocked. The fluorescent lights reflected off his round glasses, revealing fingerprints and smudges on the lenses, something that Dexter, who was never without his glasses, hardly noticed.

"Art! Come on in!" he said jubilantly. His office was decorated in a western motif. A large painting of Native Americans engaged in a buffalo hunt hung behind his desk. Several replicas of Remington sculptures sat in his office, tired cowboys on tired steeds, running cowboys on running steeds, fraternal cowboys sharing smokes, placed so that Dexter could gaze upon them after he had put down the current issue of *The Economist* or *US News & World Report.*

He stood up behind his desk and leaned across it to shake Art's hand. His angular frame, long neck, and long, bony fingers made him seem even taller. He'd always been a slender reed of a man and hadn't filled out much in middle age, but there was something in his build that hinted that he'd played some kind of ball in school. He still had most of his lank, pale hair.

SLOW SQUEEZE

Art reached his hand out to meet Dexter's across the desk. They pressed each other's flesh heartily and smiled energetically and made meaningful eye contact. Dexter's handshake was firm, but Art made sure his was even firmer, to the extent that it was almost bone-crushing.

"Sit down, sit down," Dexter said, beaming with broad, even teeth that had a slightly yellow cast. "Can I get you some coffee?"

Art sat in one of the tapestry-upholstered chairs facing Dexter's desk. "No, thanks. I'm fine. I've had plenty today."

"I know how that goes." Dexter relaxed into his chair, letting his knees fall open and clasping both hands behind his head. It was a wide-open pose that said, "Give me your best shot."

Art attempted his own relaxed posture by setting one leg on top of the other, grabbing his ankle with one hand, and hooking his other arm across the back of his chair.

"Catching up on the *Journal*, huh?" Art said amiably, nodding his head toward the pile of newspapers.

"Oh yeah," Dexter said. "I read every issue religiously. If I miss one, I save it for later. Haven't missed one in fifteen years."

"No kidding. Why?" Art asked guilelessly.

"My wife tells me I have a compulsive personality."

Art pushed his lower lip out, tightened his chin so that the flesh was dimpled, and nodded sagely, not knowing how to respond.

Dexter continued, "But I'm inclined to think I like to keep up on current events." He took his hands from behind his head, rolled his chair forward, and dropped his clasped hands on his desk with a thump. "So, Arthur, you wanted to meet with me."

Art also leaned forward, placing his arms on his legs and dropping his clasped hands between his knees. "Mr. Dexter, I've been in Sales for about six months and I've been working really hard." He paused, waiting for confirmation. None was forthcoming. He continued, "I want to be a success at McKinney Alitzer. I want to be the best salesman you've got."

"I admire your ambition. Good thing to see in a young man."

Buoyed by Dexter's response, Art became more animated. He unclasped his hands and moved them expansively. "I've landed a couple of new accounts. They're starting slow but I'm nursing them, gaining their confidence." Art shimmied forward until he was sitting on the edge of his chair. "I know I've got what it takes to be the best. I know I do." He leaned his forearms on the opposite side of Dexter's desk. The tapestry chair tipped forward slightly on its slender front legs. Dexter sat back in his own chair to avoid being nose to nose with Art.

Art rolled into his pitch, elbows on the desk and both hands held out. "Mr. Dexter, I want Sam Gold's accounts when he retires." Having reached his apex, Art collapsed back into the chair with his legs sprawled out. Too nervous to sit still, he waggled his legs in and out.

Dexter sat quietly for a painful beat or two, rubbing his chin between his thumb and forefinger. Finally, he leaned forward in his chair. "Art, I'm glad you brought that up. I'd been meaning to talk to you about this. I'm happy to say that you are getting some of Sam Gold's accounts. To be fair, I'm dividing them up among all the sales reps according to the management requirements of each account."

Art was sitting on the edge of his chair again. "That's fair."

"I'm happy to tell you that you'll be managing the Panosian Markets and the Silvers."

Art blinked his eyes as if it would help him hear better. "Panosian Markets and the Silvers?"

Dexter was again sitting with his legs spread and his hands clasped behind his head. "They're both long-standing, medium-sized accounts—good clients—and I'm confident you'll do well with them."

"The Silvers? That old couple? All they want are money markets and CDs. And Panosian's got a couple of mom and pop stores in Armenian neighborhoods like my dad's corner store in East L.A."

"These are people who have entrusted their life savings to us. It's a big responsibility and not to be taken lightly.

You have to walk before you can run, Arthur. It's hard to break in new clients."

"But I've brought in new clients. I know how to handle new business."

"You've done great, but they've all been related to you. Your uncle, your cousin. Of course, that's the way you have to start in this business. That's the way I started. But the worst thing you can do right now is get in over your head. And that's the worst thing I could let you do."

"What about Consolidated Industries and the Keyhole Fund and those pension plans Sam's got?"

"To be frank, I need a more seasoned person to handle those. They'll be split between Iris Thorne and Billy Drye."

"All right. And Amber?"

"Amber's getting six. She's been in the industry significantly longer than you have."

"And Sean Bliss gets the rest."

"That's correct."

Art stood up. "Why?" He walked to the center of Dexter's office, then turned to face him. "No. I know why."

Dexter was sitting straight in his chair again, looking as if he were preparing to stand.

"You're friends with Sean's father. You both belong to the Edward Club. Like they'd ever let *me* in that club."

"My relationship with Sean's father has nothing to do with this. Sean's background and personality are more in line with the needs of these accounts than yours are."

"His background?" Art walked to Dexter's desk and leaned on it with both hands, his shoulders pressing against the leather braces that crossed his back. "We've been in Sales the exact same amount of time." Art slapped Dexter's desk. "You must mean his race."

Dexter stood up. He was a head taller than Art, but they probably weighed about the same. "If you think your being Hispanic has something to do with this, you're sadly mistaken, fella. I put a lot of thought into matching clients with reps. I can see by your display here that I made the correct decision. Now, please step away from my desk."

Art became aware of himself and stepped back from the

desk. He looked at Dexter sheepishly, his big hands dangling limply at his sides. "I got carried away. I'm sorry."

"I'll accept your apology. I was a young turk once too. A real hothead. But that didn't fly when I was coming up and it's not going to fly around here. I'll give you two pieces of advice, Arthur." Dexter pointed one finger at him. "Lose the attitude." He straightened a second finger toward him. "Pay your dues."

He unrolled the rest of his fingers and extended his palm toward Art. Art took it. Dexter leaned across his desk and patted Art's shoulder with his other hand. "Keep up the hard work. You're doing great."

"Thanks," Art said, releasing Dexter's hand and moving toward the door. "There's only one other thing."

"What's that?"

"It's *Arturo,* not Arthur." He walked out the door.

9

JULIE'S WAS THE STREET-LEVEL WATERING HOLE IN THE McKinney Alitzer office tower. The room was dominated by an oval bar around which business people freely and unapologetically invaded one another's space. It was Friday and happy hour was just getting started. The folks who had gotten paid that day had an extra reason to celebrate. The eagle will soar.

Iris spotted an empty stool at the bar and nabbed it a second ahead of another woman. She was fifteen minutes late to meet Barbie Stringfellow, but there was no Barbie to be seen. Iris ordered a chardonnay and grabbed the last piece of focaccia from a napkin-lined basket. The flat bread was covered in an olive oil–based paste of garlic, basil, and rosemary. Iris gobbled it down, then dabbed her finger in the basket to retrieve fallen basil and rosemary fragments. She asked the bartender for more.

Several television sets were hung around the oval bar, all tuned to the Lakers game. Most of the men and some of the women had tilted their heads to watch big men skilled at running while bouncing and throwing a ball. Iris tried to become interested in the game as a way of passing the time, but watching the players run back and forth, back and forth soon bored her.

She was into her second basket of bread, the stress of the work week giving way to unrestrained consumption, when she caught a flash of purple out of the corner of her eye. Barbie had arrived, forty-five minutes late. Iris waved a piece of focaccia at her and Barbie returned the wave with fingers decorated with shiny nails and glittering rings.

The crowd prevented too breezy an entrance, but Barbie made the most of what was available. She wore a purple chiffon blouse that was sheer except for two patch pockets over her breasts. Her bra, visible through the blouse, was also purple, as was her leather miniskirt and the faux jewel–encrusted baseball cap perched at a jaunty angle on her abundant hair. She slid through the crowd, holding her hands above her head, pressing full body against the men she passed, momentarily drawing their attention away from the Lakers game.

"Iris! I love this! Out and amongst 'em!" She threw her large, white purse on top of the bar, where it landed solidly. "Whatcha got? Wine again? Barkeep! Yoo-hoo! Barkeep! Bourbon and ginger ale in a tall glass, if you please. Whatcha eatin'?" Barbie leaned close to Iris, pressing her breasts against her arm to grab a piece of the focaccia. Iris leaned away.

Barbie laughed. "Sorry, honey. These enter a room before I do." She bit into the bread, leaving a fuchsia lipstick mark. "Hmmmm . . . different," she said with her mouth full. "Sorry I'm late, sugar. This town, I'm tellin' ya. I don't know how y'all get anywhere. Well, how the heck are ya, Iris?"

"I'm good, thanks. I've done a lot of research and I've got a great plan laid out for you." Iris started to reach down into her briefcase, which was sitting on the floor.

Barbie put her hand on her arm. "Darlin'! Always the businesswoman. Always on the go. Just go, go, go. Relax! Let's have a drink. We can *always* talk about business. Good Lord, ain't it the truth?" Barbie started brushing at Iris's shoulder. "What the heck you got on ya?"

Iris looked at her shoulder. "Oh. Coffee. It's a long story."

"Sounds like a doozy. Here's my drink. Boy oh boy, is this gonna go down good. Let's toast, sugar. To the beginning of a beautiful friendship. Remember that from *Casablanca?* I *love* that movie. Cry every time I see it."

Iris lifted her glass to Barbie's.

A man wearing an expensive suit and standing next to Barbie smiled at her with amusement.

Barbie spotted him. "You got a financial manager? I got a great one. Give him your card, Iris. You got a card? Give him your card."

The man looked trapped.

"What do y'all do for a livin'?" she smiled.

"I'm unemployed," he said.

"We got somethin' in common." She pushed his arm. "I'm unemployed too!"

Iris pulled a card from her inside jacket pocket and handed it to the man. "Aren't you an attorney for O'Connell and Meyers? A friend of mine works in your office."

The man pressed his index finger against his lips as if they were sharing a secret. He looked at the card and pocketed it.

Barbie took a long slug of her drink and turned back to Iris. "Betcha he calls you. Whatcha bet?"

"Hey! Lakers!" Art Silva walked up behind Iris and put his hands around her neck and gave her a shake. "What did I miss, Iris? Give me the play-by-play. Ha, ha! Hey, Jeff!" Art reached his arm across the bar to shake the bartender's hand. "What up? What's the score?"

"Lakers, fifty-two, forty-seven." He sat a light beer in front of Art.

"Swee-eet! Awright ... here we go, boys ... two points, Lakers!" The Lakers made a basket and Art slapped high fives with the bartender and two other men nearby. Art gulped the beer. "You know what I like about sports, Jeff?"

The bartender played along. "No, what do you like about sports, Art?"

"In sports, they don't care where you come from, who you know, or what you look like. All that counts is how you play the game. Am I right?"

"When you're right, you're right."

"Damn right I'm right." The Lakers scored again. "All right!" He raised his hand for another round of high fives. Barbie put her palm in the air in Art's direction and he slapped it.

Barbie slid close to Iris's left ear. "Who's your friend?"

Iris faced her. This close, she could see Barbie's age through her makeup. "Art Silva. We work together."

"I do believe he's the *most* attractive man I've seen in Los Angle-lees."

Iris looked at Art. He evoked a sensation of cool sheets and clean sweat. "He does have a certain animal magnetism."

"He married?"

"Nope."

"Got a girl?"

"I don't think so."

"What's he do?"

"He's an investment counselor, like me."

"Really! He as good as you?"

"No. But he's good. He's learning."

"Silva. What kinda name is that?"

"Mexican-American. He's from East L.A."

Art was wedged next to Iris on her right. Barbie leaned back and looked around Iris for a complete view. Art's shirt cuffs were unbuttoned and rolled back, revealing olive skin, dark hair, and strong wrists with lean muscles running up underneath the sleeves. His suit pants revealed tight buttocks that the muscles had pulled into hollows on each side. Barbie didn't miss any of it.

"He's a young 'un, ain't he?"

"I think he's in his late twenties."

"Just a pup. I love these Latin men y'all got out here."

Iris looked at her and was about to speak when Barbie responded for her. "I know! What men don't I like?" She butted Iris's shoulder with her own, then raised her glass. Iris clinked her glass against it. "What can I say, honey? Goin' without for as long as I have can make a woman real cranky. That's one reason I wanted to get out of Atlanta. Everyone watching the Widow Stringfellow to make sure she behaved appropriately."

The Lakers scored two free throws and Art high-fived everyone within arm's reach. Barbie put her hand up again and when Art slapped it, she closed her fingers around his, winking at him before letting go.

Art leaned back around Iris and stole an appraising look at Barbie. "Who's your friend?" he said into Iris's right ear.

"My new client, Barbie Stringfellow."

"Yeah? Tell me about her."

"She's wealthy, lonely, and horny, and she's too old for you, sweet meat, *and* she's my client."

"So she's your client, so what?" Art leaned forward against the bar and looked at Barbie from the front. She leaned forward at the same time.

"Peekaboo." Barbie grinned.

Iris said, "I like to keep business and pleasure separate."

Art spoke into Iris's ear. "She's not *my* client. She's good-looking even though she's got a little age on her."

"Happens to the best of us."

"But I can do that. Especially if she's got dough."

Iris threw up her hands. "Would you like me to introduce you?"

Art's bright smile answered for him.

Iris stepped back from the bar so that Art and Barbie could face each other. "Arturo Silva"—Iris held her right hand in Art's direction, then held her left toward Barbie—"may I present Mrs. Barbie Stringfellow of Atlanta."

Art extended his hand toward Barbie and she delicately shook it.

"Pleased to meet you, Arturo."

"Everyone calls me Art."

"You *are* a work of art ..."

Iris rolled her eyes.

"But I'll call you Arturo." Barbie rolled the last *r* on her tongue. She jerked her head toward Iris. "She's not used to me. I just say whatever's on my mind. It can be a frightenin' prospect sometimes, I admit."

"I'm scared right now," Iris said.

Barbie picked up Art's tie and slid it between her fingers. "You a gamblin' man, Arturo?"

He smiled. "Roll the dice."

"Since you're a gamblin' man, maybe you'd honor us with your presence at dinner."

Art shrugged his shoulders and looked at Iris. "Sure I won't be in the way?"

"Barbie, we were going to discuss my investment strategy for you. I'd like to get going on it Monday morning."

"Well, honey, we'll snatch a few minutes. You got that cop of yours waitin' at home?"

"He's working tonight."

"Well, let's make a night of it."

"Yeah! Let's party!" Art said.

"Now I'm not so sure *I* won't be in the way," Iris said.

The Lakers game was interrupted by a news broadcast.

"What is this bullshit?" A man at the other end of the bar gestured toward the television set with a lager glass that was half full of beer. "Put the game back on!"

"The trial of four white LAPD officers accused of using excessive force in the arrest of black motorist Rodney King has been moved from Los Angeles to Simi Valley in Ventura County. Attorneys for the officers claimed their clients could not get a fair trial in Los Angeles County."

"Simi Valley!" another man said. "It's a redneck town."

The man with the lager glass shouted, "Who the hell cares? Put the game back on!"

The station played the shadowy videotape of the motorist being beaten by the police. Iris looked away. Barbie watched with fascination.

Someone else shouted, "They stopped the game to show this drunk being beat up for the millionth time?"

"If he'd stayed on the ground, they wouldn't have had to hit him like that," a woman said.

"There were four guys kicking him in the head," Art said. "He didn't know which way was up."

"It was his own fault," the woman continued.

The man with the lager glass said, "The cops should have taken out the cameraman, too."

The game resumed. Several people clapped.

"Let's get out of here before I punch somebody," Art said.

"Sounds good to me," Barbie said. "I heard about this new place . . . Tangerine?"

"We'll never get in there on a Friday night," Iris said. "They're booked three weeks in advance."

Barbie grabbed her purse off the bar and it swung heavily from its strap. She reached in, pulled out enough money to pay for all their drinks, and tossed it on the bar. "We'll just see about that. That okay with you, Arturo?" She adjusted her baseball cap.

"Whatever's your pleasure."

Barbie put her hand on Art's cheek. "I love this man." She turned on her heel and started making her way through the crowd. After a few steps, she looked back. "Y'all comin'?"

Iris grabbed her purse and briefcase. "Yes, ma'am." She turned to Art. "After you, work of art."

Art spoke into Iris's ear. "I feel like she wants to eat me with a spoon."

"She does. Sprinkled with a li'l sugah on top."

"Oohh," Art said. "That gave me a chill."

10

ART DROVE, BARBIE RODE SHOTGUN, AND IRIS SAT IN THE backseat of Art's black 1966 Mustang convertible. He drove Barbie to her car in the office tower garage so she could get her coat.

"Swee-eet!" Art exclaimed when he saw the red Mercedes two-seater with the white leather interior.

"You like it, Arturo? I'll let you drive it sometime." Barbie opened the trunk and pulled out a full-length red fox coat.

"Whoa!" Art exclaimed. "That's not real, is it?"

"Course it's real." Barbie got back in the car. Both Art and Iris couldn't resist touching the fur.

"So beautiful and so politically incorrect," Iris said.

"Since what I had to do to get this coat was politically incorrect, I figure I've earned it. If any of those animal rights people come near it, I'll tear off their heads and spit down their necks."

"I do believe you would," Iris said. "But it's not very cold out, Barbie."

"What does being cold have to do with it?"

"Let's kick it." Art sped through the garage. The Mustang's tires squealed against the smooth concrete.

Art drove down Olympic Boulevard, which traverses the city from East L.A. to the ocean. Iris lay across the rear seat with her hands clasped behind her head and her stockinged feet propped up on the side of the car behind Art. The Mustang's convertible top was down. It was a cool and clear January night, the sky lightened to indigo by natural and artificial light sources—street lamps, jets, news and police helicopters, headlights, houses, businesses, and the pure light of the moon and the few stars that managed to shine through.

The streets near downtown had a Central American flavor. The restaurants, bars, and stores were owned by local moms and pops who painted the building facades with colorful homemade pictures of the fish, rice, meat, *empanadas,* cold beer, dolls, records, boots, and dresses found inside. There were many people in the streets, walking or sitting on the front porches of grand old homes that had long ago been divided up into many apartments, talking and watching their kids play.

Farther west, they reached Koreatown. Stone Buddhas and strings of hanging lanterns decorated the small front yards of the tiny, old wood-framed houses found throughout L.A.'s modest neighborhoods, the neighborhoods changing hands over and over again as immigrant populations moved in, moved up, and moved out. New corner minimalls displayed bright plastic signs in Korean and English for acupuncturists, herbalists, designer clothing shops, small electronics stores, and Korean barbecue restaurants. A large brick church with Stars of David molded into its facade and stained-glass windows wore a new sign: KOREAN PRESBYTE-RIAN CHURCH.

At La Brea, Iris, Barbie, and Art headed north, and chichi restaurants, bakeries, and retro clothing stores appeared. At Melrose, they turned left and entered West Hollywood, a city that was once just an older L.A. neighborhood cluttered with furniture upholstery shops and kosher delis. Now in Westho, it was a full-time job keeping up with what was hot and what was not. Streets were clogged with bars catering to all flavors of gays and straights. There were art deco and fifties furniture stores, interior design shops, hair salons, coffeehouses featuring open-mike poetry readings, and more bakeries and more restaurants and more retro clothing stores. In Westho, haircuts, hair colors, and attire were cutting edge. Parking laws were strict. Neon reigned. Ennui was in.

In front of Tangerine, two red-jacketed, Hispanic valets hopped up to the Mustang. One of them opened Barbie's door; she swung an ample but shapely leg onto the sidewalk, the purple miniskirt hiked high around her thighs. The valet ogled her. She stood on the sidewalk and demurely pulled the fox closed around her.

"Jefe," Art said to the valet who had climbed into the driver's seat. "Park it up close so's I don't get ripped off."

The valet gave Art a thumbs-up and depressed the accelerator, making the Mustang's eight cylinders roar.

Tangerine was a white concrete box inset with industrial glass laced with chicken wire and irregularly shaped greenish glass cubes. The restaurant was built around an open-air courtyard and had the requisite glassed-in kitchen, where white-toqued chefs could be seen busily working with knives and fire. White wire patio chairs and metal patio tables were crammed together across the concrete floor. The primo table was next to the kitchen where one could watch the renowned head chef fret over his brood.

"So this is Tangerine," Art said. "You sit on patio chairs?"

Iris looked at the people crowded around the tiny bar. "And are grateful for the privilege."

"Look!" Barbie pulled on Iris's sleeve. "There's Chet Steele!"

"Who?" Iris asked.

"I don't know his real name, but that's who he plays on the soap opera."

"Oh."

Art made his way to the table where two black-outfitted hosts decided who sat and where. One was an angular woman with long blond hair held away from her face with a wide elastic band pulled down to her hairline. The other was an angular blond man with freshly trimmed hair cut scalp-close at the bottom and full at the top, where a shock of hair had been bleached platinum. Both of them had gold hoop earrings, long fingers, and straight, white teeth. They looked very clean.

"Uuuh!" Barbie inhaled sharply and pulled Iris's sleeve. "Look!"

"Where?"

"There!"

Iris squinted where Barbie was pointing. "What?"

"It's Charles Bronson!"

"Huh. I thought he was dead."

"Isn't it awful what happened to his wife?"

"Whose wife?"

"Charles Bronson's! She died of cancer," Barbie said soberly.

"Oh. Right. Terrible."

"I wish I had my camera."

"Excuse me, Barbie. Be back in a minute."

Iris walked through the restaurant and finally found the restrooms, discreetly tucked in a corner behind a screen. The restaurant's designer had continued the stark, white, minimalist theme here. The sole decor was a single long-stemmed, waxy, orange-red anthurium bloom in a clear glass vase with clear glass marbles at the bottom. As usual, there weren't enough stalls. Two women were waiting. One of them had her T-shirt pulled up to bare her perfect breasts.

"They look great," the other woman said.

"They're not too big? I told him I didn't want them too big, that I didn't want to look like a bimbo."

In the restaurant, Art walked up to the reception desk and was about to speak when a man shoved in front of him. He was fashionably grungy, wearing torn, baggy jeans cinched around his waist with an oversized belt, a black T-shirt with the message EXTINCT MEANS NO MORE partially tucked in, dusty boots, and a weathered motorcycle jacket. His long hair was caked with a greasy concoction.

He handed the host a neon-green plastic device and ran his hands impatiently through his greasy hair, bumping his elbow into Art.

"Hey, man," Art said. "I was here first."

"I was beeped." He drew out his lips and the word with disdain.

The host grabbed two menus and led the man and his date through the restaurant. They tried their best to look as bored as possible.

Art glared at them for a long time, as if staring would vilify the man, then turned back to the hostess, who was smiling vacuously.

"Hi. What can you do for a party of three?"

The hostess blinked her clear, turquoise-blue eyes. The perimeters of the colored contact lenses were visible just beyond her irises, which were probably blue to begin with but not the desired blue-green hue. "I'm sorry. We've been booked solid for weeks." She sounded as if she meant it.

Art leaned on the table toward the hostess. "See that woman over there?"

She looked at Barbie, who gave her a friendly smile, out of earshot of Art's conversation. Iris emerged from the restroom and joined Barbie.

"She's from Atlanta and very rich and very important," Art told the hostess. "She's a client of my friend and myself and we're trying to impress her. She has her heart set on eating here."

The hostess frowned apologetically. "See all those people waiting? I can't seat you tonight."

Art walked over to Barbie and Iris and put an arm over

each of their shoulders. "Ladies, why don't I take you to a place where we can have some real fun?"

"You're saying they won't let us in?" Barbie asked.

"Barbie, I did my best."

Barbie walked over to the table, the fox swaying with her gait, and approached the host, who had returned. She put her hand on his arm, pulled him aside without a word, turned him so that his back was to the reservation desk, and spoke confidentially into his ear. "Sir. I'm Barbeh Stringfellow of the Stringfellows of Atlanta." She paused to let her announcement sink in. The host smiled and nodded expectantly. "Your partner told my friend that you're full up."

"We're booked weeks in advance."

"I understand that, I do. I'm in the restaurant business myself, and I don't want to put you in a difficult situation darlin', but"—she unzipped her purse, reached inside, and held out a twenty-dollar bill—"I'm only gonna be in town a short while, because I—"

The host looked amused and gently pushed her hand away. "I'm really sorry."

"—flew into town to go to my sister's funeral earlier today. I leave tomorrow, and—" Barbie reached her hand into her purse and added a fifty to the twenty—"I had my heart set on dinin' at your fine restaurant before I left." Barbie's eyes filled with tears.

The host's expression changed from skeptical to surprised.

"This was my dear sister's favorite place. It would make me feel like she's still here with me." Barbie pressed the bills into the host's hand and closed his fingers around them. "This is just a li'l somethin' to compensate you for your trouble."

The host slipped the cash into his pants pocket.

Barbie touched her eye. "I'm so glad you understand."

The host slyly looked over his shoulder at the hostess, who was showing a couple to their table on the other side of the restaurant. He pointed to a corner table that the busboy was just setting with fresh linens and grabbed three menus. "Quick, before I get busted."

"Thank you ever so. I've always heard that Los Angelees was a friendly town."

"Right."

Barbie quickly walked over to Iris and Art. "Follow me." Iris and Art followed.

Once they were seated, the host handed them menus. "I'm sorry about your sister," he said to Barbie.

She looked up at him sadly.

"Can I take your coat?"

Barbie slid her fur off and handed it to the host, who walked to the coat rack holding it away from him as if he were carrying a dead rat.

"Your sister?" Art asked.

She patted Art's hand. "Sugar, a sad ol' story sweetened with a li'l honey. Find your weak link and pour it on."

"I'm impressed," Art said.

"The woman gets what she wants," Iris said.

Barbie nodded. "Ain't that the name of the game?"

The waiter came over. "Hello, my name is William and I'll be your server tonight."

"William!" Barbie exclaimed. "Ain't there any plain ol' Bills in this town?"

William smiled condescendingly. "Would you care for anything to drink?"

"Champagne!" Barbie jumped up a little, like a cork popping. "To celebrate with my friends."

"I'll bring you the wine list."

"I'm sure whatever you bring will be just fine, Billy," Barbie said, stretching out the *i* in *fine*.

"Something dry," Iris said.

"Something dry," William repeated as dryly as the champagne they ordered. He turned to walk away, making a face before his back was completely to them.

Barbie opened her menu. "Duck sausage? Now why the heck is duck sausage on every menu in this town? What kind of half-wit would make sausage out of a duck anyway? And rabbit? That's what the poor folks ate where I come from. We came all the way across town for this?"

"It's California cuisine, *ma chérie*," Iris said. "They have some things that are less ... exotic."

"How about a burger?" Art asked.

"Here's one," Iris offered, "with goat cheese and cranberry-pineapple salsa."

Barbie closed her menu, leaned her elbows on it, and rested her head in her palms. She looked around the restaurant.

"See any more stars, Barbie?" Iris asked.

"I think I seen that gal over there in a TV commercial, but that's about it."

A waiter served food to the people at the next table. Barbie turned to see what they'd ordered. The plate in front of one of the women held a cardboard container with parsley, spinach leaves, and steamed baby vegetables on the side.

"What the heck is she eatin'?"

"That's from her diet plan," Iris said. "She brought her own food."

"I guess you're better off bringin' your own food." Barbie leaned her head on her palm and drummed the porcelain nails of her other hand on the table, the tapping muted by the tablecloth. "You know, this place ain't such a big deal after all."

"It's kind of stuck-up, if you ask me," Art said.

"Well, we might as well talk about my ideas for your portfolio." Iris reached down to get her briefcase.

Barbie swatted the air. "Honey, I'm too depressed to talk about that right now."

"You want to go to a place where we can dance?" Art asked.

Barbie brightened. "Yeah! Let's dance!"

"A real L.A. place?"

"Yeah! Let's have some fun!"

"Iris?"

Iris slid her briefcase from her lap and set it back on the floor. "Sure. We could be having a lot more fun at these prices."

William brought the champagne and expertly freed the cork with only the smallest pop. He started to pour the champagne into flute glasses that he'd placed in front of them, but Barbie quickly put her hand over the top of her glass. William tipped the bottle up just before any spilled out and gave Barbie a tight-lipped look.

"We gotta go, Billy. We'll take the champagne and these three glasses too. A hundred bucks cover it?" Barbie didn't wait for William to answer. She reached inside her bag, pulled out a hundred-dollar bill, and held it toward William. He looked at it as if she were handing him a cockroach. Barbie tipped the bill up and down in his direction and waited. William reluctantly took it. Barbie stood, grabbed the bottle of champagne by the neck, and scooped up the flutes in her other hand.

"Let's go, kids." She sashayed through the restaurant, swinging the bottle in one hand and the champagne flutes, held upside down by their stems so that they rang musically, in the other.

Iris and Art looked at each other. They scrambled out of their chairs.

Barbie turned back. "Arturo, please get my coat."

When Barbie had walked out of earshot, Iris said, "Arturo, madam would like her coat."

"Shaddup," Art said. He walked to the coatrack and retrieved the coat. A woman sitting at another table hissed at the fur as he walked out.

11

CLUB ESTRELLADO WAS FAR FROM THE FASHIONABLE WEST end of Sunset Boulevard. There it met the ocean after wending through pine-covered hills and the lush, rolling lawns of gated estates. There the ocean breeze kept the temperature comfortably constant during summer. Club Estrellado was at the beginning of the boulevard, too far east of Hollywood even to have some of that notorious, sleazy charm. This part of town had never been chic. It was flat and hot and all available space had been developed and asphalted many years before. Mostly Mexicans and Central Americans lived in the small stucco houses, making livings as gardeners, housekeepers, busboys, and mechanics and saving money so that the next generation would have more.

Art found a parking place on the street across from the club. Iris waited for Barbie to get out so she could maneuver herself out of the backseat of the two-door Mustang, and Barbie waited until Art came around and opened the door for her. She threw her leg out and grunted as she stepped onto the high sidewalk from the low car, holding a champagne glass in one hand and the bottle in the other. She walked across the street to the front of the club, the back of her fox swaying.

Art offered his hand to Iris as she squeezed from behind the front bucket seat, holding her empty champagne glass.

"I can't believe you drove across town with an open bottle of booze in your car," Iris said.

"Aww, lighten up, Iris. Have some fun."

"An open-container violation is fun?"

"I'm the one who's driving, okay?"

Iris reached back into the car for her briefcase.

"C'mon, Iris! Leave it alone."

Iris looked at Art coolly. "Barbie and I were meeting tonight to discuss business."

"Yeah, but things have changed. Go with the flow. Don't be so uptight."

"That's tough talk from a guy who'd crawl naked over broken glass to land a client like Barbie." Iris grabbed her briefcase and shoved it toward Art. "Lock it in the trunk. I don't want it to get stolen." She walked across the street.

Music wafted from the club—shallow bongos, sharp, skin-tight timbales, mellow congas, and sassy trumpets. Two young Hispanic men were standing on the sidewalk, smoking. They both wore dark slacks, thick belts with big silver buckles, thin-soled boots, and lightweight, western-style, long-sleeved shirts with the top buttons open. One was short and wiry and wore a gold medallion and chain around his neck. The other one was taller and not as thin. He smoked his cigarette by holding it between two fingers, palm up, then putting his palm to his face to take a drag. Both of them shamelessly eyed Barbie then lavished the same attention on Iris after she had crossed the street.

"Good evening," Barbie said.

They smiled and said "Good evening" in accented English.

Art and Iris walked up next to Barbie. Art said, *"Buenas noches."*

"Buenas," Iris offered.

"Ooohh, Spanish," Barbie said. "What's it mean?"

"Good evening," Art shrugged.

"Buenas noches," Barbie tried inelegantly. The two men responded in Spanish, smiling even more broadly than before. Barbie beamed back. "How fun. I've never met real Mexicans before."

The shorter man spoke to Art in Spanish. Art responded and the men laughed.

"Whatcha talkin' about?"

"He says they're not Mexican. They're from Guatemala. They offered to help me out since I have more women than I can handle. I said I'll wave a handkerchief if I need them."

Barbie shimmied her shoulders with the music, the fox coat swinging around her legs. "This is gonna be fun. Let's toast!" She filled her glass from the champagne bottle and held it toward Iris.

"Here on the sidewalk?" Iris asked.

"Boy, you're straight," Art said.

Iris pursed her lips and let Barbie pour champagne into her glass.

Barbie filled Art's glass, then held hers high in the air in front of them. "To the beginning of a beautiful friendship!"

"To a beautiful friendship," Art raised his glass.

"For the second time," Iris said. They looked at Iris quizzically. "Your *Casablanca* toast."

"Good Lord, you're right." Barbie smiled. "Someone else make a toast. I ain't got any imagination."

"To money," Art offered.

"A man after my own heart."

"To money," Iris said. They toasted and drank. "Unfashionable, but honest."

Barbie topped off their glasses, "The folks who say you

shouldn't want it never had a prayer of gettin' it anyway. When you had nothin' for as long as I did, you want everything you can get and for as long as you can get it."

"Hear, hear," Art agreed. "You want money, Iris. If you didn't, then why work as hard as you do?"

"I don't know. I've been working so hard for so long, I forget why I do it."

"I want to write my own ticket, not have to answer to the man," Art said. "Like my uncle. He owns this club."

"Really?" Barbie and Iris chimed. They looked at the facade of the club again as if they were seeing it for the first time.

"He works his butt off, but it's all his. That's my dream too."

"Is he here?" Iris asked.

"Probably not. He makes his own hours, see? Calls the shots."

"How long has he owned it?" Barbie was moving her shoulders with the music.

"About fifteen years. It used to be a Mexican restaurant. My uncle worked here as the cook after he and my dad came from Mexico. When the family who owned it wanted to retire, my uncle got together the money to buy it. He put in live music and a dance floor and it really took off. He made the last payment a few years ago."

Art looked at the building nostalgically. "I worked a lot of summers here. When I was little, I worked at my dad's market in the neighborhood. When I got old enough, I came here so's I could earn tips."

"You ever think about going in with your uncle?" Iris asked.

"Yeah, but I've got something bigger in mind. I tell you what I don't want. I don't want to end up like Sam Gold. Making cold calls his whole life, taking care of his little client book until he's old enough to retire."

"I don't think he's had a bad life," Iris said.

"It's not for me. I want to make it big-time. Not just for me but for my family. I'm the first one to graduate from college. I'm a role model for the kids."

"Do the kids go with those street gangs?" Barbie asked, wide-eyed.

"Nah. We're pretty middle-class. Everyone goes to school or works." Art shrugged. "Nothing glamorous."

"You have any brothers or sisters?" Iris sipped her champagne.

"I've got an older sister. She's just a housewife."

"There's nothing wrong with that," Barbie said.

"Yeah, but my family settles for so little. They get their little store, little club, little job, little family, everything in the neighborhood, then they sit back and cruise. No one wants to make it big-time." Art jabbed his index finger into his chest. "Except me."

A group of young women in short, shiny dresses with their hair ratted high walked down the sidewalk. One of the men who was smoking outside held the door open for them.

Art continued, "I thought the securities industry would be my ticket to the next level, but I'm not gonna be able to get the dough I need within the system."

"Why not?" Iris asked.

"Because the Anglo man's got too firm a hold. I'm already hitting the ceiling."

"I agree that it's a white man's world, Art, but it's changing. You can make your mark."

"Maybe I'm out of line, Iris, but you should talk. You've done well and all, but you should be manager. Everyone knows it. Look what they did instead. They brought Oz out from New York."

Iris set her jaw. "They made the right decision. The firm needed an experienced manager in L.A. I'll get my turn."

"When? When you're forty? I don't want to wait until my life's half over before I get anywhere."

Iris laughed. "I'm almost there now, baby cakes. Trust me, there *is* life after thirty."

Barbie topped off Art's glass and held the bottle toward Iris.

She put her hand over her glass. "I'm fine, thanks."

Barbie topped off her own glass and sat the empty bottle on the sidewalk. "I'll drink to life after thirty. Hell, even forty. Fifty!"

Iris and Barbie tapped their glasses together.

"You know what was the best time in my life so far?" Art didn't expect a response. "High school. High school was great. I was captain of the football team, quarterback, got all the best girls, everyone knew me, everyone was my friend. I'd walk across campus and people would turn and stare." Art gazed down the street at nothing. "It was great."

"I was a troll in high school," Iris said.

Barbie grinned, "Hell, I never made it past the eighth grade. Kids made fun of me 'cause all I had was hand-me-downs. And I sure weren't no beauty queen."

"To getting out of high school," Iris said.

Iris and Barbie clinked their glasses together again.

"Just go ahead and make fun. It was a taste of what I know I can achieve. Talking about Oz"—Art laughed bitterly at the sidewalk—"I told you I was gonna make a play for Sam's accounts today? Oz tells me he's got 'em all split up already."

"How many?" Iris asked.

Art held up two fingers.

"Just two?"

Art nodded expansively. "The big ones are going to you and Drye, which I figured."

"You didn't figure that when I talked to you this morning."

Art ignored the comment. "Guess who got most of the rest?"

"Sean Bliss."

"See, you know the score, Iris. I told Oz, 'It's because you and Sean's father are buddies.'" Art's posture was rigid.

"Sounds like you're tellin' it like it is, Arturo," Barbie said.

"I told him all right."

The men who had been standing outside the club finished their cigarettes and went inside.

"How did he respond?" Iris asked.

Art straightened his back, smoothed his tie, and turned the corners of his mouth down, affecting a stuffy pose. "I have two suggestions for you, Arthur. One, lose your attitude. Two, pay your dues."

"Not bad advice."

Art looked at Iris incredulously. "Lose my attitude? Take the crumbs and be a nice, quiet Mexican?"

"C'mon, Art. We all know that Dexter is good friends with Bliss's father. That's the way of the world. He's not after you because you're Chicano."

"He may not be after me, but he doesn't think of me as a player either. Today clinched it. It's crystal clear now." Art paced a few tight steps back and forth on the sidewalk. "I should just go for my dream."

"What's that?" Iris asked.

"Opening my own club."

"We're out of champagne and all this talk's making me thirsty," Barbie said. "I figure they serve drinks in there?"

"Only the best kick-ass margaritas in town. Ladies." Art put an arm around each of the women's shoulders; Barbie slid hers around Art's waist. They walked toward the entrance.

"What's the name mean, Arturo?" Barbie asked.

"It means the club that's covered with stars."

"Club Estra-yell-do," Barbie mispronounced the name. "Sounds sexy."

Art removed his arm from around Iris and opened the painted, black steel door, which was lined with tuck-and-roll red vinyl on the inside. Music and cigarette smoke flooded out. The place was packed. A ten-piece combo with lots of brass and percussion was crammed onto a small corner stage in front of the dance floor. There was hardly room to stand, but the men spun the women out and around, then close and tight, sliding their hips side to side in time with the sinewy rhythm.

"Hey, Tiny!" Art shook the hand of a massive bouncer who was sitting on a stool just inside the front door.

Tiny had receding black hair brushed straight back from his forehead and a deep M-shaped hairline. His moustache grew in two long tails down either side of his round face. When he smiled, the sides of the moustache rose like quotation marks and his high, round cheekbones squeezed his small eyes into slits. "The quarterback!" He playfully punched Art in the ribs. "How's it going, *hombre?*"

"Never better," Art said.

"Two women? Some things never change, huh, *amigo?*"

Art gave Tiny a thumbs-up and led Iris and Barbie into the club.

They surveyed the scene. Men stood at the bar drinking Bohemia, Dos Equis, or Tecate beer and watched both the dance floor and the door, seeing who came and who went, looking for friends or enemies and checking out the women. The women sat at small tables near the dance floor, wearing short, tight, shiny dresses and high heels, sipping cocktails, smoking and eyeing the men at the bar. Couples sat in red vinyl booths that lined the walls; some had fifths of booze and mixers on their tables. They necked between cigarette drags.

Art worked his way to the bar, stretched between two men on bar stools, pounded on the bar, and yelled to the bartender whose back was to him, "Hey, *cabron!* Gimme drink!"

The bartender turned around, holding a bottle by the neck. Art was now facing the dance floor, his back to the bar.

"What's your problem, *amigo?*" the bartender asked. The two men on either side of Art looked uncomfortable and gave him plenty of room.

The bartender poked him in the shoulder with the hand that still held the bottle. He was shorter than Art, and his face was deeply pitted with old acne scars that a narrow *pachuco* moustache did little to cover. *"Ese!* I'm talkin' to you, man!"

Art said, "Don't touch me, man."

The bartender grabbed Art's shoulder and spun him around. He relaxed when he saw Art's face. "Artie! Don't do this shit to me, man!"

Art held out his hand. The other man took it and pulled him over to the bar, grabbing him around the shoulders.

"You son of a bitch. You heard what happened last week, that guy with a gun?"

"I know, I know. Hey! Let me introduce my friends. This is Iris and this is Barbie. This is my cousin, Hector."

Hector stood the bottle on the bar, wiped his hands on a

towel stuck into his belt, and reached over the bar to shake Barbie's hand, then Iris's. "What can I get for you?"

Barbie said, "I'll have a bourbon and ginger ale."

Art swatted the air. "Let's get you with the program. Bring her a margarita." He rolled both *r*'s. "Iris?"

"Perfect."

"Hector makes the best maggies in town."

Hector dipped the rims of long-stemmed, wide-mouthed glasses into a shallow bath of lime juice, then into a container of coarse salt, coating them. He dumped tequila, lime juice, triple sec, and ice into a blender, let it whir, then poured the slushy, yellowish concoction. "Now, don't get crazy on me."

"Me?" Art said.

"Especially you."

"I'd like to hear about this," Barbie said.

Art reached into his pocket and put a twenty-dollar bill on the counter. Hector tossed it back to him. "I'll get the first round."

"Thanks, bro. Is Tio here?"

"He never comes at night anymore. He's in bed by nine."

"The *patrón*. Makes his own hours. Sounding better and better to me." Art handed Barbie and Iris their drinks. "Another toast. To the beginning of a beautiful friendship." He jabbed his elbow playfully into Barbie's side.

"Y'all funnin' me now," Barbie said. "That's okay. I can take it." She licked the salt from her glass and took a sip. "This is different."

Iris was watching the dance floor and swaying with the music. "That's what you said about the focaccia. Does that mean you like it or not?"

"It means I'm not sure yet. I'm tryin' it out."

"Let's get some food," Art said. "I'm starved."

They pushed through the crowd, holding their margaritas by the bowls of the glasses, freezing their fingers, and snagged a booth that a group had just left. Barbie took off her coat and draped it across the seat.

A busboy cleared the table, and a waitress came over and handed them large menus covered with dark red paper textured to look like leather.

"Hi, Coco," Art said. "Howyadoin'?"

Coco was twentyish and had a pretty face with caramel skin, almond-shaped eyes, dark eyebrows and eyelashes, full lips, and white teeth. Her long hair cascaded to her waist in loose curls. She wore her simple uniform of a white blouse and black slacks with tarty aplomb. The blouse was tight and unbuttoned to reveal a hint of white brassiere lace. The slacks were skintight. She tossed her head, throwing her hair over one shoulder, rolled her hip against the table, arched her back, and stood ready with her pen and order pad.

"Hi, Artie," she cooed. "Haven't seen you. Whatcha been up to?"

"Oh, the usual."

"The usual?" She pushed Art's shoulder and giggled breathlessly. "With who?"

Iris looked from Coco to Art with her eyebrows raised. Barbie watched Coco.

"Let me introduce my friends. Iris, Barbie, this is Soccorro. We call her Coco."

Coco tossed her head again. She held out her hand, limp-wristed, and shook Barbie's hand, then Iris's. "You ready to order or do you need more time?" She giggled again and pushed Art's shoulder.

"Barbie, do you know anything about Mexican food?" Art asked.

Barbie leaned close to look inside Art's menu, and Coco caught sight of the fox on the seat next to her. "I don't understand a word in here." Barbie waved a bejeweled hand at the menu, dismissing it. "I'll have whatever y'all are havin'."

"Do you eat meat?" Art asked.

"Of course I eat meat."

"Well, some people don't."

"Not where I come from."

"Iris?"

"You the man." Iris batted her eyelashes.

Art pretended not to notice. "Coco, bring us queso fondido and some chimichangas to start. Ask Jessie to make us some plates with enchiladas, a little chicken en mole, ropa vieja, carnitas, rice and beans, of course, and flour tortillas.

Okay? And a pitcher of margaritas and a round of tequila shooters."

"That real?" Coco pointed her head toward the coat.

"Course it's real, sugar pie," Barbie smiled. "Maybe I'll let you try it on."

"Really? I'll come back." Coco rolled her hips across the club and into the kitchen.

Iris looked at Art and puckered her lips, "Oooh la la. Co-co."

"She's a cutie," Barbie said.

Art shrugged. "My cousin's wife's sister."

"Family?" Iris looked up at Art through her eyebrows. "How convenient."

"Stop giving me a hard time." Art pinched Iris in the ribs and she shrieked. "Uh-oh, ticklish!" He poked her ribs and she twisted spastically, almost knocking over her drink.

"Stop! Art, please . . ."

"I thought you guys just worked together," Barbie said.

Iris and Art stopped, both of them still laughing. Iris wiped tears from her eyes. "We do."

"I never knew Iris could be this much fun," Art said. "We call her the Ice Princess at the office."

Iris primly smoothed her skirt. "You know what they say. The bigger they are, the harder they fall."

"That sounds like a challenge."

"Art, what don't you see as a challenge?"

"Nothing," he said matter-of-factly. He slid out of the booth, pulling Iris's hand with him. "Let's see how the Ice Princess moves on the dance floor. The next one's for you, Barbie."

"Take your time, kids. Don't y'all worry about Barbeh."

Art wove Iris through the crowd.

She yelled into his ear to be heard over the music. "Good choice, Art. Great place."

"Having fun?"

"Yeah."

"Still mad at me for butting into your meeting?"

"Yeah."

They squeezed onto a corner of the parquet dance floor. Art spun Iris around and they slid their hips side to side.

Other dancers bumped into them. He spun her out and she danced around him, shimmying her shoulders.

"Go, girl!" Art shouted over the music. "Careful! Don't burn up!"

"It's the tequila talking."

"Hell, let's have another round." He grabbed her and they danced fast and close again.

Barbie skipped up to them. One of the men from outside had asked her to dance and was trying to show her how to move to the Latin rhythm. He stood with one hand poised in the air and the other on his belly and shimmied his hips back and forth.

Barbie tapped Iris's shoulder. "You take my partner."

Before she knew it, Iris was in the grip of the other man. His hands were moist and his shirt was wet with perspiration down the back. She touched him lightly at first, put off by the sudden intimacy, then more firmly as his foreignness gave way to rhythm and motion. She spun and swirled and shimmied her shoulders for several songs before she noticed that Barbie and Art weren't on the dance floor.

She eventually made it back to the table, which was now covered with plates of food. She was starving. She tore a flour tortilla in half and dipped it into the melted cheese of the queso fondido, then spooned salsa on top of it. She frantically fanned her mouth and gulped her margarita when she realized how hot the salsa was. Into another tortilla went ropa vieja, shredded beef stewed with chilis and peppers so that it ends up looking like its name, "old clothes." She tried the carnitas, chunks of pork seared in orange juice, moist on the inside and crusty on the outside, and the chicken en mole, a dark sauce of chocolate, chili, and sesame seeds. She forgot about Barbie and Art. They were in the upstairs office.

"This was the only Latin music club in the area when my uncle started it. Now everyone comes here. Gringos too. I told my uncle that we should open a mainstream club with a Latin flavor in a better neighborhood. Go big-time. But he's not into it."

The office held an old wooden desk piled with organized clutter with an equally old wooden captain's chair behind it.

There was also a worn couch that had outlived its usefulness in somebody's living room, an overstuffed easy chair, and a chrome and vinyl chair with a faded marble print that had once belonged to a dinette set. A calendar with a Hispanic girl in a bathing suit holding a bottle of Mexican soda pop was tacked to the wall. A set of filing cabinets sat in one corner and a low, heavy safe sat in the other. Some framed family portraits were on the desk.

Barbie walked around the room, surveying it. "Running a club takes a lot of energy."

Art walked to the desk and straddled the corner, leaning back on his hands. "I know one thing. Having to kiss some guy's ass to get ahead is bullshit." He held his hands up apologetically. "Excuse my language, but it is. Like I was saying outside, my dream is to own my own club. A killer Latin music club. It'll be jammin'. People'll line up to come in. I can do it, too. My uncle knows the business and I've got the energy and I know how to put it together. The only thing I don't have is money."

Barbie walked past the door, closed it, then leaned against it, posing with one leg bent, her toes pointed to the ground.

Art's full upper lip slid crookedly up his white teeth. "You've got dough."

"That money's into other things, darlin'."

"But you've got it."

She walked over to him and stood at the corner of the desk between his knees. "Such a young man. So many plans." She put her hands on his thighs and leaned toward him.

"Hello," Art said.

"You got a girlfriend, Arturo?"

"No one steady."

"A young man should sow his wild oats." Barbie leaned closer, put her hands around his neck, and kissed him on the lips.

"Wow," Art said.

"Oooh, the point of this desk is hurtin' me." Barbie moved a pile of papers to the side, pulled Art so that he was square with the desk, then put her hand on his chest and tried to push him down.

Art didn't move. "Whoa! Whatcha got in mind here?"

"Whatever you're in the mood for." Barbie unbuttoned the top button of her purple blouse.

"Here? In my uncle's office?"

"Why not?" Barbie unbuttoned the remaining buttons.

"What about Iris?"

"What about her?"

"She's probably looking for us."

"She's dancing." Barbie pulled the blouse from her skirt and opened it, revealing a sheer, shiny purple brassiere. "She's not lookin' for us."

Art scooted back on the desk, away from her.

"You aren't afraid of me, are you, Arturo?" Barbie put her hand on his crotch. "Oh, my. That don't tell me that you ain't interested." She started to unbuckle his belt. "Or did Iris's tight little body do that to you when y'all were dancin'?"

Art took her hands in his and gently pulled them away. He was blushing. "Barbie, you're very attractive . . ."

"You think I'm too old."

"No! I think you're very sexy. But we just met and this is my uncle's office and you're Iris's client."

"So?" She freed her hands from his.

"It just doesn't seem right."

She undid the front clasp of her brassiere. Her breasts tumbled out. She arched her back, picked up his hand, and put it on one breast. "Touch me, Arturo."

Art swallowed hard.

Barbie lay on top of him, pressing him onto the desk. She kissed him on the mouth, then inched her way backward until she was kneeling on the floor, her head level with his crotch.

He was breathing heavily.

She unzipped his pants and started to pull them off.

Art lifted her face in his hands. "Oh, wow. This doesn't feel right. I guess I'm used to taking the initiative."

Barbie stood up. "An old-fashioned man. I'll be damned."

Art slid off the desk and zipped up his pants. He turned around to straighten the papers on the desk.

Barbie reached between his legs from behind and squeezed him.

Art jumped. "Barbie!"

"I'm just playin'! I guess I come on too strong sometimes. We still friends?" She held out her hand.

He took it. "Sure." He shook his head. "I've never had a woman come on to me like that before."

"Life's short, sugar." She slowly reclasped her bra, buttoned her blouse, and tucked it back into her skirt while Art watched.

"You're very sexy." He lifted her chin in his hand and kissed her.

Barbie stepped back and scrutinized him. "That was a real one. You do like me, just a little bit."

"I like you a lot, Barbie. I just don't know what to make of you."

"Don't make anything of me, sugar. What you see is what you get."

By the time they got back downstairs, Iris had put a large dent in the food. She was wiping fried chimichanga crumbs from her mouth and chin with a napkin.

Barbie slid into the booth, next to Iris, smiling and twitching. "Iris, you leave us anything?"

"Where you guys been?" Iris asked.

"Taking a tour," Art said.

"I'd like to see it too."

"Didn't see it all, though." Barbie leered at Art, who slid into the booth on the other side of Iris. "Just a preview."

Iris looked from Barbie to Art, then picked up the fried chimichanga and took another bite.

Art quickly slid two of the shot glasses of tequila across the table in front of Barbie and Iris. "Tequila shooters! Watch." He shook some salt onto his wrist, slammed the bottom of the shooter glass onto the tabletop, licked his wrist, downed the tequila in one gulp, then bit into a lime wedge from a plate that was brought with the shooters.

"Thanks for the demo, Art, but tequila shooters and I are old friends," Iris said.

Barbie followed Art. She shook her head and pursed her lips. "Whoa!" She set the shot glass down. "Powerful!"

"So where were you guys?" Iris persisted.

"Art was trying to talk me into investin' in a club with him."

"Oh, really?"

Art nudged Iris's tequila shooter toward her. "Shooter time."

"Let's talk about this investment idea you have for my client. Barbie, I have to advise you that clubs and restaurants are bad risks."

"Don't worry about it, Iris," Art said.

"Worried isn't the word I would use."

"C'mon, kids," Barbie said. "This is flattering, but don't fight over me."

Art tapped the shooter glass with his finger. "Do it."

"Bottoms up, sugar." Barbie squeezed Iris's knee and gave her thigh a friendly slap underneath the table.

Iris looked at Barbie quizzically, then speared a chunk of carnitas on her fork. "The last time I did tequila shooters was down in Ensenada. It was ugly. I still don't remember everything that happened. Never again."

"New night, new crowd." Art tapped the shooter glass. "Do that shooter."

"Don't push me. Now I'm really pissed off at you."

"Honey, don't be mad at Arturo," Barbie said. "The last thing I want to do is invest in a club. We were just playin' around. It wasn't nothin' serious."

Art looked at Barbie sullenly. "You like the food?" he asked, changing the subject.

Barbie and Iris grunted their approval.

They finished eating, talking about nothing in particular, then they danced, all three of them together, jerking back and forth, trying to keep their arms entwined, sweating, until the band went home. They sat back down and Barbie asked for the bill.

"No, this one's on me," Art protested.

"I'll get it," Iris said. "This was *supposed* to be a business dinner with my client."

"You're never going to let me forget that, are you?"

"Sorry, kids." Barbie threw down enough cash to cover the bill and the tip. "This is my treat."

"I'll treat next time," Art said.

"Next time?" Iris asked.

"C'mon, you two. Play nice," Barbie said.

They left the club, saying good-bye to Tiny and Hector on their way out. Iris's shooter sat untouched on the table.

Art drove back downtown and into the underground garage. The garage had the eerie quality of familiar places after hours.

He drove to Iris's car first.

"Look at that car!" Barbie said. "That's Iris's wild side showin'."

Iris unlocked the Triumph and opened the door. The whine of the squeaky hinge sang through the empty concrete structure.

"Art, thanks for driving all over the place." Iris shook her head. "What a night!"

"A major rager," Art said. "Killer."

"Killer night," Barbie agreed, smiling.

"See you Monday, Art. I'll call you next week, Barbie, and we'll talk about my plans for your portfolio."

"It's a date," Barbie said.

Art waited until Iris had backed the Triumph out before driving Barbie to her red Mercedes convertible with the white leather upholstery. He left the Mustang's engine running and turned to face her. "I just want you to know one thing. I *am* serious about this club."

Barbie patted his leg. "I know you are, sugar."

"I want you to meet my uncle."

Barbie turned the key in the ignition and cut the Mustang's engine. "Let's talk about it later, darlin'. It's been a long night."

She leaned over and kissed him, long and sloppily. He rubbed her breasts through the sheer blouse. She unbuckled his belt and unzipped his pants. Art didn't stop her this time. She started to slide toward his crotch until the steering wheel stopped her.

Art reached down beside his seat, lifted a lever, and pushed the seat back. Barbie continued her downward slide. Art clutched the backs of both seats. His moans reverberated in the empty garage. When it was over, Barbie carefully tucked his shirt back in and zipped up his pants. She patted him.

"That's quite a thing you got there," she said. "Take care of that."

She opened the passenger door, got out of the Mustang and into her car, and drove off.

Art sat in the Mustang in the quiet garage, his hands still clutching the backs of the bucket seats.

12

BARBIE PULLED OPEN THE HEAVY GLASS DOOR AND ENTERED the subdued mauve-toned lobby of the McKinney Alitzer suite. Her red jersey dress clung unapologetically to her ample curves. She wore red high-heeled sandals and white stockings with tiny red hearts strewn across them. Her hair was teased high on top of her head, the front swept dramatically away from her face in a winged effect, displaying earrings that had different sized red enameled hearts dangling from many lengths of gold chain. She carried a handled shopping bag from an exclusive chocolate and sweet shop.

"Good afternoon," she said formally to the receptionist, who had put aside her work as soon as Barbie set foot inside the suite. "Happy Valentine's Day to you. I'm Barbie Stringfellow"—Barbie pointed a manicured and beringed finger at her chest—"and I would like to see Iris Thorne, please."

"Do you have an appointment?"

Barbie wandered to the perimeter of the lobby and peeked down the corridor in both directions. "As a matter of fact, I don't."

The receptionist picked up the telephone. "Let me see if Ms. Thorne is in."

Barbie waved dismissively. "Don't trouble yourself, sugar. I'll just go surprise her. I can find my way."

"Excuse me!" the receptionist scooted forward in her chair. "Ma'am!"

Barbie had already turned down the corridor, heading the wrong way.

"Shoot!" The receptionist punched in Iris's extension.

Barbie walked past the lobby again, now heading in the right direction toward the Sales Department.

"Ma'am!" the receptionist shouted again.

Barbie gave her a friendly wave as she flounced by, swinging the shopping bag.

Iris didn't pick up her phone. The receptionist started to go after Barbie but saw her with Billy Drye and assumed he would find Iris for her.

"Well, hello there." In her heels, Barbie was eye level with the diminutive Drye. "And who might you be?"

Drye looked Barbie up and down, then held his hand out. "Bill Drye. May I be of assistance?"

Barbie took his hand. "Well, Mr. Drye, I'm Barbie String-fellow and yes, you may. I'm looking for Iris Thorne." She released his hand.

"You're Iris's new client." He took a step closer and sniffed the air in her direction. "That's a very seductive fragrance."

"That's what I paid for. Thank you for noticin'. Well, hello, Arturo."

Art walked up to them. "What a surprise. What are you doing here?"

"You two know each other?" Billy Drye asked slyly.

"Just slightly," Art blurted. He took Barbie's arm and started walking away from Drye. "Those documents I was telling you about are over here."

"Nice to have met you, Mr. Drye," Barbie said over her shoulder.

"Pleasure's all mine." He grinned.

"Pleasant fellow," Barbie said to Art.

"He's the office gossip."

"Don't worry, sugar. I don't kiss and tell."

Iris was walking toward them down the corridor.

"There's the lady of the day!" Barbie exclaimed.

Iris extended her hand to Barbie. Barbie took it, pulled Iris toward her, and planted a kiss on her cheek, leaving a large, red lip mark.

"This is a pleasant surprise," Iris said.

"I just brought a little Valentine's cheer for you and Arturo."

"That's nice of you. Come into my office."

Art followed them to the corner office.

"Have a seat. Can I get you a cup of coffee, soda, or something?"

Art lingered in the doorway.

"Thank you, darlin', but I won't stay long." Barbie reached into the shopping bag, took out a small heart-shaped candy box, and handed it to Art. "This is for you."

"Thanks." He beamed. "I think this is the first time a woman's ever given me candy."

"Well, life still holds lots of firsts for you, don't it, Arturo?" she winked at him.

Art blushed.

Barbie reached into the bag again and handed Iris a large, elaborately decorated, heart-shaped candy box. "They're cherry cordials. My favorites. I hope you like them too."

"Love them. What a beautiful box. Thank you." Iris opened the box and offered the chocolate-covered cherries to Barbie.

Art looked at Iris's candy box, from which Barbie was carefully making her selection, and dangled his by his side, as if it were of no consequence. "Iris's is bigger."

Iris offered the box to him. "Cherry cordial?" She smirked.

He declined.

Barbie popped the chocolate into her mouth and bit down. "Mmmm ... Delicious. Arturo, I just wanted to thank Iris for all the money she's earned for me. It don't mean I think any less of you, sugar."

"Shoot, I don't care," Art said. "I was just making a comment."

Iris bit into a piece of the candy, savoring the sweet smoothness of the cherry-flavored cream, the bitterness of the chocolate, and the tart snap of the cherry. She smiled at Art, but it was still more of a smirk.

"Iris," Barbie said. "I'm just out and about and thought that if you had a moment we could grab a bite or a drink."

"Barbie, I'd love to, but I'm taking my mother to tea."

"Oh, how wonderful. How darlin' of you. Where y'all goin'?"

"The Ritz Carlton Huntington."

"Oh, delightful. I'm sure she'll love it." Barbie paused and looked at Iris coquettishly. "You got room for one more maybe?"

"Well, I'd like to do that some time, Barbie, but this is my day with my mom."

"Of course," Barbie said. "Maybe later, for dinner?"

"John's cooking dinner for me tonight."

"What a lucky girl you are. So many valentines." Barbie stood up and patted her winged hair. "Well, honey, you just enjoy yourself. We'll do it some other time."

"I'm free, Barbie, until later tonight," Art said.

"You got yourself a little Valentine's date later?"

"Well, yeah. I would have . . . If I'd known . . . I figured you had plans. I can make an excuse."

"Honey, I wouldn't dream of it. I think I'll treat myself to a massage at the spa and then just relax at home."

Iris came from behind her desk and gave Barbie a hug, tinkling her heart earrings. "Let's have lunch next week. I'll call you."

"I'll call you tomorrow, darlin'," Barbie said to her. "Enjoy yourself today." She turned to Art and scratched a polished nail against his cheek. "And I'll talk to you later."

She walked out of the suite. Art followed her to the elevator, still dangling the candy box she'd given him. Barbie pressed her finger against the heat-sensitive call button that glowed amber at her touch.

"I can change my plans," Art said. "We can do the town."

"Arturo. I'm not gonna be responsible for you breakin' a Valentine's date. I had you all to myself earlier this week. Let another girl have a turn. We'll get together some other night." She stood on tiptoes and kissed Art lightly on the lips. "I'm still recoverin'. You wore this old broad out."

"Is that the only way you think of me? For sex?"

"How would you like me to think of you, honey?"

"As a potential business partner. Did you forget about the club? You said you were going to think about it."

"I have. And I am. And I will. It's a promise."

The elevator arrived. Barbie got in.

"Let me arrange a meeting with my uncle. I'd like you to meet him, then we can really talk business."

"I'll call you. Bye-bye, sugar." The elevator doors closed.

Art slammed the candy box in the trash.

Iris came out of the suite and pressed the elevator's down button. "What's going on? You look mad about something."

A dimple formed in his cheek as he clenched his jaw. He shook his head.

"What?" Iris persisted.

"Why does Barbie have such a hard-on for you?"

"She's my client. Your clients have brought you gifts, haven't they?"

He turned and walked back inside the suite.

John and Iris were eating dinner at the scrubbed pine table in John's dining room. Iris set her fork down, leaned back in her chair, and rubbed her full belly.

"Delicious chicken chasseur. You've outdone yourself."

"Thanks. This was fun. I've been working so many hours, seems like a long time since I've made dinner like this. I think the last time was when I made chili and Penny was here."

"We could use some time off, you and me. I'm looking forward to our trip to the Mariah Lodge."

"That's a couple of weeks away."

"Well, I'm still looking forward to it."

"I have to remember to tell Penny that Chloe will be with her that weekend."

"Speaking of Chloe, did she say anything about my bracelet?"

"Why should she?" he said sharply. "I told you she doesn't know anything about it."

"Don't get your panties in a wad. I was just wondering."

Buster, the bull terrier, attempted to approach the table. He forgave Iris all her shortcomings as he turned his soft brown eye on her and begged for a scrap. Iris, ever hopeful of mending fences, pulled a piece of chicken from the bone and held it toward him. He opened his powerful jaws and gently took it from her fingers.

"Buster!" John shouted. "Iris, don't feed him. He's too fat as it is."

Buster retreated to a corner of the dining room and turned his cold blue eyes on John.

"Ready for dessert?" John asked. "I have ice cream."

"And cherry cordials." Iris left the table and returned with the elaborately decorated box.

"Secret admirer?"

"Barbie brought them to the office. Wasn't that sweet?"

"Valentine's candy? That's kind of weird."

"Why? I've made her good money. She wants to thank me."

"She sure is in your face a lot."

"She's just lonely. I have to stay on her good side, since I'm about to hit her up for the rest of the dough she was talking about. You know what happened today? My mom and I were going to tea at the Ritz Carlton Huntington, but we changed our minds at the last minute and went to the Bel Age instead. Guess who walks in?"

"Barbie."

"Isn't that a coincidence?"

"Some coincidence."

"It was a *coincidence,* okay? You've been a cop for too long."

"Did she have tea with you?"

"Yeah, then she and my mom went shopping."

"You let your mom go with her?"

"John, my mother can make her own decisions. What's your problem with Barbie, anyway?"

"There's something about her I don't like."

"You made that clear enough at dinner the other night. Just don't forget, she's one of my biggest clients."

The phone rang.

"Let the machine pick up," Iris said. "We haven't finished dinner."

They waited in silence while John's outgoing message played

for the caller. The phone was in the living room, but the amplified voice could be clearly heard in the dining room. "Hi, John, it's Penny. I'm just calling to say hello and . . ."

John got up from the table and walked toward the living room.

"John! If we'd gone out for dinner, you couldn't have answered it."

"Well, we're not out for dinner."

Iris threw her napkin on the table, walked softly out of the dining room, and stood next to the arched entrance to the living room. She couldn't hear John's exact words, but his voice was low and soothing.

"I'd better go. I'm getting ready to have dessert. With Iris, yeah."

John hung up the phone, and Iris hopped on tiptoes back to the dining room.

"Everything okay?" she asked when he entered the room.

"Fine. Ready for dessert?"

"I guess."

"Something wrong?" His shoulders tensed as if he were bracing for a fight.

Iris weighed the possibilities. Have a fight or finish dinner? She decided. They could always fight tomorrow. "I'll get bowls for the ice cream. You want coffee?"

13

SEVERAL WEEKS LATER, IRIS WAS ARRIVING HOME FROM WORK and heard the phone ringing as she unlocked the door to her condo.

"Hi, darlin'! It's Barbeh!"

"Now what!" Iris shouted at the machine.

"Just callin' to see what you're up to . . ."

Iris stood her briefcase underneath the small antique table in the entryway and sat her purse on top of the table as she did at the end of every workday. She picked up the telephone, interrupting Barbie in midsentence.

"Hi, Barbie. I just walked in the door."

"Hi, sugar! You sound tired."

"I am. I stayed late at the office to take care of a few things before I leave."

"That's right! The big romantic weekend with your cop. Happy birthday, birthday girl!"

"My birthday's actually Saturday, but thanks."

"Well, I want to take you out for a little birthday cheer, honey. You busy now?"

"Now? I have to pack. We're leaving first thing tomorrow morning."

"Next week, then. What day's good for you?"

"Barbie, can I call you? I'm so busy and I just stepped through the door and—"

"Of course you can, honey. Of course you are. I'll talk to you later. You have a good time and don't do anything I wouldn't do."

Iris hung up. "What is her problem? Can't she be alone for five minutes? Why the hell did I ever give her my home number?"

She opened the terrace doors, poured a glass of wine, took her clothes off, hung them up, peeled off her pantyhose, and threw them on top of a pile in the corner of the closet. She pulled on her old sweats that had holes worn in them and a T-shirt from a concert given by a band that had broken up eight years ago. She took off her makeup, washed her face, and brushed the mousse and hairspray from her hair. The workday was officially over.

She reached back inside the closet, grabbed the mound of soiled pantyhose, and threw them into the light of day. She'd just worn the last of the three dozen she'd ordered when they were on sale. She carried the mound into the bathroom, crammed it into the sink, and started running water, when her doorbell rang.

"Son of a bitch!" she shouted. She stood over the sink,

her hands dripping with soap suds, and debated whether she should answer it.

"Iris, you there?" She heard John's voice through the door.

She wiped her hands on a towel, ran to the door, and opened it. "Hi!" She put her arms around him and reached up to kiss him on the lips.

He halfheartedly puckered his lips in her direction.

"What's wrong?" she asked.

He shook his head and walked past her into the condo. "Nothing's wrong."

"Ooo-kay." She followed him into the living room and gestured toward the couch. "Sit?"

He paced around the room. His height made the room look small. "I'd rather stand."

"All right. How did you get past the security door downstairs?"

"Someone who was leaving held the door open for me."

"Great. You want to go out on the terrace?"

"Yeah."

"You want something to drink?"

He shook his head.

"I don't mind if I do. Something tells me I'm going to need it." Iris disappeared, returned with the glass of wine, and set it on the terrace railing.

The mid-March air was mild and warm and hinted of summer to come.

John looked over the terrace wall. "Hey! You!"

The street man looked up at him.

"What the hell are you doing down there? This is private property!"

The street man ignored him.

"Aw, leave him alone," Iris said. "He doesn't bother anyone."

"You shouldn't allow that."

"The police have already chased him out half a dozen times. He just keeps coming back."

"Santa Monica cops. Bunch of bleeding hearts."

The street man turned his head slightly to look at them out of the corner of his eye but said nothing.

"Did you come for a reason? I'm kind of busy. I need to pack for the weekend."

"That's what I came to talk to you about."

"The weekend?"

"Well, not just about the weekend."

"Are you going to tell me or do I have to drag every word out of you?"

John reached in his jeans pocket, took out a piece of paper, and handed it to Iris. "Chloe found this."

Iris read it. It was the note she'd shoved into Chloe's pajama bag. "Did she finally fess up to stealing my bracelet?"

John faced Iris with his hands on his hips. "She did not steal your bracelet."

"John, I found it hidden in her bedroom."

"What were you doing snooping in her room?"

"She stole my bracelet. You're forgetting the point!"

"The point is that you were snooping in my daughter's room."

"Well, *your* daughter stole from *your* girlfriend. I only went looking for it because you wouldn't believe me. I can't win. I'm always going to have less credibility with you than she does."

"You don't understand what it's like to have children."

"Here we go."

"Iris. This isn't working out."

"What's not working out?"

"Us."

"Oh, c'mon. Why do you take a small issue and make it a life or death thing? We can work this out."

John's eyes grew red.

"You don't mean it," Iris said. She turned away from him, leaned against the terrace railing with both hands, and looked at the ocean. She suddenly felt very light-headed and lead-footed at the same time.

"I've felt for a long time that I was giving Chloe mixed messages about premarital sex. And now, with this bracelet thing, I feel like you're putting a wedge between me and my daughter."

"That's what Chloe said, right?"

"But I agree with her."

"And Penny's view?"

"Penny says that if Chloe had a more stable family life she wouldn't be having problems."

"Like mother, like daughter. They dangle the guilt out there and you just bite right into it. Of course your own happiness is a nonissue."

"I think it's best if we break up. I'm sorry." He put his hand over hers on top of the terrace railing.

"Don't!" she said.

He stepped close behind her and put his hands on each of her arms. "C'mon, Iris. Can't we be friends?"

She lifted the wineglass toward her lips, then impulsively jerked it over her shoulder. The wine splashed in John's face.

"Damn!" John released her arms and tried to wipe the wine from his eyes.

The street man continued to look straight ahead through the bushes, giving no indication that he must have heard everything.

Iris walked back inside the condo, holding the glass upside down by its base. Droplets of white wine dribbled onto the floor. She sat on a corner of the raw silk couch, lay the glass on its side on the floor, tucked her feet under her, wrapped her arms around herself, and stared into space.

John came in from the terrace, still wiping his face with his hands. She didn't acknowledge him. He walked through the living room and down the corridor to her bedroom. When he returned, his face and hair were dry but his shirt still showed splashes.

Iris hadn't moved. She spoke without looking at him. "This is stupid, John. You caving in to Penny is not going to make a better life for anyone in the long run. You can't live a lie."

" 'Bye, Iris." He closed the door behind him.

Iris remained quietly on the couch for a long time. Finally, she unfolded her legs, which had grown cramped from sitting on them, stood up, and walked through the bedroom and into the master bathroom.

The water she'd run in the sink had seeped out, leaving

behind sudsy, snakelike pantyhose. She was running more water when she spotted the towel he'd used to dry his face. She snatched it from the towel bar and threw it into the bedroom, intending to wash it later with the hottest water possible and lots of soap. While the water was running into the sink, she turned her back and leaned against it. John had left the toilet seat up. She reached out from where she stood and tipped it down with a bang. A sob escaped. She fell to her hands and knees, grabbed the toilet seat, and lifted it and slammed it down over and over again against the porcelain. Tears streamed down her face. A crack appeared in the toilet seat's thick plastic.

She stopped only when she heard the phone ring. She stumbled to the phone on her nightstand.

"Honey, it's Barbie. You sounded so tired when we hung up, I just wanted to make sure you were okay."

Iris started sobbing.

"Sugar, what's wrong?"

Iris couldn't speak.

"Iris, tell me what it is."

"Oh, Barbie. John left me . . ."

14

ART RANG THE DOORBELL OF BARBIE'S APARTMENT. THE doorbell was a cheap, spring-activated model in a little plastic box that chimed a shallow *ding-dong* when pushed. Barbie's voice rang out through the other side of the thin door, "Just a minute!"

Art waited, facing the door, holding his hands behind his back.

Barbie's apartment complex was on Tahiti Way in Marina Del Rey, built between two basins. The complex was three stories tall, the seventies-style woodsy units built in a zigzag pattern to give each tenant maximum window exposure to the marina. Each unit had a small terrace, most of them holding a barbecue, a small patio table and chairs, and a bicycle. Many terraces were decorated with tubular wind chimes or wind socks shaped like colorful fish, flying in the wind.

The marina air resonated with tinkling noises from wind chimes ringing in the omnipresent breeze, steel fittings clanging against aluminum sailboat masts, ice clinking in cocktail glasses, and laughter rising from folks at play. A few boats were heading out for sunset sails. Most were coming back in. Many boats hardly ever left the dock but served as floating rec rooms for their owners. It was the dinner hour and owners were now screwing little portable barbecues onto boat rails. The scent of saltwater mingled with barbecue starter fluid, grilled steaks, and gasoline.

Barbie swung the door open. She cooed, "Hello, Arturo."

She was wearing a deep purple silk jumpsuit in a military style with long sleeves, gold buttons, and epaulets. A broad gold belt cinched her waist, and her flesh bubbled over it. The jumpsuit's top buttons were undone, the opening filled with round mounds of pale Barbie. A long gold chain encircled her neck. She stepped into the doorway and put her hand on his cheek. "Lovely to see you, sugar."

He stepped closer and handed her the flowers he'd been hiding behind his back. "For you."

"Aren't you just the sweetest thing?" She set the flowers on the bar of the small kitchen that was built against the same wall as the door.

Barbie's apartment was a small studio with the living room and bedroom sharing the same space, the bedroom area sitting on an elevated platform separated from the living room by three steps. The closets and the bathroom were to the left of the bedroom. The outside wall was composed of two large sliding glass doors that opened onto Barbie's terrace, which had no patio furniture, wind chimes, or wind sock. The apartment had been rented furnished, and the furniture was made out of cheap pressboard and upholstered in a sturdy, drab brown plaid fabric.

Barbie gave Art a small peck on the lips. He flung his arms around her waist, jerked her close, and locked his lips on hers. She squirmed, trying to free herself from his grasp. He held tight, standing with his legs staggered, rubbing her back and waist through the purple silk and pulling her hips against him.

"You want to fight me today, huh?" Art suddenly let Barbie go. He ran his hand over his mouth, trying to rub off the pink lipstick that was smeared there.

"Hi, Art," Iris said. She stood in the small living room wearing black leggings with a long, bright red pullover.

Barbie gave Art an I-told-you-so look.

"Hi, Iris," Art stammered. "I thought you were going up to that Mariah place with John."

Barbie put her hand on Art's sleeve. "I invited her, sugar. Her trip got canceled."

"John dumped me," Iris said.

"Dumped you? You mean like he really dumped you?"

"Right down the crapper."

"What happened?"

Iris's eyes welled with tears. She shook her head bitterly.

Barbie put her arm around Iris's waist. "Let her be, Arturo. She didn't want to come out, but I couldn't let her sit at home by herself on her birthday."

Iris wiped a tear from her cheek with the back of her hand.

Barbie patted her waist. "So we spent the day shoppin' and going around. I bought this." Barbie pirouetted in her jumpsuit. "Like it?"

"It's great."

"And Iris bought that sweater and I bought her a little gift and I bought you a little gift too, sugar."

Art leaned close to Barbie's ear and whispered, "But I'm taking you to meet my uncle."

"I know you're going to meet your uncle," Iris said.

Art looked at Iris with surprise. "You're not mad?"

Iris flipped her wrist. "If Barbie wants to invest in a club, she'll invest in a club."

"Well, okay. Great." Art walked into the small living room.

"Good. We're all friends again." Barbie leaned forward

conspiratorially and whispered, "I've got a bottle of champagne in the refrigerator. Let's have a little toast."

"Thanks, Barbie, but I don't feel like having anything." Iris sat on the couch listlessly and folded both arms across her chest.

"C'mon, honey. Just have a little glass." She directed herself to Art. "Poor thing's hardly eaten anything all day."

"Maybe you need a little tequila." Art winked at her.

"I don't want anything. Nothing sounds good."

"You're gonna be a barrel of laughs tonight." Art opened the sliding glass door and walked onto the terrace. "Hey, Barbie? Did you find a burgundy pullover? I think I might have left it here."

Barbie busied herself with the champagne bottle and glasses in the kitchen. There was no formal dining area, just two bar stools underneath a Formica bar on the kitchen's outer wall. She said, "No, I haven't, sugar." There was the pop of a champagne cork being released.

"When's that bigger apartment coming through? This place is starting to look more and more like a cheap motel," Art said.

Barbie walked out of the kitchen holding two wineglasses that were three-quarters full of champagne. "Apartment manager told me I'm the next one in line for one of the top corner, three-bedroom units. I can't hardly wait to get all my crystal and china and knickknacks and things out of storage. Go ahead and take a sip, Iris. Just for a toast."

Iris accepted one of the glasses. "So that's why there's no personal stuff around."

Barbie went back into the kitchen and got the third glass. "Of course that's why. What didja think?"

Iris shrugged. "I didn't think anything. I just wondered why someone of your means didn't have more stuff."

"Oh, I've got it all right. Once I get set up, I'll have a big dinner party for y'all. I'm a hell of a cook. Betcha didn't know that."

"A woman of many talents," Art said.

"Let's toast, to Iris's birthday."

"Let's pick something else," Iris said.

"C'mon, sugar. We're gonna have a ball tonight."

DIANNE G. PUGH

Iris raised her glass. "To my birthday. For she's a jolly good fellow, hip hip hooray, hi de ho ho, screw everything, and bottoms up." She took a sip and set the glass on the coffee table.

"So how old are you?" Art asked.

"Chronologically or mentally?"

Barbie took a small sip of the champagne, then put her glass down on the pressboard coffee table. "Honey, you'll feel better once you get a change of scenery. Let's go. Let me fix my makeup and get my coat." She pranced up the three steps that led to the bedroom, then turned left into the corridor lined with closets on either wall.

"So, what happened between you and John?" Art asked.

"Johnny thinks I'm putting a wedge between him and his daughter, the devil girl child Chloe, and that he's giving her mixed messages about premarital sex."

"But you guys have been dating for over a year. Why now?"

"His ex-wife, the high, holy, and most righteous Penny, was dumped by her own live-in boyfriend of six years, the initially clueless but finally wise Philip. So John starts to look pretty darn good to Penny again and she starts coming around, punching his guilt buttons like there's no tomorrow. And boy, has he got 'em."

"So, what's he doing tonight?"

"Who knows? Penny's probably cooking up some seared tofu steaks and wheat germ." Iris picked up the glass and took another sip. "I've had it up to here with them and their screwed-up family life. I'm not gonna beg anyone to stay with me."

" 'Atta girl." Barbie came back into the living room, her fox draped over her shoulders. "Plenty of fish in the sea for someone like you. You just wait."

Iris blew air out. "I'm done with men. I don't want them near me, touching me, talking to me, *nada.*" She gestured toward Art. "You don't count."

"Gee, thanks."

"You know what I mean."

Barbie put her arm around Iris's shoulders. "C'mon, darlin'. Don't worry about being lonely. You won't be. Everything's gonna be just fine."

102

15

EAST L.A. IS COLORED IN SHADES OF BROWN, GRAY, AND gold. It comes from the patches of vacant land covered with wild grass, wheat, and mustard that are green just briefly in spring before turning gold in summer, then churned into brown again when the city tractors the earth to reduce the fire hazard. It comes from the smallness of the houses and buildings in relation to the broad, gray asphalt streets and from the brown tint of the sky when the smog pools against the hills that are far from the ocean breeze.

There are few trees to break up the monotone of the natural landscape other than palm trees planted years ago by new residents who wanted those sunny Southern Californian icons in their own yards. The palm trees are now impossibly tall, their long trunks neatly trimmed up to the reach of a man unsteadily standing on a ladder with garden shears held above his head. Above that point the trees are cloaked with brown, dead fronds where mice and other opportunistic creatures find homes. Occasionally one of the trees catches fire in the dry heat and burns like a huge torch.

Art got off the freeway onto a broad boulevard lined with small businesses. A *pastelería* displays thickly frosted traditional wedding cakes with plastic brides and grooms on top; a tuxedo rental shop offers sky blue ruffled shirts buttoned onto molded plastic chests; a trophy shop supplies the local schools with athletic and academic awards; auto repair shops feature an impressive array of specialties. Small food stands with hand-lettered signs advertise tacos, burritos, hamburgers, and taquitos. A bar's flat stucco facade is painted with musical instruments, music notes, and long-haired, big-busted, high-bottomed fantasy women in string bikinis. The pictures imply that the bar has exotic dancers. There are none. The owner just likes the pictures.

Business owners attempt to cover the gang *placas* on their walls with neutral-colored paint, only to have the street gangs repaint them the next night. The spray-painted *placas* juxtaposed with the shades of neutral block-out paint create unintentional abstract art.

Art's parents' house was at the bottom of a hill on a corner, next door to their neighborhood grocery store. Art parked on the street in front of it. The house was small and Spanish-style, in creamy white stucco molded into smooth and rough textures, and had a tile roof. The windows and doors were built into arches. A tall wrought iron fence encircled the house, and a cement path began at the front gate and meandered as best it could across the short distance to the front door. The path was lined with well-tended tree roses in neat, circular beds, blooming showy red, salmon, pink, and violet, releasing their fragrance into the smoggy day. Art's uncle lived in a sister house across the street.

A sign made out of painted carved wooden letters stood on the roof above the market's door and announced: SILVA MARKET. The store windows had been boarded up years ago after the era arrived when storefront windows begged to be broken. Hand-lettered signs in black paint on white butcher paper were thumbtacked into the square areas where the windows had been. ORANGES .39/LB. CERVEZA $2.39. TORTILLAS 2 DOZ $1.

They piled out of the car. Barbie in her purple was as incongruous in the surroundings as a splashy orchid pinned to a favorite bathrobe. Iris laced her fingers and pushed her hands up over her head and arched her back, standing on her toes, grunting as she stretched. She brought her hands down and rubbed her belly. "When are we eating?"

"Is food all you think about?" Art asked.

"Well, I no longer have a sex life."

Art pulled open the market's screen door, which jangled a bell fixed to the ceiling. He waited for the women to enter, then released the door, which closed with a slam.

"Artie!" said a boy behind the counter, putting down his comic book. "Your father said you were stopping by." He was tall and gangly and wore a short-sleeved, abstract-print cotton shirt tucked into black jeans and enormous, spotlessly white, name-brand athletic shoes with very high tops and very thick soles. The smooth skin of his face sat close against his bones as if every ingested calorie fueled his upward growth, leaving little to flesh out the rest.

Art swung his palm toward his cousin. "Victor! What up, *carnal?*"

"I made the JV football team, first string." Victor spoke with extended vowels, an enunciation unique to the barrio. Art's speech quickly lapsed into the same cadence.

"For reals?"

"For reals."

Art high-fived Victor over the counter. "Way to go, man!"

"Course, all the coach talks about is how your team made it to the city semifinals and how the quarterback was 'poetry in motion,'" Victor teased.

"Yeah, poetry in motion until those big black guys from South Central whipped our little Mexican asses." Art laughed. "Hey, this is my friend Barbie and"—he looked around for Iris and saw her staring into the free-standing ice cream freezer—"that's Iris."

"Hi. Everyone's in back."

"Let's go. Hey, Iris!"

Iris was leaning over the freezer bin, holding its clear plastic lid open, studying the open boxes of ice cream bars and Popsicles that were displayed ends up with their lids torn off, the cool rush of frozen air on her face.

Barbie walked over and put her hand on Iris's arm.

Iris looked up with a start. "Oh, hi."

"You want to stay here or you want to meet Art's family?"

"I was just flashing back to when I was a kid and I used to walk down to our corner store with my older sister and our dog. I'd have a bunch of sweaty change in my fist and I'd walk back and forth from the toy rack to the freezer. I'd finally decide on ice cream and then we'd walk back up the hill, the ice cream melting and running down my arm, pieces of it falling on the sidewalk, where the dog would lap it up. We'd walk through these vacant fields, and dust would stick to the melted ice cream on my hands and arms. At home, I'd rinse off with the garden hose and take a drink from it. It was like drinking from a waterfall."

Iris straightened up and let the freezer door slide closed. "It seems like a million years ago. What parents would let their kids walk to the store by themselves in this town today? How did life get so complicated? Ex-wives, other people's kids . . ."

"I don't know, darlin'. I don't know. But at least you have happy childhood memories. I'd settle for that." Barbie put her hand around Iris's waist. "C'mon, sugar."

Art's father and uncle were in the back storeroom, peering into the guts of a refrigerator unit. The side panel had been removed and detached parts were arranged on square shop cloths on the floor next to an open red toolbox. Tools and refrigerator parts were comingled. The storeroom walls were lined with cases of canned goods and paper products.

The two men were clearly brothers. They were shorter than Art but had his broad white smile, square jaw, and wide forehead. His father's hair was wavy, like Art's, but his uncle's was kinky and clipped close to his head. Art's father wore khaki work pants, a sleeveless T-shirt, and functional black-laced work shoes. His uncle wore a promotional T-shirt printed with a Latin band's logo, old designer jeans, and worn athletic shoes.

"Barbie and Iris," Art said, "this is my father, Eduardo, and my uncle, George. Iris and I work together, and Barbie is the woman I wanted you to meet."

Iris shook hands with each of them. "Pleased to meet you, Mr. Silva and Mr. Silva."

"Please," George said. "First names."

Barbie extended her hand to each of them and held onto George's hand. "Arturo showed Iris and me the best time at your club. It was so lively."

"Thank you," George said. "Glad you enjoyed yourself."

"Art, I'll call your mother." Eduardo pushed open the screen door covering the storeroom's back entrance with his shoulder, leaned out, and yelled, "Sylvia! Sylvia, Artie's here!" He came back inside. "She's hanging out the laundry. She'll be right here. Please sit down."

For seating, there were a couple of beat-up wooden chairs, plastic milk crates, and boxes of different products stacked against the wall. Eduardo turned a crate on end and sat on it. George resumed his position on the floor. Barbie sat in one of the chairs. Iris perched on a stack of boxes, crossing her legs and holding her knee with both hands. Art continued to stand.

"Tio, Barbie owned a restaurant in Atlanta," he said brightly.

"That's what you told me."

"And she's thinking about going into the nightclub business with me."

Barbie was more cautious. "Well, I'm exploring the possibilities."

A woman entered the storeroom. She was small-framed and round, with thick dark hair cut short and fashionably styled away from her face. She had large eyes with bright whites that contrasted starkly with her sable-colored irises and long, dark eyelashes. They were Art's eyes. She was wearing an A-line, knee-length cotton skirt and a cardigan sweater that she took off when she came in the storeroom, revealing a short-sleeved blouse and strong arms that were very brown from yard work and from hanging out laundry in the sun.

"Mom." Art walked to her and kissed her on the cheek.

She put her arms around him, stretching to reach his shoulders. *"Mijo,* good to see you."

Art introduced Barbie and Iris.

"Artie's been telling us how he wants to open his own nightclub," Eduardo said.

Sylvia put her hand on Art's arm. "That's what your uncle told me. But, Arturo, all those years at college. For what? No offense, George, but to open a club?"

Eduardo raised his eyebrows and nodded.

"And your job at McKinney Alitzer. You were so happy when you got that job. I thought you were doing well there." Sylvia looked at Iris. "Isn't he?"

"He's one of the rising stars," Iris offered.

"See? Why do you get a college degree to own a nightclub? The hours are terrible, the money's not good. You can see your uncle's not rich. The people who come around aren't high-class. You'll have a better life doing what you're doing. Why a nightclub, Arturo?"

"I know Tio's not rich, but he's done as well as he wanted to do, right, Tio?"

George nodded. "Art's right. How much you're willing to put into it has a lot to do with it."

"To make it big, you need to think big." Art held both hands apart. "That's what I'm doing. Tio's talked about opening another club for a long time. He and Barbie have the know-how and cash and I have the energy. I can do it, Mom."

"I don't doubt you, *mijo,* I just don't know why you want to change careers so soon. You haven't tried the other thing that long."

Art shook his head. "Mom, I've already hit the ceiling there."

"The ceiling?" Eduardo said. "What ceiling?"

"The glass ceiling. The thing that's keeping me from making it to the top. They're only going to let a Chicano from East L.A. get so far."

"How do you know? You haven't done it for very long." Sylvia looked at Iris. "Is this possible?"

Iris raised her shoulders. "It's a tough business. It takes time to get established."

Sylvia pointed at Iris. "See? See? I'm not so sure if you hit your . . . ceiling or if you're just impatient. I know you, Arturo. You can't always be on top."

"C'mon, Mom. This isn't a spur-of-the-moment thing. I'm serious about this. You're embarrassing me in front of my business associates."

"I'm sorry, *mijo.* I didn't mean to embarrass you. My apologies to you, Barbie and Iris."

"It's perfectly all right," Barbie said. "I'm pleased as punch to see that Arturo has so many people who care about him. I understand your concerns about Arturo going into the nightclub business. I owned a restaurant for many years down in Atlanta, and it *is* a lot of work. But don't think for a minute that I'm absolutely convinced that Arturo's club is the place for my money. I'm just hearing Arturo out, like y'all are."

Art's father turned to George, who had been sitting quietly on the floor with his legs crossed. "What do you think, Jorge?"

George stretched his legs out in front of him and leaned back on his hands. "I think that if this is what Art really wants to do, we ought to at least think about it."

Art clapped his hands together.

Sylvia glowered at her brother-in-law.

George continued, "Next week, I'm going to Mexico. I'll be gone for about a week. Art, maybe you, Barbie, and I can talk when I get back. Is that okay with you?"

"Sure," Art said. "Barbie?"

"Be happy to get together with y'all after you get back."

"Great!" Art said. "All I want is for you to take a serious look at this. Doesn't mean we're going to do anything." He leaned over to shake his uncle's hand, then shook his father's hand. He hugged his mother.

"Have you eaten?" Sylvia asked. "Would you and your friends like to stay for dinner?"

"Thanks, Mom, but I'm taking them for burritos at Manuel's, then I'm going to show them around the neighborhood."

Barbie and Iris stood up. Art put his arm around Barbie's waist and kissed her on the cheek. Barbie quickly freed herself from his grasp and walked to the storeroom door.

"I'll look forward to seeing you, George, when you return from your trip. 'Bye, y'all." She slipped back inside the store.

Iris and Art bid their good-byes and followed Barbie.

Art's father made sure the storeroom door was closed, then he returned to his seat on the crate.

His wife looked down at him solemnly with her arms crossed over her chest.

"If it's what he really wants to do, we should support him, Sylvia."

"I agree," George said.

"He's dating the one in the purple?" Sylvia asked. "This Barbie person?"

Eduardo shrugged. "He gave her a kiss on the cheek. So what?"

"And did you see how she moved away from him? She didn't want us to know that he's with her. Why?"

"Maybe she's shy."

"That woman is not shy. Arturo can get anyone he wants. Why is he with her? She's too old for him. I know why she'd want to be with him, but why is he with her?"

"He's a young man. He sees things you don't, if you know what I mean, Sylvia," George said.

"She has money. Is that why? I don't like how he's acting. Why does he think he has to be rich tomorrow? We didn't raise him like that."

"He's young," Eduardo said. "When you're young, you want everything now. Sylvia, you can't always protect him. He's got to learn things himself, the hard way."

"But I don't think he should pay for it with the family's money."

George rolled forward onto his haunches and began sorting through the refrigerator parts on the floor. "Don't worry, Sylvia. I'm not going to give him money unless I think it's a good deal."

"When you find a good deal, let me know." Sylvia opened the storeroom's back screen door and walked out.

16

"C'MON!" ART YELLED. "PLAY BALL! FOURTH AND GOAL! It's a gut check."

Barbie ran backward a few steps, her breasts bouncing in the purple jumpsuit, her right arm holding the football aloft. She heaved the football through the air with a grunt. It twisted end over end. Art sighed dramatically.

Iris ran forward, caught it, and ran toward the goal post behind Art. He lunged for her, catching her around the waist. She fell backward, and Art fell on top of her with his hands around her hips and his face in her crotch. The ball came out of Iris's hands and Art lunged for it.

"Fumble!" he yelled. "My ball!"

"My ass!" Iris got up and stood with her hands on her hips. "This is supposed to be touch football, Tarzan!"

Art smiled broadly, his white teeth and the whites of his eyes shining in the moonlight. "Sorry. I got carried away."

Iris rubbed her hip. "I'm gonna have a hell of a bruise tomorrow."

"It was just a little tackle. Stop being such a baby."

"Screw you. You're drunk."

Art lunged for her, catching her around the calves, knocking her backward again. "*I'm* drunk? Look who's talking." He tickled her ribs.

Iris writhed on the ground. "Stop it! Art, stop it!" she screamed. "I'm gonna be sick! Barbie! Help!"

Barbie leaped onto Art's shoulders from behind and tried to pull him off, then started tickling his ribs. The three of them rolled over and under each other on the grass of the dark athletic field. They didn't see the security guard until he was standing over them.

"Hey!" he shouted, dancing around them, not knowing who to grab. "Knock it off! School's closed! You're trespassing!"

Art rolled over and sat back on his hands. "Hey, Mike! What up? It's Artie!"

Mike shone his flashlight on Art, who put his hand up to shield the beam.

"Art Silva." Mike clicked off the flashlight and extended his hand to help Art up. "What are you doing back on the home turf?"

Art shook Mike's hand. "Just foolin' around, showing my friends the old neighborhood. This is Iris and this is Barbie."

Mike held his hand out toward Barbie to help her up. She took it. Art did the same for Iris. She ignored him and unsteadily got to her feet by herself.

"We played a lot of games here, you and me." Mike looked around the dark field. "A lot of memories."

"We'll take off," Art said. "I don't want to get you in trouble."

"Go ahead and stay. No problem. Just take your empties with you." He shook Art's hand. "Nice to meet you, ladies." He walked across the field, then gave a look back over his shoulder. Art threw him a pass, long and straight. Mike caught the ball and threw it back, then left the field.

Art walked to the visiting team's bleachers, where a bottle of tequila, a round box of salt, and a stack of plastic cups stood. One of the cups held lime wedges. He gathered everything in his arms and ran up the benches, the wooden planks bending under his weight, until he was at the top. He put the things down and stood facing the wire fence that surrounded the school's perimeter, his fingers laced in the fence's basket weave.

Iris climbed up next to him. She poured tequila into a cup, put salt on the back of her hand, licked the salt, downed the tequila in one gulp, then bit into a lime wedge.

Art watched. "For someone who doesn't do shooters, you sure been friendly with Jose Cuervo tonight."

"So what?" Iris slurred the *s*. She leaned her belly against the fence.

Art shrugged. "So nothing."

Barbie finally reached them, huffing and puffing and patting the perspiration from her face with the back of her hand. "What are y'all lookin' at?"

"The city," Iris said.

The school was built on top of a hill at the city's eastern edge. It was not the classic L.A.-at-night view like the one from the Griffith Observatory. From here there was no luxury, no hint of an ocean. There were simply the lights of an overgrown and unrestrained city, cast carelessly across the hills and valleys as far as millions of dreams could throw them.

Barbie leaned against the fence next to Iris. She carefully stuck her fingers through the wires, trying not to scratch her manicure.

112

"I'm psyched!" Art shouted. "We're gonna open a club!" He rattled the fence with both hands.

"Deal's not done yet, Arturo," Barbie said.

"But the meeting went well, didn't you think? My uncle was impressed with you." Art reached his hands above his head, grabbed the fence, and put his face close to it. "This city is *mine*."

"You can have it." Iris turned around, sat on the bleachers, and leaned against the fence. She poured tequila into three cups, handed one to Art, and began to hand one to Barbie. It slipped out of her hand and tumbled between the bleachers to the ground. "Ooops."

"That's okay, darlin'. I've had enough."

"Iris hasn't had enough," Art said. "She's getting flatlined."

"How about some wine?" Iris asked. "There's wine left."

"We drank it," Art said.

"You two go ahead and enjoy yourselves," Barbie said. "I'll drive y'all home."

"Can you drive a stick?" Art asked.

"Can I drive a stick?" Barbie repeated. "Of course I can."

Art reached into his back pocket, took out his wallet, unfolded it, and dug his finger around inside, looking for something. He pulled out a marijuana joint and held it up, displaying it in front of them. "Since we're celebrating, how about a special treat?"

"I'm not celebrating." Iris leaned forward and almost lost her balance. Barbie grabbed her, putting her leg on the bench below to steady them both. "But I'll have a taste. I don't think I've smoked since I was in college. I think I first did it with John. Figures. Future cop."

Art lit the joint, took a hit, and passed it to Iris. She took a hit and immediately started choking. Art took it from her fingers. Iris grabbed her chest with both hands. "Burns!"

Art offered it to Barbie. She shook her head. He took a hit and passed it back to Iris. She took another hit and didn't cough as much.

They traded the joint back and forth in silence.

Art spoke. "What should I call it?"

"Call what?" Iris said.

"My club."

"Oh, shut up about that damn club."

"What else is there interesting to talk about?" Art said.

Iris looked at Barbie, and something on Barbie's face caught her attention. Iris slowly reached her hand up and touched a small mole. "Barbie's family."

"Why do you want to hear about that?" Barbie asked.

Iris rolled her finger around the mole. "Because you told me, 'At least you have happy family memories.' Don't you have any? Not one?"

"You don't want to hear about that. Honey, stop playin' with my face. You're gonna rub it raw."

"I want to hear about it. Don't you, Art?" Iris heavily dropped her hand back in her lap.

"Sure. Let's hear it."

Barbie crossed her arms over her chest and held herself. "Like I told you before, my three older brothers and I grew up half naked and half starved down in Mississippi. Daddy worked all day on the railroad, which was fine with me, 'cause when he got home, he'd get drunk and beat on us. Momma ran off when I was twelve. That was Daddy's story, anyway. I always suspected he got carried away one day and killed her. Wasn't like Momma to leave us like that. My youngest brother and I thought he planted her out in the yard. There was this spot out back where the wildflowers always grew real nice. After she was gone, I had to drop out of school. I lived in the dirt. Thought I'd die there."

"How awful." Iris was staring at the mole on Barbie's face again. She put her finger up to touch it but touched a spot to the left. "Poor Barbie."

"That's only the half of it. My two older brothers used to have their way with me and my younger brother."

"No way!" Art leapt up with outrage. He straddled two benches.

"Yes, they did." Barbie chewed her lower lip.

Iris stared up at Art. He seemed to be ten feet tall. She propped her head against Barbie's shoulder as she watched him. "What about Daddy?"

"He didn't get in on the action, if that's what you mean.

I don't know if he knew. My brother and I were afraid to tell him. Figured he'd just beat us. You know, blame us."

"Whatcha do?" Iris asked.

"When I was fifteen, I looked twenty-one. I left home and went to Atlanta. The only work I could get was as a stripper. It was good money. But I never prostituted myself. Some of those girls did, but unh-uh, not me. Stripped for a few years, then got a more legitimate job as a waitress for Hal Stringfellow. You know the rest."

Art grabbed the bottle of tequila and splashed some into three cups. He handed a cup to Barbie and one to Iris. "Hal deserves a toast." He held his cup out. Barbie and Iris held theirs out to meet it. "To Hal!"

"To Hal!" Iris chimed.

"May his li'l ol' redneck heart rest in peace." Barbie took a sip of the tequila, then set the cup next to her on the bench. She plucked at the neckline of her jumpsuit, straightening the collar, which had gone awry during the football game.

"Have you ever gone back home?" Iris asked.

"Nope." Barbie briskly shook her head. "Never did. Used to think I'd go back, flashin' diamonds and furs. Then I thought, what for? They'd just try to borrow money from me. Or laugh. I keep up with my youngest brother. He lives in Texas. Runs a janitorial supply business. Got a coupla little kids, wife. Turned out good."

"Hell of a story," Iris said.

"It's no story," Barbie said indignantly. "It's the truth."

Iris looked at her. "I didn't mean you made it up, I just meant it's a hell of a thing, you know? To have happened."

Art was still standing with one foot on the bench above and one on the bench below. "I've got the munchies. We got any food left?"

"No," Iris said. "I'm starving, too." She stood up and started walking down the bleachers, stepping from bench to bench.

"There's a little store down the hill. I'll make a food run."

"You ain't fit to drive, Arturo," Barbie said.

"I'll walk. What's your pleasure?"

Barbie patted her belly. "Nothing for me. I've already ruined my diet for the weekend."

Iris jumped off the last bleacher onto the athletic field.

She ran across it with her arms spread out. "Oreos!" she shouted as she ran. "Chocolate Oreos!" She turned and ran back. "And tortilla chips! Barbecued tortilla chips!" She kicked her leg and her shoe flew off, landing somewhere in the dark. She kicked her other shoe off. She pirouetted on the grass until she got dizzy and collapsed. She held her head until the world righted itself, then crawled on her hands and knees to the bleachers. She reached underneath the first bench. "Here's some wine. It rolled underneath."

Art came down the bleachers and handed her a cup. Barbie followed him.

"I'll see you later." Art walked across the field. Halfway across, he disappeared into the darkness.

Iris sat on the grass, uncorked the bottle, and poured some into the cup, spilling it on her hand.

Barbie tried to take the cup from her. "You're gonna make yourself sick, sugar."

Iris jerked the cup back. "So what if I do?" She took a sip and set the cup on the bottom bench. She suddenly got up and ran across the grass. "Fucking men! Fucking John Somers! Asshole!" She screamed at the top of her lungs. "Asshole!" A dog somewhere started to bark. Iris started to sob. She stood on the dark field and held her head in her hands.

Barbie walked over and put her arms around her. "I know, honey. I know."

"How could he leave me?" Iris sobbed.

"C'mon, sit down." She sat on the grass and Iris lumbered next to her.

"How could he leave me for that fucking earth mother?" She leaned on Barbie's shoulder and cried.

Barbie put her arms around her and rocked her back and forth. "There, there. It's okay. Barbeh's here."

"My life's going down the tubes. Nothing's gone right. It started when Alley was murdered. I can still see him lying in the street. I see . . ." Iris's voice caught in her throat. She sobbed into Barbie's shoulder. Her shoulders shook. She inhaled and exhaled trembling breaths.

Barbie rocked her back and forth.

Iris clumsily drew her fingers along the tracks her tears

made in Barbie's silk jumpsuit. "I'm wrecking your clothes. All your pretty purple clothes."

"That's okay, honey. Just get it all out."

Iris suddenly sat up. "Man, I'm really stoned. Wow. That was strong stuff." All at once, she stopped crying. She stared at Barbie's face.

"Whatcha looking at, honey?"

Iris reached out and smoothed Barbie's makeup with her thumb. "Your makeup's messed up." Barbie turned her head and leaned into Iris's touch. She put her hand on top of Iris's. Iris pulled hers away and let it drop heavily into her lap.

"I don't have any purple clothes." She shook her head sadly.

"I'll buy you something purple."

Iris looked intently into Barbie's eyes. "Thank you. Thank you, Barbie. Thank you. You're such a good friend. You're always there for me." She picked up Barbie's long gold necklace from her chest and turned it to reflect the dim light. She twisted and turned it and twisted and turned it.

Barbie watched her. She raised her hand and slowly moved it to Iris's face, which she stroked.

Iris closed her eyes. "That feels good."

Barbie slowly leaned closer and closer. She opened her lips around Iris's.

Iris suddenly opened her eyes.

Barbie moved her head back and looked at Iris without saying anything.

Iris wrinkled her brow. "What are you doing?"

"Just bein' here for you, darlin'."

"Why are you so close?"

"I'm right where I was."

Iris touched her lips. "Did you kiss me?"

"Kiss you?"

Iris stood up.

Barbie leaned back on her hands. "Why? You find the idea offensive?"

"This is weird." Iris walked several paces, rubbing her head, tangling her hair in her hands. "You did, didn't you?"

"Honey, I'm just sittin' here listenin' to you talk. I don't know what you're goin' off about now."

"Talk? About what?"

"About John."

"John? What was I saying about John?"

"About how he's always buggin' you about whether you have that embezzled money."

Iris rubbed her forehead, trying to remember. "Why would I say that?"

Barbie shrugged. "I don't know, sugar."

"Hell, he told me to keep it."

"Keep it?"

"Yeah." Iris pirouetted.

"Then you buried it."

"I didn't say that. Why would I say that?"

"I guess I didn't hear you right. What did you say?"

Iris stopped pirouetting and faced Barbie. "Just why are you so interested?"

"Honey, I'm not interested. You were the one who asked me what you were talking about."

Iris held her head back and regarded Barbie skeptically, her head wobbling on her neck. "Just why are you so interested?" she repeated.

"I told you." Barbie got up from the ground. "You were talkin' about it. Don't you believe me? You just said I was your good friend."

"But it's not something I talk about."

"You don't trust me. Must be lonely being such a distrustful person."

"I'm not distrustful."

"Maybe that's one reason John went back to his ex-wife."

"What?"

"There's gotta be some reason. I'm not being mean, honey. I'm just tryin' to help you."

Iris fell onto her knees on the grass. She started to cry again. "It wasn't my fault, was it?" She picked up the hem of her red sweater and rubbed her face with it.

She got up again and started walking toward the bleachers. She tripped over an uneven spot in the grass and stumbled for another three steps before she managed to stop her forward motion. She looked back accusingly at the lump in the grass, then looked down at her bare feet. She wiggled her toes in the cool grass. A slow smile crossed her face.

"This grass feels so cool. I can't remember the last time I stood barefoot in grass." She walked toward the bleachers, picked up a cup, and uncorked the bottle of wine.

"Honey, you're gonna make yourself sick." Barbie retrieved Iris's shoes, walked over to her, and took the bottle from her hands.

"You're right. You're right." Iris stopped and looked intently at Barbie. She put her hand to her forehead. "What were we talking about? We were talking about something."

"The money. You were telling me where the money is."

A look of recognition washed over Iris's face. "Oh, the *money*. Right. Alley." She chuckled. "He was carrying almost half a million dollars around in his briefcase." She held her ribs and laughed and looked at Barbie to share the joke.

Barbie chuckled.

Iris threw her head back, laughing. She staggered backward, gasping for breath. "In his briefcase! That Alley! I'm tellin' ya. Oh, boy." She wiped tears from her eyes, then stared across the field. "I'm gonna burn it. It's like a curse. I'm gonna get it out tomorrow and burn it." Iris frowned as she wrestled with a thought. "Wait. Tomorrow's Sunday. Can't tomorrow."

"It's in a bank, sugar?" Barbie asked.

Iris put her hands on her hips and leaned defiantly toward Barbie. "Yes, in a safe deposit box. Locked up. Safe from nosy, prying people. Okay?" Iris snatched her shoes from Barbie's hands, sat on a bleacher, and put them back on. "I don't like this conversation. I'm not so sure I like you."

"That's not a nice thing to say, especially after everything I've done for you."

"Done for me?"

Art yelled at them from across the field. "I have returned." He was carrying a brown paper grocery sack. "What have you two been up to?"

"Just girl talk," Barbie said.

"I'm not gonna touch that." He tore a piece of beef jerky between his teeth.

Iris looked expectantly at the bag.

Art reached into it and handed her a bag of Oreos and an open half-gallon of milk.

"All right!" Iris snatched them from Art, sat on a bleacher bench, took an Oreo from the package, twisted the two halves apart, then scraped off the filling with her bottom teeth. "Oh," she moaned. "This tastes wonderful." She twisted open another one and ate it. "This is so good."

She put down the carton of milk, from which she'd just taken a slug, and looked intently at Barbie, then across the darkened field. She looked back at Barbie. "What *were* we talking about?"

17

BARBIE DROVE THE MUSTANG HOME WHILE ART SLEPT IN THE front seat and Iris slept in the back. Barbie walked Iris, with one hand clinging to Barbie, the other to the cellophane corner of an almost empty bag of Oreo cookies, upstairs to Iris's condo. After Barbie left, Iris kicked off her shoes, pulled off her pants and sweater, took off her underwear, threw everything across the room, pulled up the covers, and was immediately out.

Barbie drove through the early-morning streets of Santa Monica, Venice, and Marina Del Rey. A moist fog had rolled in and the thick air was a chilly contrast with the clear, bright sunshine of the day. A few party animals were still in the streets, on foot and in cars, catching their second wind. Barbie parked in the visitors' parking area of her apartment complex.

"Arturo. Time to get up." She roughly shook his left shoulder. "Arturo! I can't leave you here all night. You might get mugged or something. Wake up!"

Art turned his head, groaned, and opened his eyes a slit. "Where am I?"

"You're in the parking lot of my apartment building. You're not drivin' home, mister. Come upstairs."

She got out of the car, then went to the passenger door and opened it. Art put his hand around the back of her neck, pulled her down, and kissed her wetly. He rubbed her breasts through the purple jumpsuit.

"Figures you'd wake up horny," she said.

"I'm always horny."

"I know. It's one of your best qualities."

Barbie released the seat to recline against the backseat. She bit the crotch of his jeans, pulling the denim with her teeth, then hitched up the thighs of her jumpsuit and climbed on top of him with one knee on each side of the bucket seat. He fumbled with the buttons on her jumpsuit, pulled taut by her breasts. He fed the top three buttons through the buttonholes and the fabric sprang open. He cupped her breasts and rubbed her nipples through her purple lace brassiere. Barbie reached up and snapped open the clasp. Her breasts tumbled out. Art rubbed his face in them, then took one of her nipples in his mouth.

She grabbed his hair with both hands, arched her back, and moaned. "Keep that up, I'll pop off."

He kept it up.

"Wait, sugar," Barbie said breathlessly. "Stop. Wait."

She pulled the jumpsuit off her shoulders, then grunted as she worked it down her hips. She took off her purple lace panties. The light from a high-intensity lamp in the parking lot reflected off her pale skin.

She unzipped his jeans and pulled him free. He slid his jeans down past his knees and put his foot on the ground outside the Mustang's door. She tried to slip him inside. She shimmied her hips around on top of him. She shimmied again.

Art put his hand on his forehead. "I can't. I've had too much to drink."

She lifted her hips and examined him clinically. "I guess this was not meant to be."

"Sorry." He leaned his head back against the seat and pulled his jeans up.

She rubbed the skin around her lips, trying to neaten her smudged lipstick, then got out of the car, stark naked. "Happens to the best of 'em." She reached over Art to grab her jumpsuit. He was breathing deeply. She pushed his shoulder. "Arturo?"

The rhythm of his breathing didn't change.

She stepped out of the car and into the jumpsuit. She pushed his shoulder again. He moaned a little, crossed his arms over his chest, and settled more deeply into the seat.

"Arturo, wake up!"

He began to snore.

"Good Lord. Pass out here in the parking lot."

She looked at his left arm, which was lying across his chest. She picked up his hand and looked at his watch. It was an inexpensive digital model with two rows of tiny buttons for programming telephone numbers and dates.

"Why you wearin' that cheap thing tonight?"

She lay his arm on his lap and picked up his right arm. The sleeve of her jumpsuit brushed his face. Art didn't twitch. She draped his fingers across hers as if she were giving him a manicure and rubbed her thumb over the insignia and initials of his class ring.

She twisted the ring on his finger. It was snug, but she could turn it. She pulled. It stopped at his knuckle. He stirred. Barbie froze, still holding his hand.

"New account . . ."

"What, sugar?"

He shifted his feet. "Five thous . . ." He pulled his hand away from hers, rolled onto his left side, put his left hand under his cheek, and dropped his right hand in front of him on the seat, his fingers curled inward. His breathing became deep and even again.

"Shoot!" Barbie whispered. She walked around to the driver's side, working her jaw. She spat into the palm of her hand, leaned over the door into the car, and worked the spittle underneath the ring and over his knuckle. She held his palm with one hand and the ring with the other. The Mustang's door pressed painfully against her middle. She held onto his palm firmly, took a deep breath, and gave the ring a sharp pull. It cleared his knuckle and came off.

Art frowned in his sleep. His expression was as unguarded as a baby's. Barbie smiled down at him. She touched his coarse hair and patted the top of his head. She put his ring on her own finger and held her hand up to examine it. The gold was still warm. She grabbed her underwear from the Mustang's dashboard and walked to her apartment.

Lorraine reached out in the darkness toward the ringing telephone. She missed it on the first pass, then tried again. "Hello?" she said thickly.

"Hi, darlin'."

Lorraine slowly sat up in bed. "Charlotte?"

"It's your Charlotte, sugar."

"What time is it?" Lorraine looked at the clock next to the bed. "It's five in the morning."

"I'm sorry. I forgot about the time. It's two hours earlier here. Figured you'd just be comin' home after our bar closed down. I was just sittin' around, missin' you. I'm so sorry, honey, for leaving you that way. I . . . I'm so sorry."

"Where are you?"

"A wonderful place. So romantic. It's dark . . ." Barbie breathed heavily into the phone. "It's dark but you can still see the outlines of the boats, so many pretty boats."

"Boats?"

"In the marina. The king's marina, darlin'. Don't you love it? My apartment's got a little balcony and big picture windows that look across the boats. I took it because it's woodsy-lookin'. You always reminded me of the woods, Rainey. The deep, dark woods." Her breathing grew quicker. "My windows are open and the air is blowin' over me, over my body. The air is so soft . . ." She whimpered.

"Are you getting off?"

"I miss bein' with you, sugar."

"Is this why you called me?"

"C'mon, honey. You still love me, don't you?" Barbie's breath was shallow.

"You've met someone else, haven't you?"

"No, no. I'm still in love with you, Rainey. In love with you like the cool breeze that's blowing over me. Like the way you used to blow on my skin, remember?" She moaned. "You still love me, don't you? Tell me you love me. Say it."

"I do. I wish I didn't, but I do."

"Tell me," she breathed. "Tell me you love me."

"I love you."

"Again."

"I love you."

"Again." Barbie began breathing harder and harder, and her moans became shrill. She gasped for air.

"Charlotte?"

Barbie's breathing was still uneven.

"Where are you, Charlotte? I'll come out."

"Honey," she panted. "I'm dying to see you but the time's not good. I've got to go now, darlin'."

"Charlotte, don't do this to me. I can't take this. I can't."

"Bye-bye." Barbie hung up.

18

"Hi, I. This is your mu-ther." Her voice was amplified through the telephone answering machine's speaker.

Iris closed her eyes tighter against the dim light that filtered through the closed drapes.

"I'm calling again, just to see how you're do-ing," she singsonged. "It's eleven now. You're still not in. I hope you're all right. Call me just as soon as you get in. I . . ."

". . . love you," Iris said the words along with her mother. The machine rewound itself.

Iris pulled a pillow over her face. "Oh, my God."

She swallowed. Her tongue stuck against the roof of her mouth. It tasted both sour and sweet. She swung her feet out and sat on the side of the bed. Her head hurt across both temples. She looked down at her nude body. Her skin felt hot and seemed flushed and troubled.

"Seemed like a good idea at the time, didn't it, Iris Ann?"

She saw her new sweater on the floor beside the bed,

turned halfway inside out. She picked it up and righted it. Blades of grass and bits of dirt fell off.

"Awww . . ." she moaned. "Football. That damned Art."

Her panties dangled from the lampshade, where they had landed after she'd thrown them. Her shoes were on opposite sides of the room, lying where she had kicked them off.

She stood up, went into the bathroom, and pulled on her terry cloth robe, the soft fabric feeling rough against her hot skin. The almost empty bag of Oreos was next to the bathroom door.

"Awww . . . not Oreos!" She paused, then slapped her hand to her forehead when she remembered another empty cellophane bag. "Barbecued tortilla chips! A whole bag." She rubbed her sour stomach. "Tequila shooters, wine, milk, and cookies . . . Ugh!"

She turned the rod to open the blinds, letting in the bright sunlight. She winced. She played the five messages on her phone machine. Two were hang-ups. Three were from her mother. She'd called every hour since nine that morning.

"Great. A nervous-mother day."

She sat heavily on the bed and punched a number into the telephone.

"Hi, Mom. I was here, I just had the phone unplugged. Out with friends. I didn't get in until late. But I didn't get mugged or raped or stabbed. I'm here. I'm fine. Yes, I heard about the girl who was murdered in her office garage. Please don't do this anxiety thing today. I know you love me. John was busy last night. He's not coming by today. He's . . . busy. Gotta go. Everything's fine. He just wanted to spend time with his daughter, okay? Gotta go. 'Bye."

Iris clicked off the phone. "Jeez! Get a life, Mom."

She made coffee. The coffeemaker hissed and belched as it sent boiled water through the grounds. She poured some into a mug and washed down two aspirins. The coffee scorched her throat and the aspirins felt oversized. She put bread in the toaster, leaned against the kitchen counter, held her coffee mug between both hands, and took small sips. The aroma of toasting bread filled the room. She started to feel hungry. It was a good sign. She took a few more sips of coffee while staring at the linoleum floor.

What the hell happened last night? Why do I feel so uneasy?

She set the coffee mug down and rubbed her eyes with the heels of her palms. It felt as if there were sand underneath her eyelids. Her eyes sprang open in terror.

"No! God, no!" She frantically searched the scattered fragments of her memory. "I didn't sleep with Art, did I?" She put her hand against her rapidly beating heart and breathed a sigh of relief. "No, I didn't." Then she touched her lips. *Something about a kiss. And Barbie. Why was I mad at her?*

The toast popped up. She spread margarine and jam on it, took a bite, and chewed while she stared at the closed cupboard in front of her.

"Forget it."

She found her purse on her bedroom floor, took it to its place on top of the antique table in the entryway, dropped her keys inside, and took her sunglasses out of it. She took the toast and the portable phone onto the terrace.

The street was full of people walking and riding bikes and roller skating and being sun-kissed and healthy and enjoying the day and the ocean and sand and life.

"Iris, you degenerate."

She looked over the railing into the thick decorative bushes below. The street man was sitting on the ground with his knees drawn up to his chest. His bedding was neatly rolled up and the dark green plastic garbage bags containing his belongings were hidden in the bushes. His long hair needed a wash but it was neatly combed and pulled back into a ponytail. His jeans and T-shirt looked fairly clean. His corrugated cardboard VIETNAM VET WILL WORK FOR FOOD sign was leaning against the wall behind him.

Sighing with exasperation, she plopped into the Adirondack chair that she'd ordered from a company in Maine. She looked at the phone dial, hesitated, then punched in John's number. In the pause before the call connected, she hung up. She bit into the toast. Crumbs fell onto her bathrobe. "Bastard." She dabbed her tears with the robe's belt. "Jerk." She punched in his number again. A woman answered. Iris quickly hung up. She sprang out of the chair and paced back and forth on the terrace.

"She spent the night!"

The street man looked up at the underside of the terrace.

Iris went inside and refilled her coffee mug. The recollection hit her like a cold wave. She slapped the counter hard enough to make her palm sting. "I told her! I don't believe it! I freaking told her!" She hit the counter again. "Shit! I was high, I didn't care, and she knew it. She pushed me. She kept asking me about it. Damn her!"

Iris picked up the coffee mug. "That's what I was mad about. Whatever. It's safe. If she tells anyone, I'll just deny it." She dumped the coffee into the sink. While she was putting the mug in the dishwasher, she suddenly straightened up and touched her lips. "*She* kissed me. Oh, man."

Iris was just stepping out of the shower when the phone started to ring. She wrapped a towel around herself and answered it.

"Hi, sugar. How ya doin'?" Barbie's voice was as clear as a bell. The energy made Iris wince.

"I have a major hangover."

"I figured you might, so I brought you my surefire hangover tonic. Fix you right up."

"You're here?"

"I'm sorry, darlin'. I should have called first. Is this a bad time? You know you got a man livin' in your bushes out here?"

"Yeah, I know. C'mon up."

Iris quickly dried off, threw on sweat pants and a T-shirt, and wrapped a towel around her hair before the doorbell rang. She opened it without looking through the peephole. John Somers was standing next to Barbie.

"Look who showed up just when I was comin' in," Barbie said.

John was carrying a large spray of red roses and assorted greenery in a glass vase. He was wearing blue jeans, a denim shirt, and athletic shoes. His coarse red hair was neatly trimmed and stood away from his scalp, as if it had been recently washed and cut.

"Pretty flowers," Iris said.

John handed her the vase. He moved to kiss her on the lips. Iris turned her head and offered her cheek.

"Wanted to wish you a belated happy birthday."

"Thank you." Iris walked across the living room and put the vase on the dining room table. "Aren't they pretty, Barbie?"

"Very nice." Barbie was carrying a large, handled shopping bag from an exclusive department store and a plastic grocery sack. She was wearing skintight stirrup pants with a long, multicolored overblouse, high-heeled slingback shoes, and her faux jewel–encrusted baseball cap. She walked into the kitchen and began taking bottles of tomato juice, Tabasco sauce, and clam juice out of the grocery sack and setting them on the counter. "Course, if you'd been with her on her birthday, you wouldn't be here with flowers in hand trying to make up for it today."

John walked to the end of the kitchen and stood in Barbie's line of vision. He put his hands on his hips and leaned his long torso toward her. "Just what business is this of yours?"

Barbie faced him, holding the neck of the clam juice bottle. "Iris is my friend. My friend's affairs are *always* my business."

"Well, *my* affairs are *none* of your business. Furthermore, Iris understands what happened between her and me."

"Oh, yeah. She understands all right. She understands so good that she cried her eyes out right here on my shoulder." Barbie indicated the location with a manicured fingernail.

They both looked at Iris, who stood watching them, her legs apart, her arms dangling at her sides, her mouth ajar, as if she couldn't believe they really existed. She finally spoke. "Barbie. Would you mind waiting in the bedroom while John and I talk?"

"No problem, darlin'." She waved at Iris. "I bought you a li'l somethin' and I wanted to hang it up anyway." She grabbed the handled bag and started to walk out of the kitchen past John. He made an insignificant move to clear her way. His jaw was fixed, which pursed his Cupid's bow lips, giving him a look that was more like a boyish pout than an intimidating glower.

Barbie brushed past him, hitting his waist with her elbow. "*Excuse* me. Not much room to pass here." In her heels, she barely reached his chin. She left the room with her slingbacks slapping against her heels. Her fragrance hung in the air.

"I can't stand that woman," John said before Barbie had completely exited the room. He stared at the doorway through which she had just passed. "I've told you before that there's something about her that's not right."

Iris closed her eyes and rubbed them with the pads of her fingers.

"Out late last night?"

"Yeah."

"Oh. With her?"

"Yeah. And other . . . people."

"Hmmm." John surveyed her puffy face and red eyes as if they would reveal what had transpired. "Where'dja go?" he asked conversationally.

"John, you've lost information privileges. Especially if you're sleeping with your ex-wife."

He paled underneath his freckles.

"Did you do it before we officially broke up or did you at least wait until after?"

"Last night was the first time."

"Oh. You waited. I feel *so* much better." Iris walked onto the terrace and leaned her back against the railing. "Why did you come? You were the one who wanted to end it."

John stood next to her, gripping the terrace railing with both hands. He shook his head. "I'm so confused. I thought I'd made the right decision, but when I read your card, I was really moved by some of the things you said."

"I didn't send it to try to change your mind. I was just finishing business. Just wanted to say a few things."

"Want to hear something funny?" John laughed. "Penny opened it by accident."

"By accident?"

"Well, she wouldn't have opened it on purpose," he said with a defensive backpedal in his voice.

"Oh, not Penny." Iris heaved out a sarcastic burst of air.

"C'mon, Iris. You don't know her very well if you think . . ."

Iris turned to face him. "No, *you* don't know her very well. How can a man who's so tough and astute in his professional life be so mamby-pamby in his personal life? Why don't you ask yourself why you feel so ambivalent about taking up with her again? Why don't you ask yourself why you're here now?" She tore the towel off her head and threw it on the Adirondack chair.

"I know why I'm here." A small tear caught between his eyelashes. "I still love you, and I was thinking maybe . . ."

"John, don't." Iris grabbed the railing as if to steady herself. "It's either me or her. If it's her, then please don't come around anymore"—her voice broke—"because I can't take it." The tears came quickly.

He wiped his eyes with his hand. "Well, I guess I better go. I hope you like the flowers."

"They're beautiful, but it's a hell of a way to get you to bring me flowers." She looked at him and laughed. He laughed too. It was horrible to have shared a joke.

He looked out at the ocean again, then looked around the terrace, as if he were trying to imprint the scene in his mind. He glanced underneath the terrace. "Hey!" he shouted. "Hey, you! Iris, I thought you were going to get the police to get rid of him."

"I told you, it's pointless. He just keeps coming back."

"These bums, they're not saints, you know." John's tears had dried. "It's not like in the movies where the homeless man becomes your buddy."

"John." Iris sighed with fatigue. "I'll deal with it, okay?" She walked back inside the living room and slowly to the front door. She opened it and stood beside it with her hand on the doorknob.

He followed her through the living room and stopped when he saw the open door. He looked at the rectangular opening and the dim hallway beyond it, knowing that passing through it would change his life forever. He angled his body slightly forward and walked past her through the doorway and kept walking, not looking back, until he was halfway down the corridor and heard the door close quietly behind him.

Iris blew her nose on a paper towel from the kitchen and threw cold tap water on her face. She felt even more tired than she had earlier. She stood in front of the sink and tried to comb her wet, tangled hair with her fingers, mindlessly occupying herself for several minutes. Then she remembered Barbie roaming somewhere in her home and immediately walked toward the bedrooms, her bare footsteps muted on the carpet.

She peeked into the guest bedroom, which she used as an office and saw Barbie looking through one of her desk drawers. Iris stood in the doorway and watched her for a brief moment before Barbie noticed her and quickly closed the drawer.

"Hi, sugar," she said brightly. "I was looking for a pair of scissors." She displayed her left hand, in which she already held a pair of scissors. "I bought you something and I wanted to cut the tags off." She set the scissors on the desk and walked toward Iris with open arms. "Oh, darlin'. You've been cryin'. What happened?"

Iris took a couple of steps backward and put her palm out in front of her. "I'll be fine. John and I were just talking."

Barbie stopped in the middle of the room. "About what? What made you so upset?"

"Oh . . ." Iris shook her head and wrinkled her nose as if it were nothing. "Just things."

"What kind of things? Something made you upset."

"I'm hungover, I'm feeling kind of fragile anyway. It's nothing."

"You're sure you don't want to talk about it?"

"Positive." Iris smiled cheerfully. "So, you said you needed a pair of scissors?" She glanced around the room, taking everything in.

Barbie shook her head bitterly. "I'm sorry, honey. Maybe you thought I was out of line, but I don't like it when people don't treat my friends right. And I don't like cops. They have an attitude I don't care for. I know John's got some good qualities but"—she waggled her finger at Iris—"honey, you could do a lot better. And you *will*."

"So, you said you bought something?" Iris's voice was bright, but her eyes were cool. She surveyed the office one more time, then turned and walked toward the bedroom. She stopped at the doorway. "You made the bed and picked up. How nice." She looked around the room.

Barbie peeked in the doorway behind her, putting her hand on Iris's waist. Iris stepped away from her.

"You know I can't sit still. I'd rather be busy." Barbie

skipped into the walk-in closet and retrieved a long-sleeved, purple silk blouse on a hanger. "What d'ya think?"

"It's beautiful." Iris walked up to it and fingered the material.

"Let me cut the tags off first. Now, don't look at the price."

"What's the occasion?"

"Don't you remember, honey? Last night you were telling me you didn't have nothin' in purple and I told you I'd buy you somethin' and here it is."

"Thank you. That was very nice." Iris rubbed her temples. "Frankly, I don't remember too much from last night."

Barbie took the blouse off the hanger and held it toward Iris. "Here, try it on."

"I'm sure it'll fit. It's the right size."

Barbie walked toward her, holding the blouse out. "Don't you want to try it on?"

Iris took it and held the shoulders against her own shoulders. "See. It'll fit fine." She handed it back to Barbie and watched as she walked into her closet and hung it up.

"Boy, I was really out of it last night. I don't remember hardly anything. What *were* we talking about?"

Barbie sat on the bed. "Oh, all sorts of things."

Iris gestured toward the hallway. "Weren't you going to make me your hangover tonic?"

"Sure, darlin'. Let's do that." She walked out of the room in front of Iris.

"I'll be right there. I need to step into the bathroom." As soon as Barbie left, Iris quickly looked around the bedroom and in the closet. She shrugged and walked back into the living room, still barefoot.

Barbie jumped when she saw Iris. "You scared me out of my wits!" She was holding Iris's key ring in her hand. "Darlin', I found these on the carpet against the wall over there. You probably dropped them when you came in last night." She held up the rectangular brass fob, which was engraved with Iris's name. "This is nice."

"Thanks." Iris took the keys and put them in her purse sitting on the small hallway table, its zippered top open like she had left it earlier that morning.

"Let's get to that tonic." Barbie bounced into the kitchen.

Iris followed. "Barbie, what was I crying about last night?"

"Oh, you were upset over John. You know. How he did you dirty."

"A funny thing happened. I woke up this morning thinking about Alley, the mailroom boy at the office who was murdered. Was I talking about him last night?"

Barbie twisted the metal lid on the jar of clam juice until the suction released with a pop. "Oh, honey. I had too much to drink myself. I don't exactly remember what we were talkin' about either." She began opening cupboards and looking in them.

Iris hopped in front of her and pressed the cupboard door closed. "Shoot! I forgot! I promised my mother I'd go shopping with her. I'm late! I've gotta go."

"Oh, I'd love to go with y'all. I'd love to see your mom again."

"Why?"

"Why? Well, I guess because I lost my momma at an early age, like I was tellin' you last night." She put her hand to her forehead. "Or, like I *thought* I was tellin' you. Like I said, I had a lot to drink, too."

"We're going over to my sister's house for dinner and it's sort of a family thing."

"I thought you were goin' shoppin'."

"After we go shopping."

"Sure, sure, darlin'. I'll just put all this in the refrigerator. It'll keep." Barbie opened the refrigerator door and put the tomato juice, clam juice, and Tabasco sauce away. She walked into the living room and picked up her purse from the couch, then walked to the front door.

Iris followed right behind her.

"I'll give you a call later, darlin', okay?" She patted Iris's cheek.

"Okay. Thanks for the blouse and thanks for coming by."

After Barbie left, Iris turned the bolt lock and leaned against the door. "Lady, what do you want from me?"

19

"She's the yellow rose of Texas, da da da da dada. She's the ..."

Barbie set a vase of flowers on the rickety pressboard coffee table in her living room. She stood back and admired them.

"... yellow rose of Texas, da da da da dada."

She looked around the small apartment. "What a dump! That's okay, Barbeh girl. Movin' soon! Movin' up!"

She climbed the three stairs that led to the platformed bedroom area and turned left to enter the corridor that was lined with closets. On one of the shelves she found a small, white cardboard box, took off the lid, and removed a square of cotton. She dipped her finger inside and crooked Art's college ring over the first knuckle of her index finger. She held her hand out to admire it, then bent her finger up and down to test the ring's weight. She put the ring back and poked her long, hot pink fingernail around the other pieces of jewelry. There were a pair of earrings, a brooch, and several rings, both men's and women's.

She lifted her long overblouse, reached into the waist of her tight stirrup pants, which seemed fuller than usual, and pulled out a gold and enamel brooch in the shape of an iris bloom. She held it in front of her by the stem, then pressed it against the side of her chest to see how it would look. She put it in the box, carefully placed the square of cotton back on top, replaced the lid, and put the box back in its place on the closet shelf.

She lifted her long overblouse again, reached her hands inside her stirrup pants, pulled out a folded square of cobalt blue cloth, and threw it on the bed. From her pants on the other side of her belly, she pulled out another cobalt blue bundle and shook it out. It was a suit jacket. She picked up the square from the bed and shook it out. It was the jacket's matching skirt. She held the skirt's waistband against herself. It barely covered half her girth. She put the fabric against her face and inhaled deeply, picking up a residue of Iris's cologne. She walked to the closet and carefully hung the suit among her other clothes. She pulled out a hanger that held a man's burgundy pullover, put the sweater against her face, and inhaled deeply before rehanging it.

She walked out the open sliding glass door onto her terrace. The setting sun cast an orange glow on the water whose ripples broke the light into myriad slivers. Barbie listened happily to the Sunday sounds of boat engines, sails flapping in the breeze, Sunday sailors speaking nauticalese, bicycle wheels clicking, and people talking about nothing. The boats rocking in their slips implied opulence and spare time. Barbie threw her head back and took a deep breath, holding both arms out in a V.

Her stomach rumbled loudly. She grabbed it. "Stick to your diet, girl! Just mind over matter."

She went inside, got a diet soda from the refrigerator, pulled a bar stool onto the terrace, climbed up, rested her back against the wall, hooked the heels of her slingbacks on the bar stool rungs, and comfortably lost herself in her thoughts. She sang a hymn in a low voice: "How great thou art . . ."

The doorbell clanged its shallow *ding-dong*. Barbie looked at it. It clanged again. Still humming to herself, she walked across the small apartment's living room and swung open the door without looking through the peephole.

Barbie's happy smile froze.

Lorraine's tired blue eyes traveled across Barbie's face, and her lower lip worked up and down.

Barbie blinked a few times. She unfroze her smile and stretched it into a broad grin and raised her eyebrows. "Well, Rainey! I'm so surprised I could just choke a goat!" She held her arms open and Lorraine walked into them. Barbie reached one arm behind Lorraine and pushed the door closed.

Lorraine was not dressed for the warm Southern California spring day. She was wearing a long-sleeved flannel shirt and had a wool sweater tied around her waist. Her denim jeans were loose around her thin waist, where they were held with a belt. She was tall, slender, blond, and pale. She wore no makeup. Her facial bones were prominent in her thin face. Her hair hung straight and lank to her shoulders.

At Barbie's touch, the tears that were brimming in Lorraine's eyes spilled down her cheeks. "Oh, Charlotte."

Barbie recoiled slightly at the name.

"I can't believe I found you."

"You sure did, Rainey."

Lorraine leaned back to look at Barbie's smiling face. "Are you glad to see me?"

"Darlin'! Doesn't it look like I'm glad to see you?"

Lorraine hugged her. "We're together now."

"That's right." Barbie pulled Lorraine closer. She stared over her shoulder. "We're together now."

Lorraine stood on the terrace and watched the sun's last rays sparkle on the water. She breathed in the salty, fishy, green ocean smell. She was wearing a cotton T-shirt and shorts that Barbie had lent her. The belt from her jeans held Barbie's ample shorts around her waist. She sipped the champagne that Barbie had poured for her from the bottle that Iris and Art had half emptied the previous night.

Barbie walked out onto the terrace with a plate that held a sandwich and a few carrot sticks. "Here you go, honey. It's diet bread and it don't have a lot of flavor, but the turkey meat's good. You know me, always dieting."

"You look great." Lorraine took the plate and sat on the bar stool that Barbie had left on the terrace. She looked up gratefully. "Thanks. I'm starved. I only stopped once the whole way."

Barbie sipped her diet soda. "So, you just got in your car and drove the whole way from Salt Lake City? Just like that?"

"I couldn't sleep after you called me . . . this morning." Lorraine looked at Barbie with amazement. "I can't believe it was just this morning. I threw a few things in the car, got gas, and took off. It took just ten hours."

"How did you know where to come?"

Lorraine smiled mischievously. She flipped one side of her hair out of her face and hooked it behind her ear. "Well, you said it was two hours earlier here, so you had to be on the West Coast. You said you were in the king's marina. So I got out my map book, found Marina Del Rey, and said, 'This is it!'" Her broad smile lit up her pale features.

"That's a long way to come on a hunch, honey."

"You know how sometimes you just know something?" Lorraine set the plate on the terrace railing. It still held an almost complete half of the sandwich. "Then I just drove around all the apartments near the water, looking for one that was woodsy with big picture windows and balconies. I saw this one and got out of the car and started walking around and I saw you sitting out here, up on the third floor."

"I'll be damned."

"Then I rang doorbells on the third floor until I found yours."

Barbie shook her head. "Rainey, I never would have guessed you had it in you. Just goes to show you, you think you know all about someone, and there you are."

Lorraine took a sip of champagne. She giggled. "This champagne's going to my head. I'm not supposed to drink with my medication."

"Medication?"

Lorraine's amusement faded. "I guess a lot's happened since you left."

"I thought you looked a little thin. What's goin' on?"

Lorraine held her wrists up to the fading light. She turned them as if she were admiring bracelets. The slash marks had healed but the scar tissue was shiny, taut and bright red.

Barbie placed her fingertips against her face. "Good Lord!"

"After that, they put me on medication. I feel better now . . . most days, anyway."

Barbie picked up Lorraine's almost empty glass and walked into the kitchen. "Let me get you some diet soda, honey. That sandwich is too dry to wash down with dry ol' champagne."

She returned with a glass tumbler of ice and cola. Her own glass held an amber-colored liquid and ice.

"Thanks," Lorraine said. "What're you drinking?"

"A li'l bourbon and water. A welcome drink to you." She raised her glass toward Lorraine. "To your health, darlin'." She took a long drink. "But sugar, why would you do such a thing?"

Lorraine looked guardedly at the ground. She worked her face as if a response was difficult. "Well, it wasn't the first time. I tried once before. About ten years ago."

"You never told me."

Lorraine fixed Barbie with her tired eyes. "There's things you never told me either, Charlotte."

Barbie gulped the rest of her drink.

"Things were going good when we met, Charlotte. I had an apartment, a job at the insurance company, my dad bought me a car. I was dating. Things were going real good. I didn't want to drag up all that old stuff. I wanted to put it behind me."

Barbie looked at the plate. "You didn't finish your sandwich. No wonder you're thin as a cat's tail."

Lorraine's eyes brimmed with tears. "My life hasn't been too good since you left me."

A man working on his sailboat, which was docked in a slip below Barbie's balcony, looked up at the two women.

"Darlin'," Barbie picked up Lorraine's plate. "Let's go inside."

They sat on the brown plaid couch. "How's your mother?" Barbie asked.

"Fine."

"Daddy?"

"Said he'd kill you if he ever found you."

"Nice talk."

"Well, you know my dad."

"Do your folks know where you are?"

"No."

"But you'll have to call them. You know how they'll worry. But I guess you'll see them tomorrow when you drive back home to go to work. That's what you're planning, isn't it? Driving back home tomorrow?"

Lorraine shook her head. "I don't have to go back to work. I've been out on disability. Because of . . ." She glanced at her wrists.

Barbie got up from the couch, walked to the center of the room, and turned to face Lorraine. She put her hands on her hips. "What do you mean you don't have to go back?"

Lorraine scooted forward onto the edge of the couch. "Charlotte, this was the best thing I ever did. It felt so good to get in that car and just leave. Leave all my problems. Leave everyone who's hassling me. It made me feel powerful, like I was in charge. I figured that's how you must have felt when you left. I was jealous of you for that. Now I've done it, and it wasn't that hard. It really wasn't that hard!"

"But you *have* to go back. What about your parents and your apartment and car and job and all those things you were talking about? What about your kitty cat?"

"Spooky got hit by a car."

"Honey, I'm sorry."

Lorraine laced her fingers in her lap and began twiddling her thumbs. "These past few months, I've been doing a lot of thinking about how things happen, how people come and go and how things change." Lorraine rolled her thumbs rapidly around and around and stared ahead as she talked. "And sometimes things change too much and you can't ever go back to your old life. You shouldn't even try."

Lorraine stopped rolling her thumbs and began tapping the top of one thumb with the other, over and over. "These past few months I've been waiting for . . . *something*. A sign to guide me, to tell me what the next step was. Then you called and it was clear. You called and I knew."

Barbie suddenly ran toward the couch, shoved the wobbly coffee table out of the way, causing the vase of flowers to rock back and forth, and threw herself onto her knees. She pressed her hands over Lorraine's hands, stopping her fidgeting, and looked into her eyes. "You know why I left you, sugar? You know the real reason I left? Because I'm not good enough for you. You deserve someone better than this beat-up old broad." She laid her head in Lorraine's lap.

"I came home from work and you were gone. That was cold, Charlotte."

"I . . . I wanted to forget the past. I even changed my name when I came out here. I couldn't stand being Charlotte Caldwell anymore." Barbie lifted her head and looked into Lorraine's eyes. "I wanted to freeze our life together in time. Leave it just the way it was. Charlotte belonged to you. Charlotte will always be yours."

Lorraine slowly pulled her hand from underneath Barbie's and moved it toward her head. She picked up a strand of Barbie's black hair and drew it between her fingers.

Barbie closed her eyes. "I always loved it when you did that."

Lorraine picked up another strand of hair and pulled it out slowly.

Barbie let out a small sound of pleasure.

Lorraine picked up another strand of hair, wrapped it around her index finger, and pulled.

"Owwch!" Barbie scampered away from Lorraine on her hands and knees and put her hand to her head.

Lorraine displayed her index finger with the lock of hair wrapped around it. She smiled malevolently. "Your leaving so fast couldn't possibly have anything to do with that man who came looking for you, could it?"

"What man?"

Lorraine tapped the finger with Barbie's hair around it against her cheek. "Let me think." She looked at the ceiling. "Just what was his name? Goins, that's right. Jack Goins. He called you by a different name, but he definitely described you. Said he'd come to get the money that you promised to pay him when he'd stopped by the day before. He'd come all the way out from Atlanta. You told me the knock on the door was someone selling encyclopedias."

Barbie rubbed the sore spot on her head. "He was a bad man, honey. I only left to protect you, to keep him from you."

Lorraine flicked the hair off her finger. "What kind of fool do you think I am?" She asked the question without emotion, as if she were asking the time. "No, I know what kind. A big fool." She spoke in a quiet, staccato monotone.

"I had my apartment, my car, my job, my cat and had just met a wonderful woman and I don't know why I gave her up for you. I don't know why I took something that was real between me and her and gave it up for"—she stretched her hands toward Barbie—"something that didn't exist. A dream. You came into my life and filled up all the spaces. You were over all the time, calling me all the time, doing things for me, buying me gifts. I didn't have time to think. I got to where I couldn't imagine life without you. The shrink told me it's like brainwashing. I thought it was the way true love was."

Barbie crawled over to Lorraine. "But honey, it *was* love."

Lorraine grabbed a gold charm on a chain around her neck and began pulling it back and forth. "I still believed you even when you stole from me. I wrote bad checks for you because you said you'd wired the money to my account. When I'd call the bank, they'd say the money was there but when the check hit, it wouldn't be. So the bank would use my overdraft protection and take it from my savings account." The charm made a whizzing noise against the chain. "When I wouldn't write checks for you, you forged them. Then you stole my bank statements so I wouldn't find out. The same thing with my credit cards. By the time you were done, my entire savings were gone. Thirty thousand dollars. Then you charged another five thousand on my credit cards."

Barbie stood up and rubbed her knees. She faced Lorraine with her legs apart and her hands on her hips. "Well, Lorraine. You got it right. That's exactly what I did."

"I'm not done. You stole the diamond and sapphire ring my grandmother left me, didn't you?"

Barbie held her hands up. "You've caught me red-handed. But I tell you what, I'll give you back the ring and I'll pay you back double for everything I took. In cash."

Lorraine breathed out in disgust. "You think I want money?"

"Why else are you here?"

Lorraine looked dully at Barbie. "My life in Salt Lake

City is ruined. You revealed my . . . sexuality . . . to my family. I never wanted that."

"You'd rather keep the real you hidden?"

"It was better than having my family disown me. Better than having my father tell me that I'm no longer welcome in the house where I grew up." She abruptly stood. "I sacrificed everything for you!" she shouted. "Everything! And then you left me! Alone! With nothing! You didn't just steal my money, you stole my family, my dignity, my self-respect"—she swung her arm out and sent the vase of flowers tumbling over, spilling water and petals on the table and floor—"my sanity! You can't write a check big enough to cover that."

"Well, what in God's name do you want from me?" Barbie whispered.

"What I want, Charlotte, or whoever the hell you are, is the dream. I want the dream. I want what I gave up my old life for. What you promised me. You *owe* me that. You owe me *you.*"

"You're nuts."

"Yeah. And you know what?" Lorraine walked slowly toward Barbie, who stepped backward. "I don't care. I'm tired of trying to live how other people tell me to live, of being poked at and prodded and having people dig through my head and my dreams, telling me, 'Don't do that, do this, don't say that, say this,' and trying to make me into something I'm not. If I'm crazy, I'm gonna stay crazy. Sanity is too much work."

Barbie caught herself walking backward and stood her ground. Lorraine walked close to her. She reached her hand up and put it on Barbie's hair and stroked it. Barbie recoiled.

"You know why they think I'm crazy? Because in spite of everything, I still love you. Now, *that's* crazy."

Barbie circled her hand around Lorraine's head and pulled it down to meet hers. They kissed. Barbie broke the kiss first.

"You're right, sugar," Barbie breathed. "We were meant to be together. We'll be together now. It'll be just like it was."

"I'm the only one in your life, aren't I?"

"You're the only one."

"I was afraid you'd found someone else. You know what I thought?"

"What, sugar?"

"That you'd come to L.A. to be with that woman we saw on television the day before you left. I even got a videotape of that show so I could hear your voice from when you called in, so I could have something of you. You never let me take your picture. The tape was the only thing I had. I couldn't bear it if you'd found someone else. I just couldn't bear it."

Barbie took Lorraine's face in her hands. "Barbeh's here now. Don't you worry about a thing."

20

IT WAS MONDAY MORNING. IRIS WAS LATE. SHE SHOWERED and decorated herself, splashed a second cup of coffee into her commuter mug, scooped makeup into her purse, grabbed her briefcase and pull-out stereo, speed-walked down the corridor, forwent the elevator, and skipped down the stairs instead. She walked through the lobby and into the garage of her building, where the Triumph waited silently under its shroud. She set the commuter mug on the ground, rolled off the TR's canvas cover, stashed it in the trunk, got in the car, pulled out the choke, stepped on the accelerator twice, and turned the key in the ignition. The engine turned over and the Triumph's baritone, heightened with the choke out, reverberated through the garage.

She reached into her purse and threw assorted tubular, square, and cylindrical makeup containers onto the passenger seat, got a flashlight from the glove compartment, turned it on, and held it up between her knees. She twisted the rearview mirror to face her and applied her makeup, working around the flashlight's eerie lighting.

She threw the car into reverse, backed out, put it in first, rolled down the window, and shone the flashlight beam on the drip pan. It was splattered with more black and amber globs than the day before but nothing outside the normal range.

She waited for the garage security gate to slowly slide open. She rolled the car out and was startled by a bundle in the bushes on her left that writhed underneath a blanket. Then she remembered that the street man was still in residence.

Freeway traffic on Mondays is light, and Iris's drive downtown was uneventful. She opened the heavy glass doors of the McKinney Alitzer suite and quickly walked down the corridor that led to the Sales Department. She shot a glance at Dexter's office. His door was closed and his lights were off. She breathed a sigh of relief and sped to her own office.

Art was already at his desk. When he spotted Iris, he stuck his palm into the corridor, perpendicular to the floor. She slapped it as she walked by. Amber was already on the phone. Sean Bliss didn't look at Iris's face but focused on her chest. Iris unconsciously touched the buttons on her blouse to make sure they were fastened. The last cubicle was where Billy Drye lived. He pointedly ignored her and she offered the same sentiment back.

She unlocked her door, put her things away, turned on her computer, pulled files from her briefcase, opened one on top of her desk, and moved some of its papers around, then threw a yellow pad and pencil on top of that. She rolled her chair out at a careless angle to the desk. She surveyed her work, decided it provided an appropriately busy aura, grabbed her BUDGETS ARE FOR WIMPS mug, walked back down the corridor and into the lunchroom. She opened the refrigerator door. There was no leftover cake. It held only neat lunches. She rolled open one of the crisp paper bags and had a look at a different lifestyle. She refolded the bag and surveyed the snack machine. She dug a thumb into her skirt waistband, which was tighter than it had been the previous week.

"Hell."

With tremendous resolve for a Monday morning, she turned away from the snack machine and walked to the coffeemaker and poured a cup with her back to the door. She heard the lunchroom door open and close and heavy footsteps approaching her. The footsteps were a clue, but the cologne cinched it. She finished pouring her coffee.

"Happy Monday, Drye."

He stood beside her, impolitely close. She faced him. Not being on top of her game so early in the morning, she took a step backward. He merely made up the distance with a step forward.

"You mean you plan on speaking to me?" Iris said. "I thought you were punishing Amber and me with your silence. Don't stop on my account."

When Billy Drye smiled, his pointed ears, diamond-shaped face, upward-angled eyes, and arched eyebrows created an effect that was puckish and endearing. When he scowled, the effect was demonic. He was scowling now.

"Garland Hughes is flying out from New York to meet with you and Amber today over at the Edward Club."

It was too early to face both Drye and his sour breath, so she took a sip of coffee and casually walked over to a table where the daily newspaper had been placed. "I'm glad to see you're still plugged into the information pipeline."

"I'm impressed that the firm's second-in-command is coming out for you two broads."

"Not just for us, Drye. For you, too."

"I happen to be very tight with Hughes. If you think he's gonna sell me out, you're in for a surprise."

"Tight with Hughes?" She casually turned a page of the paper. "What? You shook his hand at a sales meeting?"

"I'm not losing my job because of you two bitches. I'm not going down without a fight."

She looked up at him and smiled. "Good! Wouldn't be as much fun if you just lay down and rolled over."

"Just go ahead, Ice Princess. Just keep talking." He left the lunchroom.

"That's what they pay me for," Iris said to the closing door.

She went back to her office. At her desk, she logged onto the word processing program and started to write a client proposal. She rewrote the first two sentences four times. She gave up and spun her chair around to look at the cityscape from her western-facing window. Dark clouds were in motion across the sky. A storm was predicted for later in the week, just in time for Easter. She looked out the window to her right at the other worker bees in the office tower across the street. She spotted someone in one of the offices gazing out the window at the Monday morning, just like her.

She left her office, walked to the storeroom, and pulled open the double doors of a tall cabinet. Thick telephone books were stacked inside, spines facing out. Several different filing methods appeared to be in effect: geographic, alphabetic, and random. She walked her fingers across the book spines, then started over and tried again. She finally located the book for Atlanta and took it back to her office.

The book was over a year old. Hal's restaurant had a quarter-page ad featuring a drawing of a columned mansion with a wide porch. The copy read:

> Hal's offers you French cuisine in a classic Old South setting. Your host, Hal Stringfellow, invites you to join him in his restored plantation house in an experience of dining elegance.

Iris tore the page from the book and dialed the phone number listed with the ad.

A woman answered. "Minnie's Porch."

"This isn't Hal's?"

"No, we're Minnie's Porch now. But if you enjoyed Hal's, we're sure you'll enjoy us."

"What happened to Hal's?"

"Mr. Stringfellow died about a year ago and the restaurant was sold."

"Did you know him?"

"No, but the owner might have. Name's Jack Goins. He's not here right now."

"How about Mrs. Stringfellow? Did you know her?"

"I didn't know about a Mrs. Stringfellow."

Iris said she'd call back later. She returned the phone book to the cabinet.

"Closed for a year." Iris muttered to herself. "That checks."

She resumed work on her proposal and worked for fifteen minutes before she caught herself staring out the window again. She opened her personal phone book, found a number, and made a call.

"Research Library."

"Tom Butler, please."

"Who's calling?"

"This is Iris Thorne. I'm an old college friend." Polite classical music played on the phone while she was on hold.

"Iris! It's been too long! To what do I owe the pleasure?"

"Hi, Tom. I'm sorry to say I'm not calling just to chat. I need a favor."

"I didn't expect anything else," he said playfully.

"You've known me too long, Tom. There's lunch in it for you."

"Sounds like a deal."

"Does the library carry newspapers from Atlanta, Georgia?"

"Sure. The ones that aren't current are on microfilm. We go back a couple of years."

"I'm looking for an obituary that ran about a year ago. A man named Harold or Hal Stringfellow."

"I'll put someone right on it."

Iris gave Tom the number to the office fax machine and made lunch plans with him for the following week. She looked at her watch. It was ten o'clock and she had done virtually no McKinney Alitzer work the entire morning. She focused on the client proposal and forced herself to finish it. As she was struggling with a snappy closure, a secretary came in and handed her a fax.

The obituary read:

Harold Stringfellow, seventy-one years, lifelong Atlantan. Proprietor of the well-known restaurant, Hal's, which he opened twenty-five years ago. Avid golfer and bowler. Revered boss, beloved brother and uncle. Survived by his sister, Margaret Conners of Nashville, niece Lucy Fields of Fort Worth, Texas, nephew Allan Conners of Springfield, Missouri, and grandnephews Tyler and Colin. In lieu of flowers, please make a donation to a favorite charity.

Iris picked up her telephone and punched in three numbers.

"I see you survived," Art said. "You were fun-ny on Saturday."

"You weren't exactly the picture of moderation yourself."

"I was totally hungover at my golf lesson on Sunday."

"Golf?"

"Lots of business conducted on the golf course, Iris. You should get with the program."

"Right. Hey, can I talk to you for a few minutes?"

"Sure, I'll be right down."

"No, in the stairwell."

"One of those. Oh-kay."

Iris folded the fax in half, grabbed the ad for Hal's, slipped them both between the pages of a yellow pad, and picked up a pencil. With sufficient props to look busy and purposeful, she walked briskly out of her office, down the hallway, and into the stairwell.

The stairwell's raw concrete and plain white walls were a stark contrast to the plush carpeting, wall coverings, and artwork in the suite. A woman stood on the landing, smoking. The raw concrete floor was covered with cigarette butts, ground-in ashes, and Styrofoam cups coated with brown coffee stains. The woman gave Iris a rebel-with-a-cause look. The building's nonsmoking policy had forced smokers either to the stairwells, lobby, or outside the building where they huddled together, having only their shared habit in common.

Iris walked through the smoke cloud and down a flight of stairs to the floor below.

Art waited a couple of minutes, then followed her. When he didn't see her inside the stairwell door, he walked down to the next landing. He pointed at her and snickered. "You said it, the bigger they are . . ."

"How long before I live this down?"

"Never."

"Did you spend the night at Barbie's?"

"Sort of. I passed out in the Mustang. She couldn't wake me up."

"You slept there all night?"

"I woke up a couple of hours later and drove home. So, to what do I owe the pleasure of this meeting?"

She pulled the fax from the yellow pad.

Art read it and handed it back to her. "Good old Hal."

"You don't find anything unusual about it?"

"No, what?"

"Where's the widow? And Barbie said he had grown kids."

Art shrugged. "It's the newspaper. They make mistakes. What's your point?"

Iris stepped closer to Art and lowered her voice. "I think you should seriously check out Barbie before you go into business with her. I don't think she's everything she says she is."

"Iris, I know you don't want to lose Barbie as a client, but don't you think this is a little desperate?"

"Art, I've had some weird things happen with Barbie lately, and I don't want you to get burned."

"What kinds of things?"

"I caught her in a lie about something she and I talked about on Saturday night after you went to the store."

"A lie about what?"

"She was trying to pry information out of me when I was out of it."

"What kind of information?"

"I can't tell you. But she definitely lied."

Art folded his arms across his chest and raised one side of his upper lip, revealing his even, white teeth.

"And then on Sunday she stopped by, spur of the moment, and I caught her going through my desk drawers."

"Did she have a reason?"

"Said she was looking for a pair of scissors to cut the tags off a blouse she'd bought me." Iris raised her hand as if it held scissors. "But she already had scissors in her hand!"

Art leaned against the wall. "Nice of her to buy you a

blouse. Of course she wanted to take the tags off. What's the problem?"

"It was a smoke screen to give her an excuse to go into my bedroom. You know what else she did? She made my bed."

"That made you mad? I wish someone would make my bed."

"I had a feeling she'd gone through all my stuff." Iris took a few frustrated steps away from Art. She turned and walked back to him. "Listen to this. I caught her with my keys in her hands. She said they were on the floor, but they weren't. She took them out of my purse."

"Iris, you were so out of it on Saturday, how do you know you didn't drop them on the floor?"

"Because I picked them up Sunday morning and put them in my purse."

"I was still drunk when I got up. How do you know what you did Sunday morning?" He slapped his hand against his thigh. "You're spinnin' out, girl. Just chill, okay?"

"How about this?" She balled her fist and pointed her thumb over her shoulder as if Atlanta were next door. "Hal's restaurant." She pulled the ad from between the pages of the yellow pad. "Look. The ad doesn't mention Hal and his wife, it just mentions *Hal.*"

"So Hal got married and never redid the ad. So what?" He put his foot on a step to start walking up, then turned to face Iris. "Are you jealous of Barbie and me because John dumped you?"

"Oh, Art. I just want you to check this woman out before you . . . hop into bed with her, so to speak. It's sound business practice. You don't know anything about her."

"Bullshit. She and I have done a lot of talking."

"Yeah, pillow talk? Speaking of which, you know what else happened on Saturday? She kissed me. On the mouth."

Art threw his hands up. "Now I know you've lost it. I don't know how you remember anything from Saturday. You didn't know your ass from your elbow." He started walking up the stairs.

"Fine. I'm done. I'm through. But I suggest you call some of Hal's relatives listed in that obituary."

Art turned back. "Did Barbie tell you we're meeting my uncle tonight? Is that why you're all over me?"

"I thought you were waiting until your uncle got back from Mexico."

Art leaned his hand against the wall. "We had to push it up. Barbie's got some people in Phoenix, some potential investors, that she wants to talk to before they leave the country for a couple of months. She wants to iron out specifics with me and my uncle first."

"Is she going to ask you for money?"

He raised his lip again. "We're just laying out some plans so she has something to talk to these people about. There's no money involved." He took his hand from the wall and twisted the skin where his ring used to be.

"Where's your ring?" Iris asked.

"I must have lost it when we were playing football."

"That's weird. Why would it just come off like that?"

"Maybe *Barbie* stole it from me." He laughed sarcastically and continued walking up the stairs. The smoker had already gone inside. Iris remained standing on the landing.

Art opened the door of the suite and looked down at Iris. "You think I don't know what I'm doing. Hey, that's okay. Soon people are going to be standing in line to kiss my ass. You'll see." He went inside.

"I hope so, Arturo."

She walked up the stairs and back to her office. Her phone rang. The LED display said: A. AMBROSE CALLING.

"Hi," Amber said. "Ready to go to the power lunch?"

"Yeah. Just give me five minutes."

Iris slid the ad for Hal's in front of her and punched in the number for Minnie's Porch. "Jane . . ." Iris looked around her desk. "Pad, paddle . . . book, booker. Jane Booker."

"Jack Goins, please." In the background there was the tinkling sound of silverware and china in use and a low hum of voices peppered with laughter.

"Hello, Mr. Goins. I'm Jane Booker from Better Mortgages out here on the West Coast. I'm assisting my client, Barbie Stringfellow, in obtaining financing for a residence she'd like to purchase. Do you know Mrs. Stringfellow?"

His voice was robust. "Of course I know Barbie. She used to own this place with her husband, Hal. Then old Hal passed on and Barbie sold it."

"I see. How long did Barbie own the restaurant?"

"Oh, I don't know exactly. Happy to find that out for you."

"I'm just doing a preliminary report. Can I call you if I need more information?"

"Be my pleasure."

Iris ended the call. "Maybe I am spinning out." She put the fax and the ad in her desk drawer. "Or maybe Barbie's smoother than I thought."

She got her purse and started to leave to meet Amber. She turned back, took the fax and the ad from her desk drawer, folded them in half, and dropped them on Art's desk on her way out.

"It's your baby," she told him.

He looked up at her and smiled as he balled up the papers and threw them in his trash can.

"Good afternoon!" Barbie sang into the phone.

"It's Jack Goins."

"Hello, Jack," Barbie said icily. "Don't tell me you're running short again."

"Lucky for you, your last payment arrived on time. I just hung up with someone checking on Barbie Stringfellow. You remember Barbie, Hal's widow?"

"Man or woman?"

"Woman. Said she was Jane Booker with Better Mortgages. You must be doing pretty well if you're buying a house out in L.A."

"That woman was lyin'."

"It takes one to know one."

"How do you keep findin' out where I am?"

"You've never learned the fine art of discretion. Any private investigator worth his salt could find you. You should be more careful. Whoever else you did dirty to may not be happy with just being repaid, like me. Remember, a cat's only got nine lives."

"I've been meaning to talk to you about that, Jack. I figure we're square now. I've paid you more than the fifty thousand I borrowed from you."

"Borrowed? Is that what you call it?"

"Of course it was borrowed. I paid you back."

"You paid me back, all right, only after I almost wrung your neck. Sorry, my dear, but you still owe me plenty for pain and suffering, especially if you want me to cover your lies for you."

"I no longer have any use for your services. Our business relationship is over."

"Remember, dear, you can run but you can't hide."

"Good-bye, Jack. And best of luck to you."

21

IRIS AND AMBER WALKED INTO THE LOBBY OF THE EDWARD Club, whose unceremonious entrance was located off the garage, where members once arrived by horse-drawn carriage.

Amber said, "I'm impressed they sent Garland Hughes out. Have you ever met him?"

"No."

"Think he's in the Dexter mold?"

"Probably. I think all the wheels in the New York office are cloned."

"I heard he just got divorced."

"Great. That can only improve his objectivity toward us."

The Edward Club's high-ceilinged lobby was crisscrossed with carved wood beams, each squared-off section decorated with red, green, and gold fleurs-de-lis on a midnight blue background. The gray-veined, white marble floor was strewn with floral-patterned oriental rugs. A tremendous ceramic vase with a tall and wide arrangement of flowers, ferns, and twigs stood on a round table in the middle of the lobby.

Iris and Amber were spotted by a dark-suited Hispanic man as soon as they entered the lobby.

Amber spoke under her breath to Iris. "Didn't they used

to have a policy about no women, Jews, blacks, no ... you know ... as members?"

"They claim it wasn't a formal policy. It's just that no one who wasn't white-bread male with the appropriate background was ever nominated for membership. The outside world has encroached on the membership a bit."

The Hispanic man walked energetically toward them. "I presume you're Herbert Dexter's guests for lunch? Please follow me."

They entered an old wood-paneled elevator with brass fixtures that slowly cranked to the second floor. The elevator doors opened onto a corridor illuminated by a brass chandelier with electric candles that had replaced gas jets after it appeared that electricity was going to be more than a passing fad. To the left was a room furnished with brown leather chairs and deep couches, each with its own table and green-shaded lamp. To the right was a room with a long, cherrywood bar against one wall. Behind the bar was a beveled-glass mirror with a carved cherrywood frame. Small cocktail tables and tapestry-upholstered sofas and chairs were arranged around the room. A bartender wearing a dark suit was polishing the bar's gleaming surface.

Straight ahead were tall double doors opening onto a large, high-ceilinged room with floor-to-ceiling windows dressed with burgundy velour drapes pulled back with gold-tasseled stays. The floor was of intricately patterned inset wood. Round tables appointed with crisp white linen and complete silver, china, and crystal place settings were positioned at discreet distances from one another. The diners, mostly men, spoke in subdued tones, which lent an aura of conspiracy to the conversations, as if takeovers of corporations or small Third World countries were being planned.

Their guide walked ahead of them into the room. Iris angled a comment to Amber. "They're probably into their second martinis. Heard these guys from New York like to drink their lunch."

"What do you think we're going to get from this?" Amber asked.

"Probably lunch."

"You're not serious."

Herbert Dexter was sitting at a table by a window and stood when he spotted them. The other man at the table also stood.

Dexter made the introductions. "Garland Hughes, this is Amber Ambrose and Iris Thorne."

Hughes was of medium height and build, but he looked short standing next to the tall and lanky Dexter. He was fiftyish, trim and energetic. He had a pleasant face that was rubbery and animated. His eyes were round and blue and took in everything. He extended his hand to shake the two women's. He had a confident, firm, dry grip.

They sat and a waiter took their drink order. Both women ordered iced tea, which was what Dexter had in front of him. A tall green bottle of mineral water and a glass with ice sat in front of Hughes.

Iris glanced at a basket of rolls and flatbread on the table. The look didn't go past Garland Hughes, who lifted the basket toward her. She took a whole-grain roll and met his eyes. He held the contact for just a beat longer than necessary, a beat that was practically undetectable, so small that Iris thought that maybe she had imagined it, but she blushed slightly anyway as she quickly thanked him and placed the roll on her bread plate.

Hughes offered the basket to Amber, then casually sat back in his chair and crossed his legs. "I hate to ruin a nice lunch talking about business, so let's get our discussion topic out of the way before we enjoy the Edward Club's fine cuisine."

Herbert Dexter leaned back in his chair, crossed his legs as well, dropped one hand on his lap and the other on the table. Amber didn't make an attempt to disguise her edginess but sat erect in her chair, her ankles crossed, her back washboard straight, her fingers laced tightly in her lap. Iris adopted Dexter's casual pose, but one leg underneath the table was in furious motion.

Hughes continued, "I want you both to know that I don't consider your allegations regarding our colleague, Bill Drye, to be spurious. I wouldn't have given it my personal attention otherwise." He opened his blue eyes wide, looked from

Amber to Iris, and allowed the import of his message to sink in.

"Amber and I appreciate the time you've invested," Iris said.

"And I appreciate the professional manner in which both of you have approached this issue. Your documentation is very thorough. You've presented it through the proper channels and have maintained confidentiality. Your well-being is, of course, our primary consideration. However, the firm's image is a close second, and I'm pleased to see this demonstration of not only your personal integrity but also your loyalty toward the firm." He paused and again looked from Amber to Iris. Herb Dexter nodded his concurrence.

Amber guilelessly asked the question on both her and Iris's mind. "Are you going to fire him?"

Garland Hughes pursed his lips thoughtfully and leaned forward onto the table. A few seconds passed before he looked up at Amber. "Over the next few days, Herb and I are going to discuss the best resolution. We hope to come to a decision by next week. Primary among our goals is to reduce the level of trauma to *all* parties concerned. After a decision is made, you and Iris will be the first to know."

He clapped his hands together as if he were breaking a spell. "Enough talk." He picked up the menu that was lying across his plate. Everyone else followed his lead. The menu was tall, in proportion to the room. "Now the last time I was here, I had the most marvelous John Dory."

They ordered. Iris selected a fish fillet, avoiding the linguine special, the Cornish game hens, and anything else that was difficult to maneuver. They talked about current events, movies, books, and business, everyone holding a view but not pressing it too strongly. Iris noticed Garland Hughes casting an occasional glance in her direction, which made her wonder whether, in spite of her best efforts, she was wolfing her food.

After coffee and dessert, which Iris was going to skip but indulged in anyway, Iris and Amber thanked the two men and stood to leave. Dexter and Hughes stood too and everyone shook hands. Hughes again held eye contact with Iris for what seemed to be a beat too long, but it was so subtle that she decided she was reading too much into it. She seemed to be doing a lot of that lately.

When the elevator doors closed and Iris and Amber were alone, Amber said, "That's it?"

Iris shrugged. "It was lunch."

"Aren't they going to fire Drye?"

"I don't know."

"But they *have* to."

"They don't have to."

"What if they don't do anything? Do we handle it outside the firm? File charges?"

"That's always an option. But we'd have to seriously consider how much our careers are worth to us."

"Think so?"

"Are you kidding?"

Amber was silent.

"What did you think of Garland Hughes?" Iris asked.

"He's not at all what I expected."

"Me neither."

They walked out of the Edward Club, whose plain facade belied the opulence within, and back into the real world.

"You mind walking back by yourself?" Iris asked. "I have an errand to run."

The Great California Bank was a few blocks away. Iris walked slowly, feeling weighed down by the rich lunch. The bank was in a stately older building. A street man roamed the granite steps that led to the bank's large doors, his dirty slacks slung obscenely low on his hips. He shook a paper cup at Iris, rattling the few coins at the bottom. Iris found some change in her jacket pocket and dropped it into his cup. He blessed her.

It was well past the lunch hour and there were few customers in the bank. Iris walked past the teller windows and went to a side counter where nonmoney bank business was transacted.

Howard spotted Iris as soon as she came in. He was waiting on a customer at the teller window when he looked up and saw her, shooting past her eyes to a point over her shoulder. He made a gesture with his hand to indicate he'd be with her soon.

157

Iris smiled and said "Great" through clenched teeth.

Howard had boyishly disheveled, sandy brown hair, pale blue eyes, and a receding chin that dropped straight from his mouth to his neck, where the field of skin was peppered with old acne scars. His soft, round waistline and pale coloring suggested nights in front of the television with many snacks.

Iris leaned her back against the counter as she waited and looked out the large glass doors at the clouds moving across the sky. She glanced over her shoulder and caught Howard staring at her in that way that made her feel as if he wanted to crawl inside her skin, consume her, put her in a box to be his forever. Quiet, polite Howard gave Iris the willies. She halfheartedly pasted a pleasant expression onto her face.

Howard finished with his customer, sat a wooden NEXT WINDOW PLEASE sign in his window, and walked over to her.

She was still leaning against the counter with her back to him, daydreaming. She felt something warm and moist on her hand. Instinctively, she snapped it back. Howard had touched her.

"Hi, Iris." He said her name as if it were delicious.

"Hi, Howard," Iris said brightly. She tilted her head in the direction of the street. "Looks like we're going to get more rain."

"Yes." He was staring at a point to the left of her ear.

"They say the drought's finally over. We'll be able to flush the toilet whenever we want."

He nodded and watched her.

Iris cleared her throat. "I'd like to get into my safe deposit box."

"Certainly." He buzzed her into a high-walled cubicle to her right and entered his side from a door behind the counter.

Iris unzipped her purse, dug her hand inside its bowels, and finally located her key ring with the brass fob. She sorted through the keys.

"You sure have a lot of keys."

"I shouldn't carry them all. I think it gives me a false sense of security to know I can unlock so many doors." She chuckled.

Howard smiled after a delay, not getting it.

She found the small key embossed with the number 106, separated it from the pack, and handed the key ring to Howard.

He took it and returned with a long, steel box, which he sat heavily on the counter.

"Thank you."

He gave her a final glance from underneath his eyebrows and turned to leave.

"Hey, Howard?"

He turned back with a hopeful look in his eyes.

"How hard would it be for someone other than me to get into this box?"

"Impossible. If we didn't know them, we'd verify their signature with the other signatories on the box."

"What if they had the key?"

"Doesn't matter," he said indignantly. "There are important bank procedures that have to be followed."

"Just checking. Thanks."

He turned and left her alone.

She looked at the steel box. Its appearance was unremarkable in relation to the large space it had held in her mind during the past year. She flipped open the lid.

At least I was neat, she said to herself.

The four hundred thousand, six hundred and eighty dollars were organized by denomination and bound with rubber bands. The neatness made sense. Whenever her life was in shambles, Iris organized the inanimate things around her, the things she could control. She took out a bundle and rifled it with her thumb. The bills were old, wrinkled, and dirty. She unzipped her purse, and shoved in a bundle, then took out two more bundles and shoved them in.

Burn this crap.

She stopped, holding a bundle in midair, and shook her head angrily. She took the bundles from her purse and jammed them back into the box.

Being paranoid. It's locked up. She can't get it.

She looked down at the money. "Oh, hell!" she said out loud. She crammed a few bundles back into her purse.

Get the rest later. I don't want it, but she's not getting it either.

She stopped and grabbed her hair with both hands. "Chill out!" she exclaimed quietly.

She took all the bundles from her purse, put them back in the box, and closed the hinged lid.

She doesn't know where I bank. Even if she did, she can't get in. I am going nuts.

She peeked her head over the cubicle wall. Howard was counting out cash at a teller window, laying it on the counter in the shape of a fan. The customer was a twentyish woman in a conservative dress who'd probably come down from one of the tower office buildings. Howard finished counting out her cash, looked up through his eyebrows, and smiled too crookedly and too long at her shoulder. The woman returned a tense smile, clutched her purse to her body, and left quickly.

Howard brushed perspiration from his upper lip and noticed Iris.

She waved him over.

Procedures, huh? Like to see Barbie try a procedure on you.

Howard entered his side of the cubicle, and she pushed the safe deposit box across the counter toward him.

"Finished!" she said brightly.

22

IRIS FINALLY ARRIVED HOME. SHE TOOK OFF HER CLOTHES, peeled off her pantyhose and started a new pile on the closet floor, put on her bathrobe, scrubbed off her makeup, and brushed the mousse and hairspray out of her hair before she could face the messages on the phone machine. There were two.

"What happened at the meeting, Iris?" Billy Drye said with a sneer in his voice. "I know what happened. A big nothing. Zero! *Nada!* So, one for me and zip for you." He hung up.

"Asshole!" Iris shouted at the machine as she unlocked the terrace door. She walked outside. The street man's bundles were neatly organized, but he was not around. She went back inside.

"Hi, darlin'!" Barbie's voice rang through the condo.

"Oh, great. Miss Congeniality. I guess you're still my big client."

"I want ya to come on out with me and Arturo tonight."

"What?" Iris whined at the disembodied voice.

"I don't know if he told you, but we're going down to the Club Estra-yell-do to meet with his Uncle George . . ."

"Sorry, I'm in for the night." She grabbed a handful of crackers.

". . . and I got an old friend of mine in town and I'd like you to meet her."

Iris stood in the middle of the living room floor, facing the phone machine and eating a cracker. "You have old friends?" she asked the machine.

"She just came into town on a whim yesterday."

"I'd like to meet one of your old friends."

"Her and me were waitresses at Hal's. I'm pleased as all get-out to see her and I'd like to show her a good time."

"Yeah. Sure. Let's show her a good time."

The message ended and the tape rewound. Iris dialed Barbie's number.

"Hi, Barbie! Sounds great. When are you coming by? Why? But I'm right on the way. Okay, okay. I'll drive over. See you in a bit."

Barbie's doorbell discharged a thin *ding* when Iris pressed it and a thin *dong* when she released it. She'd dressed in black jeans, black cowboy boots, and the purple silk blouse that Barbie had given her on Sunday, the day before. It fit perfectly. Iris heard voices on the other side of the door.

She couldn't make out the words, but the tone sounded angry. She was moving her head closer to hear better when Barbie swung the door open.

"Well, hi, sugar!" Barbie threw her arms around Iris and gave her a big hug. Iris hugged her back, immune to any warmth from Barbie and appreciating the extent of her girth instead.

Barbie was dressed in a full floral print skirt whose hem extended past her knees, a purple linen unstructured jacket, and a soft blouse in petal pink that didn't reveal a hint of cleavage. Her shoes were simple navy blue pumps without a bow, buckle, or faux jewel.

"You're dressed conservatively," Iris remarked.

"This is my business look, honey. This is a side of me you don't know."

"The multifaceted Barbie." Iris glanced behind Barbie and saw a woman standing next to the couch with her arms folded across her chest, one foot in front of the other and one hip jutting out rakishly. She was as tall as Iris and as slender. She eyed Iris haughtily.

"Ain't it the truth?" Barbie put her hand on Iris's back and guided her into the small apartment. "I'd like to introduce you to my good friend, Lorraine. Honey, this is Iris Thorne, the gal who's been managing my money for me."

Lorraine unfolded her arms and limply extended her hand palm down to Iris. Iris had extended her hand perpendicular to the floor and was caught off guard by Lorraine's gesture. Lorraine impatiently dropped her eyelids. Iris finally clasped the tips of Lorraine's fingers, feeling like one of Scarlett O'Hara's beaus coming to call.

"Pleased to meet you," Iris said.

Lorraine wore a tight black, leather miniskirt, a black mock turtleneck sweater, black stockings, and strappy high-heeled sandals. Her hair had been cut short and painted with highlights, her face dramatically made up and her nails done in long, candy-apple-red enamel. Her lipstick was the same color as her nail polish.

"I feel like I already know you." Lorraine refolded her hands across her chest.

"Really? Why?" Iris asked.

162

"From the Susie Santé show."

"I'm surprised at the number of people who saw that show."

"You'd be surprised to know the effect you had on some people."

"Really? How?"

Barbie rushed between the two women, fluttering her hands. "I've just been telling Lorraine how we met and all and how much you've helped me since I've been in town, you know, and how close we are now."

"Just exactly how close?" Lorraine asked.

"Close enough to share secrets," Iris said.

"Rainey, Iris and I are just good gal friends." She put her hand on Lorraine's arm. "I told y'all about that."

Iris noticed Barbie's hand. "You get a new ring?"

Barbie centered the diamond and sapphire ring that was snug on the little finger of her left hand. "Yes! I . . . uh . . ."

Lorraine took Barbie's hand in hers and rotated the ring back and forth so that the stones reflected the light. "I gave it to her."

"It's beautiful," Iris said. "Is it an antique?"

"It is." Lorraine released Barbie's hand. "It's a family heirloom. Barbie tried to give it back to me. But I made her keep it. She'd always admired it."

"So!" Barbie clapped her hands. "Can I get y'all a soda or a glass of wine while we wait for Art?"

"Nothing stronger than diet soda is going to cross my lips for a while," Iris said.

"Okay," Barbie said. "And a diet soda for you, too, Lorraine."

Lorraine sat on the couch and crossed her long legs. She picked at the porcelain nails, scraping at one hand with the thumb of the other, then reversing hands. "I'll have a glass of wine, myself."

"Lorraine, I think you'd be better off with a soda." Barbie noticed Iris's quizzical look. "Lorraine has a . . . she's allergic to alcohol."

"But I've been feeling so much better. One li'l ol' glass of wine's not gonna hurt nothin'." Lorraine mocked Barbie's accent.

Barbie gave her a long look. "Careful you don't ruin your fresh manicure, darlin'." She went into the kitchen.

Iris sat on the bulky chair that was upholstered in the same drab, brown plaid as the sofa and crossed her legs. She smiled at Lorraine, who had crossed her arms and tucked her hands underneath each forearm. Her hands now quieted, she began to waggle her top leg rapidly. She gave Iris the same icily appraising look as when she had first come in the door.

"You just arrived yesterday?" Iris asked conversationally.

"Yes."

"Are you staying through the weekend, through Easter?"

"Yes. I'm staying for a long time."

"Have you done any sight-seeing?"

"Barbie and I went shopping in Beverly Hills today."

Iris laughed. "Barbie's favorite place."

Barbie shouted from the kitchen. "We did it up. Hair, nails, facials, new outfits. The whole shebang."

Lorraine uncrossed her arms and began scratching the nails of one hand with the thumb of her other hand. "Barbie made me have these nails put on. They feel gross." She put her finger in her mouth and clicked the nail between her teeth.

"Honey, stop pickin' at 'em," Barbie said from the kitchen without seeing what Lorraine was doing. "You'll get used to them. They make your hands look sexy. You ought to get some, Iris."

"That's exactly what I need, one more appointment every week," Iris said.

"Barbie's taken you shopping, huh?" Lorraine folded her hands in her lap.

"A couple of times."

"I wondered about that blouse."

Iris put her hand on her middle, touching the purple silk. "Barbie bought it to cheer me up when I was having a bad day."

Lorraine began twiddling her thumbs. "That was nice of her. She bought me one that was almost the same when we lived together."

"I didn't know you were roommates."

Barbie shouted from the kitchen. "We lived together for a while when we both worked at Hal's."

"We were room-*mates.*" Lorraine tilted her head down and looked up at Iris meaningfully.

"That's . . . nice. Are you originally from Atlanta, Lorraine?"

"Salt Lake City. That's where I live now." She looked toward the kitchen, raised her voice slightly, and spoke as if she were reciting something. "I was only in Atlanta for a few years. That's where I met Barbie. We were both waitresses at Hal's."

Barbie walked into the living room, carrying glass tumblers of ice and cola.

Lorraine pointed a long fingernail at the glasses. "What's that?"

Barbie threw paper napkins on the rickety, stained coffee table, then set the sweating glasses on top of them. "Diet soda, darlin'. You know that bottle of wine I had? I just opened it and it's vinegary. Just ruined. I'm takin' it back tomorrow."

Lorraine stood up and started walking toward the kitchen. "Let's just have a look. How bad could it be?"

Barbie grabbed Lorraine's arm. "Don't you believe me, sugar?"

Lorraine looked at Barbie and slowly blinked her eyes. "Why wouldn't I believe you? I just want to taste it for myself."

Barbie followed Lorraine into the kitchen. Barbie's voice was too low to be heard. Lorraine's tone was sarcastic: "Whatever you want, darlin'."

The doorbell clanged. Barbie danced out of the kitchen and over to the door and swung it open. Lorraine walked back into the living room. She smiled at Iris.

"Hey," Art said. He put his arm around Barbie's waist and started to kiss her on the mouth.

Barbie quickly turned her head so that the kiss landed on her cheek, then pranced away from his grasp into the middle of the room. She held her arm out in a grand gesture, and Lorraine walked toward her as if on command. Barbie put her arm around Lorraine's waist.

"This is my good ol' friend Lorraine. Honey, this is my potential business partner, Arturo Silva."

Lorraine held out her hand limply, palm down.

"Nice to meet you, Lorraine," Art said, taking her fingers. "Welcome to L.A. Hey, Iris."

"Artie." Iris got out of the chair and stood next to Lorraine.

Art looked from Iris to Lorraine. "Hey, you know you guys look alike? You could be sisters."

Iris and Lorraine looked at each other.

"I guess we do at that," Iris said.

"I noticed it right off," Lorraine said.

"You know, you're right. Isn't that a coincidence?" Barbie took her purse from the bar, draped the strap over her shoulder, picked up a leather portfolio that was leaning against the bar, and put it underneath her arm. "Shall we go, kids?"

"Aren't we going to finish our drinks?" Iris asked.

"I don't want to make Uncle George wait," Barbie said.

"He's at the club anyway," Art said.

Barbie stood in the doorway. "Iris, I know you and Arturo have to get to bed early for work tomorrow, so let's go."

"Who's driving?" Iris asked.

"I'm the only one with a car that's big enough," Art said. "Big enough for all kinds of activities." He leered at Barbie.

Barbie clutched the portfolio tighter to her chest. "Let's go, kids."

"At least someone's having sex," Iris said.

"Who's having sex?" Lorraine asked.

"Iris and Art," Barbie answered.

Iris and Art gaped at Barbie.

Barbie started walking quickly down the corridor. "Will one of y'all pull the door closed and lock it?"

Art shrugged and looked at Iris and Lorraine. "I guess we're going."

"Madam does not desire her coat?" Iris asked stuffily.

Lorraine sniggered. "That damn coat!"

Art gestured for the two women to walk through the doorway and pulled the door closed behind them.

23

It was early Monday night and the Club Estrellado was slow. The band was setting up. A few couples were seated at the red vinyl booths, having dinner and margaritas. The singles would start arriving after ten o'clock, operating on a more bohemian schedule. Even on a Monday night, the Club Estrellado drew a crowd.

Coco, the waitress, latched onto Art as soon as he walked in the door. The collar of her white blouse was pulled up at a jaunty angle, the fit tight enough to make little holes in the side seams where the thread entered the fabric. She held onto his arm for balance as she stood on tiptoes to reach his ear, as if it were loud in the club, which it wasn't, and whispered animatedly to him.

Iris slid in one side of the circular booth, Lorraine in the other. Barbie sat next to Iris.

Coco slapped Art on the arm, giggled, and spun away with a shower of long hair flying over her shoulder, bouncing her tray on her hip as she walked. Art started to slide in next to Barbie, when Barbie suddenly leaped out of the booth.

"Art, sit in the middle so we can share you." She gestured with her thumb for Iris and Lorraine to get up. "C'mon. Out."

Iris and Lorraine crawled out of the booth. Barbie nudged Art toward the now vacant vinyl. He dutifully climbed in.

"Now, Lorraine, you sit on Art's left and Iris on the right, and I'll sit next to Iris. There! Isn't that better?"

"I guess," Art said.

Barbie anxiously twisted the face of her watch. "I thought you said your uncle was already here."

"Coco told me he had to go out. He'll be back soon."

A busboy began to set the table.

Barbie put her hands out to stop him. "That's not necessary, sugar."

The busboy stopped his work and looked uncomprehendingly at Barbie. Art asked him to continue, in Spanish. Barbie persisted, making a brushing motion with the back of her hand. He quickly finished laying out the place settings and left.

"Why didn't you want him to set the table?" Art asked.

"Aren't we eating?" Iris asked. "I'm starving."

"We're here for a business meeting, not to eat," Barbie said.

"Iris and Lorraine can eat," Art said. "They're not coming upstairs with us."

"Sure they are."

Lorraine was nibbling the tip of one of her nails, clicking it against her bottom teeth.

Art put his forearms on the table and leaned toward Barbie. "Isn't that why you asked Iris to come? To keep Lorraine company?"

"Yeah," Lorraine said. "Then Iris and I can get to know each other."

Barbie folded her arms across her chest. "I just thought it'd be interestin' for Lorraine and Iris to observe the meetin'. This is a big step in our lives."

"No offense," Iris said, "but I'd rather observe a big plate of enchiladas."

"I can do that," Lorraine said.

Art looked at Barbie and shook his head. "You're acting weird tonight."

"I'm just a little nervous, honey."

"Barbie nervous?" Iris said. "This is a first."

"Iris! This is an important meeting. Of course I'm a little nervous. Anyone would be." Barbie plucked at the front of her blouse, straightening it.

"It *is* an important meeting," Lorraine said. She slid her hands underneath her thighs, to quiet her fingers. "You need to know whether you're getting the dough for that important Phoenix trip."

"That's the spirit," Art said. "Let's get some food and drink over here."

He gestured for Coco to come over. Iris, Lorraine, and Art ordered food. Art ordered a pitcher of margaritas.

"Margaritas," Lorraine said. "Yummy."

"I'm sticking with ice water," Iris said.

"I can't eat or drink a thing." Barbie pointed a finger at Lorraine. "You'd better watch your drinkin', missy. She's allergic to the stuff," she explained before anyone asked. Demonstrating, she ran her hands over her arms as if they itched. "Breaks out all over. Terrible."

"Bullshit!" Lorraine leaned toward the table as if she were preparing to share a confidence. "The truth is"—she looked at them conspiratorially—"the truth is, I'm on medication. But one drink's not going to do anything. I've done it before."

"Medication for what?" Art asked impulsively.

"So that I don't see the little green aliens," Lorraine said.

Iris, Art, and Barbie looked soberly at Lorraine.

Lorraine reflected their serious expressions, then suddenly clapped her hands and laughed gleefully. "You should see your faces!"

Art and Iris laughed nervously along with her.

"As long as it's just one, darlin'," Barbie said through a tense smiled.

Lorraine snapped back, "Charlotte, mind your own fucking business."

Both Iris and Art looked at Barbie, whose smile drooped like yesterday's daisies.

Lorraine gave her head a shake. "Barbie, I mean."

Art winced with confusion. "Charlotte? Who's Charlotte?"

Barbie found her smile and pressed a hand to her ample chest. "Charlotte's my middle name. Lots of my old friends know me as Charlotte. It's a bit of the Old South flavor." She wrinkled her nose playfully. "That's all."

"Barbie Charlotte?" Art asked.

"Barbara Charlotte," Barbie confirmed.

"What's your maiden name?" Iris asked.

"Maiden name? Why, it's . . ." Barbie looked in the direction of the bartender across the room. "It's Beer."

"Barbie Beer?" Art laughed. "Like drinking beer?"

"My family's from the country. You have to understand that they're not real sophisticated."

"So, Lorraine," Iris said. "What do you do for a living in Salt Lake?"

"I'm a medical claims analyst at an insurance company."

"Oh. So you must have known Hal when you were in Atlanta."

"Hal?"

Barbie looked at Lorraine with a hesitant smile.

"Hal Stringfellow. Barbie's husband. Your boss."

"Oh, Hal! Sure. Good old Hal. Sure, I knew Hal."

Iris persisted. "So, what's old Hal up to these days?"

"I-ris!" Barbie exclaimed, giving Iris a slap on the thigh underneath the table. "Where's your mind? You know Hal's passed on."

"Ooops!" Iris in turn slapped Barbie's lush thigh underneath the table. "Of course! Where *is* my mind?" She rubbed her temples. "It's been a *long* day."

Art looked at Iris with one side of his upper lip raised.

"Well, Iris, aren't you just full of questions tonight?" Barbie said.

"You know I have a natural curiosity about people. So, Barbie. Tell us about these rich friends you have in Phoenix."

"Oh good, the band's startin'." Barbie shimmied her shoulders with the music, which was now loud enough to make conversation difficult.

"C'mon, Barbie. Let's dance," Art said.

"No, no! Dance with Lorraine. Show Lorraine how to dance Mexican-style."

"There's my uncle. Tio!" Art tried to stand up but was pinned in the middle of the booth. "Tio!" he shouted over the music.

Coco caught George before he started to go upstairs and directed him across the floor. He walked over, smiling.

Barbie slid out of the booth and extended her hand. "George, so nice to see you again." She shouted to be heard over the music.

George smiled, put his hand on top of Barbie's, and shouted back, "Good to see you again, too."

Lorraine slid out of the booth to free Art. Art shook his uncle's hand and mumbled a greeting that was lost in the music. George gestured toward the stairway on the other side of the bar.

Barbie dragged her purse by the strap and reached down to the floor where she had left her portfolio. "We may be an hour or so. Why don't you two have some fun and dance?" She pulled Art's sleeve. "Arturo, find someone to sit with them." She looked anxiously around the room.

"Why?" Art said.

"You can't let two ladies sit by themselves in a club."

"Why not?"

"Honey, I guess I was just raised different. It just don't look proper. See those two men over there? Get them to entertain the ladies."

Art protested, "The *ladies* will be fine. Trust me."

He put his hand on Barbie's back and started guiding her toward the staircase. When they passed the bar, Barbie abruptly took a right and walked up to the two men who were sitting there. She pointed out Iris and Lorraine, reached into her purse, pulled her hand out, and opened it into the palm of one of the men. She climbed the stairs that led to the office. At the top, she shot a final glance back at the table and smiled when she saw Iris and Lorraine getting up to dance with the men.

Upstairs in the office, Barbie sat in the chrome and vinyl kitchen dinette chair with a faded marble print, George sat behind the large wooden desk in the aged captain's chair, and Art pulled up a worn, overstuffed easy chair.

Barbie crossed her legs at the ankles, pressed her knees together, laid the portfolio on her lap, clasped her hands on top of it, tilted her head, and smiled at George.

Art glanced at the corner of the desk, then looked at Barbie with a lascivious smile playing on his lips. Barbie ignored him and continued focusing her attention on the man behind the desk.

George rolled back in the captain's chair and rested a foot

on the desk. He was wearing tennis shoes. "My nephew tells me you want to talk dollars and cents."

Barbie sat straighter. "George, when we last met, we chatted a bit about Arturo's dream to open a club. Arturo mentioned my experience in the business, but we didn't discuss my ability to lay my hands on capital for such a venture. Not just my own, but from many business associates throughout the country. My late husband, Harold Stringfellow, bless his heart, was a prominent Atlanta businessman with many influential friends who have become my trusted friends." Barbie placed her long fingernails against her heart. "They have confidence in me. They know what I can do." She pointed at George. "I want you to be confident in your decision to go into business with Barbie Stringfellow and I'm gonna do that by lettin' you know just who Barbie Stringfellow is."

George removed his foot from the desk and rolled his chair up. Art continued sitting with one knee crossed on top of the other, his lips barely closed over his broad smile.

Barbie sat back in her chair, paused, then slowly unzipped the black portfolio she held on her lap. She took out a restaurant menu. It was tall and covered in padded forest green leatherette. She put one hand on the top edge and one on the bottom and held it next to her face, like a product demonstrator, keeping her face and the product in view at the same time. HAL'S was embossed in gold script underneath a gold drawing of a stately, pillared mansion. AT-LANTA, GEORGIA was embossed in smaller letters on the lower right-hand corner.

Barbie shifted her eyes and glanced affectionately at the menu. "My baby." She handed George the menu. "I held lots of jobs, some of which I'm not too proud of, comin' from humble beginnings myself, just like y'all. Fortune finally smiled upon me when I took a job waitressin' for Hal Stringfellow. After a coupla years, Hal and I made it legal. Got married. Hal always told me I had a good mind for business. I didn't believe him, but he believed in me, and that was all it took. Like you and me believin' in your nephew. Just takes someone givin' you a chance."

George handed the menu to Art.

"I ran Hal's for five years. Hell of a joint." Barbie pursed her lips and looked down wistfully at the beat-up linoleum. She lowered her voice. "After Hal died, I tried to keep it goin', but there was no joy. So I sold everything, lock, stock and barrel. I'm childless, so there was nothin' to keep me in Atlanta. Came west, where I've been tryin' like crazy to be a lady of leisure." She leaned forward and cupped her hand to the side of her mouth. "Between you and me, I was startin' to lose my marbles with boredom."

George chuckled and nodded.

Barbie pointed at him. "You know what I'm talkin' about, don't ya, George! But fortune smiled upon me again and I met your charmin' nephew. He's got the energy and the ambition. George, you and I have the know-how *and*"—she dropped her voice to a whisper—"the capital."

Art handed the menu back to Barbie. She slid manicured fingers lightly across the embossed name, smiling sadly, slipped it back into the portfolio, slowly rezipped it, and clasped her hands on top of it.

"Gentlemen, I can come up with a million dollars. Cash. Right now. With a li'l work, I can get more."

George broke his stoic expression and raised his eyebrows slightly.

"You'll need at least that just to get started on the kind of venture that Arturo has in mind—an upscale Latin-flavored dinner club with top-notch food and entertainment. We'll be unequal partners, based on what everyone kicks in. How much can I count you in for?"

Art crossed his legs in the other direction. George leaned back in the captain's chair, whose old joints teetered precariously, crossed his arms, and looked at his nephew. Barbie looked down at the portfolio in her lap and remained silent.

Finally, George inhaled deeply. He righted the chair and placed his hands flat on the desk, shoulder distance apart. "You've made a very interesting proposition, Barbie."

Art started to waggle the foot that was resting on his crossed knee.

George stood up. Art and Barbie followed.

George walked from behind his desk. "I'm going to have to think about this. But I *will* think about it, very seriously."

"You're absolutely right, George," Barbie said. "Consider

everything very carefully, because if we go, we go one hundred percent."

"Absolutely," Art said.

Barbie held a cautioning index finger in the air. "But if you do decide to jump in, there's one thing we need to seal our commitment." She paused and looked from George to Art. "Good faith money." She unrolled her fingers and held her open hand, palm out, toward George. "Just to prove that we're serious. See, I'm gonna be contactin' folks, gettin' investors lined up, and I don't want to raise the subject unless I know you're committed. I have a reputation to protect."

"What sort of good faith money are you talking?" George asked.

Barbie rubbed her chin. "Due to the magnitude of the project, I don't think fifty thousand dollars is unreasonable."

George frowned slightly.

Barbie put her hand on George's arm. "Fifty from you and Arturo and fifty from me, deposited in an escrow account." She gestured toward Art. "Or we can give it to Arturo to manage. I know you trust your nephew. Deal?" Barbie held her hand toward George.

George shook it. "I promise you I'll give this some serious thought. I'll call you in a couple of days, before I leave for Mexico."

Barbie bit her lower lip.

"Something wrong?" George asked.

"I'm leavin' town Friday afternoon to meet with old friends in Phoenix who just might be excellent investors in our project. They're going abroad for several months and I have *got* to get to them before they leave. I'll have to have your commitment by Thursday night, at the latest."

George patted his kinky black hair. "I didn't expect that. Let's see. This is Monday. That's not very much time, but I can at least give you a thumbs-up by Thursday." He looked at Art. "I'd like to be able to give my nephew a chance to live his dream and not have to do it the hard way, like his father and I did."

Art clapped his hands and hugged his uncle. "You won't regret it, Tío."

"It's not done," George cautioned.

"I know, I know. But at least you're going to think about it."

"That's all we can ask," Barbie beamed. She shook hands with George and Art.

"Now, enough business," George said. "Go downstairs and enjoy yourselves."

24

"BARBIE, IT'S TEN O'CLOCK." IRIS WAS SITTING ON THE BROWN plaid couch in Barbie's living room. "I've got to go home. I have to be at work at six-thirty in the morning."

The room was dim. The sole artificial light emanated from a small light bulb inside the oven that shone through the grease-splattered glass door. The apartment's drapes and sliding glass doors were open, and the full moon cast a milky beam across the gold shag carpet.

Art and Barbie slow-danced in the moonbeam to music from a boom box sitting on top of the bar that rimmed the kitchen. Lorraine was sitting in the easy chair, watching Art and Barbie. She took a sip of her diet soda.

"So does Arturo," Barbie said over her shoulder.

"But he's younger than I am," Iris responded. "Hell. Doesn't matter anyway. I've hardly been able to sleep since John dumped me."

Lorraine looked at Iris. "Can't sleep?"

Iris shook her head.

Lorraine pulled her purse, which was sitting by her feet, onto her lap. It was a small, brown shoulder bag in an inexpensive grade of leather that was worn bald in spots. It was very full. She unzipped it. Brown plastic prescription containers with white caps were crammed inside, along with an overstuffed wallet held together by a rubber band and a hairbrush that needed cleaning.

Iris eyed the mysterious containers. "I guess you *are* on medication. What's it for?"

Lorraine took out one container, looked at the label, put it back, then took out another one. She pressed down and turned the child-proof cap. After several tries, she got it off. "It's a long story."

"I don't want any pills," Iris said.

"Go ahead."

"I really don't want any pills. Thanks anyway."

"Don't you want to sleep?"

Iris held her palm out with resignation. Lorraine tapped several small, bright blue tablets into it.

"What are they?" Iris asked.

Lorraine shrugged. "Take one. You'll sleep."

Iris dumped the pills into the pocket of her purple silk shirt. She stood up and put her purse under her arm. "Barbie, I'm leaving."

"Stay," Barbie said. "Don't be a party pooper."

Art murmured into Barbie's ear, "Why don't you get rid of them?" He pulled her closer.

Barbie pressed distance between them. "I can't do that to guests. And please watch your hands, mister. We're not alone."

Art pressed his hips against Barbie. "Let's go down to the car. I like the way you get in cars." He put his face close to her ear, his nose in her hair. "If we work together in business like we do in bed, this is going to be hot."

"You love me, sugar?" Barbie whispered in his ear.

"Love?"

"You love me, Arturo, don't you?"

"Well, I . . . uh . . ."

She leaned back and looked in his eyes. "If I had just wanted a business partner, I could have found one with better credentials than you."

"What do you mean?"

"I thought we had somethin' special."

"We do."

"But you don't love me."

Art put his lips close to Barbie's ear. "I do love you, Barbie." He moved his lips close to hers. "I love you." He opened his mouth to kiss her.

She quickly pressed her fingers against his lips. "My love, the next time we kiss, it's going to be in private and it's going to be a forever kiss."

"Let's go down to my car." Art slid his hand down to the full part of Barbie's hip and squeezed.

Barbie saw Iris and Lorraine watching them. She pushed Art away. "Arturo!" she loudly exclaimed. "You'd better act like a gentleman or I'm not gonna dance with you."

Iris was still standing. "I'm leaving. It's getting a little too steamy in here for me."

"We haven't had a dance, darlin'."

"I think you've danced enough, Barbie," Lorraine said.

"Lorraine, I'll be the judge of when I've danced enough." She pulled Iris's purse from under her arm and set it on the counter.

Iris picked it up, but Barbie wrenched it from her hand and put it back down on the counter.

"Iris," Barbie said. "That's no way to treat one of your best clients."

Lorraine opened one of the other pill containers and swallowed a white tablet with a swig of diet soda.

A cloud crossed in front of the moon, dimming the already thin light.

"Barbie, I don't want to appear rude, but I have to go."

Barbie put one hand around Iris's waist and took her hand in the other. "Just one little dance."

"I've lost my partner," Art said. "Lorraine, c'mon."

Lorraine stood up and smoothed her tight miniskirt over her hips. "Sure. I'll dance with you." She glanced out the window at the full moon shining through the clouds. "Remember the wolfman? Do you think he was happier as a wolf or as a man?"

A commercial came on the radio.

"That's it," Iris said. "I'm going."

Barbie held on to Iris's wrist. "Honey, just one dance. If Arturo and I go into business together, I'll have to close my account with you. It's a kind of endin' and beginnin'. It needs a dance!"

Art searched through the radio stations on the boom box until he found a slow song.

"A dance. It needs a dance," Iris said. "Okay. One freaking dance. All right, Barbeh?"

Barbie smiled coquettishly. "Okay," she said in a little voice.

Lorraine melted into Art's arms.

"You know, you're pretty good-looking," Art told her.

"Thanks." She turned to watch Barbie and Iris, who were dancing with a good arm's length between them.

"Think you could go for a guy like me?"

Lorraine looked at Art. She touched her tongue to her upper lip. "You're not my type."

"No? What is your type?"

She smiled at him and turned to watch Iris and Barbie.

"So you're closing your account with me, huh, Barbie?"

"Sorry, sugar. But you knew it was comin' if Arturo and I did this club deal."

"Since our professional relationship may be ending"—Iris looked into Barbie's eyes—"maybe we can talk on a personal level. You know, just as girlfriends."

"Love to."

"I've been thinking about that kiss on Saturday night."

"You were?" Barbie's eyes traveled across Iris's face.

"Why didn't you follow through?"

"Because you were gettin' kind of skittish on me and I didn't want to scare you off."

"Why did you lie about kissing me?"

"I didn't exactly lie. I just didn't answer your question. How much of a follow-through did you have in mind?"

"So you remember what happened that night and you lied about it. You also lied about prying me for information about the missing dirty money."

Barbie looked surprised. "What dirty money?"

"Barbie, don't bother. I remember the whole conversation."

"C'mon, Iris. Aren't you makin' a mountain out of a molehill? Everyone likes to be lied to every now and then.

It gives people what they want, even if it's for just a minute." Barbie leaned her head back and looked at Iris through slitted eyes, her heavily made-up eyelids almost closed. "You still didn't answer my question. How far did you want me to go with that kiss?"

Iris released her tenuous grip on Barbie. "I'm leaving. I'll cash out your account tomorrow. I can't manage your money anymore."

Barbie slid her eyes to the side and looked levelly at Lorraine, who hadn't stopped watching them. Barbie returned her gaze to Iris. "Since you won't answer my question, my darlin' Iris, I'll answer for you." She abruptly grabbed Iris's shoulders, jerked her close, and kissed her hard.

Iris pushed her away roughly. "For Chrissakes!"

Lorraine screamed something. The words were lost in the scream's ringing shrillness.

Barbie put her hands on her hips and faced Lorraine. "No one tells *me* what to do, missy!"

Lorraine ran up the three steps to the bedroom and turned left into the hallway, screaming, "Liar! Fucking liar!" She ran into the bathroom, slammed the door, and pounded her fists on the other side.

"Wow," Art said. "What's gotten into her?"

"I'm out of here," Iris said.

Barbie looked at her watch. "Yes. You'd better go now." She picked up Iris's purse from the counter, handed it to her, and held her hand out. "It's been a pleasure doing business with you, Miss Iris Ann Thorne. You may give the proceeds of my account to Arturo."

Iris just looked at Barbie's outstretched hand. She opened the door and slammed it closed behind her, the cheap door emitting a thin bang.

She quickly walked down the corridor, muttering to herself. "Freaking chamber of horrors. How the hell did I *ever* get involved with people like that? I'm through! Done! Finished!"

Iris pulled the Triumph into its spot in the garage. It was eleven-thirty, and the cars of the other worker bees were already snug in their spots, their drivers snug in their beds upstairs, resting for the next workday.

She got out of the Triumph, set her purse on the ground, opened the trunk, and started to take out the canvas car cover. She threw it back inside.

"The hell with it."

She grabbed her keys from the trunk lock, closed the trunk, and picked up her saddle leather purse, hanging the strap over her shoulder. Suddenly she felt compelled to turn around. The street man was standing close to her. She pressed the hand that still held the keys to her pounding heart.

"You scared me!"

He looked into her eyes for a brief moment, and in that moment the empty garage felt huge and lonely, and she thought she knew his intentions. She pushed past him and started to run. He grabbed the strap of her purse, jerking her toward him. Iris swung her right hand and slashed her keys across his cheek. He pulled the purse free of her arm and tried to take the keys from her hand, but she wouldn't let go. He threw his elbow into her chest, knocking her and the keys to the floor, the cement scraping her outstretched palm.

In the second it took for her head to clear, he was gone. She hadn't even had time to scream. She pushed herself off the floor with her stinging right hand and walked back to the Triumph.

She clambered on the Triumph's hood, reached up to the top of the wood storage cabinets that were built over each garage space, and felt around in the dust and crawlies until she finally located her spare set of keys.

Upstairs, after she had called the police, she sat in her living room in the wingback chair and gingerly examined her aching shoulder and hand.

The police arrived quickly, but the street man was gone, having already removed his bundles from underneath the terrace.

25

"I TOLD YOU, THEY'RE BUSINESS ASSOCIATES!" BARBIE TOOK a can of diet cola out of the refrigerator and flipped open the top. It was the wee hours of the morning. "Sex is the only thing that gets Arturo's attention. And sports."

Lorraine was sitting on Barbie's brown plaid couch, hugging her knees underneath her chin, rocking back and forth. She was still wearing the black leather miniskirt and the mock turtleneck sweater. "What about that purple blouse? You buy that same blouse for all your women?"

Barbie went up the three stairs into the bedroom and began to undress and hang up her clothes.

"You came all the way out here just to find her after you saw her on television. Why? To see if she has that dead guy's money or to make it with her?" Lorraine stopped rocking. "Don't answer. It was the money *and* to make it with her. You like to make it with the people you rip off. It's the frosting on the cake for you."

Barbie peeked her head out of the closet area. "I don't have to explain myself to you."

"Don't bother. I don't want to hear any more of your lies."

Lorraine went into the kitchen and got the bottle of wine from the refrigerator. She took a glass tumbler from a cabinet, pulled the cork from the bottle, and tipped some wine into the glass. She took a sip. "There's nothing wrong with this wine."

Barbie padded quickly down the three stairs and across the living room in purple slippers with pink pom-poms on top. She was wearing a purple negligee of sheer chiffon with shiny satin trim. A satin sash encircled her waist and was

181

tied in a bow. She grabbed the neck of the bottle as Lorraine was pouring and pulled it from her hand.

"Hey!" Lorraine tried to snatch the bottle back.

Barbie turned her back on her and started pouring the wine down the sink. Lorraine reached around her and grabbed the bottle, wrenching it from Barbie's hand.

"You almost twisted my wrist!" Barbie cried.

Lorraine took the half-full tumbler and the almost empty bottle back into the living room. She tucked her feet under her legs and nestled into the corner of the couch, the wine bottle snug next to her.

"Ain't this pretty?" Barbie faced Lorraine on the other side of the rickety coffee table with her hands on her hips. "Mixin' booze with that pharmacy in your purse."

Lorraine unfolded her legs and put her stockinged feet on the coffee table.

"Just how do you get so many pills, anyway?"

"Shit. That's easy. Just need to know the right doctors."

"There's gotta be more there than you could ever need."

"It gives me peace of mind to know I can check out any time. No razor blades. No guns. I can be all laid out, nice and pretty."

"Remember one thing, missy, before you head off to la-la land. This is my house, and in my house you follow my rules."

"You *were* in charge. No more."

"Just go ahead, girl. Just keep goin'. You're gonna mess up everything I've been working on for months. If you're not gonna help me, you're gonna have to get out."

"I'm not going anywhere. You try to get rid of me, all I have to do is make a little phone call to the police. Hell, my father would be happy to come out here and ring your chubby neck himself. Or how about that Jack Goins guy?" Lorraine held the tumbler up to Barbie in a toast, then took a long sip. "I don't know what you're so pissed off about. I'm doing everything you asked me. I'm telling all the right lies."

"Sure you are. What was that business about calling me Charlotte?"

Lorraine looked into space, trying to remember the incident. She sputtered through her lips. "Oh, right!"

"Fortunately, I covered it up. All I need is for Iris to put doubts in Arturo's mind and he'll never turn that money over to me. She's already checked out my Atlanta story. What did you tell her while I was upstairs with Art's uncle?"

"Nothing. We were dancing. You took care of that, remember? You're messing yourself up more than I'm messing you up."

"I gotta move fast. Faster than I'd planned, but I can still pull it off." Barbie walked up the steps into the bedroom area and returned with her can of diet cola. "This is exactly why I've always worked alone."

"Maybe it's time to take on a partner."

"Well, Rainey, I never would have thought you had it in you, but I've seen a side of you the past few days that I never knew existed."

"Teach me."

Barbie stepped around the coffee table and sat next to Lorraine on the couch. She spread out the folds of her purple chiffon negligee. "Maybe I should at that. I'm gettin' old. Losin' my looks. I can't do this forever. That checking account and credit card stuff is penny ante. This was gonna be my last job. Get me enough to retire in comfort. Maybe I should take on a younger associate."

"If you teach me, I'll give you a cut of everything I earn."

Barbie ran her fingertips across Lorraine's face. "You may have something at that."

Lorraine closed her eyes as Barbie moved her hand to her breast and rubbed it through the clingy jersey. Lorraine suddenly grabbed Barbie's hand and kissed her palm. She looked at Barbie. Her eyes were moist.

"Do you like sleeping with Art?"

Barbie quickly shook her head. "Honey, no. I told you about that." She picked up Lorraine's hand and put it on her face. "Touch me."

"You're not in love with him?"

"Good Lord, no."

"What about Iris?"

She moved Lorraine's hand over her body. "Honey,

there's no one but you. Art and Iris are just business. Let's go to bed."

Barbie lay in bed, listening to Lorraine sleep. Her breathing was deep and even and had been for a long time. Barbie had almost dropped off a few times but forced herself awake. She watched the minutes click by on the illuminated dial of the digital clock on the nightstand. Finally she climbed quietly out of bed.

She walked in bare feet to the closet, which she had left slightly ajar, and picked up the jeans, top, and shoes that she'd neatly folded and placed on the floor when Lorraine was in the bathroom. She took the clothes into the living room and quickly dressed in everything except the shoes. She rolled up her purple chiffon nightgown and stuffed it underneath one of the couch cushions.

Still barefoot, she walked into the kitchen and opened the cabinet underneath the sink. She took out a folded brown paper grocery bag that she'd placed there earlier in the evening and pulled her bright yellow, rubber household gloves from where they were draped across one of the sink pipes.

She picked up her large hobo-style purse from the bar, put the yellow gloves inside, held the paper bag under her arm, being careful not to rustle the stiff paper, grabbed her shoes, and quietly left the apartment. She left the door unlocked.

Barbie drove her red Mercedes convertible with the top down through the quiet streets of Santa Monica. She drove past Iris's building, paused in front of it, and looked up at the windows. They were dark. Barbie drove on.

She parked on the street in front of Palisades Park, the long strip of grass and trees fronting a cliff that dropped off steeply to the ocean and the Pacific Coast Highway below. Wrapped bundles were nestled underneath trees and on park benches. The park, a favorite of street people, was a short distance away from the Santa Monica Pier and its antique carousel with its carefully restored horses and calliope. A new extension had been built on to the pier after a rough storm several years ago had unceremoniously knocked half of it into the ocean. A fresh storm was on its way, and the ocean was already churned up in anticipation.

Barbie hummed to herself.

After a few minutes, the street man walked out from behind one of the pier pilings, up the steps that led to the street, and over to Barbie's car.

She said nothing as she pulled the rubber gloves from her purse and put them on.

He handed her Iris's expensive saddle leather handbag.

Barbie took it and looked inside. She found the wallet and opened it. The gloves were clumsy.

"Everything's there," the street man said with irritation.

Barbie counted the money in the cash compartment. "Eleven dollars?" She tsk-tsked. "Iris, honey, you should always carry enough for cab fare home."

"Where's my money? I have to beat it."

"Don't worry. I'll give you your money." She continued looking through the purse. "Where are the keys?"

"Oh, right." He reached inside the pocket of his denim jacket, pulled out the keys, and threw them on the Mercedes's passenger seat.

Barbie frowned at him. "You a local boy?"

"Yeah. Why?"

"I figured as much. None of y'all out here have been raised with any manners."

"Just give me the money." He looked around nervously. "I can't stand here all night."

Barbie reached into her hobo bag, pulled out a wad of bills that were folded in half and fastened with a rubber band, and handed it to the street man.

He took off the rubber band and started counting the money.

"It's *all* there," Barbie said.

He continued taking his time counting it, refastened the rubber band around the bills, shoved the wad into his jacket pocket, saluted Barbie, and walked back toward the pier, down the steps, and into the shadows underneath.

Barbie took the eleven dollars from Iris's wallet and put it into her purse. She opened the section that held Iris's checkbook and pulled a check free. That done, she opened the brown paper bag, put Iris's purse inside, and folded the bag over it.

She started the car and drove until she found a mailbox in which she crammed the bag with the purse inside, opening the hinged door again to make sure it had gone down all the way.

She sat in her car and picked up Iris's key ring from the passenger seat. It held a large bunch of keys. Barbie smiled to herself as she turned them, one by one, around the ring.

26

HOWARD SAW IRIS WALK UP THE GRANITE STEPS LEADING TO the bank. He almost didn't recognize her because she was wearing a beret and had her hair twisted up into it. He'd never seen her wear a hat before. But he recognized the cobalt blue suit that she wore frequently. He figured it was one of her favorites.

He watched her frown extravagantly at the street man who shook a paper cup that held a few coins at her, his soiled pants slung low on his hips. She clutched her large handbag to her chest, scurried up the remaining steps, and pulled open one of the bank's tall glass doors.

The bank had just opened for business. Howard was working the teller windows with three women. He was counting out cash for his first customer, laying it down carefully in the shape of a fan, when Iris came in. She was hesitating just inside the doorway. Since the dimness of the bank contrasted with the bright sunlight outside, he figured she was letting her eyes adjust.

The queue fed another customer to Howard's window. He ignored the elderly man facing him and looked over his shoulder at Iris standing just inside the door on the other side of the bank. He looked up at her from underneath his eyebrows, trying to catch her eye. He knew she'd eventually look his way and smile at him and maybe even wave, and he didn't want to miss the moment.

Finally, she glanced in his direction. He angled a crooked smile at her. When she didn't respond he immediately wiped the smile from his face and blushed, the red flush starting from the top of his head and moving down his neck. Humiliated, he quickly looked down.

She walked to the counter where the nonmonetary transactions were conducted and set the large Louis Vuitton satchel that she'd been clutching close to her body on the counter. A woman sitting at a desk on the other side of the counter whose plastic name tag announced she was Mrs. Harris, got up and walked up to her.

"Hi," Mrs. Harris said amiably. "Nice to see you again. How are you today?"

"Fine."

Mrs. Harris watched her run her hands up and down the satchel's leather strap, then suddenly fold her arms across her chest with her hands tucked underneath each forearm. "I want to open my safe deposit box. Now."

"Certainly."

She unfolded her arms, reached into a pocket of her suit jacket, and retrieved a key ring with a brass fob that was heavy with many keys. She fumbled through the keys and finally located the small key that was embossed with 106.

"I have as many keys as you," Mrs. Harris said. "You just keep putting them on and before you know it, there you are." She reached her hand under the counter, and the door to the high-walled wooden cubicle where folks conducted their safe deposit box business in private began to buzz.

"I'm sorry I startled you," Mrs. Harris said when her customer flinched. "I guess I should warn people before I do that. I'll meet you inside."

She left then returned with the safe deposit box, which she sat on the counter. "Just give me a holler when you're finished."

Howard saw Iris leave the bank without saying good-bye, clutching the satchel close to her body. She walked down the granite steps and continued down the street, out of How-ard's view. After a few blocks, she entered a multilevel park-ing garage. She walked up to a red Mercedes convertible and got inside. Barbie was sitting in the car.

"Well, Iris?" Barbie grabbed the satchel and eagerly pulled it open. "Oh, my Lord." She fished her hand around inside the satchel, churning the bundles of cash.

"I was so nervous. I didn't think I could pull it off. But then the money was right there in front of me."

"Rainey, we did it! We did it!" She grabbed Lorraine's arm. "*You* did it, darlin'. I'm so proud of you."

Lorraine beamed at Barbie. "It was great!"

Barbie held her palm out toward Lorraine. "Put it there, partner!"

27

ON TUESDAY MORNING, THE LOCKSMITH LEFT AFTER REKEY-ing all the locks in the condo. Iris had canceled her credit cards, told the bank that her checks and safe deposit box key had been stolen, and had arranged to leave the Triumph with the mechanic to have its locks rekeyed later in the day. She'd done laundry, straightened up her condo, unloaded the dishwasher, called in the order to close out Barbie's account, left instructions to give Barbie's check to Art Silva, and gathered together a bundle of clothes for the dry clean-ers. She'd looked high and low for her cobalt blue suit, which she was certain she'd thrown in the pile of clothes for the dry cleaners. She decided she'd probably already taken it to the cleaners.

It was just midmorning. She'd gotten an early start be-cause she'd hardly slept a wink. She'd forgotten about the tiny blue tablets that Lorraine had given her until she'd picked up the purple silk shirt and thrown it into the bundle for the dry cleaners. Not that she would have taken the pills anyway. She tossed the tablets into a drawer of her jewelry box.

Herb Dexter called her at home and asked her if she would help him out and attend a two-day seminar in his place. Iris knew it was just a way of giving her a couple of days away from the office, and she was grateful. While she didn't feel up to facing the office, she was not enjoying being left alone with her thoughts.

During the next two days, the only call she took was from her mother, to whom she revealed the mugging and her break-up with John, confirming all her mother's worst fears in one blow.

She did not hear from either Barbie or Art, not that she would have taken their calls if they'd attempted to contact her. She had a wild thought that Barbie was behind her mugging, that she'd done it just to nab her safe deposit box key, but felt reassured when she called the bank and was told that her safe deposit box would be sealed until she was able to move everything to a new one.

The seminar was held at a hotel near the airport. For each of the two days, Iris dressed casually, in slacks and a jacket. She met some people, made a few friends, and began to put Barbie, Lorraine, Art, and John behind her.

On Thursday morning, she dressed for the office.

In the garage, she waited in the Triumph for the security gate to slide open at a speed relaxed enough to let in anyone who was so inclined. She pulled the car beyond the gate and paused as she always did before making her left turn. She glanced into the bushes underneath her terrace. The street man had taken all his belongings except one. She had looked at it for the past two days. She put the TR in neutral, set its parking brake, got out, picked up the corrugated cardboard VIETNAM VET WILL WORK FOR FOOD sign, and put it on the TR's passenger seat.

She carried the street man's sign into the McKinney Alitzer suite and into the administrator's office, where she picked up a new set of office keys. She unlocked the door to her office. The new door key had an odd, sharp-edged feel in the lock.

Her office felt reassuring. There was plenty of work to be done, relentless work that demanded attention in spite of the events of her personal life. The work was heartless and unsympathetic and required only cool intellect and verve. Iris looked forward to losing herself in it.

She put away her purse, positioned the street man's sign on top of her credenza, turned on her computer, and answered calls from well-wishers who wanted to know how she was doing. She was gazing out her western-facing window and daydreaming when she heard a shallow knock on the metal door frame.

"I heard about the mugging," Art said. "Terrible."

"I'm glad it wasn't a lot worse."

"Really. I wanted to let you know that the Accounting Department gave me the check. You did well for the Widow Stringfellow."

"I hope she puts her earnings to good use."

Art sat down without being invited. "She will. She's got a club to invest in." He gestured toward the street man's sign. "Different, but I like it."

Iris shrugged. "Who knows? I might need it someday." She paused. "I'm asking against my better judgment, but are you saying that you got your uncle to commit?"

Art smiled broadly. "Of course."

"What's the plan?"

"I'm meeting him after work, getting the dough, then meeting Barbie tomorrow morning, when I'll give her the cash-out check from her McKinney Alitzer account and the fifty grand in good faith money, in cash."

"Cash? Does your uncle know you're giving her cash?"

"No. He's too conservative. He wouldn't understand."

"What happened to the escrow account?"

"Barbie thought it would make more of an impression on her friends if she brought cash."

"Why? Are they drug dealers?"

Art's smile faded. "Iris, can't you take anything at face value?"

"Not when it involves money in the five figures."

The skin of his face drew taut.

"Art, don't you find it odd that Barbie never mentioned these Phoenix friends until Lorraine showed up? And if she's such good trusted friends with these people, why does she have to flash cash?"

"I don't question her methods. You didn't question her when she wanted to work with you."

"There's a big difference. She was giving *me* money."

A vein in his forehead pulsed. "I can make a good business decision, Iris."

"No doubt. But you're not making one this time, because you're thinking with the head between your legs and not with the one on your neck."

Art abruptly stood up.

"Art, why has Barbie's whole demeanor changed since Lorraine arrived? First, Barbie has all the time in the world to do the club deal, and now she needs everything yesterday. And who is this nut case Lorraine anyway? Why does she make Barbie so nervous? Have you *ever* seen Barbie nervous before? Does Lorraine know something we don't? Something that Barbie doesn't want us to know? And what was this Charlotte business?"

"Barbie explained that."

"Oh, of course she did. The woman thinks on her feet. I have to give her that. One thing's for sure. Lorraine and Barbie are lovers."

"You're sick!"

"Then why couldn't Lorraine take her eyes off you and Barbie, and what was that screaming fit? And why does Barbie avoid you when Lorraine's around? And why does Barbie keep making passes at me?"

"You know, Iris, I'm tired of your feelings this and your feelings that. If you can show me solid proof, I'll listen, but otherwise I don't know what your problem is unless you're jealous of me and her because your boyfriend dumped you or you don't want me to be richer than you or something." Art walked to the window, his back to her, and ran his hands through his hair.

"Art, I just don't want you to get hurt. You're a pain in

the ass, but I like you." She pointed at his back. "See! You're worried, aren't you?"

He turned to face her. "I can take care of myself, Iris. No one's going to take advantage of Art Silva. Got it? No one." He left her office.

Iris stood up and opened her filing cabinet next to the window that overlooked the suite and busied herself with nothing.

You never learn to mind your own business.

She looked out the window and watched Art disappear into his cubicle.

Her phone rang again. It was an outside call.

"Iris Thorne."

"Ms. Thorne," this is Detective Verdugo from the Santa Monica Police Department. We've recovered your purse. There's no cash in it, but it looks like your credit cards and everything else is there. We didn't find your keys. Did you recover them?"

"No."

"He must have dropped them somewhere."

"Doesn't matter. I've already had everything rekeyed. I'll come down this afternoon and pick it up. Any sign of the bum?"

"No, he's long gone."

28

EARLY FRIDAY MORNING, BARBIE STOOD IN THE LIVING ROOM and watched Lorraine sleep. They'd spent the past couple of days shopping, sight-seeing, and doing the town. Last night they'd dressed up for dinner and gone to a fine restaurant. Lorraine wore the slinky black cocktail dress with spaghetti straps that Barbie had bought her. They had gotten home very late. Barbie didn't balk when Lorraine ordered two cocktails at dinner, and she later encouraged Lorraine to take a few sleeping pills before she went to bed since they'd got in bed very late the night before and had risen early to get started on their sight-seeing.

Barbie made Lorraine a fresh pot of coffee. The guttural noises of the automatic drip coffeemaker boiling and expelling water did not stir her. Barbie wrote a note on a pad: "Sugar, went to the market. Back soon. Here's some money in case you go out." Barbie put a pile of bills next to the note.

Dressed in a purple suit with big gold buttons, Barbie walked through the apartment in her stocking feet. She propped the note against a cup and saucer that she'd set on the sink. She'd also put out nondairy creamer, a spoon, the artificial sweetener that Lorraine liked, and a package of bear claws that she'd bought especially for Lorraine. She touched her hair, which she'd pulled into a neat French roll.

She picked up a large local telephone book, quietly opened a kitchen cabinet, and replaced it in its spot. She studied the cabinet's contents. She closed the door and opened the cabinet next to it. She had few housewares, just the bare essentials she'd bought after she'd moved to Marina Del Rey. She smirked at the contents and closed the door.

She picked up a broad-brimmed white hat with a purple ribbon from the coffee table, fastened it on her head with a pearl-tipped hat pin, put her overstuffed makeup bag inside her purse, slung it over her shoulder, put her car keys in her pocket, and tiptoed up the stairs past the bed to the closet. The closet door was already open. Barbie looked through the few garments that hung there, moved one from the group and hung it farther down the closet rod, removed one more and rehung it, then grabbed the rest of the garments in her arms and lifted them off the rod. She leaned back inside the closet, managed to free a hand, and spread out the remaining hangers.

She peeked into the bathroom, looked at the bathroom counter, on which she'd left a few miscellaneous toiletries and makeup containers, then turned and tiptoed past the closets. Lorraine stirred. Barbie stopped. She looked to her right at the still open closet door and took a tentative step backward, closer to it. She raised the bundle of garments as if she were going to toss them inside. Lorraine turned over and pulled the sheet up around her neck. Barbie waited. Lorraine's breathing again became slow and steady.

Barbie carried the clothes out the front door, which she closed but did not lock, avoiding any extra noise. She wiggled her feet into her conservative pumps, which she'd left standing side by side just outside the door.

In the garage, Barbie opened the trunk of the Mercedes and threw the garments on top of a mound of clothing, shoes, and purses that was already there. She emptied her purse of the makeup bag and other sundries and shoved them next to the overstuffed Louis Vuitton satchel. She closed the trunk and ran her fingers lovingly along the car's thick wax.

"Well, Ol' Paint. Looks like you and I are gonna be partin' company soon."

She drove a few blocks and parked in the lot of a convenience store on a busy, ugly intersection where a complicated street light system directed traffic through the several streets that converged there. Cars, trucks, and buses created a din of squealing brakes, engaging gears, and revving engines as the vehicles stopped, then restarted from inertia.

Barbie looked at her watch. It was eight o'clock in the morning. The streets around the convenience store were clogged with morning drive-time traffic. She went inside the store, got ten dimes in change, then walked outside to the phone booth in front. It was an open-air model with just a half-egg of plastic surrounding the phone and no doors or glass to tempt vandals. She stacked the dimes loosely on the small metal shelf that extended from the lower half of the plastic cocoon and took a pad of paper and a pen from her purse. The pad had several phone numbers written on it.

She dropped two dimes into the phone. They rattled as they followed a mysterious course through the guts of the machine. At the dial tone, Barbie punched in the first number on her list.

"Hi. Can you tell me your flight schedule from Salt Lake City to Los Angle-lees today?" Barbie turned back the top page of the pad and wrote down the flight times. "Are there seats available? Thank ya kindly."

She dropped in another two dimes and punched in the next number.

"Hi. Can you tell me your flight schedule from Salt Lake City to Los Angle-lees today? Seats available? What other airlines fly from Salt Lake to L.A.? Uh-huh. I got that one. Can you give me their phone number? You can check for me? Thank you ever so." Barbie jotted down the flight times.

She looked at her watch again. "Hour to get ready." She tapped the watch face with a long fingernail. "Half hour to the airport. Could make these . . ." She circled two of the flight times. "Transportation from the L.A. airport, half an hour at least. Couldn't get here before two at the earliest."

She reached into her purse, took out her personal telephone book, found the page she wanted, dropped two dimes into the telephone, and dialed the operator. The two dimes clattered back down into the change bin. Barbie dug her finger inside the bin and retrieved them.

"I'd like to make a collect call to Salt Lake City. Earl or Evelyn Boyce. Tell them it's Lorraine."

Barbie danced her fingernails against the phone booth's metal shelf as she waited. The phone clicked several times and the operator announced that her party was on the line. Barbie held the phone receiver slightly away from her mouth.

"Daddy? It's Lorraine. I'm in L.A." Barbie raised her normal tone to a higher pitch. "I am talking as loud as I can. I think it's a bad connection. Come get me, Daddy. I want to come home. I'm sorry . . ." A big truck drove by, making the asphalt quiver. "I said I'm sorry I scared you and Mom but I want to come home now. Hi, Mom. I don't know, I just wanted to come here. I sound funny? I feel kinda funny. Here's where I am. Two-ten Tahiti Way. Apartment three-two-two. Can you come now? Are you gonna fly or drive? I'll be waiting. Look for me at the pool if I'm not there. 'Bye." Barbie hung up the phone.

"That ought to do her." She shook her head. "Barbeh girl, you somethin'!"

She dropped in another two dimes, dialed directory assistance, and got the toll-free telephone number for the Mariah Lodge in Las Pumas.

"Is your best room a li'l ol' cabin out in the woods? Is it available this weekend? You had a cancellation? Great. Make the reservation under the name of Iris Thorne. Two nights. I'll be there about six o'clock. I'd like a bottle of your best champagne waiting. You heard right. Your *best* champagne. I don't care what it costs."

Barbie dropped two more dimes and made one last phone call. The phone rang five times, then the answering machine picked up. "Lorraine, honey? You up? Pick up the phone. Hi, sugar. You have a good sleep? I'm running some errands. I may not be back until two, three o'clock or so. So just stay there and relax. I'm sorry, honey, but I gotta take care of some business. Go out by the pool. Honey, if I weren't comin' back, why the hell would I bother callin' ya? Just put those negative thoughts out of your mind. See you soon."

Barbie replaced the receiver. "Well, that's that."

29

ART WAITED FOR BARBIE AT THE STREET CORNER SHE'D SPECIfied. He'd checked his watch almost every minute of the twenty-two that Barbie was late. He finally caught a glimpse of purple and saw her quickly sashaying toward him, darting around the business folks in their conservative browns, grays, and navy blues that blended with the concrete, asphalt, and granite of the financial district. She spotted him and waved. He walked quickly to meet her.

"Hey, buddy," Barbie drawled. She stood on her toes and kissed the air to the side of his cheek. "I don't want to send you back to the office with lipstick on your face. They'd think the worst, which would only be the truth."

Art caught a glimpse of the blouse she was wearing under her suit jacket. "What have you got on?"

"Just a li'l something I picked up." She pulled one side of her jacket away from her chest. The blouse had a low scoop neck that displayed cleavage suspended in a sheer lace bra.

"Shit, Barbie. You can almost see your nipples. Why do you dress like that?"

She caressed his cheek. "Darlin'. Don't tell me you're jealous. You used to like me to dress like this."

"I'm just surprised."

"Aren't you jealous, just a little?"

"I guess maybe I am."

"I thought so." Barbie puckered her lips in his direction. He leaned down and very lightly touched them with his. Barbie rubbed the lipstick residue from his lips with her thumb. "Well, sugar, I've got a zillion things to do before I catch my plane at three. Did you bring everything?"

Art stood his briefcase on the ground, reached inside his jacket and took out a white envelope. "From your account."

Barbie took the envelope and peeked inside. "Iris did good." She looked at Art expectantly.

Art didn't move.

"The good faith money?"

Art's shoulders sank.

Barbie's eyes narrowed. "Uncle George backed out."

"No . . . No, I have it."

She reached up and turned his head toward her. "You're not lookin' in my eyes. What's wrong?"

He met her eyes. "We need to talk about how the finances are going to be managed."

"What do you mean, darlin'? We have talked about it."

"I think we should put the money in an escrow account, Barbie. That's the standard way of doing something like this."

"You don't have it."

"I already said I did."

"Let me see it."

Art squatted on the sidewalk, opened his briefcase, took out a manila envelope, stood up, showed Barbie the contents, then clutched it in his quarterback's hand to his chest.

"Arturo." Barbie looked into his eyes. "Now that we've come all this way, why are you havin' second thoughts? Iris been puttin' ideas in your head?"

"I've been thinking, Barbie. Why do you have to show these Phoenix people cash?"

Barbie looked down at the ground, pursed her lips, and slowly shook her head back and forth. When she looked up again, her eyes were filled with tears. One spilled over the rim of her eye and traveled down her face.

Art's expression softened.

"I'm such a fool. I never learn." More tears flowed. "Man tells me he loves me and I believe him." She dug her hand into her bag and retrieved an embroidered handkerchief. "I always get 'I love you' and 'I want to sleep with you' confused in my head. When am I ever gonna learn?" She blotted her face and turned accusing eyes on Art.

"C'mon, Barbie. I wouldn't have said it if I didn't mean it."

She shook her head. "You don't love me. All men have ever wanted from me is money or sex. Why should you be any different?"

Art rubbed Barbie's arm with his free hand. "C'mon, Barbie. You know that's not true." Passersby watched them with interest. Art put his arm around Barbie's shoulders, put the manila envelope under his arm, picked up his briefcase, and walked with her to a bench in a small patio between two office buildings. They sat down.

She shook her head sadly. "You don't know the first thing about love. Love is about trust." She rested her elbows on her knees and put her head in her hands and sobbed.

"You've got me all wrong."

"I just can't win at this game. Why did I think a young buck like you'd be interested in a broken-down ol' broad like me? I guess there's no fool like an old fool." She stood up, dried her eyes, refolded her handkerchief, and smoothed her clothing.

Art looked alarmed.

She held her hand out. "It's been fun, sugar."

Art stood. "What do you mean?"

She shrugged. "How can we go on? You don't trust me and now I don't trust you no more, so what's the point?"

"Just like that?"

"I don't know what else we can do."

He handed Barbie the manila envelope.

She pushed the envelope back and waggled a manicured finger at him. "You can't unscramble an egg. It's *over.*"

"Barbie, I'm sorry. This is so much money for my family, I got cold feet. But I'm back with the program now."

Barbie pursed her lips, hesitated, then reluctantly took the envelope. She put it in her bag. "I'm sorry I went off like that. It's just ... when you've been knocked around in life as much as I have ..."

Art pushed back a lock of Barbie's hair that had come loose from her French roll. "Let's just forget this conversation. I really like your hair like this and your hat."

Barbie smiled demurely. "Thank you."

"When are you coming back from Phoenix?"

"Day after tomorrow."

"Call me tonight after you get there?"

"You better believe it." She took his chin between her fingers and shook his head back and forth. She stroked his cheek. "You sweet thing. I'll call you tonight."

Art kissed her lightly on the lips, taking some of her bright pink lipstick away with him. He held her by the shoulders, looked down at her chest again, moaned theatrically, then turned and walked down the street. He looked back at her. She crooked her fingers at him. He winked at her, then continued walking. He took a handkerchief from his pocket, rubbed it against his lips, and looked at the pink stain on the white cotton.

Barbie walked to the bank that her McKinney Alitzer payout check was drawn on, cashed it, then walked to her car in a nearby garage. She opened the trunk and shoved the additional cash into the Louis Vuitton satchel. Looking behind her to make sure no one was watching, she dug her hand into the middle of the neat, rubber-banded bundles.

"You did it, Barbeh girl! Where to put you? Under my

fox, of course." Barbie dug through the pile of garments in her trunk.

"She's the yellow rose of Texas, da da da da dada!"

She stopped singing. She frantically looked through the clothes in the trunk.

"I couldn't have . . ."

She straightened up and stamped her foot. "Can't be!" She chewed her lower lip. "Good Lord, girl. You can buy another fur." She knitted her eyebrows. "But I want that one!" She looked at her watch. "Still time. I'll just go fetch it."

30

IRIS DECIDED TO TAKE A BREAK AND FINISH HER BANK BUSI-ness. She grabbed her purse from the filing cabinet and walked the few blocks to the Great California Bank.

Climbing the bank's granite steps, she passed the street man, who shook his cup of change at her. Since she'd contributed last time, she ignored him. Inside the bank, she walked to the counter for noncash transactions to the right of the teller windows.

A woman sitting at a desk behind the wooden barrier asked Iris if she needed assistance.

"Mrs. Harris, please," Iris said.

Iris saw Howard working his window. She quickly looked away, anticipating his creepy stare, then looked back with curiosity when she realized he was ignoring her. She continued to stare at him, trying to see if she could get his attention, just for the hell of it, but he continued to ignore her.

A woman walked up to Iris on the other side of the counter. "Hello. I'm Mrs. Harris. I took your call about the stolen key. That's a shame, having to replace all those keys you had."

Iris smiled guardedly. "How did you know I had a lot of keys?"

"We laughed about them when you were here the other day."

"Howard helped me the last time I was here. You've helped me before, but it's been awhile."

"Really? I'm positive I helped you the other day. You were wearing a pretty, bright blue suit."

"Then it must have been a while ago, because the dry cleaners lost that suit."

Mrs. Harris shrugged. "I guess you're right. Some days I don't know if I'm coming or going."

"Anyway, about my safe deposit box, I've decided to move everything to a new box."

Mrs. Harris buzzed Iris into the cubicle, left momentarily, and returned with box 106. She supported it easily with one hand. She set it on the counter in front of Iris and left her alone.

Iris lifted the box by its handle. "Son of a bitch." She took a deep breath and pulled open its hinged top. It contained her insurance policies, will, trust deed, and other documents and nothing else. The almost half a million dollars in dirty money was gone.

Iris stared into it. She wanted to scream or shout but ended up just slowly closing the metal lid and shoving the box across the counter, away from her. She left the cubicle and waved at Mrs. Harris.

"You said the box was sealed as soon as I called."

"That's right. Immediately after you reported your key missing. Is something wrong?"

"But I called first thing Tuesday morning, right after you opened at ten o'clock."

"We open at nine o'clock. Is there a problem?"

Iris waved her hand distractedly toward the box. "I'll change everything later. I have to go now."

She walked out of the bank and down the stairs, methodically putting one foot in front of the other as if she didn't trust the ground to support her weight.

Finally reaching the McKinney Alitzer tower a few blocks away, she walked to a group of telephones against one wall of the lobby, dropped in two dimes, and punched in a number. Art's LED display indicated that the call was from an outside line, so he answered formally. "Art Silva."

"It's Iris. Meet me in the stairwell off the ninth floor."

"Iris, some of us have to work."

"You wanted solid proof. Well, I've got it. In spades."

Art walked to the stairwell. A cloud of cigarette smoke flooded out when he opened the door. He swatted at the air and walked past the smokers and down three flights of stairs. Iris was standing on the ninth-floor landing. Art stood with his legs apart and his arms crossed over his chest.

"Okay. What?"

Iris spoke in a calm, low voice, but her hands were trembling. "Barbie and Lorraine robbed my safe deposit box. They must have paid that guy to mug me to get the key, then Lorraine posed as me. And I yelled at the poor dry cleaners for losing my blue suit."

"Say again?"

Iris's sangfroid was fleeting. The words spilled out. "Barbie took my keys from my purse. She was looking for the safe deposit box key. Then she lied about it." She was talking faster and faster. "John warned me about that guy. When I got my purse back, everything was there but the cash. Who cares about the cash? And the keys, but I thought he'd just dropped them. The purse was a cover-up. She paid him to get the keys." Tears streamed down her face. "She did it for the money. Everything! Every gesture. Every word. Lorraine's in it, too. And now they're gone. They're gone, Art! They're gone."

"Slow down! I can't understand you." Art took a folded handkerchief out of his back pants pocket and handed it to Iris. "Here, let's sit down."

They sat on the concrete steps.

"Tell me again, slowly."

Iris wiped away tears that were blackened with eye makeup. "Barbie paid that homeless man to mug me. She stole my blue suit from my closet and gave it to Lorraine to wear to the bank. The woman at the bank told me I'd just been there, wearing my blue suit, but I can't find my blue suit! Lorraine robbed my safe deposit box." She refolded the handkerchief and noticed a smear of pink lipstick on the white cotton next to the red of her own lipstick.

"What would she want in your safe deposit box?"

Iris looked at Art, her face and eyes red and swollen. "Alley's dirty money."

Art widened his eyes. "You have it?"

"Not a million, like everyone thought, but almost half a million." She put her hand on his. "You can't tell anyone, Art. Promise. Promise you won't tell anyone."

"Damn! You had it all the time!"

"Art, promise me. Promise you won't tell anyone. I'll get into big trouble."

"I promise. Iris, I do. I promise."

Tears sprang into Iris's eyes again. She held herself with both hands. "I feel like I've been raped or something."

"I can't believe you had it all this time."

"Don't you get it yet? Where's the good faith money?"

"C'mon. You don't think . . . ?"

"We have to find them."

"No. I don't believe you."

"Art! Barbie got the street man to mug me. I could have been killed!"

Art stood up. He raked the fingers of both hands through his thick hair. "I've got to think. Give me a few minutes."

"We don't have a few minutes!"

"She better think again if she thinks she's gonna steal from me!"

"Let's call them. Maybe they're still packing. You call. Talk to Barbie. Don't alarm her. Just tell her you . . . you wanted to say good-bye again. Act normal."

They skipped down the nine flights of stairs to the bank of telephones in the lobby. The phone rang five times before Barbie's answering machine clicked on.

"Hey, baby. It's Arturo. I just called to say good-bye again. I miss you already. I love you, baby. I really do. We're gonna have a great life together. Call me as soon as you get home." Art hung up. "I'll drive. I have to go back upstairs and get my keys. I'll tell Dexter I'm going to see a client."

"I'll call up my excuse from down here. Get my briefcase from my office. It has my mobile phone in it."

"We're going to have some explaining to do on Monday."

"I'll meet you in the garage."

Within half an hour they had retrieved the Mustang and were driving down the Ten west. They didn't speak for a long time.

Halfway to Barbie's, Iris broke the silence. "Do you really love her?"

Art raised his upper lip against his teeth. "Shit." He shook his head. "If she walked, my nightclub walked. Hell, I would have said anything. Now I feel like wringing her neck."

"I'm having a homicidal moment myself."

31

"CALL ME AS SOON AS YOU GET HOME."

Barbie heard Art's voice through the thin front door of her apartment. He was on the answering machine. She knocked.

"Lorraine, darlin'. Open up."

She put her ear to the door. There was silence. "Good. She ain't there." She started to put the key in the lock, stopped and frowned when she heard Art's voice again.

"Hey, baby. It's Arturo. I just called to say good-bye . . ."

Barbie pushed the door open and gasped.

Lorraine was sitting on the floor with her legs sprawled out, wearing only the slinky black cocktail dress that Barbie had bought her. The dress was hiked up around her waist, and one of the straps had slipped and lay loose against her upper arm. Barbie's bottle of bourbon and a glass were on the carpet next to her. The answering machine set on the floor in the V of Lorraine's legs.

Lorraine pressed Play, and Art's message began again.

"Hey, baby. It's Arturo . . ."

Lorraine looked up at Barbie. Her head wobbled on her neck. Her eyes beneath her half-closed lids were glassy.

Barbie recovered and breezed into the room. "Hey, Rainey! Whatcha up to?"

Lorraine unsteadily watched Barbie's movements through the apartment. When Art's message had finished, she rewound the tape and played it again.

"Hey, baby. It's Arturo . . ."

Barbie walked up the three steps to the bedroom area and turned left into the hallway that was lined with closets. She slid open one of the doors and saw the fox in its zippered bag.

"You forgot your fur," Lorraine shouted.

Barbie reappeared. "I didn't forget it, honey. I was gonna get it when I came to pick you up. I just didn't want to drive around with it in my car."

Lorraine sloppily tipped bourbon into her glass. She raised the glass to her lips and sipped. "Buncha dead animal skins mean more to you than people."

"Well, Lorraine, that's an unkind thing to say. Especially when we're just about to start our new life. I made a reservation at the Mariah Lodge for the weekend. It's a very exclusive resort. We have their *best* room. It's a little cabin right on a cliff with the ocean below."

Lorraine's head swayed as she looked up at Barbie. "Our life? You mean, *your* life . . . with Ar-turo." She turned up the volume on the answering machine.

"We're gonna have a great life together . . ."

"I love you, baby," Lorraine mocked Art's voice. "We're gonna have a great life together."

Barbie marched down the three stairs and over to Lorraine. She bent over and clicked off the answering machine. "I *told* you about Arturo. The man just handed me fifty thousand dollars in cash. Isn't that worth a li'l 'I love you'? Huh? Isn't it? Words don't cost nothin'."

"Don't they? They cost me over thirty thousand dollars. The money you stole from me."

"I'll *give* you fifty. Okay? Then we'll be square."

Lorraine stood up. She staggered before she found her balance. "I told you before. Money's not enough." She slurred her words. "You promised me a life. And I'm gonna get it."

Barbie put her arms around Lorraine. "Sugar, that's where we're headed. What's got you so upset? I left you a note. Told you I had to run some errands. And here I am, back again."

"You weren't coming back. You took all your clothes. You just left the stuff you never wear anyway."

"Lorraine, you're never gonna be happy until you start to trust people."

"I saw the fur and I cracked up. I wondered whether you had the guts to come back for it."

"Honey, what in the world are you talkin' about? I packed up my clothes just to save time." Barbie looked at her watch. "Now let me help you pack your stuff so we can skedaddle outta here."

"What's your hurry, *Charlotte?*" She spat out the name. "I think we should have a toast first." Lorraine tottered to the kitchen and got a glass from the cupboard, knocking a second glass into the sink, where it clattered ominously but did not break.

Barbie nervously twisted her watch. She ran up the three steps to the bedroom, got Lorraine's suitcase from the closet, threw it open on the bed, and began haphazardly packing Lorraine's things.

Lorraine poured bourbon into the fresh glass, spilling some. She set the glass on the coffee table and leaned over to pick up her dirty glass from the floor. She lost her balance and stumbled into the coffee table, putting her hand on it to break her fall. One of the wobbly legs gave, toppling her, the full glass of bourbon, and a vase of flowers onto the floor.

Lorraine began to laugh. She clapped her hands and laughed harder and harder.

Barbie ran down the steps. She leaned over and tried to pick Lorraine up. "How much have you had?" She looked at the bottle. Most of it was still left. "You don't hold your liquor too good, do you?"

"I took a couple of magic pills."

"Good Lord." She tried to lift Lorraine. "Darlin', you have to help me."

"I don't care if I'm sick. I don't care if I die." She sat inert against Barbie's efforts. "I don't care if *you* die."

Barbie straightened up. "Now that's nice talk, missy."

Lorraine looked up at Barbie and laughed. "You're just so proper, aren't you? Just a nice Southern lady."

"Honey, we've got to go. Now!"

"What's your hurry?" Lorraine rolled onto her hands and knees and managed to stand up. She clawed at the hem of the cocktail dress, pulling it down, her lacquered nails leaving red welts on her legs. "Afraid Earl and Evelyn are gonna show up?"

Barbie paused, as if to make sure she'd heard right. "Your parents? Why would they come?"

"You're such a fucking liar."

Barbie winced at the vulgarity.

"I called them today, just to let them know their precious daughter was okay. Such a good daughter." Lorraine clawed at the fallen dress strap and pulled it onto her shoulder. "Was I surprised to find out I'd already called them this morning!" She slapped her thigh.

"You'd already called them? What do you mean?"

"You know what I mean." Lorraine pointed a swaying finger at Barbie. "You're good. You don't miss a beat. You're gonna teach me *everything.*"

Barbie looked at Lorraine speechlessly.

Lorraine clapped her hands and snorted through her nose as she laughed. "See what you get for fucking with fucked-up people?"

"Lorraine, I'm leaving."

"No you're not."

"You're too drunked-up to stop me." Barbie ran up the three steps, grabbed her fur from the closet, and ran back downstairs.

Lorraine held on to each side of the door frame, blocking it. "Go ahead. Leave."

"Get out of my way."

Lorraine smiled crookedly.

Barbie put the fox in its zippered bag on the floor and tried to pry Lorraine from the door. She didn't budge.

"You didn't realize how strong a crazy person could be, did you, Charlotte?"

Lorraine pushed Barbie backward. Barbie lost her balance on her narrow pump heels and toppled to the floor. She looked up at Lorraine.

"You afraid of me? Yeah, you're afraid. I've never seen you afraid. I kinda like it."

"What do you want from me?" Barbie whispered.

"I already *told* you," Lorraine said with exasperation. "I told my parents not to come. Doesn't mean they won't. So you're right. We'd better go now."

Barbie stood up and smoothed her clothes. "I'm going to the bathroom first. You'd better get changed and finish packin'."

Lorraine pulled the cocktail dress over her head. She stood nude in the middle of the living room floor. "What do you think? Who looks better? Art, Iris, or me?"

"Don't you worry yourself about Arturo and Iris. I'm done with them."

"If it wasn't for Iris, you might have stayed in Salt Lake. Huh? Wouldn't you?"

"Yes, if it wasn't for Iris, I would have stayed in Salt Lake. Of course. I'll be out in a minute." Barbie went into the bathroom and closed the door. A loud fan switched on automatically when she turned on the light.

"All Iris's fault. Miss Prissy-ass. Some people think they can get away with anything." Lorraine put on underwear, jeans, and a blouse.

The phone rang.

"Lorraine? It's Art." The remote phone amplified the sounds of the freeway.

"Arturo! Lover man!"

"Is Barbie there?"

"Uh-huh."

"Let me talk to her."

"Unh-nh."

"Why not?"

"Because she's done with you. Got it? And we're goin' away, on your money, honey. And Iris's too."

"What do you mean, going away? Let me talk to her!"

"You two had a hot time, but you should know one thing. She likes girls better."

Art handed Iris the phone. "I can't deal with this."

"Lorraine, it's Iris."

"I-ris. Little Iris. Hi, Iris."

"Where are you going?"

"To a cabin on a cliff where I'm gonna make her forget she ever saw you."

"Where is it?"

"That's for me to know and you to find out."

Barbie came out of the bathroom. "Who are you talking to?"

"Lorraine, let me talk to Barbie. Art! Watch where you're going!"

"Sorry, wrong number." Lorraine hung up.

Barbie looked steadily at Lorraine. Lorraine smirked back.

"Let's go," Barbie said. She pulled the incoming message tape from the answering machine and flushed it down the toilet.

In Art's car, Iris clicked off the remote phone. "She hung up."

Art sped around a corner, flinging Iris against the passenger door.

"Let's get there in one piece, okay?"

"Where are they going?" Art asked.

"She said a cabin on a cliff. It's probably the Mariah Lodge. That's where John was taking me on my birthday. Barbie knew that. She even ripped off my place."

"Where is it?"

"Las Pumas. About a four-hour drive. I'll see if she made a reservation."

Iris got the lodge's number from directory assistance and called the reservation office. "Hello, this is Iris Thorne. I'm calling to check on a reservation . . ." Iris looked at Art. "You have the Cabin in the Woods ready? How many nights did I say I was staying? Friday and Saturday. Great. Thank you."

She disconnected the call. "So I guess she's done with Barbie Stringfellow and now she's going to be Iris Thorne."

Art darted through the marina's street traffic, speeding down Via Marina and making a tire-squealing left on Tahiti Way. He parked in front of Barbie's apartment building, halfway on the sidewalk. He jumped out and ran toward Barbie's carport. Iris ran into the apartment complex.

The carport was empty. Art ran up the stairs to Barbie's apartment. Iris was knocking on the door.

"Barbie! Open up!" she yelled. She pounded on the door with her fists.

"Her car's gone," Art said.

"Shit!"

"Lying bitch!" Art pounded on the door.

"Art, she's gone!"

He kept pounding. Red imprints of the side of his palm appeared on the door. He'd split the skin on his hand.

Iris tried to grab Art's arms. He shook her off, then took a step back and charged the door with his shoulder.

"Art! She's gone!" Iris yelled.

"Bitch!" He charged the door again. "Whore!" The frame broke and the door flew open. Art's momentum carried him almost through the sliding glass door on the other side of the apartment.

Iris went inside and surveyed the broken coffee table, the spilled flowers, the bottle of bourbon, and the glasses. The phone machine was still on the floor, the hinged plastic lid over the tapes standing open.

"What a mess."

"Let's get out of here." Art ran out the front door.

Iris followed, pulling the broken door closed as best she could. Art was well ahead of her. He'd already started the car by the time she'd run down the stairs. She got inside the Mustang.

"We can catch her on the road or at that . . . lodge," Art said.

"Art, call the police about your money." Iris punched 911 into the mobile phone.

Art snatched the phone from her hand and disconnected the call. "I can't call the police."

"You have to."

"I can't let anyone know what happened. How can I let my family know what a fool I was?"

"Art! She stole fifty thousand dollars from you!"

"What about what she did to you?"

"What can I tell them? I don't have any proof about the mugging other than Lorraine having the key to my safe deposit box. Then they'll ask what was in the box. And I'll say, 'Oh, half a million dollars in embezzled money.' I'm sure. I'd be bounced out of the industry so fast my head would spin."

"How did you get that money, anyway?"

"That idiot John Somers. Alley left me an envelope with this cash in it. I tried to give it to John; he's the police, after all, and he goes, 'Just keep it. It won't get past the cops who process it.' That was a bad call all around."

Art drove back down Tahiti Way. "We have to get the money back ourselves."

"No. *You* should call the police, then we should both go home. Hell, let her have the dirty money. If it brings her one iota of the bad luck it's brought me, that'll be revenge enough."

"If she was after your half million, what was I? The hors d'oeuvre? The two-point bonus? I'm sorry, Iris, about how I went after Barbie with that nightclub idea. It was stupid, stealing your client for that. It was just ... all the sex and gifts and plans. ... She set me up."

"She set us both up. You know that first instant you set eyes on a person, that gut reaction? It's like the essence of them is there, if you just pay attention to it. My gut reaction to Barbie was, 'This woman's not for real,' then I spent the next four months convincing myself otherwise. Hell, it was real for a while. She gave us what we wanted. Then the bill came due."

32

BARBIE PULLED INTO THE MARIAH LODGE'S CIRCULAR DRIVE-way. Two well-groomed, fresh-faced young men wearing khaki pants, pink polo shirts, and webbed, military-style belts with shiny brass buckles ran up to each of the Mercedes's doors. The one who ran up to Lorraine's door stopped before opening it. Lorraine was leaning against the inside, asleep.

"I'll park it," Barbie said. "Just let her alone."

Barbie walked inside the high-ceilinged lobby, registered as Iris Thorne, and paid in cash in advance for two nights. Armed with a map of the grounds, she got back in the car.

Lorraine stirred. "Are we here?"

"Yes, ma'am."

Barbie drove down the gravel road that wound around the hotel grounds. The golf course was to their left, bungalows were well spaced from one another on their right, and the ocean was just beyond the bungalows. The road twisted and turned. At the end was a lone cabin surrounded by trees.

Barbie got out of the car, unlocked the cabin's door, and pushed it open. Still standing on the doorstep, she exclaimed, "Rainey, look at this! It's just beautiful! Charmin'!"

Lorraine got out of the car and stumbled inside.

Barbie went through the bungalow, opened the back door, and walked down a gravel path edged with rocks, which led from the doorway to the cliff thirty feet away. A sturdy wood fence coated with many layers of white paint bordered the cliff, keeping the blue-blooded guests from accidentally toppling into the surf during the black nights. Flowers grew in well-tended beds on either side of the path—gold marigolds, candy-striped petunias, pink vincas, blue salvia, and white and purple alyssum. A rustic wood patio table and chairs sat on the grass to the left of the bungalow. Pine, eucalyptus, and cypress trees surrounded it, the fragrance of the eucalyptus overpowering that of the other trees. The ground under the trees was littered with pine needles, pine cones, long, pointed eucalyptus leaves, strands of bark, and hard, round eucalyptus and cypress seed pods.

A few bungalows were clustered to the north. The lodge's main building was further north still. The tall trees hid the Cabin in the Woods from the rest of the complex. To the south was a state forest and wildlife preserve.

"Lorraine! Come out and see this."

Lorraine plodded out.

Barbie breathed in the ocean air. "Isn't this beautiful!" She pranced to the railed fence at the edge of the cliff and looked over. "Pretty far down there."

Lorraine followed her. "Maybe we can try to push each other off."

Barbie put her hand on her hip. "Is this how it's gonna be? You think we can at least be nice and enjoy this place?"

"How'd you find out about it?"

"Iris stays here."

"Of course. I-ris. I guess I have to hear about fucking Iris for the rest of my fucking life." Lorraine walked back inside the bungalow.

Barbie turned her back to her and continued looking out across the ocean. The sun was beginning to set and was sparkling the last light of the day across the surface of the water through breaks between the dark storm clouds that were moving inland.

"You can do this, Barbeh girl," Barbie said in a low voice to herself. She clasped her hands in front of her chest and squeezed her eyes closed. "You can free yourself from that terrible woman. You can!"

"Over there, I guess." Barbie heard Lorraine's voice from inside the bungalow.

Barbie walked back inside. A uniformed waiter had rolled in a cart with a bottle of champagne in a silver bucket, two cut-crystal champagne flutes, and a large platter of assorted fruit, cheeses, crackers, and rolls.

"The fruit and cheese platter is compliments of the manager, Mr. Stanford, for guests in our deluxe rooms. Shall I open the champagne now?"

"See what I got us, Rainey!" Barbie said brightly. "Please do."

He pulled off the cork with a pop, half filled the flutes, buried the bottle in the ice bucket, and wrapped a towel around the neck.

Barbie signed the check. "Say, could y'all bring us a bottle of bourbon and some ice and soda water?"

"Right away, Ms. Thorne." The waiter bowed and left.

Lorraine raised her eyebrows. "I'll put on her suit again if you want to pretend you're with her."

"Darlin', we've had our differences, but we're in this beautiful place. Let's enjoy it. To your health, sugar." Barbie raised her glass toward Lorraine.

Lorraine met Barbie's glass with her own. "And to yours."

"Umm-mmm. Isn't that good?" Barbie topped off her glass again and held the bottle out toward Lorraine. "There's nothing like good champagne. Just kind of tickles your mouth and eases on down."

"First you don't want me to drink and now you do. You trying to get me drunk so I'll pass out and you can split?"

"I just want to have a li'l celebration. Or are you gonna ruin our entire holiday?" She shoved the bottle back into the ice. "Why don't you put on somethin' more comfortable, Rainey? I'll unpack the car."

She went out to the car and brought in Lorraine's suitcase. Lorraine poured herself another glass of champagne.

"Help yourself, darlin'. Once it's open, it's just gonna go to waste."

Barbie went out to the car again and dug through the mound of garments. She returned with a purple silk blouse, jeans, cowboy boots, her purple chiffon and satin negligee, and her fur-topped, heeled boudoir slippers. She carried a small cosmetic bag under her arm. She casually tossed the clothes over a rough-hewn chair that stood next to the door. The chair's frame was made of varnished tree branches and it was upholstered in a fabric printed with a guide to horses that looked like a color plate from an old encyclopedia. Each drawing was labeled: Morgan, Tennessee Walker, Arabian.

Lorraine sat in a matching chair beside a small lamp table. Her legs were crossed; she swung the one on top. She finished the rest of her champagne and held the empty glass toward Barbie.

"More?" Barbie asked gaily.

"Yes, please."

Barbie refilled her glass.

"You didn't bring in very much stuff, Charlotte."

"I can't bring it all in. I've got so much, and it's not packed good."

"So you're thinking of cutting out on me in the middle of the night. You've had enough practice lately."

"Lorraine! Stop this, now."

Lorraine raised her hips from the chair and reached into her jeans pocket. She pulled out her hand and pointed her index finger toward Barbie. Barbie's car keys dangled from it.

Barbie put her hands on her hips. "You've been digging through my purse!"

"No, *darlin'*. You left them right here on the table." Lorraine raised her hips and shoved the keys back into her pocket. "Shouldn't matter, since you're not gonna need your car tonight anyway. Right?"

"That's not the point." She picked up the purple negligee. "It's the principle. You shouldn't mess with other people's belongings."

Lorraine started swinging her leg again and chewing on her nails. "Look who's talking."

"I'm gonna freshen up." Barbie took the negligee, slippers, and cosmetic bag into the bathroom.

The room service waiter knocked on the door again and brought in the bourbon, ice, soda, and two squat glasses.

After Barbie heard the waiter leave, she came out of the bathroom. She pirouetted in front of Lorraine in the purple negligee. "Remember how we were the last time I wore this?" She knelt on the ground in front of Lorraine, took the champagne flute out of her hand, and sat it on the lamp table. "Think how romantic making love's gonna be in a place like this."

She drew her finger down the side of Lorraine's face, unbuttoned her blouse, stood, and tugged on her hands. Lorraine got up. Barbie pulled the blouse out of her jeans. Lorraine pushed it off her shoulders and let it fall to the ground. Barbie kissed her neck. Lorraine held Barbie's head to her chest and leaned her own head back.

Barbie straightened up and licked Lorraine's lips. She looked at her with heavy-lidded eyes and murmured, "Why don't you get into that little pink thing I bought you?"

Lorraine picked up her suitcase and took it into the bathroom.

As soon as Barbie heard the door click closed, her eyes darted around the cabin. She spotted Lorraine's purse on the bed and ran to it, frantically pulling out different brown plastic prescription containers and looking at the labels.

She found the small blue tablets, opened the container, took out several pills, put them in the bottom of one of the squat glasses, and mashed them with the handle of the knife from the fruit and cheese tray. She poured in bourbon and soda and mixed it with the knife, holding the glass up to the light and swirling the liquid until the pills appeared to be dissolved. She dropped a few ice cubes into the glass, then set the drink on the lamp table. Then she made herself a drink, going easy on the bourbon.

Firewood and kindling were already arranged in the fireplace. She took a long match from a box next to the fireplace, struck a flame, and put it to the kindling. The dry wood caught easily and began snapping as it burned.

She plumped the pillows on the bed and lay back against them. She spread the negligee's layers around her and adjusted her breasts in the bodice so that they pressed against the sheer chiffon and spilled over the purple satin trim. She took a sip of her drink.

The bathroom door opened.

"Finally. I was gettin' lonely out here." Barbie abruptly sat up on the bed. "Where you goin'?"

Lorraine was wearing the slinky black cocktail dress with

black stockings and black high-heeled sandals. She'd done her hair and put on heavy makeup and red lipstick. "Out."

Barbie pouted. "I thought we were havin' a private party here."

"I'm tired of partying with you. You're a drag, Charlotte. All you do is order me around."

"At least have a drink with me before you go out. I made you one, over there on the table."

Lorraine picked up the bourbon and soda and took a sip.

Barbie crawled forward on her hands and knees on the bed. "Rainey. Don't leave me. You always hated to go out alone."

"I've gotten used to it since you left me. I might even get lucky." She took another sip of the drink, then set the glass on the nightstand next to the bed. "I could do better than you."

"Won't you at least finish your drink with me?"

Lorraine puckered her lips. "Tastes funny." She poured some champagne into the empty flute and took a sip. "Get the taste out of my mouth." She set the champagne flute back on the rolling cart next to Barbie's.

She walked outside. Barbie heard the Mercedes's trunk release. Lorraine came back in with the zippered bag that held the fox.

"What are you doin' with that?"

Lorraine took the fox out, threw the bag on the floor, and put the coat on. She modeled it for Barbie. "Looks good on me, doesn't it?"

"All right. Go ahead and wear it. But I want you to sit here and have a civilized drink with me first."

"I've already had enough drinks with you tonight." Lorraine picked up her purse, made a display of dropping Barbie's car keys inside, then swung open the cabin door.

"You shouldn't drive!" Barbie shouted.

"You know, it feels good to be in charge. Instead of sitting around letting life happen to me, I'm controlling what's going on. I guess I can thank you for opening my eyes. Things are going to be different for me from now on." She stepped through the doorway and reached back in to close the door behind her. "Have a nice evening." The door slammed closed.

Barbie picked up Lorraine's cocktail from the nightstand. White sediment had settled to the bottom. She put it down, threw herself against the plumped pillows, and crossed her arms across her chest.

Last call for alcohol was at two in the morning. Shortly before three, Lorraine stumbled back down the road to the bungalow. She wasn't alone. An executive on a weekend business trip had taken his tie off, rolled up his shirtsleeves, and spent a good portion of the evening on a bar stool next to Lorraine, trying to put his hands up her dress. They had many drinks. He insisted on walking her back to her room.

They were halfway down the dark gravel road.

"I can walk the rest of the way alone," Lorraine said.

"C'mon. Don't you want some company?" He put his hands inside the fox and jerked Lorraine toward him.

She tried to pull his hands off. She twisted and broke free of his grasp.

"C'mon, honey. In the bar you acted like you wanted some company." He lunged at her again.

Lorraine scampered away on heavy feet, unsteady in the high-heeled sandals on the gravel road. He easily caught up with her. He grabbed her again, and she walked backward into a hedge that bordered the road. He pushed her against it and slid his hands underneath her dress.

"Stop it!" she screamed. There was no one else on the lonely road.

He leaned on top of her against the hedge. The fox cushioned her against the sharp branches. She reached her hand down and felt the long wooden handle of a pair of garden shears left behind by a careless gardener. She twisted away, grabbed the shears, and snapped them open and closed in his direction.

He jumped backward. "Hey! Careful with those! Someone could get hurt!"

Again she pulled apart the long wooden handles and snapped them quickly together. "Yeah. You!"

He took a step toward her with his hand out. "C'mon, honey. Don't be that way."

She snapped the shears at his outstretched fingers.

He yanked his hand back. "Hey!" He examined his fingers to make sure they were intact. "Why, you . . ." He made a motion to grab the clippers, but Lorraine stepped out of his grasp.

"Okay, all right. I'm going." He turned and began to walk back down the road. "I don't need this shit."

After he'd rounded a bend, Lorraine continued walking. She held the shears by one of the long handles and dragged the blade behind her in the gravel, raking a path in the pebbles.

She finally reached the bungalow. A Do Not Disturb sign hung from the doorknob.

"Oh, fuck you, Charlotte."

Lorraine unlocked the door of the dark bungalow and went inside.

33

BARBIE STRINGFELLOW LAY IN BED ON HER BACK WEARING her purple negligee, as she had been for the past day and a half. Her lush figure pulled at the seams of the negligee's sheer chiffon and slick satin. She had a pleasantly surprised look on her face, but she had always had a cheerful disposition. A spring storm had blown through Las Pumas over the weekend on its way south and had kept the cabin cool and Barbie's body intact during the many hours that had passed since her murder.

Police Chief Charles Greenwood looked down at Barbie's body. He pulled a foil-covered chocolate Easter egg from the pocket of his suit jacket and offered it to his assistant chief, Jerry Kosnowski. Kosnowski shook his head, declining the offer.

"It's the good chocolate."

Kosnowski pursed his lips as if the idea were bitter to him.

Greenwood shrugged and peeled the foil from the egg with fingers that were as broad as sausages and the same rich, dark color as the chocolate. He popped the egg into his mouth and rolled it against his fleshy cheek, where it made a small bulge.

Kosnowski looked at Greenwood with amazement. "How can you eat?"

"It's chocolate."

"Looks like she liked chocolate a little, too. A little too much."

Greenwood slapped his ample belly soundly with both hands. "Careful." He walked around to the other side of the bed and scrutinized the body from that angle. "Did you notice that the little finger on her left hand's been cut off?"

Kosnowski walked closer to the bed and looked at Barbie's hand lying palm up next to her on the patchwork comforter. Her fingers were curled inward, as was the stump of red flesh and white bone where her little finger had been. Blood had pooled on the comforter under her hand. Kosnowski frowned, pulling together his overgrown brown and gray eyebrows and deepening the vertical folds down each side of his face. "Wonder where it is?"

Greenwood shrugged and began to peel the foil from another egg. "Probably turn up when we start digging around."

Kosnowski deepened his frown and walked to open the front door. "Isn't it stuffy in here?"

"When's the last time you've seen a homicide, Jer?"

"Never."

"But you've seen some pretty bad accidents out on the One-oh-one."

"That's different."

"This is nothing compared to when that guy used a shotgun on himself and his wife fifteen years ago. Boy, was that a mess."

"That's good to know."

Greenwood stood with his hands clasped behind his back

and his legs spread and looked down at the still pleasantly smiling Barbie. He shook his head sadly. "Lady, why did you come to Las Pumas and get yourself murdered? Just couldn't keep driving to the next town."

"Funny that the first murder in fifteen years wasn't between some drunks at Slappy Mack's but at the famous and elegant Mariah Lodge."

"I'm sure the irony won't be lost on Mayor Lou." Greenwood looked at the clock on the nightstand. "When's the county coroner getting here? Hope this doesn't take all day. I promised my kids an Easter egg hunt in the backyard."

"Maybe you'll find the finger."

"That's sick, man." Greenwood pulled two chocolate eggs out of his suit pocket and again offered one to Kosnowski.

Kosnowski accepted the offer this time. "See what happens when these L.A. people come up."

"Don't let His Mayorship hear you say that. That's the new plan. Bring 'em in and take their money."

It was midmorning. Sunlight streamed through the window on the cabin's eastern wall. The maid had discovered the body when she finally dared to enter the room, not having cleaned it on Saturday because of the Do Not Disturb sign on the door. Greenwood was paged at church, where he had been singing his heart out at the Easter Sunday service with his wife and three kids, all dressed in fluffy Easter clothes. His voice was a clear, ringing tenor.

He walked to a rough-hewn wood table standing underneath the window, his heavy-soled cowboy boots resounding solidly on the hardwood floor, and bent over to get a closer look at a pair of long-handled gardening shears leaning against the table, their point scratching the floor.

"Look. Blood." He drew his hands together quickly as if he were working the shears. "Snap! Good-bye, finger."

"Isn't it stuffy in here?"

"Man, had I known you had such a weak stomach, I wouldn't have hired you."

"It's about eleven years too late for that."

Kosnowski walked to the cabin's rear door and opened it, holding the sleeve of his regulation windbreaker over his hand.

Greenwood looked at a cloth-draped rolling table that held a platter of shriveling fruit and drying cheese, bottles of bourbon and club soda, squat glasses, an ice bucket, and a half-empty bottle of champagne. Two cut-crystal champagne flutes sat next to it. One had been drained dry, and the other held a couple of fingers of flat champagne. Both had lipstick marks on the rim. Greenwood matched the hot pink tone with the lipstick on Barbie's mouth. The other mark was red.

"Negligee, champagne, fire in the fireplace," Kosnowski said. "Looks like a seduction scene."

"And two lipstick marks."

"Maybe Ernie was up here, having one of his dress-up nights."

Greenwood shook his head. "Nah. Red's not his color."

Kosnowski looked down at the body. "Some set of hooters. Her and another chick. . . . Kinda different, huh?"

"Wonder if a woman strangled her?" Greenwood said.

"Why not? They want their equal opportunities. Maybe someone was hired to knock her off and took her finger as proof."

The phone rang. Both men jumped. It rang again. They looked at each other.

"I guess we should answer it," Kosnowski said.

Greenwood pulled a handkerchief from his pocket, shook it open, and wrapped it over his hand before picking up the phone. "Greenwood. Morning, Lou."

Kosnowski pulled the sides of his mouth down into a sour face.

"County should be here any minute. Driver's license says she's from down south." There was a pause. "I know the tourist season is coming. I know Mr. Yajima's concerned, but we're not turning this over to the county. Lou, the Las Pumas Police Department will handle it. I've got to go now. Happy Easter."

Greenwood hung up the phone and hitched up his pants by pulling on his hand-tooled leather belt, which fastened with a silver buckle inscribed with his three initials. He ran his hand down the shiny, bald path between the fringe of kinky black hair rimming his head. A few strands of gray were woven through the black. "That weasel. He's afraid of Mr. Yajima."

"Yajima?"

"The new guy the Kawashima Company sent over from Japan to run the resort. He's not a bad guy. But you know Lou Fox. Doesn't want to put off the deepest pockets in town. We're not turning this case over to the county. We can handle it."

"Can we?"

"Jer!"

"But Charlie, you need special skills for this."

"Baloney. I have more at stake than the county does. My family lives here."

"People would understand."

"My kids wouldn't understand."

Tires rolled on the gravel road in front of the cabin. Two sedans marked with the insignia of the San Luis Obispo County Sheriff's Department and a square truck with CORONER painted on the side stopped abruptly in front of the bungalow. Car doors were opened and slammed closed, and soon the quiet bungalow was filled with people and activity.

A thirtyish Asian-American man wearing Levi's, worn tennis shoes, and a T-shirt from Slappy Mack's, the local watering hole, got out of the coroner's truck. He jerked his head back to swing his overgrown, lank black hair from his eyes and waved a pair of latex gloves at Greenwood and Kosnowski.

"Hey, Charlie, Jer. Happy Easter."

"Coroner Kenny," Greenwood said. "I've had better ones."

Ken flicked his black hair out of his eyes again and pulled on the latex gloves. "Let's have a look." He walked over to the bed and lifted Barbie's head back, displaying the red and purple bruises around her throat. "No finger marks. Looks like it was done by a cord or something. Find it?"

"Nope," Greenwood said.

The noise and bustle accompanying the arrival of the county people had roused some of the lodge's guests, who were now creeping toward the cabin, looking both curious and afraid. A deputy sheriff was positioned outside the cabin to keep them away.

Ken picked up Barbie's left hand. "Hey! Check it out! Her pinky's gone. Gnarly. Who would have thought, here in sleepy Las Pumas?"

"Who would have thought?" Greenwood said, sounding annoyed.

"I guess times are changing on the central coast."

Greenwood hitched his thumbs into his belt. "Not this way. Not if I have anything to do with it."

34

THE LED DISPLAY ON THE TELEPHONE INDICATED THAT THE call was from outside the office. Iris reached to pick up the receiver without stopping her work. "Iris Thorne."

"Ms. Thorne, this is Charles Greenwood, the Las Pumas chief of police."

Iris set her pen on her desk and leaned back in her chair. "What can I do for you?"

"Did you know a woman by the name of Barbie Stringfellow?"

"She's a client of mine."

"I'm afraid I have some bad news for you. She's been murdered."

"Murdered?" Iris said softly.

"We found her body yesterday in a cabin at the Mariah Lodge up here. She had your business card in her wallet and made the room reservation in your name."

"What happened to her?"

"She was strangled."

"Do you know who did it?"

"We don't, ma'am. I'm coming to Los Angeles today. I'd like to meet with you."

"Of course."

"Is there anyone else down there who knew Ms. Stringfellow who I should speak with?"

"Well . . ." Iris worried the phone cord between her fingers. She pulled on it too hard, and the phone connection crackled.

"Ma'am?"

"I'm sorry. I'm a bit stunned. She was friendly with one of my colleagues here, Art Silva."

"Is he there today?"

"Yes. His extension is four-forty."

"Anyone else?"

"The only other friend of hers I met was a woman named Lorraine. She came to visit Barbie about a week ago and was staying at her apartment."

"Last name?"

"I never knew her last name. She said she was from Salt Lake City."

"Could she have been with Ms. Stringfellow at the lodge?"

"She could have."

"Did you know that Ms. Stringfellow was going out of town?"

"She told me she was going to Phoenix on business."

"When was the last time you saw her?"

Iris paused for a second and lied again. "Friday evening. Before she left."

Greenwood was silent, as if he were jotting it down. Suddenly he asked, "What does this Lorraine look like?"

"Late twenties, about five-seven, slender, short blond hair, blue eyes, light complexion."

"Thank you, Ms. Thorne. I'll be in town late this afternoon. Shall I come to your office?"

"I'd prefer that you came to my home in Santa Monica, if that's okay. My day ends early."

"I may call you again, if I have more questions."

Iris gave Greenwood instructions to her condo and hung up. She leaned back in her chair and swiveled it to face her western window. The storm that had pounded the central coast over the weekend was heading south. Dark clouds were moving quickly across the sky. Still looking out the window, she picked up the phone and punched in three numbers. The LED display showed A. SILVA BUSY.

Iris waited, swinging her chair back and forth. After a few minutes, she tried the three numbers again.

"What up?" Art answered.

"Did he call you?"

"Just hung up. Wow."

"Let's talk."

"Yeah, let's talk."

Iris spoke in a low voice, her mouth pressed close to the receiver. "Meet me in the stairwell. I'll go first."

Iris grabbed a manila file folder as a prop and left her office. She walked down the corridor past Art's cubicle, where he was filling in the grid of one of the many sales reports that Dexter now required from the investment counselors. After a minute or two, he got up and took a different route to the stairs. Iris was standing just inside the stairwell, among cigarette butts and Styrofoam coffee cups.

"I can't believe it," Iris whispered.

Art shook his head. "Unreal. Bitch got what was coming to her, though, huh?"

"I never wished this on her. Is this Greenwood guy meeting with you today?"

"Yeah. Iris, don't tell him about me and Barbie."

"He already knows you knew her."

"You know what I mean."

"Art, I'm not going to lie to the police."

"C'mon, Iris. I don't want anyone to know about the money. It'll get back to my family."

"They're going to find out sometime. The money's gone."

"I'm working on something to cover it up."

"What?"

"Iris, just mind your own business, okay?"

"No, it's not okay. This whole thing is my business."

Art ran his hands through his hair. "What about you? You want everyone to know about your safe deposit box?"

Iris sighed. "No. It was stupid to have kept that money

in the first place, but I don't want my career ruined because of it. Damn! You tell one lie, then you have to tell another to cover up the first one and then another . . ." Iris rubbed her forehead.

"What about this? We tell him everything. Everything about you, me, Lorraine, and Barbie except about the money. We'll just leave it out. It'll be simple."

"If we do it, we have to keep it simple. Okay. So where were we Friday afternoon?"

"You know where we were."

"C'mon. We have to get our story straight. I dated a homicide detective, remember? Greenwood asked if I knew that Barbie was going out of town. I told him she said she was going to Phoenix."

"You didn't tell him you knew she was going to Las Pumas?"

"I didn't want him to know what happened that afternoon."

"See, you've already lied to the police," Art said loudly.

"Shhh! I just didn't tell him the whole truth. That's not exactly lying."

"Now we're into the fine shades of definition."

"Art, are we going to stand together on this? Because I have half a mind to tell the cops everything. Even if I do lose my license, at least my conscience will be clear."

"Don't do this holier-than-thou thing with me. You're up to your neck in this too. Especially if they find out about the money."

Iris turned away from him in frustration and looked at the stairway's unpainted concrete wall.

Art spoke to her back. "Are you really willing to risk your securities license over some stupid mistake you made a year ago when you weren't thinking straight because your friend was murdered?"

Iris turned to face him. "Let's try it again," she said calmly. "Where were we Friday afternoon?"

"At work."

"But I already told Greenwood we saw Barbie on Friday."

"Why?"

"I don't know. I panicked. I was thinking someone could have seen us at her apartment." She threw her hands down. "This is exactly what I'm worried about. We have to get our stories straight. Let's try it again. Where were we Friday afternoon?"

"We went to say good-bye to Barbie. She said she was going to Phoenix." Art sat on the stairs. "We said, 'Bye, Barbie. Kisses. See you next week.' "

Iris sat next to him. "What if they ask Lorraine?" Iris was rubbing her palms together, over and over.

"It's her word against ours. Relax, Iris! Just tell the police to find Lorraine. She was so wigged out, she probably did it."

"You think so?"

"Sure. Or maybe it was someone we don't even know about. Who else did Barbie rip off?"

Iris stared at Art. "You went straight home after you dropped me off on Friday, didn't you?"

Art raised his upper lip indignantly. "What do you think? Straight home to my apartment. Didn't talk to anyone. What about you?"

"I went home, took a bath, didn't see or talk to anyone either."

"That proves we're in the clear. Two smart people like us would have at least lined up some alibis if we were going to murder somebody."

"Sorry, Art. I just . . . I don't know."

"Like you said, we have to stand together on this." He rubbed her back. "It's okay. So, after we saw Barbie, we drove back to the office. That's weird. Why drive all the way from downtown to Marina Del Rey to say good-bye, then all the way back?"

"It was a nice day and we felt like playing hooky from the office."

"Okay. Then we both went straight home, watched television, and went to bed. Got it?"

"Got it," Iris said. "What if Lorraine did do it? She didn't like us too much either. Kind of gives me the creeps, thinking of her on the loose."

"Does she know where you live?"

"No. Barbie never brought her by, thank goodness. Of course, my phone number's listed, but my address isn't."

"Same here. Don't worry about it. She probably went home to Salt Lake. What did that Greenwood guy sound like to you?"

"Like a big cowboy."

"That's what I thought. Great. He probably hates Mexicans."

Iris returned to the office first. Art waited a few minutes, then followed.

A couple of hours later, Greenwood called Iris from his car phone while he was on the road to L.A. and asked more questions about Barbie, Lorraine, and Art. Iris didn't mention the money and was relieved when Greenwood didn't ask her if she had any idea why someone would want to kill Barbie.

35

AFTER WORK, IRIS HEADED HOME ON THE WESTBOUND TEN, driving at a moderate speed and in a modest style. Her thoughts were elsewhere. She was conscious only of forward motion. After ten miles, she realized another vehicle was tailgating her. It was a power play. She tried to ignore it. The other vehicle was a pickup truck with two long-haired guys, both wearing baseball caps turned backward. The machismo level in a pickup truck with two guys exceeds that of a pickup truck with a single guy by a factor much greater than two.

Iris, exasperated, held up her hands, looked in her rearview mirror, and yelled, "Can't we just cruise in this city?"

They thought she was flirting with them and pulled next to her. She ignored them in a way befitting an ice princess.

Having a Generation x short attention span, they soon tired of her and moved on.

In the garage of her condominium complex, Iris opened the Triumph's trunk to take out its canvas cover. She saw the purple silk blouse twisted together with other garments headed for the dry cleaners, its color segregating itself ostentatiously from the polite grays, pinks, and blues of her work clothes.

She grabbed a corner of the blouse and pulled it out of the bundle, walked to the driver's door, opened it, and pulled hard on the hood release cable. She walked to the front of the car, the blouse gathered in her hand, freed the hood latch with her index finger, pulled the hood open, and fixed it in the air with a steel pole. She pulled out the oil dipstick and dragged it across the blouse, replaced the dipstick, pulled it out again, and checked the oil level.

She clasped the blouse over the cap covering the brake fluid, twisted off the cap, and checked the level. She checked the clutch fluid as well, then gently closed the Triumph's hood, which clicked back into place with a small snap. She walked to a large Dumpster, pushed up the lid, tossed the blouse in, then let the lid drop with a bang.

Inside her condominium, Iris threw a pile of mail onto the small lamp table in the entryway, put her briefcase on the floor next to it and her purse on top, then walked through the living room, her pump heels clicking when they connected with the hardwood floor, muted when she walked over the oriental rug. She opened one of the wood and glass French doors that led out onto her terrace, rattling the string of brass bells. A brisk breeze blew through the condo. She walked outside. The ocean churned troubled blue-gray waves in anticipation of the storm.

There were five messages on her phone machine. She listened to them as she moved through the kitchen. The first was from her mother, checking in. Iris took a hunk of cheese from the refrigerator and a carton of crackers from the cupboard. The second call was a hang-up. The third call was from Billy Drye.

"Have any news from Garland Hughes, Iris? No one rushed to rescue the two poor little girls?"

"Asshole!" Iris shouted in reply.

The fourth call was a hang-up. So was the fifth, but there was an angry noise as if someone had cried out and slammed the phone down.

"That's lovely! Very nice!"

Iris finished making a plate of cheese and crackers and distractedly put the cheese away in the cupboard and the crackers in the refrigerator. She grabbed a wineglass and opened the refrigerator again. She saw the crackers and opened the cupboard to put them away when she saw the cheese.

"You're losin' it, girl."

In her bedroom, she furiously tore off the pantyhose that she'd been wearing for thirteen hours, balling the legs inside one another and throwing them into the pile in the corner of the closet. She took off the rest of her clothes and hung them up.

"There's no purple in this closet!" Iris jammed the hangers onto the rod. "And no Barbie!" She jerked a blouse from the rod, put it on, and buttoned it. Her hands trembled. She tore a pair of jeans from their hanger. "Darlin', sugar, honey-pie. Liar!" After struggling, she managed to pull the jeans on but couldn't zip them up.

"Son of a bitch!"

She threw them into a corner of the closet. She looked down at her belly. She grabbed a big handful of flesh. She clutched her rear end. It seemed to go on forever.

"Dammit!"

She pulled another pair of jeans from their hanger.

"The faithful fat jeans."

To her dismay, they fit perfectly. She looked at the plate of cheese that she'd sat on the bed and the glass of wine on the dresser.

"Oh, hell."

She took them with her into the living room anyway.

"Okay, girl. Calm down. Relax. Deep breaths."

She sat on the living room sofa with her hands calmly folded in her lap and deeply inhaled and exhaled a few times. She clicked on the television. The programming took a news break and the shadowy, badly focused videotape of the black motorist being beaten by the baton-wielding policemen came on.

"Good God."

She clicked off the power.

The phone rang. It was the intercom downstairs; the police had arrived. She released the lock on the main door, put the plate and the wineglass in the refrigerator, smoothed her hair with her hands, and opened the door.

Two big men were standing there.

"Hello, Ms. Thorne. I'm Charles Greenwood." He held out his hand. Iris took it. It was big, soft, and warm, and the skin felt dry. Her nerves got the better of her and she giggled.

Greenwood looked at her curiously.

She giggled more. "Forgive me. I'm so sorry."

"Something wrong?"

She covered her face, still laughing, and tried to compose herself.

Greenwood exchanged a bemused look with the other man and said, "Sometimes people tell me I intimidate them, but I've never had anyone respond to me quite like this before."

"I'm so embarrassed." Iris wiped tears from her eyes. "I'm really nervous and upset and ... you don't look *any-thing* like I imagined." A couple more giggles escaped. "I apologize. How rude of me."

"It's okay," Greenwood said. "Cops affect people funny sometimes."

"I'm glad you're being so nice about it."

"I save my tough side for the hardened criminals in Las Pumas. You know, the speeders out on the One-oh-one." He winked at her. "Let me introduce Detective Tom Fillinger of the Los Angeles Police Department."

Fillinger was a tall, lanky man who had adopted a spread-legged stance to bring him down closer to the rest of the world. He had blond hair and pale eyebrows and eyelashes on freckled skin. The same pale hair covered the backs of his wrists and the tanned V of skin visible behind the undone top button of his shirt. Iris took Fillinger's hand. It was long and bony.

She invited them in and offered refreshments. Greenwood accepted a glass of water. When she came back into the living room, they were casually roaming around. She knew they weren't looking for anything in particular, they were just looking. John Somers did the same thing when he entered an unfamiliar room.

She seated them on the raw silk couch and herself on the more commanding wingback chair. She bounced her legs on her toes, then caught herself in the nervous gesture. She crossed her legs, casually dropped her hands in her lap, and slouched down a little in order to appear relaxed.

Greenwood took a small spiral-bound notebook and a pen from his inside jacket pocket, turned over some of the notebook's pages, and reviewed the facts gleaned from his two phone conversations with her. He occasionally took notes as Iris clarified a few points. Fillinger sat quietly with his long legs apart and his clasped hands dropped between them.

When Iris had finished her story, she let out a long breath. Her shoulders dropped.

Greenwood flipped back and forth through the notebook pages without speaking. He rubbed his face with his hand, the ample skin bulging through his fingers. Fillinger crossed his arms over his chest, leaned back in the couch, and waited.

Greenwood finally spoke. "Ms. Thorne, you said that when you first met Ms. Stringfellow, you wondered whether she was for real, but you were good friends at the time of her death. What made you change your mind about her?"

Iris pulled at a strand of loose skin on her finger. "I developed the business relationship because I needed her dough. She encouraged the friendship."

"Did you suspect her motives for doing this?"

"No. She'd just got in town and I was one of the only people she knew." Iris shrugged. "I met her at a time in my life when I needed a friend. She was a friend. I needed fun. She was fun. When Lorraine showed up, I started to reflect on my first impressions and wonder if they weren't right. Barbie seemed nervous after Lorraine arrived. I couldn't quite get a handle on their relationship, but I think they were lovers. A few days later, they were both gone."

"You didn't know Ms. Stringfellow had moved everything out of her apartment?" Greenwood asked.

"No." Iris hated lying to him.

Fillinger leaned forward with his elbows on his long legs. "A woman comes out of nowhere, enters your life, then leaves."

"Right."

"Why?"

"I only know what she told me."

Fillinger scratched his forehead. "Ms. Thorne, can you think of anything you said on the Susie Santé show that would make Ms. Stringfellow want to contact you?"

Iris's shoulders tensed. "Barbie just said she was impressed with me."

"Were you asked about the McKinney Alitzer murders?"

"Of course. That was the real reason they invited me. I have a videotape of the show I can lend you, if you're interested."

"Did they talk about the money that was never accounted for, the money that people accuse you of having?"

"Sure."

"Do you think Ms. Stringfellow might have thought you had the money or could lead her to it?"

"I don't follow this line of questioning, Detective Fillinger," Iris said brusquely. "Barbie Stringfellow was my client. She gave *me* money to invest."

Greenwood intervened. "Ms. Thorne, Barbie Stringfellow looks as if she could have been a con artist. We know she's not who she claimed to be. There was a Hal Stringfellow in Atlanta and he did own a restaurant and he did die last year, but he was a lifelong bachelor. One of Hal's employees, Jack Goins, bought the place after Hal died. He remembered a woman fitting Ms. Stringfellow's description working at Hal's for a brief time as a waitress a couple of years ago but she went by a different name. She left without warning one day and was never heard from again.

"A couple of years later, she shows up in L.A. as Barbie Stringfellow. She flashes lots of cash, cultivates a friendship with you and Art Silva, and is everything a good friend is supposed to be. I think she was biding her time until the right moment to strike. Question is, what was her plan?"

Iris shrugged.

"Did she ask you to invest in a business opportunity with her?"

Iris shook her head.

"What about the McKinney Alitzer million that's missing?"

"She asked me about that, but so does everyone."

Greenwood took a few notes. "What about Art Silva? Did she ask him to invest in anything?"

Iris looked down. "You'll have to ask him about that."

"You don't know or you don't want to tell us?" Fillinger asked.

Iris met his eyes. "I don't know everything that went on between Art and Barbie."

Greenwood flipped through the pages of his spiral notebook.

Fillinger stood. "Can you come to the station tomorrow and help an artist do a likeness of Lorraine?"

"Sure. But I can help you out there. She looked like me. People said we could have been sisters."

Greenwood looked up at Fillinger.

"It was uncanny," Iris said.

"Did Barbie ever come on to you?" Fillinger folded his arms across his chest, as if to protect himself from the thought.

"Barbie came on to everyone."

"Did you have a physical relationship with her?" Greenwood asked.

"No."

"But Art Silva did."

"I suspect so."

"You have no idea where Lorraine is? She hasn't contacted you?"

"Happily, no."

Greenwood chuckled and closed his notebook.

Iris smiled.

"One more thing." Greenwood reached into his jacket pocket and took out a small white cardboard box. He opened it, pulled off a square of cotton and showed the contents to Iris. It held several small pieces of jewelry. "Recognize any of these?"

Iris picked up an enameled brooch in the shape of an iris bloom. "This is mine."

"Was it a gift to Ms. Stringfellow?"

"No. She must have stolen it."

"Do you recognize anything else?"

Iris picked up a man's class ring. "This looks like Art's." She looked closer. "These are his initials." Iris put the jewelry back in the box. "I guess I can't take my pin back."

"I'm sorry," Greenwood said. "I'll send it back to you once the case is closed." He took a card from his jacket pocket and wrote a number on the back. "Here's my home number. Call me if you think of anything or if Lorraine contacts you."

"Thank you. I will."

Greenwood stood. Iris walked both of them to the door.

"One last thing," Greenwood said. "We have to ask you not to leave town for the next few weeks or to keep us apprised of your plans. We may have more questions or . . ."

"No problem," Iris interrupted. "Unfortunately, I've been through this before."

The storm rolled in during the night. The rain pounded against the windows in waves of greater and lesser intensity as the wind kicked up, then died down. Iris lay in bed and listened to it. She couldn't sleep.

She'd tried reading something dry. She'd drunk herbal tea, warm milk, then a shooter of Scotch. She'd turned the clock to the wall so she couldn't watch the illuminated display mark the minutes and hours of her insomnia. She finally got out of bed and pulled open a drawer of her jewelry box where the polished surface of the tablets that Lorraine had given her shone a bright robin's egg blue, like mysterious gems. She broke one in half and held the powdery edge to her lips, tasting its bitterness with her tongue. She hesitated, then put it back next to the other bijous.

She lay in bed another hour before getting up again and swallowing the broken pill half. Soon, she was sound asleep and slept until the phone rang.

"Bitch. Goddamn fucking bitch."

Iris struggled to clear the drug-induced sleep from her head. "What? Who is this?"

"Take a guess. Take a wild guess."

"Lorraine?"

"Who'd you think it was? Barbie?" Lorraine spat out the name.

"Where are you?"

"I'm on the road. In a phone booth. That's all you need to know."

"Are you going to Salt Lake?"

"What do you care? Barbie's dead. You must be happy now."

"That doesn't make me happy."

"Right. You fucked up everything between Barbie and me. If it wasn't for you, we'd be fine."

"Where are you?"

"You think I'm stupid or something? I know the score."

"What's the score?"

"Hello!" Lorraine shouted. Iris heard banging, as if Lorraine was hitting the phone receiver against the phone booth. "Hello! Earth to Iris!" She banged the phone again. "Hello!" She laughed hysterically. "You think everyone's stupid except you. You need a good spanking, that's what you need."

"Lorraine, I'm hanging up now."

The line went dead.

36

THE DAY AFTER CHARLIE GREENWOOD GOT BACK FROM L.A. in the wee hours, he rose later than usual. The marine layer that rolled in from the ocean each night still hung in the air, thick and white, filling the spaces between the pine and eucalyptus trees and settling in the streets and between the buildings of Las Pumas. Most Las Pumas mornings began this way. People spoke in subdued tones, stepped lightly, and moved slowly until the thick mist burned off around ten o'clock.

Greenwood drove to the Las Pumas police station. He turned onto Olivos Avenue, lost in thought, then suddenly punched the accelerator and pulled into the parking lot of Bowen's Hardware with squealing tires and brakes, surprising a group of teenage boys who were tagging the store's wall with cans of spray paint. They scattered when Greenwood jumped out of the car, but he managed to grab one, subduing the boy in his bearlike grasp and twisting the can of paint out of his hand.

"I been busted!" the boy yelled after his friends, who looked back, then kept running. "The hero got me, man!"

"Some friends you got there," Greenwood said.

"I'm down with my crew," the boy said with his bottom lip extended.

Greenwood started to release his grip on the boy, who tried to make a run for it. Greenwood lobbed his big hand onto the boy's arm. "Your crew's gonna be watching you cool your heels at the police station."

The boy twisted in Greenwood's grasp. "They're not rankers. They'll be back tonight to mob that wall. Seek and destroy."

"The only thing that's gonna be destroyed is the paint on that wall ... by you."

"No way! I'm not buffing my own tag."

"Are you going to get in the car or do I have to handcuff you?"

The boy looked up at Greenwood. "You really gonna make me buff my tag?"

"The whole wall, my friend."

The bravado passed out of the boy like the departure of a possessing spirit. He glanced at the small crowd that had gathered. "I'll get in the car."

Greenwood walked the boy to the passenger door and sat him inside. He started to back the car out. "What's your name?"

"Frisbee."

"What's your name?" Greenwood asked again with irritation.

The boy made a sucking noise of disgust and writhed his

head back and forth as if he were in pain. "Darryl. Darryl Thompson."

Greenwood pulled into the police station's driveway and parked in the lot in back.

The station was a 1960s-style white stucco, flat-roofed cracker box built to replace the original 1888 station a few blocks away, which was now a tourist attraction. Even though the current station had been built in the sixties, it was still known around town as the "new" station. The new station's sole external decorations were the two knee-high, brick flower boxes on either side of the front door, which Greenwood personally kept in bloom with seasonal flowers.

Frisbee spotted Barbie's red Mercedes convertible with the white leather interior. "Cool steel. But the red and white looks a little nigger. It yours?"

"That tore it," Greenwood said, picking up a leather portfolio from the front seat. "You're cooling your heels with us today."

"You can't do that. I have things to do. You're violating my civil rights."

"So sue me." He took the boy inside, pulled out a hard wooden chair, and pointed at it. The boy sat.

Greenwood handed him a piece of paper and a pen. "Write down your address and a phone number where I can reach your parents. Jerry, I caught this fellow spray-painting on Bowen's Hardware. Name of Darryl Thompson, aka Frisbee."

Kosnowski squinted at the boy, arching one of his overgrown brown and gray eyebrows, the skin above his eyebrow folding into the same shape. "Destroying private property, huh, young man?"

The boy copped a jaded attitude, looking bored and staring out the window.

"How was L.A., Charlie?" Kosnowski asked.

"I probably should have stayed another day, but I couldn't take it. The whole place feels like a balloon that's been blown up too tight. Got some good leads, but I might have to go down there again. Hi, Marion," Greenwood greeted the dispatcher on the morning shift, who sat in a glass-enclosed office.

"Better do it before that trial's over," Kosnowski said. "If they let those cops go after beating up that black guy, there's gonna be hell to pay down there."

Greenwood turned on a boom box that sat on top of a bookcase. Heavy metal music blared from it. "Officer Coleman changed my station again." Greenwood rolled the dial and located his sunny country station. A song twanged about love that was soon to be lost. "That's better. Hear back from your father-in-law over at the Highway Patrol?"

"Yep. There just might be a place for our Officer Coleman."

"That would suit our officer. He could carry a gun *and* drive fast." Greenwood unzipped his portfolio and took out a stack of papers. "I've got Barbie's phone bills."

"Anything interesting?"

Greenwood shuffled through the bills. "There's only four months of them. Lots of calls to Art Silva and Iris Thorne. One very interesting call. To Lorraine in Salt Lake City. About two weeks ago at three on a Sunday morning. I called the number and got Lorraine's answering machine. If it's not an emergency, you only call someone at three in the morning if you're sittin' around, maybe feeling a little lonely, a little sorry for yourself ..."

Marion leaned through her office window. "Or checking to see if someone's home."

"Or you're drunk enough to call an enemy," Kosnowski said.

Greenwood walked the phone bills to Kosnowski's desk, which faced his own. "Follow up for me?"

"Sure. What else happened?"

Greenwood described his meetings with Iris and Art. "Their stories jibed, almost word for word. It seemed a little too pat. I watched the video from the Susie Santé show this morning. Iris was fine, cool and calm, until that Susie Santé kept prodding her about the McKinney Alitzer murders. Then she lost it."

Marion leaned through her office window. "Charlie, you think this Iris is hiding that embezzled money somewhere?"

"I don't know. The important thing might be whether

Barbie thought she had it. Fillinger thinks Barbie was a con artist. If so, she was good enough never to get arrested."

"She only had about three hundred bucks on her," Kosnowski said. "Where's her booty?"

"Either the murderer robbed her or she's got it stashed somewhere." Greenwood took the small white box out of the portfolio and opened it. "Both Iris and Art are sticking with their story that they weren't conned. So why did Barbie take souvenirs?"

Greenwood scooped Art's college ring onto his index finger and held it toward Kosnowski. "Art looked at the jewelry a long time before admitting this was his. Said he'd given it to Barbie as a gift."

"His class ring?" Kosnowski asked.

"What every lady over the age of sixteen desires, right? But Iris admits that Barbie stole this brooch from her." Greenwood put the lid back on the box and set it on his desk. "Called Lorraine's parents. They haven't heard from her for a couple of days. Iris has. Lorraine called her last night and threatened her."

The station's back door opened and slammed closed. Heavy footsteps pounded down the corridor and turned into the kitchen. The refrigerator door opened.

"Putting away the sack lunch his wife made him," Kosnowski said.

The refrigerator door slammed closed.

"Man can't close a door without slamming it," Greenwood said.

The kitchen was quiet for a minute.

"Popping open his can of Coke," Kosnowski said. "Now he's gonna come in here and change your radio station."

Officer Coleman clumped down the corridor, holding a can of Coke Classic in his paw, mumbled "Good morning," avoided looking Greenwood straight in the eye, walked to the bookcase, and reached his hand toward the boom box's tuning knob.

"Anh, anh, anh," Greenwood warned.

Coleman made a face as he pulled his hand back. He flopped into a Naugahyde and chrome chair in the corner of the room; it squealed in complaint. Coleman was a big

241

guy, not overweight but thick, with a broad neck and heavy eyelids. He wasn't yet thirty. He'd carried his boyish squat nose and apple cheeks into adulthood. They were always sunburned.

"You're late again, Officer Coleman." Greenwood punched in the number that Darryl had given him.

Coleman sat in the chair with his legs sprawled out. He took a drag on the Coke. "Wasn't late, Chief. Was checking out a traffic accident up on the One-oh-one." He sucked on the can until it was empty, then crushed it with his hand.

"You should have called it in."

"Fender-bender. Wasn't nothing." He dragged himself out of the chair and started to clump back into the kitchen. He noticed Darryl sitting on the hard wooden chair. "Frisbee! What up, my man!"

"Hey, Coal-man," Frisbee uttered. "The hero busted me for tagging."

"Charles Greenwood. Las Pumas's long arm of the law."

"Your mom told me to let you sit there until she gets off work at five," Greenwood said.

"Five!" Frisbee protested. "That's all day!"

"If you can't do the time, don't do the crime," Kosnowski said portentously.

"Old fart," Frisbee said.

"Yep." Kosnowski walked to the coffee station, which was set up on a little table in the corner, and poured coffee into his mug, then held up a hot pot. "Tea?"

Greenwood shook his head.

Kosnowski walked back to his chair and set his mug on a windowsill stained with many brown coffee rings. He snapped open the *Las Pumas Star*. "Did you see today's paper? 'Progress Slow in the Purple Negligee Murder.' The guys down at the *Star* are having a field day with this."

"Did you see anything about the murder in the L.A. papers, Charlie?" Marion asked.

"Just a tiny article in the back of the first section. But over the weekend down there they had five drive-by shootings, busted a neofascist group that was planning on starting a race riot, and had a murder-suicide where a guy took out his whole family and the baby-sitter. Guess they had bigger fish to fry. But it's sure getting the press up here in the central coast."

Officer Coleman finished his second can of Coke, crushed it, and threw it in the bin Greenwood had set up for recyclable refuse. He stood up, stretched, and yawned expansively, displaying his dental work. "Think I'll go work the One-oh-one. Found a new hiding place, just past the Mariposa off ramp."

"Good," Greenwood said. "The city can use the revenue."

The station's front door swung open and Mayor Luther Fox came in carrying a flat of strawberries. He was wearing golf pants in a pink and lime green plaid and a lime green knit shirt. His year-round tan had grown deeper during the few days of spring sunshine they'd had before the storm had rolled in, especially on top of his bald head, where his remaining white hair was combed down into a neat fringe around the perimeter. Mayor Fox's midsection was flat and smooth but had an overstuffed look. There was speculation around town that he wore a girdle.

Mayor Fox slid the strawberries onto Greenwood's desk without asking permission and began to speak without a greeting or preamble. "Ken over at the county coroner's office asked me to give these to you. His family owns that strawberry ranch in Arroyo Grande."

"I'll have to call and thank him," Greenwood said. "Officer Coleman, would you mind putting these in the kitchen on your way out?"

Officer Coleman picked a big strawberry off the top and took a bite. "Delicious," he said with his mouth full. He grabbed the shallow, square box under one arm and walked toward the back of the station.

Mayor Fox handed Greenwood a copy of the *Las Pumas Star*. "I imagine you've seen this. I was just over at the senior citizen's center and they're very upset that this Lorraine person is on the loose. They didn't retire in Las Pumas to be terrorized by a murderer in their midst."

"Lou, Lorraine is long gone from Las Pumas," Greenwood said. "And the only one she's terrorizing is Iris Thorne. There's an all points bulletin out. We'll get her."

"Before our reputation as a safe community is ruined?

That reminds me, Mr. Yajima would like you to remove that blasted police ribbon from the Cabin in the Woods. The tourist season is starting. Certainly there's no further need to keep it roped off."

"I will, just as soon as I determine there's no further evidence to be found."

"I want that police ribbon off that bungalow. Remember, I still write your paycheck, and I can still turn this investigation over to the county. I'll expect to hear back from you later today." He turned on his heel and stomped out the front door, closing it solidly behind him.

"Well, I guess I've got my orders," Greenwood said.

"I'll get started on these phone bills, Charlie," Kosnowski said.

"I want to go home," Frisbee wailed.

"Okay, Darryl. I'll drive you to school. But we've got a date Saturday morning to repaint that wall."

37

GREENWOOD WALKED ACROSS THE MARIAH LODGE'S FLAG-stone lobby, past the Navajo rugs decorating the walls, in search of the lodge's manager, whom everyone called Mr. Stanford and only Mr. Stanford. No one in town knew anyone who addressed Mr. Stanford by his first name.

The concierge told Greenwood that Mr. Stanford was making his rounds, greeting guests as they breakfasted in the restaurant. It was a display of the personalized attention that had helped the lodge earn its three-star rating in a respected travel guide. In Mr. Stanford's ten years at the lodge, however, try as he may, the distinguished four-star rating had eluded him.

The restaurant had an outside deck. Lodge guests sat at

stylish, pale wood tables and chairs, lingering over coffee and enjoying the spring flowers that bloomed in the well-tended flower beds and the ocean spray released by the crashing waves below. Polo shirts, khaki, and madras plaid abounded. In the evening, the guests dressed for dinner and the deck was lit with candles. If a gentleman was not wearing a jacket, one was provided.

Greenwood spotted Mr. Stanford standing next to a table between a seated man and woman, a hand on each of their shoulders. He was smiling broadly, laughing pleasantly and sincerely. His smile faded slightly when he saw Greenwood. Greenwood took a step toward him but stopped when Mr. Stanford held up his index finger. He left his guests, and walked quickly toward Greenwood. He placed his hand against Greenwood's back and kept walking, steering him out of the restaurant and away from any guests.

"Good morning, Chief Greenwood," Mr. Stanford said, smiling tightly. "Thank you for coming by." He was middle-aged and from one of the neighboring central coast towns but his mannerisms had an old-world quality. He had affected a British lilt in his speech. "Let's talk over here so that we don't alarm the guests."

"Alarm the guests?"

Mr. Stanford looked intently at Greenwood. "You're a popular figure in our city, Chief Greenwood. I'm sure you're more notorious than you realize. In a positive way, of course."

Greenwood looked over his shoulder at the restaurant to confirm his suspicion that there were no blacks either dining or serving.

They reached Mr. Stanford's office. He closed the door behind them and sat at his desk. Greenwood remained standing.

"Mayor Fox has told you that we would like to remove those crime scene seals from the door of the Cabin in the Woods and"—he shook his head as if he were smelling something distasteful—"get rid of that yellow police ribbon around the outside." He lowered his voice to a whisper, even though they were alone. "It's upsetting the guests. You understand."

Greenwood nodded and lowered his voice to match. "I

understand completely. I'll make a determination today whether we need to leave the area sealed a bit longer or not."

Mr. Stanford pulled his lips into a tight line. "A bit longer?"

"It wouldn't be more than a few more days."

"As you will, Chief Greenwood." He picked up a pen, directed his attention to the papers on his desk, and spoke to Greenwood without looking up. "Please don't disturb the lodge guests."

Greenwood had been dismissed. He opened his mouth to make a retort but closed it again and left the office.

Most of the lodge's guest rooms were in the main building, but there were several free-standing bungalows nestled in the forest. They were well-spaced, with dense pine, cypress, and eucalyptus trees between them and were not visible from the road that traversed the lodge grounds.

Yellow police ribbon was pulled around the base of the trees encircling the Cabin in the Woods. Greenwood ducked underneath and walked up the path leading to the bungalow's front door. Two well-fed squirrels sitting at the base of a tree rolled onto their hind legs as Greenwood approached. They were used to the lodge guests and watched Greenwood with curiosity rather than fear. A jaybird in a nearby tree scolded him. Other birds sang gaily. The morning air was crisp. It was a beautiful day.

Greenwood took a small penknife from his pocket and slit the block of yellow adhesive paper that warned, CRIME SCENE. DO NOT ENTER. He pushed the door open.

The air did not smell of death; it merely smelled stale. The body was gone. Barbie's clothes and other effects were gone. So were the champagne glasses, the fruit and cheese platter, and the gardener's shears. All that remained was the bare mattress stained with a small circle of blood from Barbie's severed finger: a macabre chocolate brown Rorschach test. Even though the remnants of the crime had been removed, the atmosphere retained an uneasy tension, as if the walls had absorbed the horror that had transpired therein.

Greenwood took a perfunctory look around, then dropped to his hands and knees and looked under the bed. He lifted the braided rag rug and had a peek underneath. He walked into the dressing area off the bedroom. There was a small refrigerator on the floor. He opened it, knowing it was empty.

He walked into the bathroom. All the used towels had been bundled up and packed off to the county crime lab. They had found blond hairs that presumably belonged to Lorraine, and particles of vomit.

"Nothing here," Greenwood said to himself. "Guess they can have their room back."

He unlocked the back door and walked outside, inhaling the storm-cleansed air, trying to shake the bungalow's atmosphere. The ground had been raked clear of needles, cones, leaves, and seed pods. The fine dirt displayed the even marks of rake tines.

Greenwood walked out to the cliff, leaned against the sturdy wooden fence that bordered it, and looked down at the surf crashing on the rocks a hundred feet below. To his right, he could see the main building where gulls circled the deck. A guest threw bits of food to the gulls, who expertly snatched them from the air.

Greenwood sat on the ground and slid his legs underneath the fence so that they dangled over the edge of the cliff. He leaned his upper body against the fence and watched the ebb and flow of the surf below, hypnotically flowing in and out. He sat for several minutes, feeling the warm sun on the back of his head and neck, listening to the gulls cry, watching the water, until a busy trail of black ants caught his eye.

They marched in a dense line across the ground on his right. Their destination was the underside of a flat rock that lay on the slope a bit beyond the fence before the cliff dropped steeply. Greenwood watched them industriously working. He drew his finger in the dirt across the ant trail, careful not to mash any of them. The ants paused at the schism, then started running wildly in larger and larger circles. Before too long, the trail had been repaired and the traffic flowed smoothly again. Greenwood smiled.

He held on to the fence with his left hand and slid his rear on the ground until he was closer to the rock that was the source of the ants' attention. It was flat, about a foot long and six inches wide, with an uneven bottom edge that tipped away from the ground. He stretched to reach the rock and managed to get his fingertips underneath the edge. He flipped it over and watched it roll down the cliff, gathering speed, until it finally bounced into the ocean with a satisfying splash.

Underneath the rock was something that looked like a small mouse. Ants swarmed over it. Greenwood watched with interest. He found a twig on the ground and poked it, scattering the ants. He poked it again and then saw a hot pink fingernail and almost lost his balance. He slid down the cliff, holding on to the fence with his left hand, his back almost flush with the ground, and gingerly grabbed the finger. Ants crawled up his arm and over his pants. He flung the finger behind him and quickly pulled himself up with both hands on the fence rail. When he was standing, he started swatting at ants that crawled over him.

A sea gull who saw the commotion from the air landed and began walking toward the finger, which had fallen about ten feet behind Greenwood. Greenwood ran at the bird, waving his arms and shouting. The bird hopped a few feet away and stood his ground and was soon joined by another.

Greenwood pulled out one of the Ziplock bags that he had shoved inside his pocket before he left the police station and closed it over the severed finger, which still had ants crawling on it. He shook his hand, trying to shake the ants off, then slapped one hand against his pants, changed the bag to the other hand, and slapped the free one. He walked quickly back to the bungalow, holding the closed bag away from his body, and stepped back down the road toward the main building, slapping his legs and shaking his arms. A curious gardener watched him. Greenwood stopped and looked for the ants that he was certain were covering him. There was nothing there. He nodded to the gardener with dignity and kept walking.

He stepped into Mr. Stanford's office, who looked at him with a patronizing smile.

"Mr. Stanford, I'm sorry to say that the bungalow has to remain blocked off for another few days."

"Chief Greenwood, this is unacceptable."

Greenwood took a step closer and held the bag toward

him. Mr. Stanford gave the bag a look of irritation that changed to horror.

"I've found some more evidence there. I can't take the risk of disturbing the area."

"Where was that?" Mr. Stanford pointed a reproving finger at the Ziplock bag.

"On the cliff, underneath a rock."

Mr. Stanford leaned heavily back into his chair.

Greenwood left the building and chuckled to himself on the way to his car. He got in on the driver's side, then got out, unlocked the trunk, dropped the finger in, and gingerly closed the trunk lid over it, putting a safe distance between himself and Barbie's extremity.

38

LORRAINE'S HEAD BOBBED WITH THE MOTION OF THE BUS. SHE slept, dreaming she was at work at the insurance company in Salt Lake City. The office smelled of diesel fumes, like a bus. She brought a medical claim up on her computer screen and determined whether to pay, suspend, or deny each line item. Claim after claim rolled before her. She should have paid some but denied them all. Then she was at the front door of her apartment. She unlocked it, and Spooky, her cat, ran out. She called, "Charlotte! You home? Charlotte!" as she walked through the apartment. In the bedroom, she saw the empty closet. She ran out of the apartment and saw Spooky run into the path of an oncoming car.

Lorraine started awake. It was bright sunshine outside. The bus drove through a landscape of low hills covered with tender spring grass, yellow wild mustard, and California golden poppies. The pollen made Lorraine sneeze. She got up and went into the bathroom of the rolling bus. The toilet seat and floor had been fouled with drops of urine from careless fellow travelers. She knelt down on the false floor and hung her head over the toilet and vomited. She staggered back to her seat, opened her purse, took out one of her many plastic prescription bottles, removed four pills, and swallowed them with diet cola from a can that sat near her feet. She picked up the package of Twinkies next to the soda, ripped it open, ate half of one, then put the remaining half back into the package.

She craved dense unconsciousness but began to dream again as soon as she fell asleep. She was dressed in high heels, glittery stockings, and a tight, shiny tube dress. Purple. She was with Charlotte at the bar where they had first met. Charlotte had taken her to have her nails done that day, and the porcelain felt thick and odd on her fingers but gave her hands a seductive length that she couldn't stop looking at. She and Charlotte danced, and the other women watched them, and Lorraine felt conspicuous and uncomfortable and excited and sexy all at the same time. Charlotte ran her hands down Lorraine's hips in the tight dress and Lorraine became aroused.

Then she was at the bar and her friend Barbara's face was close, looming in front of her eyes, blocking out everything else, and she was saying, "Something about her I don't like. There's something about her . . ." over and over again, and Lorraine was fascinated with the fine vertical lines in her lips. Then Lorraine's father's face was in front of her. Lorraine stared at the large pores across his nose. He had his big hand around her thin wrist. She tried to twist away from him but he held tight, hurting her, calling her names, telling her to leave, that she wasn't welcome in their Christian home. Then he started pulling off the porcelain fingernails, leaving her own fingernails torn and bloody underneath.

Then his hand turned into Charlotte's. She was lying on her back in bed wearing a purple negligee of sheer chiffon and slick satin. She was pulling Lorraine toward her, saying, "You'd do it if you loved me, darlin'. Show me you love me." Then Lorraine was holding gardening shears. She snapped the shears closed, and Charlotte's finger flew in an arc onto the floor.

"Hey," a voice said. "Hey, lady."

Lorraine started awake. A young man with goofy long hair that stood at a forty-five degree angle from his head was shaking her shoulder.

"Hey! You all right? You were moaning. You must have had a major dream."

Lorraine pushed her damp hair out of her face. Her forehead was slick with perspiration. "Yes. I'm fine."

He looked at her curiously, then returned to his seat across the aisle.

Lorraine shook her head, trying to shake the dream from it. She sneezed at the pollen in the air, her hand working a diamond and sapphire ring on her finger. She became aware of the action and released the ring as if it were hot. She reached for the can of cola near her feet and jumped when she saw a porcelain nail on the floor next to it. Another lay on top of the Twinkies package. Another was in her lap. She looked at her hands. Two others dangled from her fingers. Her own nails were bloody and torn. She covered her face with her hands and began to sob.

39

CHIEF CHARLES GREENWOOD WAS STUDYING THE COLORFUL plastic-topped push pins scattered across a large map of California that hung against a wall of the Las Pumas police station. Each pin pierced a small flag of paper that had a date and time scribbled on it. A hand-lettered sign was tacked above the map: LORRAINE SIGHTINGS.

"Another call for you, Charlie," Marion said from behind her glass-walled dispatcher's office. "Newspaper."

"I'm not talking to any more of those people. We're trying to get some work done here."

Jerry Kosnowski was seated at his desk, talking on the

telephone to someone who reported seeing Lorraine. "Thanks for calling. Bye-bye." He hung up the telephone. "This one's in Chula Vista, Charlie. Way down by the Mexican border."

"The last one was up in Humboldt County. Now, how the hell could she get from the Oregon border to the Mexican border in half an hour?" He looked at Kosnowski accusingly.

Kosnowski raised his hands. "I don't know, Charlie. I'm just taking the calls."

Greenwood grimaced. "I'll mark it down. Notify the Chula Vista authorities."

They heard the back door screen open and slam closed. Heavy footsteps started down the hallway, then veered left into the kitchen. The refrigerator door opened and slammed closed.

"Coleman!" Greenwood bellowed. "You break that GD door and you're going to be buying the department a new refrigerator!"

The heavy footsteps approached the front of the station. Officer Coleman loomed in the doorway. His pug nose had grown even more sunburned during the week of bright sunny weather they'd had since the storm. He dropped heavily into the Naugahyde and chrome chair, which squealed in protest, took a long drag on his can of Coke, half emptying it, then held the can in his big paw against the chair arm. "You've got a bug up your butt today."

Greenwood shot a glance at Coleman over his shoulder. "Where've you been? What've you been doing?"

"Following up on that purse-snatching down on the Embarcadero."

"That's all?"

"C'mon, Greenwood, get off my case. Someone has to be the law in this town. Alvarez and I are the only ones out there. You two are spending all your time trying to catch Looney Lorraine. By the way, Mayor Fox wants to know what's taking so long. He gave me an earload when I cruised by the golf course this morning."

"His Mayorship can go F himself. It hasn't even been a week yet."

"GD this and F that," Kosnowski said. "That's more profanity than I've heard you use in eleven years, Charlie."

"It's going to get worse before it gets better," Greenwood said.

The front door of the station opened, and Mayor Luther Fox came in carrying the latest edition of the *Las Pumas Star*. He waved it at Greenwood.

"We saw it, Lou."

Mayor Fox read the headline anyway. " 'Hunt Still On for Purple Negligee Murderer.' "

Officer Coleman stood up and took the paper from Mayor Fox. "Hey! Check out this picture of Lorraine. She's a babe. That artist's rendering they had before made her look like a douche bag."

"They quoted Iris Thorne in there," Kosnowski said. "Did you see it, Charlie?"

"I haven't had time to read the whole GD paper! What does it say?"

Coleman read aloud, " 'Investment counselor Iris Thorne, Barbie Stringfellow's money manager, had met Lorraine Boyce socially on several occasions. Thorne described Boyce's behavior as nervous and erratic. When asked whether she thought Boyce could have murdered Stringfellow, Ms. Thorne had no comment.' "

"Lorraine's our murderer, all right," Mayor Fox said. "And the public wants to know when she'll be apprehended."

Greenwood held a push pin above the map. He turned to look at the mayor. "Lou, it's only a matter of time. Furthermore, Lorraine is only a suspect. We just want to question her."

"If she didn't do it, why is she on the run?"

"Maybe she's afraid."

"She's afraid, all right. Afraid she'll go to the gas chamber. Keep me posted." Lou Fox walked out of the station. The door closed by itself behind him, then suddenly swung open again. He poked his head back inside. "Did you hear? The verdicts are in."

"Verdicts?" Greenwood said.

"The four LAPD cops. The beating."

The room fell silent as everyone looked at Mayor Fox.
"What happened?" Kosnowski finally asked.
"Four acquittals."
"Oh, shit," Greenwood said.

Lorraine stood in the women's restroom of the San Jose bus station and examined herself in the mirror. Her image doubled and looped back over itself. She ran blood-caked fingers through her uncombed and greasy hair as she studied herself with trancelike detachment. The elegant, antique sapphire and diamond ring looked out of place on her battered and dirty hand.

Other women were using the restroom. They hurried to finish their business when they spotted Lorraine.

She unzipped her purse, dug her hand around the many prescription containers, and located a penknife. She pulled the blade from its casing and held it near her face. She lifted a hunk of hair and sawed the knife through it, dropping the hair on the floor. She cut off another hunk and another until she'd hacked all her hair off and the stubble jutted irregularly from her head.

She kneeled on the dirty hexagonal white floor tiles, opened her suitcase, and took out the slinky black cocktail dress. She pierced it with the knife, then pulled the opening with her fingers, the fabric singing as she tore it in two. She couldn't tear the black leather miniskirt, but she was able to stab holes in it and in the mock turtleneck sweater. She gashed the patent leather of the strappy sandals. She pulled a long, purple satin sash from her jeans pocket and pulled it from end to end between her hands, savoring the cool, luxurious fabric. She put her foot on one end of it, held it tight with her hand, positioned the knife over it, then changed her mind and released her grip. She rubbed the satin against her face and nose, inhaling deeply.

She dropped the sash and took out Iris's cobalt blue suit. She pulled off her jeans and pulled on the skirt, tucking her sweater into it, put on the jacket, picked up the purple sash, and shoved it into a pocket.

She gathered the ruined clothing, unsteadily straightened up, and shuffled to a large, open trash bin standing next to the wall. She lifted the bundle and positioned her arms over the top, then abruptly dropped the clothing. Some of it landed in the bin, but mostly it fell around her feet. She reached into the bin and grabbed the image of her own face. She opened the newspaper.

"Nervous! Erratic!" Lorraine smashed the newspaper, crumpling it into a ball, covering her already bloody hands with newsprint. She slammed it into the trash can.

Greenwood and Kosnowski made the half-hour drive to the San Luis Obispo bus station just before the bus that Lorraine was suspected to be riding pulled in for its scheduled stop. Many city and county law enforcement personnel, many more than were necessary to apprehend the presumably unarmed Lorraine, were already in place, hiding behind parked buses and cars and in the station so as not to make Lorraine or the other passengers suspicious.

The ticket agent at the San Jose bus station, about a three-hour drive north of San Luis Obispo, reported that a disheveled and disoriented woman matching Lorraine's description had bought a one-way ticket to Santa Monica. When the torn clothing and hunks of hair were found, Greenwood grew confident that he had his woman.

The bus driver had already made one scheduled stop before the police radioed their information. However, the driver always kept count and knew that all the passengers who were continuing through had returned to the bus. He insisted that there was no one on the bus who matched Lorraine's description. The police assured him he was mistaken and told him to get off the bus with the other passengers in San Luis Obispo.

Mayor Luther Fox had illegally parked his late-model Cadillac in the bus loading area. The car's silver color was flattering to his remaining fringe of silver hair. He briskly approached Greenwood and Kosnowski.

Greenwood dully greeted him. "Hi, Lou."

Mayor Fox rubbed his hands together and surveyed the scene. "Looks like we got our murderer, huh? Good news for the citizens of La Pumas."

"It ain't over till it's over," Greenwood said.

"But she's on the bus."

"We suspect she's on the bus."

Kosnowski nudged Greenwood's thick waist. "Here it comes."

The bus rolled in, emitting diesel fumes. The manual transmission gears thudded dully. The hydraulic brakes gasped. The bus let out a final shudder and sigh before it stopped. The front door accordioned open. The bus driver was the first one off. The other passengers slowly filed out and were quickly ushered into the bus station.

Greenwood kneaded the fleshy skin on his face and strained his eyes, peering into the face of each passenger. After the last one had disembarked, he looked at Kosnowski, and Kosnowski looked back.

"Where the hell is she?" Mayor Fox said, walking in double time toward the bus. A San Luis Obispo police officer restrained him before he could board it.

Several officers were already on board, checking the restroom and looking under the seats. One of them came out and stood in the open doorway. "Empty," he said.

40

WORD OF THE LAPD VERDICTS SPREAD QUICKLY THROUGH the McKinney Alitzer suite. There was a television in the conference room where Iris and Art joined the other employees.

Daytime programming was preempted by breathless local news broadcasts that shifted from event to event as the city began to come apart. An angry crowd gathered at the LAPD headquarters' bulletproof doors, just blocks away, and shouted, "No freedom! No justice!" in the faces of square-jawed cops in riot gear. Mobs pulled motorists from their cars and beat them senseless. Stores were looted and burned. Police disappeared into the mass of the city like rainfall in the ocean. Firefighters were shot at by snipers. Vigilante citizens stood in front of their businesses with firearms, demonstrating the extent to which the population was armed.

Panic set in among the McKinney Alitzer employees worried about children who were still at school and loved ones at work throughout the city. Herbert Dexter sent everyone home.

Iris rushed to retrieve the Triumph and queued up to get on the freeway, feeling conspicuously white and well dressed. The freeway became a kind of demilitarized zone, above the turmoil of the streets below, but it still suffered from its own type of anarchy implemented by motorists who, realizing the cops were deployed elsewhere, drove as recklessly as they wished. From the vantage point of the Ten, Iris spotted flames across the city.

In Santa Monica, there were lines at the gas stations and supermarkets. Everything was closing early due to the dawn-to-dusk curfew. Everyone wanted to get the hell home. Iris managed to get cash from an ATM machine and gas but gave up on food.

When the evening drive time finally arrived, the streets were eerily clear.

At home, Iris ventured onto her terrace. Police helicopters beat the sky. The air smelled of smoke. Gray ash settled everywhere. The ocean glowed a troubled copper, and the sun shone red. Disoriented birds flitted every which way, looking like windblown scraps of fabric.

She secured all her doors and windows and sat in the middle of her living room floor in her bathrobe with a wooden baseball bat across her knees, the remote control at her side. She ate a Sara Lee butter pecan coffee cake with her fingers while she watched the city burn on eight local and many cable channels.

Night fell. Sleep was out of the question.

News helicopters gave bird's-eye broadcasts across the city. Julie's, the street-level bar in Iris's office building where Iris had often dined with John Somers, was ablaze. In Mid-Wilshire, a man had been shot to death in a supermarket parking lot near Iris's first apartment. In Hollywood, the pink granite and brass-inlaid stars along the Walk of Fame were crisscrossed with fire hoses. Frederick's of Hollywood, a favorite Saturday night stopping point for Iris and her college friends, had been looted of its fur- and feather-trimmed lingerie. A fire burned out of control nearby, threatening Frederick's garish purple tower, which now seemed precious. The camera caught a glimpse of Musso and Frank Grill, the venerable old-Hollywood eatery down the street from Frederick's where Iris had dined after her high school prom.

Firefighters were guarded from snipers by the police, both uniformed and plainclothes. One plainclothes officer stood in the middle of Hollywood Boulevard with feet firmly apart, a shotgun held in both hands, his eyes scanning the street. The camera took a closer look. It was John Somers. Iris shoved the coffee cake and bat off her lap and crawled to the television on her hands and knees to get a closer look, but the tenuous image disintegrated into pixels. She didn't recognize this dangerous man.

The telephone rang.

"Ms. Thorne, this is Chief Greenwood."

"Hello." She sniffed and wiped her face and nose with her hand.

"Are you all right?"

"No."

"Are you in trouble?"

"No. It's just . . . the city's burning."

"I know. I'm sorry."

"So am I."

"Ms. Thorne, we believe Lorraine is on her way south. She bought a bus ticket in San Jose for Santa Monica but never boarded the bus. Someone at the bus station reported seeing her hitch a ride on a big rig. Has she called you again?"

"No."

"We've got an APB out on her, but with everything that's going down in L.A., I doubt there'll be any action on it. So stay inside, keep your doors locked, and don't open up unless you know who it is."

"I'm already doing that."

"Call me if you need anything."

* * *

It was sometime in the early morning hours. The aluminum coffee cake pan sat on the carpet next to Iris. Its contents had been stripped of its filling and frosting and reduced to crumbs. The baseball bat was squared on the floor in front of her. She was eating saltine crackers, one after the other, from a long, rectangular package and watching the news.

She became aware of a noise. She didn't know when it started but she heard it now, like an alarm clock finally buzzing through a sleeper's dreams. Someone was trying to put a key into her front door.

She set the crackers on the floor, stood up, picked up the bat, leaned it against her shoulder, and held the base with both hands. She crept up to the peephole in the door and quickly looked out. The corridor was empty.

She jumped when she heard someone trying a key in the bolt lock. Her heart pounded against her ribs. She looked through the peephole again and saw irregularly cut blond hair.

"Lorraine?" Iris said through the door in as assertive a voice as she could muster. "Lorraine, is that you?"

A key jiggled in the lock. "Goddamn son of a bitch!"

Lorraine flung her hand away from the lock, and Iris saw a flash of cobalt blue.

"Lorraine, I've had all the locks changed. I have a gun and I'm not afraid to use it."

Lorraine put her face up to the peephole, startling Iris, who jumped away. She flattened her back against the door, then thought better of it and crouched down, anticipating gunfire.

"I-ris, open the door," Lorraine said in a saccharine voice. "Don't be afraid."

Iris stood and looked through the peephole.

Lorraine was hurling herself at the door. Her eyes were wide and she looked peculiarly alert, in spite of the dark circles under her eyes, as if she were more than awake. The impact startled Iris, and she dropped the bat, which rattled noisily on the hardwood floor.

"Fucking bitch!" Lorraine screamed. "Art told me you'd be hiding!"

Iris ran to the telephone and pressed 911. It was busy. She tried again. Still busy. She put the phone down, half crawled to the door, snatched the bat, and stood with her back flat to the wall for many minutes. She heard no sound, and her peephole view of the corridor was empty. None of her neighbors had come out to see what was going on.

She sat back down on the floor in front of the television. The butter pecan coffee cake and the crackers suddenly seemed disgusting. She pushed them away. She clicked the television's volume down to a whisper and sat alert, with her back rigid and the bat across her knees.

She attempted 911 again and again until she got through. She was put on hold. She waited. Someone finally answered.

"A woman's trying to break into my condo. She intends to harm me."

A fatigued female voice asked, "You're not hurt now? This woman's not in the house now? I'll put you on the list, ma'am, but I don't know when someone's going to get there. We've got a riot going on."

Iris gave the operator her address and hung up. There was nowhere to go. There was no one who could come. She got up and checked all the doors and windows again, her legs trembling and the bat shaking in her hands. Everything was secure. She took deep breaths to calm herself down. She stopped shaking.

"The Triumph!" she moaned.

She stood in her living room and wrestled with the decision.

It's just a car.

She sat back down in front of the television with the bat across her knees and clicked through the flaming images on the television without seeing them. Half an hour passed.

She's got to be gone by now.

Iris waited another half hour, watching the minutes click by. "But it's not just a car!"

She went into the bedroom, took off her bathrobe, and pulled on a pair of jeans, a sweatshirt, and sneakers. She took her house keys and the bat, checked the peephole and listened at the door, then quickly opened it and thrust her head into the corridor. It was empty. She heard a television through her neighbor's door loudly broadcasting the news.

She quickly locked the bolt lock and ran down the corridor. She decided to take the stairs rather than the elevator and jerked the stairwell door open. The stairwell was empty. She jogged down the stairs, burst through the door into the lobby, jogged across it, and hit the door to the garage running. She didn't look back to see if anyone was standing behind the door until she was in the middle of the garage. She jogged through the garage, looking between the cars and behind the supporting columns. She seemed to be alone.

She ran to the Triumph, held the cover up, and looked underneath as she walked around the car. It was fine.

She heard glass breaking. The garage's cement floor and walls distorted the noise, making it sound as if it had come from inside the garage. Iris skipped down the driveway between the cars, turning back and forth. She didn't see anything. She walked through the door that was cut into the garage's security gate and went outside onto the sidewalk. Then she heard the string of brass bells on her terrace door rattling.

Iris ran into the quiet street to get a better look. Her terrace door was open. A pane of glass near the doorknob had been broken.

"Son of a bitch!" She swung the bat hard onto the asphalt. The impact of the wood made her hands ache. She swung the bat again. "Damn her!" She put her hands on her hips and looked around the empty street. She looked back at the terrace.

A large plastic trash can had been upended and placed in the shrubs underneath the terrace. A hard plastic milk crate sat on top of it. Those two items alone weren't tall enough to reach the terrace, but it put someone within reach of a low branch of the pine tree that grew in front of the building.

Iris saw Lorraine walk past her terrace windows.

"Get out of my house!" Iris screamed.

Someone in a neighboring building peeked out from behind their drapes. Someone else did the same thing. No one offered assistance.

I have my car keys. I should just leave. Lorraine passed her windows again. "The hell I am!"

She walked resolutely to the building's front door, unlocked it, marched back up the stairs and down the corridor to her condo. Her front door was still locked. She opened it and stood in the entryway.

"Lorraine!" she yelled. "Get out of my house!" She stepped through the kitchen, then through the dining room and the living room, holding the bat in both hands over her shoulder. There was no Lorraine. Smoke and the smell of burnt wood traveled in on the wind.

Iris threw on lights as she walked. The guest bathroom and second bedroom were empty. She heard noises in her bedroom. She didn't see anyone there. Then she saw motion in the walk-in closet.

Lorraine grunted as she tore one of Iris's blouses. Several other torn garments were on the floor.

"Lorraine!" Iris yelled. She squatted and held the bat ready "Get out! Now!"

Lorraine looked up as if awakened from a trance. She dropped the blouse she had been tearing and lunged at Iris. Iris swung at her with the bat, hitting her in the side, then swung the bat to hit her again. Lorraine kept coming. She plowed into Iris and knocked them both onto the floor. The bat rolled under the bed. They writhed on the floor in the narrow area between the bed and the dresser. Lorraine pulled Iris's hair and lifted her head up and down, smashing it against the hardwood floor. Iris tried to dig her thumbs into Lorraine's eyes. She got a fix on one eye and pressed. It felt springy and resilient.

Lorraine let go of Iris's hair to pull the hand from her eye. Then she put her hands around Iris's throat and squeezed. Iris tried to pull her off, digging her fingernails into Lorraine's hands, piercing the skin. Lorraine continued to squeeze. Iris began to see spots. She felt for the bat, which was underneath the bed. The large end was toward her. She got her hand around it and banged it against the back of Lorraine's head, but she couldn't put any force behind it. Lorraine writhed against the blows but still maintained her grip on Iris's neck.

Iris put one hand on each end of the bat, put it between them and pushed against Lorraine's neck as hard as she could. The black spots grew larger but still she pushed. Lorraine began to choke, but she maintained her grip. Iris kept pushing. Her arms trembled. She wasn't aware of herself. All that existed was the bat. She gave it one final push. Lorraine let go.

Iris blinked to clear the blackness. She had a sensation of Lorraine stumbling past her and down the hallway, wailing in a way that sounded angry and mournful at the same time. Iris managed to stand and stumbled down the hallway after her, dragging the bat by the end, not having the strength to lift it.

Lorraine was gone.

Iris picked up the phone to call Greenwood. The phone company said the circuits were busy. On the third try, she got through.

"I'm on my way," Greenwood said. "I can't get there in less than three hours. Maybe I can find Fillinger and get him over to you. He's got to be someplace in that mess down there."

41

LORRAINE MEANDERED DOWN THE MIDDLE OF THE STREET. The few cars that passed drove around her. She carried her suitcase, which she'd stashed in the bushes in front of Iris's building, and flailed her free hand in the throes of some internal conversation. She looked up at the sky as she walked, ignoring the cars.

She saw a large hotel and walked to it. A single, brave taxi was parked in front. She asked the driver if he would take her to Marina Del Rey. He looked her up and down and asked her if she had any money, then wanted to see it. Lorraine reached into her pocket, took out a roll of bills, and handed it to him. He peeled off one bill too many and told her it costs extra tonight because of the risk.

The streets were quiet until they drove through Venice Beach, where crowds of people milled around. The cab wove through them. In Marina Del Rey, the streets were again quiet. The driver left Lorraine in front of Barbie's old apartment building.

Lorraine walked up the side stairs to the third floor, then down the corridor to Barbie's apartment. Yellow police ribbon made an X over the door. A large adhesive label that said CRIME SCENE DO NOT ENTER was pressed in the corner between the door and the frame. Lorraine grabbed the police ribbon and pulled the bottom free, letting the two strands dangle from the top of the door. She tried to break the adhesive crime scene label with one of her remaining fingernails, but the label wouldn't give. She looked around. In front of the apartment across from Barbie's, someone had set out a plastic bin containing refuse to be recycled. Lorraine dug through it and found a tin can with its circular lid still partially attached. She pulled the lid free. It cut through the label easily.

The door opened on its own. The crime scene label was the only thing holding the door closed against the broken frame. Lorraine went inside. She propped a bar stool against the door to keep it closed.

The air was stale. Silver-gray dust from the police's fingerprinting efforts was thick on the counters, woodwork, and table tops.

Lorraine opened the sliding glass door and let in the marina air and smells and tinkling sounds. She stood on the terrace and began to cry. Her shoulders shook. Mucus rolled down her face. She wiped it with her hands then took out the roll of cash, pulled off a bill, and used it to blow her nose. She threw the bill off the terrace, and it landed in a wad on the walkway below.

She went back inside and pulled the sheer inner drapes across the open sliding glass door. They billowed in the ocean breeze. She walked into the kitchen, where a roll of paper towels was still neatly in its holder underneath a cabinet. She pulled off a few towels and wiped her face. She opened the cabinets. They contained the few household items that Barbie had purchased to set up the apartment. Lorraine opened the refrigerator. It held a half-eaten cantaloupe, nonfat yogurt, cottage cheese, and a small piece of the bear claws that Barbie had bought for her. The freezer held some diet frozen dinners. Lorraine touched them.

"Charlotte," she sobbed. Her legs folded under her and she slid down the refrigerator onto the floor. She laid her cheek against the linoleum and cried.

"Why am I such a fuck-up?" she sobbed. Eventually, she got up and walked into the living room. The telephone answering machine still sat on the floor where they had left it the previous Friday. She circled it a few times.

She pulled the purple sash out of the suit jacket pocket. It grew longer and longer, like a magician's scarf trick. She threw it on the couch. She undressed. She neatly folded the suit and sweater and put them on a corner of the couch, then picked up the pile and the sash, walked up the three steps to the bedroom area, and put the clothes underneath the bed, out of sight.

She rubbed the sash down her sides and across her body, pressing the smooth fabric against her skin, then dropped it on the bed.

She upended her purse. The plastic containers tumbled out onto the bed. She stood them on the nightstand, went into the kitchen, found a tall glass, half-filled it with water, and topped it off with bourbon from the bottle that still sat in the middle of the living room floor. She walked back to the bedroom and put the glass on the nightstand. In the nightstand drawer she found a pad of paper and a ballpoint pen that Barbie had used for phone messages.

Lorraine sat on the bed, clicked open the pen, drew a few small circles to get the ink flowing, then started to write.

I'm sorry. I didn't mean for it to turn out like this.
I love you, Mom and Dad. I wish I could have been a better daughter.

Lorraine set the pad on the nightstand. She picked up the satin sash, tied it in a bow around her neck, then examined the pill containers, taking the child-proof caps off certain ones. She plumped the pillows against the headboard, then abruptly got up and went into the bathroom to pee. Sitting back down on the bed, she leaned against the pillows and arranged the satin sash around her neck so that it draped smoothly down her bare chest.

She picked up a container of pills, poured some into her hand, tossed them onto the back of her tongue, and took a big gulp of the bourbon and water. Finishing the pills in that container, she went to the next one and the next one until the last of her selected drugs were gone.

She leaned back on the pillows and crossed her hands across her chest. She watched the drapes billowing through the open patio door. They looked like white clouds. Billowing white clouds that she was riding on, riding away.

Officer Jerry Kosnowski came in the back door of the Las Pumas police station.

"Hey, Marion," he greeted the dispatcher, walked to his desk, picked up his favorite mug, and carried it to the coffee-maker.

Chief Charles Greenwood was sitting at his desk, holding a white piece of paper that had been folded and unfolded many times.

"Hey, Charlie. You made it back from L.A. I was worried about you down there." Kosnowski patted Greenwood's shoulder as he walked by. He sat down at his desk and set his coffee mug on the window ledge on top of the many brown coffee rings. He ran a hand through his damp hair. "Gettin' hot. Tourists are starting to come. Embarcadero was pretty crowded. Hey! I just saw my father-in-law over at the highway patrol. They're going to take Officer Coleman off our hands. He can start Monday. Let's go get a beer over at Slappy Mack's to celebrate. I'll call ahead and give them a chance to stop any illegal activities they've got going on. Everyone gets a break today."

Kosnowski squinted at the boom box, which was playing a cassette. "Who's that you got on? Hank Williams, Senior.

Uh-oh, Marion. He's got on Hank Williams, Senior. What's wrong?"

Marion answered, "They found Lorraine. She killed herself."

"Really? How?"

"Asphyxiation." Greenwood got up and walked to Kosnowski's desk. "Here's a photocopy of her suicide note."

Kosnowski screwed up his face. "How the hell did she manage to do that?"

"Fillinger just called me with the coroner's report. Said she'd taken enough pills to choke a horse. When we found her, she had the sash that was probably used to strangle Barbie tied in a bow around her neck. She was also wearing a ring that Iris saw Barbie wearing—on Barbie's little finger. Probably had herself all laid out on the bed to be found just so, you know? But the pills and the booze she washed them down with made her sick. She got up to throw up, didn't make it, passed out on the floor on the way to the bathroom, and smothered in her vomit."

"Man, oh, man. She don't say much in her note, does she?"

Greenwood paced through the station with his hands behind his back.

Kosnowski handed the note back to him. "Looks like we got our perpetrator."

"That's what the mayor thinks."

"Congratulations!"

Greenwood smirked. "Thanks."

"You don't seem too happy about it."

Greenwood put Lorraine's suicide note and his completed report inside the accordion file for the Stringfellow case. He walked to a metal filing cabinet against the wall, opened a drawer, and filed it. "I don't know, Jer. Something doesn't gel."

"What?"

" 'I didn't mean for it to turn out like this?' That's no murder confession."

"Sure it is. It's not as straightforward as you might want, but . . . aaaah. C'mon. It's over. Life in Las Pumas goes back to normal, huh?" Kosnowski got up, walked over to Greenwood, and clasped his hand on his shoulder. "We lucked out on this one. Everyone wins."

"Except Barbie and Lorraine."

"C'mon. Let's go get that beer. Or better yet, aren't they changing the flavors down at the ice cream shop today?"

42

AFTER THE RIOTS ENDED, THE CITY SETTLED INTO A SKITTISH calm. Gang-related murders in the city decreased. A rumor that two prominent gangs, the Crips and Bloods, had joined forces and were planning a joint assault on the city once the National Guard had pulled out was just a rumor. The vacant, weed-covered lot in the suburb where the motorist had been beaten became an informal tourist attraction. "Rebuild L.A." was the new catchphrase, even though most of the population had been only marginally inconvenienced by the riots.

People were gentle with each other. Drivers patiently waited for other drivers to merge. No one tailgated. Folks held doors open for strangers. The afterglow lasted for about a week before everyone went back to pushing and shoving again.

At McKinney Alitzer, business quickly returned to normal. A week after the riots, Herbert Dexter called Iris and Amber into his office for a closed-door meeting. He greeted them at the door warmly, then sat behind his desk, smiling at them.

"I have some news from New York about your grievances against Billy Drye."

Both Amber and Iris leaned slightly forward in their chairs.

Dexter clasped his hands on top of his desk and twiddled his thumbs briefly. The gesture sent a chill down Iris's spine.

"I'm confident you'll both be pleased with the outcome. Effective today, Drye will be given the opportunity to transfer to the Denver office. The official reason for the transfer will be philosophical differences with the staff in L.A. If he declines the transfer, he'll be terminated." Dexter sat back in his chair, looking satisfied.

"That's it?" Amber said, scooting to the edge of her chair. "No sanctions, no apologies, no nothing? He just gets transferred out of L.A.? I know ten other people here who are trying to move out of L.A."

Dexter's satisfied look faded. "I'm disappointed that you're not pleased with the outcome, Amber. Garland Hughes and I worked very hard on a resolution that was beneficial to everyone. Drye will be notified that if he has problems in Denver, he's out of the firm."

Amber opened her mouth to speak again, but Iris touched her arm and Amber settled back into her chair.

Iris said, "I think I can speak for Amber as well as myself when I say that we're pleased with the level of attention you've given this situation and how hard you've worked for a quick resolution. Of course, we'd hoped for something more punitive, but we understand your constraints and appreciate the work you've done. It's been a difficult situation all around."

"I did the best I could to make the situation win-win for everyone." Dexter clapped his hands. "Drye will be cleaning out his desk today. He doesn't know this yet. So that you don't have to be around when this takes place, why don't both of you take the afternoon off? You've earned it."

He stood up. The meeting was over. He shook hands with both of them.

Iris and Amber didn't speak until they were alone in Iris's office.

"A transfer to Denver?" Amber said incredulously.

"It wasn't what we wanted, but it's something."

"It's something? Didn't you want more?"

"Frankly, I'm surprised we got that much. Shows you how jaded I've become."

"It's just not fair. Drye will go to Denver and do the same nonsense out there."

"Maybe he will, maybe he won't. At least we don't have to deal with him anymore. In this life, all we can do is count our wins, learn from our losses, and keep on moving."

"I'm out of here," Amber said. "See you tomorrow."

Iris sat down at her desk. A courier package had been placed on it while she was gone. She pulled the string that slit the package open and reached inside. A note was taped to a small bundle of white tissue paper. Iris pulled the note free and opened it: "It was a pleasure working with you. Good luck. Charles Greenwood."

Iris unrolled the tissue paper. It held her enameled iris brooch.

She picked up the phone and punched in three numbers.

"Hey," she said when Art answered. "Did you get a package from Greenwood?"

"I got it."

"Aren't you happy to get your ring back?"

"Sure. Why wouldn't I be?"

"You want to go out for lunch?"

"Nah, I've got a lot of paperwork to do."

"C'mon, Art. You've been in the doldrums ever since Lorraine killed herself. What's going on?"

"Nothing. I've just been really busy."

"You can tell me. After everything we've been through?"

"Iris, nothing's wrong. I just don't want to have lunch."

"Too bad. I wanted to celebrate. They're transferring Drye to Denver, and Dexter gave Amber and me the afternoon off."

"Drye. That idiot. He told me he was cruising around during the riots and he stole a leather jacket from a store that was being looted. He said, 'Everyone else was doing it.' He was mad because it was dark and he grabbed an extra large by mistake."

"Figures. So, c'mon. Let's go."

"I already told you, Iris. I don't want to go. I have to meet a prospect."

"You just told me you had paperwork to do. You wouldn't be trying to avoid me, would you?"

"See you. Good-bye."

Iris walked to the window that overlooked the suite. She saw Art stand up, put on his jacket, and walk down the corridor. She quickly put on her jacket, grabbed her purse, and followed him.

"Hi," she said, standing next to him at the elevator.

He looked at her without saying anything.

The elevator doors opened and they both got in. Neither of them spoke, Art punched in a button for the lowest parking level. Iris didn't punch in a floor.

"Aren't you getting off?" he asked.

"My car's on the same floor as yours."

He nodded. A dimple appeared near his jaw. He was clenching his teeth.

The elevator doors opened. He pushed in front of her to exit first and started walking quickly. She struggled to keep up with him.

The parking level was almost empty. The building had office space available, like many commercial buildings in Los Angeles, leaving this lowest and most remote level virtually unused. The cement was still pristine. Art's Mustang was parked in a far corner, away from the few other cars that were there.

"Why are you parked way down here?" Iris looked around uneasily.

"I got tired of my doors getting dinged." He unlocked the driver's door, opened it, and turned to face her with the door between them. "I thought you said your car was down here."

She smiled tentatively. "Last chance for a lunch date."

"I don't want to have lunch. Just tell me what you want, Iris."

"Don't you want to talk about everything? You know. Now that it's all over?"

"Exactly. It's over. Barbie's dead. Lorraine's dead. There's nothing to talk about."

"But I'm still here and you're still here."

"So?"

"So, as long as we're both here to tell the story, it's never quite going to be over."

He closed the Mustang's door, removing the barrier between them.

She took a step away from him. "There are still loose ends. Like I'm wondering what you told your uncle about his fifty grand."

He twisted the class ring on his finger.

"So, what did you tell him?" She took another step back until she was well out of arm's reach.

"Why don't you ask him, Iris?"

"As a matter of fact, I did. He said you told him the deal with Barbie fell through and you gave him his cash back."

He nodded quickly. "Yeah. So?"

"Where did you get fifty grand?"

He ran both hands through his hair. "I know people. It's really none of your business, Iris."

There were footsteps in the garage, and they both turned in that direction. A man got in a car a few yards away from them, started it, and drove off.

"Okay. Let's talk about the night Lorraine broke into my condo. That's my business. Don't you have anything to say about that?"

He raised his voice. "Why should I? Lorraine was a nut. She killed Barbie."

"And you put her on to me."

His face hardened. "What are you talking about?"

"The night Lorraine broke in, she said, 'Art told me you'd be hiding.' You told her where I lived."

The dimple in his jaw grew deeper.

"Okay, Art. Since you won't tell me what happened, I'll tell you. That Friday, after I finally persuaded you to drive me back to my car, you drove to the Mariah Lodge, found Barbie's bungalow, and killed her. Lorraine saw the whole thing. You kept her quiet by promising to get her ring back, but when you couldn't pull it off Barbie's hand, you cut it off. Then you found your money, gave Lorraine some, and you both split.

"When Lorraine started flipping out and calling me, she also called you. That's when you thought of a way to get rid of me, the only credible person who knew your motive to commit murder."

Art suddenly looked sad. "That's what you think of me? That I'd drive over two hundred miles to kill someone? That I'd send a crazy woman to get you?"

"I don't know what else to think, Art."

He turned and leaned against the Mustang, put his elbows on the hood, and rested his head in his hands. "Iris, I didn't plan it. I didn't. You have to believe me." He looked at her. "I just wanted my family's money. I was so ashamed, I even thought about disappearing to Mexico or someplace. After I dropped you off, I drove to the lodge, thinking I'd just talk to her. I found the Mercedes, parked, and hung out in some trees next to the cabin, wondering what I was gonna do. Then Lorraine came out, all dressed up, and I saw Barbie on the bed, wearing this purple nightgown. Lorraine took off down the road, walking. So I knocked on the door. Barbie said, 'Oh, I knew you'd change your mind, darlin'.' " Art spitefully imitated Barbie's accent.

"When she saw me, she just turned her back and said, 'So you found me. Now whatcha gonna do?' Like I didn't count for shit. Then she poured herself champagne, like I wasn't even there."

Art's voice grew bitter. "I came inside and told her I wanted my money. She goes, 'I'm not giving you any money.' I said, 'But you stole it from my uncle.' She says, 'I didn't steal it. You gave it to me, remember?' She put the glass down and walked to the center of the room. This sash on her nightgown came loose. She pulled it off, real slow, dropped it on the floor, and started dancing around. I could see everything she's got. She says, 'I don't look so bad, do I, Arturo? I've still got it, don't you think?'

"I'm starting to get pissed off." His body stiffened. "I told her the only reason she made friends with us was to rip us off. Then she goes, 'No. Iris was work. You were a freebie,' and she laughed, real snotty.

"I said, 'I'm not leaving without my money.' I looked around, saw her purse on the floor, kneeled down, and started digging in it. She goes, 'Don't you dare look through my purse,' and came up behind me and kicked me in the kidney. While I'm trying to catch my breath, she says, 'My poor, sweet Arturo. The sex was great, but people as simple as you and your li'l ol' family deserve to be parted from their money. The way I see it, I did y'all a favor,' and she walked away."

"Then everything happened so fast, it was like it was happening to someone else." The words came rapidly now but his gaze remained steady. "I picked up the sash and threw it around her neck when her back was to me. We started jumping around, and she's kicking me and stuff, then she fell on the bed and I sat on her back. She tried to scratch me, so I put my knees on her arms and just kept pulling. Finally, she stopped. I rolled her over and propped her up against the pillows. I don't know why."

Art was out of breath. "Next thing I know, I'm looking through the trunk of her car. I find this bag that's got all the cash in it. I put out the Do Not Disturb sign, threw the bag in my trunk, and came home. I guess Lorraine came back later and cut off her finger and took the ring."

He reached his hands toward Iris. She flinched as he grabbed her affectionately by the shoulders. "Iris, I'm sorry I told Lorraine where you lived. When she called me, I freaked out. I didn't even realize what I'd said until she'd hung up."

His face was flushed and his eyes shone. "I'm glad I told you everything." He was panting and smiling. "I avoided you because I knew you'd make me tell you. But now I'm glad you know. After all, we've been in this together from the start."

"But you killed somebody," she whispered, almost to herself. She glanced around the garage. There was no one in sight. "Art, once people know what Barbie did, they'll understand."

"People don't need to know. I figure I did the world a favor. Just like Barbie said she did me a favor and she did. I'll never be that stupid again." He playfully shook her shoulders and grinned. "Iris, it's okay. Don't look so serious. We'll just go on, like normal. Here ..." He walked to the Mustang's trunk, opened it, and took out the overstuffed Louis Vuitton satchel.

She looked at it with disgust. "I don't want that!"

He held it toward her. "Just put it back in your safe deposit box. Then everything will be the way it was, like it never happened."

"But you killed Barbie!"

"Now we both have a secret."

"There's a difference between hiding that"—she flicked her hand toward the bag—"and strangling someone."

He shoved the bag toward her. "Take your money, Iris."

She stepped away from him. "No."

"You're not gonna tell the police, are you?"

They stared into each other's eyes for several long seconds. She turned abruptly and started walking quickly toward the elevator. He dropped the bag on the ground.

It didn't take him long to catch up with her. He grabbed her by the shoulders and spun her to face him. "Don't tell anyone, Iris."

"Let go of me," she said firmly.

He started to shake her. "It's over! They're both dead! It doesn't matter!"

She tried to twist out of his grasp but couldn't. "Art, stop! You're hurting me!"

"She deserved it! They both did!"

Her neck snapped back and forth against her shoulders. She lost her balance, and her pump heels slid from underneath her. She slipped from his grasp when she fell to the ground. She tried to wiggle away from him, but he straddled her on his knees. He held his outstretched hands above her neck.

"Look at you!" she cried. "What's happened to you? You're no better than she was!"

Art slowly turned his hands toward himself and studied them. He sat back on his heels, still crouched over her. She scrambled out from under him, got to her feet, grabbed her purse, and ran to the elevator.

He stood, still looking at his hands, then threw them down, clenched his fists, and started walking toward his car.

Iris pounded the call button. It was lunchtime, and the elevators were busy. She looked at the stairs a short distance away and was starting to run toward them when she heard the Mustang's engine turn over. As her outstretched hand touched the doorknob at the stairwell, she heard the V-8 engine speeding toward her. She pulled the door open and flung herself inside the stairwell, but not before something smacked against the back of her legs, knocking her onto the stairs.

After the sound of the engine faded, she got up and peeked into the garage. The Louis Vuitton satchel, which had hit her when Art flung it from the car, lay on the ground.

43

THE DAY BEFORE CHIEF GREENWOOD WAS GOING TO HAVE Barbie Stringfellow's body cremated, a man identifying himself as Ms. Stringfellow's brother called the Las Pumas Police Department. The story had made it as far as a local newspaper in Dennison, Texas, where Leon Calhoun recognized his sister, Louise, from a photograph that had run with the article.

Greenwood and Calhoun both looked down at the metal table that held Louise's remains.

"You taking her to Dennison?" Greenwood asked.

"No. Back to Coffman, Mississippi, to a little hillside cemetery where my momma's buried. Where I finally had her buried. Daddy had her stuck out in the yard. After he died, I gave Momma a proper funeral. Louise'll be next to her. She loved her momma."

"Your mother was buried in your yard?"

Leon Calhoun nodded sadly. "Yep. Daddy told us she just left one day, but the way he used to beat the bejesus out of her, we figured he just finally killed her." His eyes glazed. "Louise and I grew up in a hell house. My two older brothers used to molest me and Louise from when we were just little kids. Our daddy knew, but he didn't stop 'em.

Louise left home when she was a teenager and never came back.

"Louise was the only one in the family I kept up with. The rest of 'em can go to hell. Louise used to send gifts for the kids. Expensive things. Cash sometimes. Lord knows, we could always use it. She was kind of sketchy about how she made her money, so I never pressed it. I had a feeling she didn't want me to know. I guess I didn't want to know either. She was such a sweet girl. Friendly, popular. A real personality kid. You can break a child, you know?

"Seein' her here, I feel like part of the past has died too. Because she was there with me, witnessed it with me, I knew it happened the way it did. Maybe it's best. Some things are better off forgotten."

Still shaken, Iris's hands trembled as she hurriedly opened the door of her condo and locked it behind her. There were two messages on her answering machine.

The first one was from Charles Greenwood. "I wanted you to know that Art Silva just confessed to murdering Barbie Stringfellow. He moved in on your client behind your back to invest in a nightclub scheme of his and when she ripped him off, he killed her in a rage. Fillinger and I had suspected she was a con artist. Well, best of luck to you, Iris, and give me a call the next time you're up this way."

Iris spoke to the machine. "Well, Arturo, you did the right thing."

The second message played. "Hello, Iris. Garland Hughes from the New York office here. I hope you don't mind me calling you at home, but I didn't think it was appropriate to call you at the office. Maybe it's not appropriate to call you at all, but I'll let you decide. I'm going to be in L.A. next week and I'd be honored if you'd have dinner with me. I've checked the employee handbook to make sure there's no policy against this, and everything appears to be copacetic. If you have the time, I'd look forward to it. Give me a call."

She stared at the machine as it rewound the tape. "Best offer I've had all week."

She took the Louis Vuitton satchel into her kitchen, sat it on the sink, took a folded brown paper grocery sack from the cupboard where she kept them and put the satchel inside. She carried it into her office, taped it closed, and wrote on it with a black marker:

> John,
> I'm returning this to you.
> Love, Iris

She drove north on Pacific Coast Highway with the top of the Triumph down. The normally brown hills showed their spring green and were dotted with patches of California golden poppies. Iris turned her face into the sun.

At Topanga Canyon Boulevard, she turned east and headed up through the mountains into the canyon. The road twisted and turned and she finally reached the gravel clearing down from John Somers's house. She carried the paper bag up the road.

A mailbox painted with primitive white and yellow daisies with green stems on a yellow ground was perched on a pole at the end of his driveway. Iris pulled open the mailbox door, which gave with a metallic grate, and took out the mail. There was a handful of slick department store ads, bills in neat white envelopes, and small cards with ads for carpet cleaning, closet redecorating, maid dust-busters, or some other small business enterprise printed on one side. The other side asked, HAVE YOU SEEN? and displayed poorly reproduced photos of toothy pre-adolescents or younger children with showy grins. Several of the bills had yellow post office forwarding labels affixed to the front.

"Didn't waste any time getting settled, did you, Penny?"

Iris crammed the mail back into the box and slammed the door closed. She marched down the driveway toward the house. The dog, fenced in the backyard, started to bark huskily.

Iris yelled, "Buster! Shut up!"

The dog was momentarily silenced, startled by the sound of his name, then started his lusty barking again. He began flinging his solid body against the fence.

Iris sat the grocery bag on the woven hemp front door mat, making sure the label faced out.

"Like opening John's mail, do you, Penny? Have a gander at this."

She walked to the Triumph without looking back and sped down Withered Canyon Road, sending the gravel into a satisfying spray behind her. She made quick business of Cat Canyon Road, turned onto Topanga Canyon Boulevard with a squeal of tires, then headed south on Pacific Coast Highway, heading home. She glanced at the ocean as she drove. It shone a hopeful blue.